REFLECTOR

BY C. X. MYERS

No part of this work may be reproduced or transmitted in any form or by any means, electronic or mechanical, including photocopying and recording, or by any information storage or retrieval system without the proper written permission of the copyright owner unless such copying is expressly permitted by federal copyright law.

REFLECTOR

Copyright © 2022 by C. X. Myers. All rights reserved.

Design and lay-out by Catspaw DTP LLC

Cover art by Kat Powder

For Sheena and Kyla, without whom Reflector *would not exist, and for Kat, who brings the fever dreams in my mind to life in true color and lousish smiles.*

CHAPTER 1

"Name?"

That wasn't a difficult question for most people but for the young woman standing in front of the reception desk, it was . . . complicated. She wrinkled her nose as she made a couple of abortive attempts to answer the question, but it was difficult to order her thoughts because of the smell. The grungy reception room stank of smoke, the all-encompassing scent of decaying, years-old periodicals, and burnt, week-old caff which had all but sunk into the fabric of the building.

"Wally," is what she finally said.

"Your full and legal name, Miss." The clark didn't say it cruelly, but there was an edge of weariness to his voice that stuck a knot of guilt in Wally's throat.

Still, she hated saying it out loud.

"S-Sorry." Wally fished through her pockets for her wallet before drawing it out and tugging her cheaply laminated ID from one of the sleeves. "It's, uhm . . . it's easier to read it." Really she just didn't want to have to say it.

The clark raised an eyebrow but took the card. It wasn't as though it made much difference to him. His eyes scanned over the image on the ID, matching it to the girl in front of him out of habit more than necessity.

Sex: Female
Gender: Feminine
Lineage: Half-Elf (Human [Pat], Pykan [Mat])
Hair: Brown // Green (Secondary)

Despite having gotten her ID two years ago she hadn't grown any more over the five-foot and two inches it read on the card, and although she had lost weight, down to one-thirty-three from the card's one-forty, it hadn't been for her health. She just forgot to eat more often than not.

But her name.

That's what caught the clark's eye, just like Wally knew it would.

"Really?" He raised an eyebrow at her and she frowned, and the clark held up an apologetic hand.

"Sorry, sorry, it's ah . . . well it's just kind of an unusual name, isn't it?"

"Can . . . Can't you just put down Wally?" She asked.

His frown deepened as he looked back down at the card for a moment before looking back to the young woman with dirty brown hair and streaks of muted green and shaking his head.

"No, I'm sorry." He actually sounded like he meant it. "As I said before, we need your full and legal name."

Wally nodded sullenly. She hadn't really expected him to budge, but it wasn't as though she had anything to lose by asking.

The clark flattened out the hiring register he'd been filling out, copying down the bits from her ID that were available to save himself some time with questions, and then put the pen to the top of the paper and scrawled out the name.

Walythea Wilhelmina Willowbark

Gods' *hooks*, but Wally hated her name. She took the registration sheet from the clark with a muttered thanks, retrieved her ID card, and turned to start walking the hall that stretched down past his desk. The rest of the building smelled no different than the reception area. Or if it did smell different it was only that the smells became concentrated more heavily the further back she went. It was all filterless cigarettes and caff left to go cold and stale a hundred times too many, day after day, in an overused break room.

Wally swallowed again and tried not to breathe too deeply.

She would have to get used to the smell eventually, she reasoned. At least, she would on the assumption that they actually hired her.

The clark had given her a short set of directions to the interview room before returning to his dog-eared paperback, and Wally followed them as carefully as she did with anything someone told her to do. The way she reasoned it, if she did it exactly the way she was told then, even if something went wrong, at least it would mostly not be her fault.

Mostly.

For the tenth time, Wally tugged at her dress tunic and patted away what were probably imaginary wrinkles on her slacks as she continued to walk down the eerily silent halls. Admittedly, it was the middle of the day which, for this particular place, was more or less the equivalent of the graveyard shift, but the silence was almost palpable. The only noise that disrupted anything was the faint susurration of the fan vents which, she suspected, hadn't been cleaned or meaningfully seen to since the Sunfall Rebellion, and served less to clear the air than they did to move the stink of talba smoke and old caff around like a geriatric patient getting his daily constitutional.

She reached the door too soon and swallowed thickly as she raised a hand to rap her knuckles against the cheap wood.

"Come in."

The voice was deep but had a subdued quality to it and Wally thought it wasn't such a bad sound as she opened the door and stepped inside.

"Good afternoon, Miss Willowbrook."

"Oh, it's uhm . . . W-Willow*bark*." Wally held out the paper as if she needed documentation to prove that she knew her own name.

The man was tall, easily over six and a half feet tall. He was a broad-framed and full-blooded human, and his complexion was almost the same tawny shade as hers, but a bit darker—or maybe just less pallid. He wore a cream-colored tunic with the logo of his workplace on it, one of the many mass-stamped company linens that stretched a bit at his shoulders, and a pair of sturdy pants made from dark denim and leather.

The beaten and ratty blue couch he was sitting on could have belonged to any apartment in the lower east side of downtown Colvus, and a quick glance around, at the couch, and the stained counter with two caff-pots that were inexplicably both half-full and probably cold, plugged into the wall, told Wally this was probably the infamous break room and the source of the smells.

Wally wrinkled her nose again.

"Ah, my mistake." He grinned and carded his fingers through his short, messy brown hair. It was an oddly boyish expression for someone who was supposed to be the head of the precinct house. "Willowbark, got it . . . so, please, take a seat!"

He gestured to one of the lumpy easy-chairs across from him, and Wally took the one he pointed to.

To her surprise, it was actually fairly comfortable.

"My name is Erik Mizer, but just Mizer is fine," he said. "Now, Walythea—"

"Wally," she blurted out, and then went rigid as she realized she'd interrupted him.

He didn't look offended, though, just a bit surprised.

"Wally," he repeated. "You prefer Wally?"

"Uhm . . . y-yes, please." Wally tried to inject some oomph into her voice, but it didn't really come through.

Fortunately, he didn't seem put off by her request.

"Right, okay, no problem." His smile was as warm as his dark brown eyes, and Wally found herself, uncharacteristically, liking him quite a lot. He was easy-going, and she appreciated that. "So, Wally, do you mind if I level with you before we start this interview off, just so we know where we both stand?"

That was either a good thing, or a very bad thing, and Wally hoped that the fact that he was actually bothering to talk to her at all suggested the former.

"Sure."

He nodded.

"Alright, well, in the interest of expediency," he gave a faintly wry grin, "you've pretty much got the job, assuming you want it."

Wally frowned.

"But I haven't even done my aptitude tests," she said. "You don't even know if I'll be any good."

Mizer shook his head.

"But you're a reflector," he countered, "and they're so rare it's not even funny. We've had this job posting up for six months, and yours—" he gestured with the register sheet in Wally's direction— "is the first and only application we've gotten."

Wally's eyebrows inched upwards.

"The simple fact is that unless you've got some catastrophic liability issues or your background check comes back with Sunfall Cult affiliations, we literally can't afford to turn you away, regardless of your aptitude scores," Mizer continued, then gave another boyish grin. "And honestly, at this point? The cult thing could go either way for me . . . we're in pretty dire need of your talents, so wherever your ap-scores are low, we'll shore up with on-site training, assuming that's alright with you."

Wally nodded along. To be honest, it was fine. The fact that her below-average physical abilities wouldn't necessarily be held against her was a load off of her back. She wasn't what anyone would call physically capable.

"So?" Mizer smiled hopefully, and Wally nodded.

"Yeah—I mean, yes, I still want the job," she replied quickly. "I . . . I can't really afford to turn it down either, to be honest."

He snorted and nodded back at her.

"Alright, then," he replied with a small laugh. "So, as I'm sure you're aware, reflectors don't occur naturally. They're the result of an Astral talent being exposed to high levels of miasma at a young age, so . . . may I ask?"

It wasn't her favorite thing to talk about, but this *was* an interview, and if anyone had the right to know it was the person who was going to be making use of her talents. Wally took a deep breath, and said, "I was born in Bressig."

Erik Mizer flinched.

"Oh." His mouth flattened to a hard line, and the humor

fled from his face. "Okay . . . yeah, that uh . . . Gods' hooks, yeah, that would do it. Were you near the epicenter?"

Near? Wally had to work to suppress a grimace. Yeah, 'near' was a word that described where she'd been.

"I was," was what she actually said.

"And you're—" he glanced down at the register sheet— "twenty-four, so that would have made you about nine years old at the time, right?"

"Right."

Mizer blew out a breath and leaned back against the couch, lowering the register sheet to the table as he did and shaking his head in disbelief.

"Wow," he muttered, then dragged a hand down his face. "Bressig . . . what a mess, I'm sorry you had to go through that, Miss Willowbark."

"Can we uhm . . . move on?" Wally asked quietly.

"Of course." Mizer straightened and took a steadying breath. "Okay, so, we'll have to test your reflection to make sure you can handle the work, but, like I said, you're our only option so even if your talent is C-Grade or lower, we'll work with you to raise it."

Wally raised an eyebrow, then reached into her pocket for her wallet and produced a small, more cleanly laminated card from it than her ID had been.

"Sorry I . . . I thought you would have had a copy of this," she said sheepishly.

She handed over her license of practice. It was small and contained only a few marks on it: the nature of her power—reflector—as well as the base power grade she operated at when at rest. Environmental factors could shift the strength of a talent up or down, but rarely more than half a grade's worth, so it worked well as a baseline.

It was also one of the few things she was proud of.

"Antegrade B." Mizer looked genuinely impressed as he looked up from the license to Wally. "So your power is still growing? At your age?"

"That's what the licensure office said," Wally confirmed.

Mizer shook his head in disbelief.

"That means you could be upper A-Grade or even S by the time you're fully-fledged," he replied as he passed back her license. "Our last guy was middle-C all the way, so this is fantastic news!"

Wally dared to show a hopeful smile and laughed weakly.

"Uhm, don't get too excited . . . wait til you see my stamina scores." The laugh was a little forced because she wasn't really lying. Her physical abilities, from main strength to stamina to her hand-eye coordination, were all abysmal.

"You could be stone deaf and blind as a bat and I'd still take you on," Mizer assured her.

Which led to the crux of Wally's only real question about this job. Specialized magical talents were valuable, of course, but even by those standards the passive ability to reflect curses was *so* hyperspecialized that it struck Wally as odd that anyone would specifically hold a slot open for someone with that ability. Reflecting was rare, but it also wasn't what anyone would call particularly useful. It was so niche that Wally had always struggled to think of a job where anyone would care how strong her reflection was.

Even this one felt like a stretch.

"Why *do* you need a reflector so badly, M—uhm, Mizer, sir?" Wally asked flatly. "Really, I mean."

The humor faded from Erik Mizer's face, and he wrung his hands for a moment.

"That's uhm . . . complicated," he said, finally. "You know we deal with necrotics exclusively, right? Lots of curses are involved in that kind of work."

"Only from spectrals, really," Wally countered. "I wrote my undergrad thesis on Spectral phenotypes, and those can get bad, I know, but they're so rare compared to corporeals—"

"—Corpses."

Wally frowned.

"Corporeals is kind of a mouthful," Mizer explained with that same sheepishly boyish grin. "Spectrals and corpses are what we call them."

"Oh." For some reason that felt disrespectful given the

nature of the work, but that was the culture, she supposed. Maybe it was just desensitization. "Okay, well, uhm . . . corpses—" she *really* didn't like that word— "are a lot more common, and only the oldest or most powerful demonstrate any curse-making abilities."

Mizer smiled wanly.

"You know," he said with a chuckle. "I'm starting to think you might be underselling yourself in this interview, Miss Willowbark. Honestly, when I saw that a reflector had applied, I didn't even look at your degree. What's it in?"

Wally shuffled her feet nervously as she considered lying. Honestly, it hadn't been her brightest idea to go with that degree. It made her look even weirder than she actually was, which was saying something. But in the end, it was the only thing other than her gardening hobby that actually held her interest.

"Theoretical Necromancy," Wally replied after a moment of contemplation.

A flicker of something odd passed over Mizer's face, but it was gone just as quickly. The expression left behind wasn't one of surprise. Rather, it was one that was almost solemn.

"You know," he began softly. "One of my first assignments after starting the sixth was as part of the Bressig dispersal."

That wasn't shocking. Bressig was such a mess that anyone and everyone who'd been in this line of work fifteen years ago would have been called up to help with it in some capacity. It was the biggest disaster in the area in decades.

"My understanding is that a lot of the survivors ended up in the various temples . . . trying to find peace, maybe?" Mizer said.

Wally gave a noncommittal grunt. He wasn't wrong. Almost everyone she knew from back then was Sister-this or Brother-that, or some other lay title if they didn't get their proper orders. Most of them flocked to the Solar Temples of Ys, a few went to the Halls of the Moon. Seeking the protection of the gods was natural when faced with that kind of horror. Wally understood that and she didn't begrudge them it, but . . .

"Not you, though," Mizer continued. "You wanted to understand, I guess, huh?"

Wally nodded.

"Well, you're definitely overqualified for this role, but with all due respect I'm not going to turn that down." Mizer's laugh was a soft and oddly stony sound that welled up from his barrel chest.

"You still haven't answered my question, though," Wally said.

"About why we need a reflector?"

"Yeah."

Mizer crossed his arms, pursing his lips as he did which gave him an almost petulant expression completely at odds with his frame and build. It was almost enough to make Wally laugh, and she would have if she weren't so nervous.

"Hold on."

He stood up and walked over to the coat rack at the corner of the room and began fussing around with what Wally could only assume was his jacket.

"Forgot to pull this out," he said as he retrieved a folded sheet of paper from one of the pockets, turned, and held it out.

Wally stood and walked over, took the paper, and unfolded it. She scanned it line by line. It was a short, dry, boilerplate NDA of the kind she'd seen once or twice during her mortuary residencies.

"Trade secrets?" Wally said, more than asked.

"Sure."

That wasn't the most encouraging answer. It certainly wasn't a solid 'yes'. At the same time, he hadn't been anything less than upfront with her about most of the aspects of this job. The only things he was being cagey about—and that wasn't necessarily even being fair—was the exact sorts of things an NDA would exist to protect.

"So . . ." Wally looked over the NDA again, then looked back up at Mizer. "If I sign this, can I see what I'm walking into before I say 'yes' for sure?"

Mizer's mouth flattened to a hard line and he carded his fingers through the slightly greasy strands of his hair. Despite that, he still managed to come off looking carelessly handsome rather than messy. He was just one of those people who could pull the look off, Wally supposed. As it was, he was a disarming sort of fellow, whether or not it was intentional, and Wally had a feeling it wasn't. For better or worse, Erik Mizer struck Wally as the sort who *got* taken advantage of, if only for his kindness, rather than the other way around.

"Yeah, that's fair I guess," Mizer replied. "The way I see it, if you really hated what you saw, you'd just end up quitting anyway, and that'd be bad business all around."

Wally breathed out a quiet sigh, then turned back to the low table, pulled a pen from her pocket, and bent down to scribble her signature at the bottom and date it before handing it back to Mizer who looked it over, nodded, then folded it up, pocketed it, and gestured for her to follow him.

"Okay," he said brightly, "let's go meet the team."

CHAPTER 2

The building that Dispersal Precinct Six occupied was one of the older structures in the eastern part of downtown Colvus near the edge of the Colver River, from which the city derived its name, so its structure was a little . . . eclectic. The door to the lower level was as grungy and faded as the rest of the building, but the fact that it opened to a dimly lit stone stairwell made it look like the sort of thing she'd walk down into only to never emerge. Building codes were a looser back then, but the majority of the original foundations were set down by the Earthshapers who'd built most of the four cities of the Union, rather than dug by hand. It left the majority of the older quarters like the one this building occupied as paradoxically safer in the basement levels than anywhere else.

"It's not as bad as it looks, I promise."

Mizer grinned as he squeezed into the narrow passage of the stairwell. His broad-shouldered frame and the non-standard sizing meant he had to shuffle a bit to maneuver downward. The low murmur of conversation filtered up from the depths which did a lot to soothe Wally as she followed Mizer down even as it ramped up her anxiety. She wasn't the best when it came to meeting new people but if she did take the job then she'd be working with them in close quarters whether she liked it or not.

She resolved to do her best to leave a good first impression, at the very least.

"Uhm, Mister Mizer—"

"Mizer, Gods' hooks, please, just Mizer," he laughed, waving a hand at her as he glanced over his shoulder. "Or even Erik, anything but Mister."

"M-Mizer, then." It felt weird, but Wally didn't really have a leg to stand on for judging names. "You uhm . . . you still haven't answered my question, about why you need a reflector, I mean."

"Mmm, yeah, sorry it's just complicated, that's all."

He ran his fingers through his hair again and Wally was starting to realize why his hair was always so messy. It was funny to think of someone as big as Mizer being the anxious type, but he *did* seem pretty nervous.

Nice, but nervous.

They reached the door at the bottom of the stairs and Mizer had to muscle it open. It looked like it was the sort of old door that got jammed a lot because of either temperature or the wet. Following him through the door, the sounds of conversation and industry suddenly surrounded her; a dull clinking noise, like the sounds of a chisel hitting metal was the closest, but before she had a chance to find the source, the source found her.

"*That's* the new hire?" The voice was dry and dripping with acerbic humor, and Wally's ears pinned back at their tone.

"Ease off, Jemma, at least let her get her feet on the ground."

The replying voice was higher-pitched and came from near Wally's elbow, and she startled back as the door closed. Sitting at a desk near the basement door was a short young woman—gods she couldn't have been older than eighteen— with bobbed, flaxen-blonde hair. She wore a white blouse over sun-bronzed skin and had a lovely, heart-shaped face, baby-blue eyes, and a full mouth that formed into an easy, charming smile, which broadened a little as a red flush crept into Wally's cheeks.

"Hi, and sorry about Jemma—" she jerked her head towards the back— "she suffers from a terminal case of resting bitch-mouth."

Wally followed her gesture to the rear of the room.

Standing in a dimly lit quarter of the back was a compact woman with a dark, olive complexion clad in a black muscle shirt and grey fatigues. Her straight black hair was pulled into a neat, shoulder-length ponytail which left her tapered, half-elven ears on full display. Showing off her ears like that was uncomfortably brazen—especially pinned back in annoyance as they were.

In one hand, the glowering woman gripped a heavy engineer's hammer, and in the other was a long, notched chisel of dark metal.

"I suffer from jack shit," Jemma shot back. "I'm just saying she looks like a stiff breeze could knock her over . . . at least Dolin had some meat on him."

"And he up and abandoned us, so shut up maybe," the blonde girl said sharply before turning back to Wally. "Sorry about that," she held out a hand, "I'm Paulina Truelight, but call me Polly. It's good to meet you, the witchy walking chip-on-her-shoulder is Jemma Corsivo, I'd say you get used to her but I'm contractually obligated not to lie to fellow employees."

"Oh, uhm, call me Wally, and I haven't actually accepted the job yet," Wally replied as she shook Polly's hand weakly.

Polly nodded and smiled.

"In that case, you'll definitely get used to her."

"Ladies, can we *please* try not to scare off the only reflector in the city who's given us the time of day in six months?" Mizer pleaded.

"Pffft, as if it matters, you know she's gonna pitch a fit about the new hire one way or the other," Jemma said as she went back to knock the tip of her chisel against the body armor cuirass.

Mizer shook his head and stalked over Jemma, crossed his arms, and stared down at her. She was only about five-foot and five, so Mizer *towered* over her, but Jemma had a weight and heft to her body which, along with the definition of muscles in her arms, suggested that she was significantly stronger than she looked.

"And *she's* just going to have to get used to it," Mizer replied sharply. "Just like she got used to Dolin."

"She *tolerated* Dolin."

Polly grimaced as she moved away from her arguing co-worker and boss, and closer to Wally who was beginning to feel increasingly awkward just listening to all of it.

"I'm sorry about this," Polly said quietly, putting a hand on Wally's shoulder. "I promise, it's not usually this bad . . . Jemma's a good woman but she's a little short-tempered at the best of times, and we've been down two people since Dolin quit, which left us pretty short-staffed."

"It's okay." Wally wasn't actually sure it was okay, but it seemed like the right thing to say. Plus, Polly did seem genuinely nice.

"So uhm, can I ask—"

"—how old I am?" Polly finished before Wally could get the rest of the awkward question out, and Wally flushed.

Polly's laughter was high and cheeky, and she patted Wally on the shoulder.

"S-Sorry."

Polly waved the apology off. "Don't be, everyone asks that question, and I'm thirty-seven."

Wally goggled, then the coin dropped. "You're a biomantic," she said quietly.

"Mhm," Polly nodded. "Manifested when I was fifteen and, well, bios age slower based on the grade of their power and I'm pretty up there, so in twenty-two years I've only aged about . . . three-ish, I think? That's based on my cell degradation, or lack thereof."

There was nonchalance in her tone, but the cadence of it sounded practiced. It seemed like the sort of thing that Polly had to explain every time someone got a good enough look at her. It was also something that probably caused her a lot of problems.

"I'm sorry, that sounds awful."

Polly raised an eyebrow.

"Really?" She snorted softly. "I think you're the only one to ever say that to me . . . everyone else is always—" she put on a painfully simpering voice— "like '*oh! I wish I had that!*' and just, no, trust me, you *don't*." Her easy smile got folded away like an old jacket, and lines of bitterness carved themselves over her face. "Do you have any idea how hard it is to have a relationship with someone when you age at a tenth their rate? Or even just make *friends?*"

Wally shook her head. "I can't imagine."

Polly sighed softly.

"No . . . you can't, but it's kind of nice that you know that, at least, because your predecessor never really caught on."

The bubbly exterior faded a little, but not entirely. Wally had the feeling she was a relatively upbeat person in general. How she managed that with the knowledge that she'd probably outlive everyone she knew by an order of magnitude, Wally had no idea.

Leaving Wally to her musings, Polly turned to face the two arguing members of the Sixth and cupped her hands around her mouth.

"Hey, kids!"

Jemma and Mizer both looked up with equally curious expressions as Polly wrapped both of what turned out to be surprisingly muscular arms around one of Wally's, and beamed at them while Wally stared down in a mixture of surprise and embarrassment. Polly looked soft but she was . . . dense was the best way Wally could describe it.

"I wanna keep this one!"

Mizer arched one eyebrow while Jamma's ears pricked up in surprise, and the grouchy woman huffed.

"That was fast," Jemma said. "But I guess you're her type, huh?"

Wally flushed a deeper scarlet and sank back while Polly scowled, let go of Wally, and stomped up to Jemma. It was *almost* petulant but, just like the way she'd casually described her condition, it was like a performance.

The anger wasn't.

Polly jabbed a finger under Jemma's nose.

"What is your problem today?" Polly snapped. "You can be pretty unpleasant, Jem, but today you're particularly crap form."

Finally, Jemma showed something other than anger. Her ears flicked straight up, then pinned back, and when she bared her teeth, small fangs poked out from under her lips. Wally kept her own mouth shut. The last thing she wanted to do was drive even more of a wedge between these three than she apparently already had.

"Screw off, Polly!" Jemma spat, and turned on her heel to stomp off down a side hall.

Mizer sighed then turned back Wally with a grimace. "I'm sorry, really . . . Jemma's been under a lot of pressure because she's been pulling double duty for six months. She can be abrasive but she's not usually this bad."

"It's okay," Wally said softly.

"It's not, but since you haven't turned tail and run can I assume you want to continue?" Mizer gave her a sympathetic look, and Wally nodded.

"Alright, well, you've met Polly, obviously," Mizer gestured at Polly who beamed that friendly smile back at Wally. "She and I started the Sixth together almost two decades ago, and she's forgotten more about corpses and specs than you or I will ever know."

"Bold of you to assume I forget anything," Polly quipped.

Mizer chuckled and nudged her shoulder with an elbow.

"We all pitch in, but my main role is research and prep," Polly continued. "Once we've ID'd a target, it's my job to make sure you go in with the right equipment to disperse them."

Wally nodded along, actually getting to know the job itself was much more comfortable.

"I . . . I suppose I'll be counting on you a lot if I join up," Wally said, bobbing her head in a brief bow.

"Jemma—" Mizer nodded down where Jemma had stalked off— "is our exorcist, she's the one who performs the actual rites and rituals of dispersal, and don't let her temper fool you, once she's in the field she's the best there is, and I mean that."

Wally tried to smile, she really did, but she didn't quite manage it. It showed on both Polly and Mizer's faces. They grew a bit softer, and a lot more apologetic.

"Look, if you . . . if that was too much, we understand," Polly started quietly. "But for what it's worth, and despite how Jemma behaved, we *do* need you pretty badly."

"Why?"

Polly looked to Mizer who blew out a breath.

"Follow me." He turned and began walking toward the same hallway that Jemma had taken, gesturing to Wally who fell in behind him.

As they reached it, Polly called out. "Wally!" The young reflector turned to look over her shoulder, and Polly offered an encouraging smile. "When you meet her, don't let her make you flinch."

Wally furrowed her brow, but nodded, then turned to catch up to Mizer. His long-limbed strides carried him far and quickly, so Wally had to almost jog to keep up with him.

"There are two other members of our crew," Mizer said as they turned a corner.

"And one of them is who Jemma was talking about?" Wally asked.

"Yeah, here."

Mizer stopped in front of an enormous door that looked like the gate of a bulkhead on a naval vessel, and clearly wasn't an original occupant of this building but rather something that had been installed whenever the Sixth had made their home here.

"What in the . . ." Wally reached out to run a hand across the symbols that had been carved deep into the metal of the door.

Eyes.

Dozens upon dozens of eyes.

There were certain pieces of symbology that crossed the boundaries of every culture and system of magic from the most ancient days to the modern era. Some things never changed, and among those was the symbol of the open eye. The depictions were as varied as they were numerous; here, the simple circle and dot, the hydrogen molecule, the first element, and also the symbol of the monad—the theoretical divine 'first being'. It was also the symbol for circumference, but in occult practice it simply meant: totality.

Eyes upon eyes. The eye of god, of a dozen different gods in fact, from a dozen different kingdoms and cultures. There were twice as many variations on the solar disk. All circles and dots and open eyes.

They were *all* the same thing. Gods of protection. Gods of aversion. Ancient apotropaic symbols that all meant the same thing.

I can see you. I know who you are and I know what you're doing. I can see through to your soul and through this, I know you.

I can see you.

Wally shivered. These were seals. Old ones. Simple but powerful, and meant to cast back bad luck. To bounce ill magic away. It was the sort of thing you put in front of something you considered to be precious beyond all doubt.

Or dangerous, beyond all reason.

Mizer took a grip on the handwheel of the door, then frowned and wiggled it. There was plenty of give which clearly wasn't normal if Mizer's reaction was anything to go by, and he sighed quietly.

"Stay here, alright?" Mizer nodded to the hallway. "I'll make some introductions and shoo Jemma out of the—"

The door swung open with a lazy strength and Mizer's eyes widened. A soft 'oh shit' slipped out of him, and that was the only warning Wally got before Mizer stepped back, and a horror emerged from the shadowed doorway.

It was a titan. Not titanic, although it *was* large. It was a titan in the old sense. A monster. An inhuman throwback of primordial violence that towered clear to seven feet tall, or maybe even a little over, but it was hard to tell because it had hunched to get through the doorway.

The thing wore stained denim overalls and a ragged black-and-red striped sweater over pallid, bloodless flesh that bore scars from battle and surgery alike over every visible inch of its body. Thick, steel-toed boots covered feet that preceded it through the door, followed by shoulders that were as broad as Wally was tall, and borne over one of those shoulders was a wicked-looking wood-axe.

Her—if the shape of its body could be said to be relevant to gender anymore—face was veiled by a matted tangle of hair that might have been vibrant red in life, but now, in death, was washed out and almost orange.

And she was very dead.

"Damn it—!" Mizer hissed. "Siobhan what are you doing here?!"

'Siobhan' didn't answer, she just turned with aching slowness toward Wally, and as her eyes fell across the young reflector . . .

Wally vanished.

CHAPTER 3

The world washed out into sharp-split monochrome. Black and white. Light and dark. Nothing in between. The world was painfully sharp and it was all Wally could do to keep breathing.

In front of her, the horror was frowning. It looked left, then right, seeking her. Hunting for her. It couldn't see her, though. No one could see her and if she stayed very, very still, and if she didn't breathe and didn't blink, then it would stay that way. The monster wouldn't see her, the daemon wouldn't see her.

He wouldn't see her.

Sound was muffled, but Mizer looked shocked as he shouted something—not at her but at the horror, who, surprisingly, seemed to obey. It gave a stilted bob of its head, turned its back on both Mizer and Wally, and began walking away. As it did, Jemma stepped out, or a shape that Wally thought was Jemma. She wasn't sure. She couldn't be sure of anything anymore. Panic and fear was gnawing at her guts and chewing on her bones. She had to ignore it, though, because she couildn't move. She would only be safe if she didn't move.

Mizer called out again. He said something but Wally couldn't hear him. She couldn't hear anything. She could barely see anything but the stark outlines of the world.

And the monster.

Its bulk receded slowly until it faded away, and the moment it did Wally let out a sobbing breath and collapsed to her knees.

All at once, the world slammed back with the force of a battering ram. Color flooded her vision and every sound, from the creak of the ancient building's settling bones to the shouts of her name, to a yelp of alarm from Jemma,

"Gods' hooks!" Mizer stumbled back.

"Where the hells did you come from?!" Jemma's ears were pricked almost straight up as she leaned in to examine Wally with wide eyes.

"Aighira's love, Jemma, will you give the girl some space?!" Mizer grabbed her by the shoulder and pulled her roughly back before kneeling in front of the hyperventilating Wally.

"Gods, I am so sorry about that, Wally," he continued softly, holding a hand out but not quite touching her as he did. "We try to ease people into meeting Siobhan but you've just got all the bad luck today, I guess . . . really, though, I'm sorry."

"Hey! Don't go talking about Siobhan like you're ashamed of—"

"Enough!"

Jemma started violently at the blade-sharp fury in Mizer's voice. It was loud and hard enough that even Wally let out a frightened squeak. It was eased by the fact that Mizer wasn't aiming his anger, or even looking, at her. He was staring down at Jemma who was wilting back. Her ears pinned back lower than Wally had ever seen a pair of elf ears go, and although Jemma tried to put up a brave front, the shaking in her legs betrayed her.

"Enough, Jemma," Mizer said slowly as he raised a hand and pointed a finger past her. "Please, just . . . just go find Siobhan and stay with her, alright?"

The anger went out of both of them, and Jemma let out a small, shaky nod, turned, and began jogging down the hall as quickly as she felt she could without giving up any more of her dignity.

Mizer turned back to Wally and held out a hand while wearing a genuinely pained look on his face. "Miss Willowbark, if you want to back out of this I completely understand," Mizer said calmly. "I have no excuse for what just happened."

Wally stared at the proffered limb for a long moment as she pulled her breathing back under control. It took several minutes and, thankfully, Mizer didn't try to hurry her along. He just waited as calmly as possible until Wally finally worked up the strength to speak, and the words that came out were half disbelief and half accusation.

"That was a dreadnought."

"She is," Mizer admitted. "Siobhan is sanctioned."

Sanctioned; one of the conscious dead. A corpse who had come back with their memories more or less intact. Wally had always been distantly aware of them, but they were vanishingly rare—even moreso than reflectors—so she'd never met one. For some reason, she'd always assumed they'd look more . . . normal.

"Siobhan is actually quite nice, and I promise she won't hold your reaction to her against you so long as you don't . . . well, so long as you're willing to talk to her, I guess."

Wally finally took Mizer's hand, unsure if she had an answer to that particular question yet, and levered herself up. She almost felt numb. Between Jemma, the generally odd manner of the rest of the Sixth, and now this encounter with a walking corpse, she wasn't sure if she should run for the hills or just double down and see it through.

It really couldn't get worse, could it? And if it did, it would at least be a hell of a story. The worst job interview in the history of Colvus.

"You . . . you're a dispersal unit, and you employ a necrotic?" Wally had to ask. It was buzzing in her head like a bloated horsefly.

Mizer sighed and crossed his arms.

"Siobhan didn't ask to be the way she is, Wally," Mizer said. "She's had a run of bad luck the likes of which even you couldn't possibly imagine, and whatever her appearance she's a good woman and a good employee."

Wally recognized the gentle admonition and nodded.

"I . . . okay, yeah, I'm sorry."

"It's alright." Mizer put a hand on her shoulder and smiled gently. "You're rattled, that's understandable, plus, you came out of Bressig so I understand the prejudice, but trust me when I say that when the guts hit the fan, there's no one better to have at your back."

"Don't you mean 'shit' hits the fan?" Wally asked with a weak smile.

"Not in this job."

"Oh . . . right."

"Mhm."

Mizer's smile widened, and he nodded at the still-open door.

"So, you wanna back out?" He asked.

Wally turned to look into the room beyond the seal. It was pitch black inside, and even from the doorway she could feel how cold it was inside. At least ten degrees colder than anywhere else in the precinct. She'd met a near-immortal Biomantic, a surly exorcist, a walking corpse, and the way they talked about whoever was in this room, that wasn't the worst of it. Or maybe just not the most serious, and Wally just couldn't get the memory of those warding eyes out of her head.

I see you.

She shivered.

Was this it? Was this all she had in her? After everything that had happened, after surviving Bressig and enduring fifteen years' worth of looks that ranged from pity to fear to disgust, she had finally graduated, gotten her degree, *and* found a place that was willing to take her on despite lacking a useful magical talent. Sure it . . . it wasn't *ideal*, but Mizer seemed like a good sort of person to work for, and she really liked Polly. She was pretty sure she and Jemma wouldn't be friends anytime soon but co-workers didn't have to all be bosom buddies or anything. They could have a functional, working relationship, right?

And Siobhan . . .

Wally bit down on her lip.

Mizer was right. Siobhan hadn't asked to be like that, just like Wally hadn't asked for Bressig to happen. Maybe she was just being thoughtless. She should at least give the . . . the woman a chance.

"No, I'm not backing out," Wally turned to look at the doorway again. "I want to know why you need a reflector because I want this job and I want to know that I can . . . that I'm right for it." To know that everything that had happened to her meant something.

Mizer eyed her cautiously for a few moments, then nodded.

"Alright, I'm sure Jemma gave her an earful of gossip about the new 'hire' but don't worry." He grinned and jerked a thumb towards the room. "She knows when Jemma is full of it better than most."

Wally hoped so, otherwise it wouldn't really matter if she wanted to stick around. From the sounds of it, this person was going to be the real deciding factor because—however Mizer tried to assure Wally—something about 'her' is what necessitated Wally's hiring in the first place. If she didn't want Wally around, then that was probably going to be that which, in the end, meant that it was out of Wally's hands, and that took a lot of the stress out of the matter when Wally realized it, and she nodded with a faint smile as Mizer left her in the hallway. Nothing Wally could do could really fuck up her chances. Mizer had all but promised her the job if she wanted it, so now she just had to be weighed and not be found wanting.

Wally snorted softly.

"First time for everything, I guess," she muttered.

She strained her ears to listen in on the conversation she was sure was happening beyond the door, even going so far as to brush her hair away from them and prick them up. Unlike Jemma, she didn't mind passing as human. It was easier in most cases, even though the Pykan elves had a decent reputation.

Some people just didn't like elves.

She couldn't hear a word. Had he been lying? That didn't seem right, but she didn't know Mizer very well. This certainly didn't seem like a prank, so—

The door creaked open and Wally yelped as she jumped back, and Mizer chuckled as stepped out of the doorway.

"Eavesdropping?" He asked with a smirk and a quirked

eyebrow.

Wally shuffled nervously before deciding honesty was probably the best policy in this case, and nodded. "I was just curious . . . sorry."

"It's fine." He waved it off. "There was nothing to hear, just go on ahead, she's waiting for you."

Wally nodded and stepped past him, only to pause at the doorway and look back.

"Any advice?"

Mizer scratched at his jaw for a moment, made a thoughtful hum, and then nodded back to her and said, "Don't let her make you flinch."

That was the second time she'd been given that advice in about ten minutes and she wasn't sure how she felt about that. Oh well, in for a ducar, in for a ducalt, as the dwarves said.

The room was freezing, and Wally wrapped her arms around herself as she stepped into the darkness. Her breath misted in front of her and she found herself wishing desperately that she'd brought some warmer clothes even though it was a warm spring day outside. A stiff breeze crossed Wally's face, forcing her to blink rapidly to clear the sudden, reflexive tears that leapt to her eyes, and the door clanged shut, cutting off the dim illumination from the hallway and dousing Wally in shadow. She spun about, desperately trying not to start hyperventilating again. That wasn't as easy as it sounded. It was pitch black and ice-cold, and Wally was having a hard time focusing on anything at all because of the sudden sensation of being watched.

It wasn't anything to do with the fact that she knew the room wasn't empty. It was the fact that she could *feel it*. She could feel eyes on her. A kind of flaying regard that was opening her up and picking around in her soul.

And breathing.

There was breathing.

Soft and constant, in and out. Somewhere in the room, somebody was breathing.

Don't let her make you flinch.

The advice came back to Wally in a rush. Whoever this was,

she was messing with Wally. She was trying to scare her, and that . . . that made her *mad*. Squaring her shoulders, Wally swallowed back her fear and turned to face the darkness with her feet planted and her fists clenched.

"Well?!" Wally snapped. "Come out already!"

Today had been an objectively awful day. She'd been yelled at, been fought about, had to face down an *actual dreadnought*, and now some two-bit telekine was fucking with her by slamming doors!

She was *done!*

'*Oh, I like you already~*'

Wally screamed.

The voice hadn't come from any one direction. It hadn't even come from all around her like she'd been expecting after the theatrical slamming of the door. It had come from inside of her head.

A telekine *and* a telepath? That was terrifying.

'*What's wrong? Lost your nerve?*'

"N-No." Even Wally didn't buy that, but whoever this was at least was polite enough not to point it out. "I uhm . . . telepathy is rare, I just wasn't expecting it," she said, finding her mental footing—and her anger—again, as she frowned. "And it's incredibly rude to mind-speak at someone who hasn't consented, you know!"

She said those last words sharply, and the voice rippled out in waves of laughter in her mind. It was a woman, she already knew that, but rather than Jemma's rasp or the bright and bubbly tones of Polly, this voice was . . . if Wally had to put a word to it, she would say 'husky'. Or maybe 'cocky'. It was the voice and the laugh of someone who looked you in the eye, cracked their knuckles, then jutted out their chin to give you the first swing.

'*Hmm . . . so Mizer wasn't lying. He really didn't tell you anything about me at all, did he?*'

Wally refused to flinch.

"No, he didn't."

She also refused to engage mind-to-mind.

'*Then the flat of it is that this is my only means of communication unless you're interested in a particularly morbid staring contest.'*

Some fifteen feet from Wally, a faint glow sputtered to life, outlining some kind of apparatus in the darkness, and she had to squint and hold her hand up against the sudden intrusion of light. It wasn't bright but the room was so dark that it still made her eyes ache.

"Why is it so dark?" Wally asked as she blinked rapidly, trying to force her eyes to adjust without straining them.

'Because I blow out sparklight bulbs by existing, Miss Willowbark, why else?'

Wally lowered her hand.

"Overcharge?" She asked softly.

The woman must be insanely powerful, then. To overcharge and blow out powered magical circuits just by being near them was the sort of phenomenon common only to powerful spectrals, and only because they were like an uninsulated wire themselves.

For a living person to do that? It was almost unthinkable.

'Come closer, let me get a better look at you.'

The way she said that made Wally shiver, but not necessarily in a bad way. From everything the others had said, she expected whoever this was to sound crueler.

Or to sound mean, at the very least.

Aside from a little light poltergeisting—and what telekine *hadn't* indulged in that? It was half the fun of the discipline—she'd been relatively cordial.

Wally stepped forward, crossing the short distance to a small and slightly raised platform at the end of the room. As she did, the light grew a bit stronger, and she was able to make out the shape of a metal cylinder that was partially set into the wall and which rested at a forty-five-degree cant. There was a chair beside it to the left, and an alcove built into the same side with a monitor and tower setup attached to the system. Every few seconds a soft hiss emitted from the cylinder, and Wally chuckled softly as she realized *that* was the sound of breathing she'd heard earlier.

"Is this . . . ?" Wally started.

'Me? After a fashion, yeah. Hit the glowing green button on the keyboard in front of you.'

Swallowing back her fear, Wally moved to the computer and tapped the button, and a series of clockwork clicks emitted from the cylinder. Slowly, the top third of the cylinder's front metal plate began to detach on a set of miniature hydraulic arms and slid down the length of it revealing a smooth, plate glass window that was fogged with frost.

Unable to resist, Wally moved around to the other side of the cylinder where she could reach it without crawling over the access monitor, gathered up some of her sleeves, and rubbed at the frosted window.

"Gods' hooks~" Wally stared down at what she found.

She was *beautiful*.

The woman inside the cylinder had a face that was strong and patrician with a straight duchess nose and high cheekbones, but still soft for all of that. Her eyes were closed as if she were sleeping, and her hair . . . *Gods*. It was the most vibrant shade of auburn that, in the low light, almost reflected crimson, and it fell in messy waves to frame that perfect face all the way down to the expanse of her strong shoulders.

She was wearing a light linen tunic with a chain of fine silver links looped about her neck. Something small and jeweled was attached to the necklace, but it plunged down past her collar to vanish between her—

'Flattering as this is, you might want to close your mouth before you drool on my sarcophagus.'

Wally clicked her mouth shut and flushed bright red at her cheeks. Her ears were burning and pinned back in embarrassment under her hair as she stepped away while laughter echoed in her mind, warm and confident.

"Sorry," Wally muttered.

'Don't be' the mind-voice replied, and Wally could swear she could hear her smiling. *'You're a cutie, and a helluva reflector, you're not even nauseated yet, huh?'*

"Hmm?" Wally frowned as she brushed a few strands of brown hair from her eyes, and crossed her arms over herself. "Should I be?"

Silence answered her, then more laughter. This time the

voice sounded genuinely impressed. *'Wow, you . . . you haven't even noticed, have you?'*

A shiver of apprehension settled over Wally's shoulders as she took a step back from the cylinder—no, the sarcophagus, and her frown deepened.

"N-Noticed what?"

Another wave of laughter.

'Hey, cutie, you've heard of bait-spectrals, right? Like, will'o'wisps? Ones that use a beautiful or attractive lure to get you close enough for their monstrous forms to jump you?'

"I'm not sure I like where that question is going," Wally said quietly.

More laughter.

Suddenly the room almost seemed to *flex*, and Wally clapped a hand over her mouth as a wave of vertigo washed over her, only to quickly vanish, leaving her gasping for air as a cold sweat broke out across her brow.

"What—?"

'Don't look up.'

A chill went down Wally's spine that had nothing to do with the temperature plunging another ten degrees, and the sensation of being watched doubled over on itself. A predator's gaze was boring into the back of her neck from the shadows in the corner of the room behind her. Something hungry. Something unnatural. Something *evil*. She could feel it as surely as she could feel her own hands and feet!

Wally turned her head—

'—don't do it—'

—and looked up into the shadowed corner of the ceiling.

. . .

A daemon.

It was a daemon.

Wally's mouth went dry.

Ragged sweat-matted locks of auburn hair hung like chains over a pair of cerulean embers that were burning in the shadows behind her set into a twisted mockery of the face belonging to the beauty in the containment unit. Her skin was ruddy red and veined with the same fiery blue as the light in her eyes, and her hands . . . claws? Knives, maybe. They were hideous, hooked things made to flay skin from muscle and muscle from bone. Shadows clung to her body like a greatcoat, and wavered in a psychic wind around arms that were spread to anchor herself into the corner as she stared down at Wally.

Her smile was the worst, though.

She had teeth like a deep-sea predator—thin, triangular and notched for ripping flesh in the messiest and most painful possible way.

'Hey, cutie.'

CHAPTER 4

"N^{O!"} Wally shrieked as she stumbled back from the apparition in the corner, and the air flashed silver between them.

The daemonic shape flinched and wavered but didn't fade. She just laughed. It was a chain-smoker's rasp, and it scratched at the inside of Wally's mind as much as it did at her ears as the daemon twisted bonelessly in the corner and began crawling on all fours along the ceiling towards her.

'What's wrong? Aren't I still pretty?!'

Her voice was freakishly distorted in a way that made Wally's stomach heave and twist. That wasn't telekinesis! It wasn't telepathy either!

Holomancy? *Cerebramancy?* Did she somehow get all the way into the visual centers of her brain to project an image? No, she was a reflector! That shouldn't be possible! Wally backed into the sarcophagus hard and froze as the daemon continued to scuttle disjointedly across the ceiling. Its eyes were alight with sadistic glee, and everything about it seemed too impossibly real.

"Snap out of it." Wally swallowed thickly. "G-Gotta snap out of it!"

CRACK!

She slapped herself across the face in an attempt to jar her senses. It didn't help. The click-clicking of taloned fingers on metal was still there. Those eyes—cerulean eyes like dull-flame embers—were still there!

Again! She had to snap herself out of it!

Wally raised her other hand, wound it back, and—

A telekinetic grip like iron caught her wrist, and Wally's stomach did a backflip.

Too real! TOO REAL!

'Stop that.'

The daemon was standing on the ceiling, with her hair remaining defiantly at her back despite her being upside down, and her eyes meeting Wally's evenly. The manic, sadistic gleam in her gaze was gone, as was the too-wide, shark-toothed smile.

'Mizer said you wanted to know why we need a reflector?' She asked flatly.

A strangled croak escaped Wally's lips.

The daemon released Wally's wrist, leaving a faint black mark on it that wasn't a bruise. It flaked like soot or ash. Even her kine-touch had been fever-hot, something Wally only realized beneath the veil of her terror because her wrist felt colder than the rest of her.

'Let me show you why we need a reflector.'

It was eerie, hearing her speak without speaking despite seeing her face—or at least *a* face—but before Wally could say anything, before she could plead or protest, the upside-down daemon flung its arms wide, stretched open her mouth, and *roared*.

It wasn't a sound.

It was a sensation.

Wally could feel it in the foundation of her soul as hoarfrost stained the ceiling around the daemon's feet and corpusant crackled along the metal and glass frame of the containment unit behind her, sparking like electric flames, and suddenly the whole of the room was illuminated by witchlights.

"Gods' truth . . ." Wally breathed the words out as her jaw went slack

They were *everywhere*.

Gods of aversion.

Apotropaic symbols.

Eyes upon eyes upon eyes were carved into the walls, all looking inward, all staring at the containment unit. The Eye of God. The Monad. The Solar Disk. They were all pointed directly at the figure lying supine behind Wally. It was the kind of warding that could only be meant to turn back the darkest of curses—the sort worked by cursemongers whose names were synonymous with pain and horror; names like Aibon, Mizrahi, and Pikkeman.

Silver light coruscated around Wally casting back flashes of brackish light even as the warding eyes began to glow white-hot from the effort of bouncing back the sheer weight of miasma that she was hemorrhaging out. The stink of burning metal was filling the room along with the smell of sulfur and fire-blackened bone.

Eventually, though, the wards did their work, and the roar tapered off, leaving the apparition in front of Wally looking winded and spent, and after a moment she simply faded away like mist. The hoarfrost melted, the temperature rose by increments, and the electric crackle of corpusant vanished leaving behind only the iron-tang of ozone on Wally's tongue as she slowly turned to look back down at the woman in the containment unit with wide, disbelieving eyes.

'Do you see, now?' The voice was noticeably quieter. Weaker, Wally thought. *'I vent necrotic miasma just by existing. I leave curses like footprints wherever I go . . . no one can endure my presence for long unless they're a reflector, and without a handler I can't use a lick of real magic.'*

"What are you?" Wally whispered.

'I'm a bad star.'

Wally shivered.

"Were you . . . trying to scare me?" Wally asked.

Silence followed her question that stretched on for a full minute. The faint drip-drip-drip of water from the melted frost on the ceiling was the only sound that disturbed the air. It was a heavy kind of quiet, the kind that Wally wasn't sure she could lift, but she didn't leave.

Nothing about this made any sense.

'Was I?' She sounded uncertain of her own motives. *'Why*

would I do that?'

"I don't know."

Wally was proud of how steady her voice was. She wouldn't, even on her best days, consider herself to be a brave person. She wasn't the sort to stand up to anything. Bressig had made it abundantly clear that her only talent, if indeed she could be said to possess one, was surviving in the most undignified way possible.

The apparition flickered into existence again, this time without the aura of terror and hate that it had previously worn like a villain's cape-and-mantle in some cheap, ha'ducar paperback horror. There was no scrape of claws or crackle of corpusant this time, just the sound of a greatcoat flapping faintly in the wind, and then she was there.

Wally wasn't afraid of her this time, although she couldn't quite put a finger on why. Maybe it was the very human exhaustion in the daemon's black-pinned, blue-ember eyes, or something about the way her auburn hair hung lankly around her face, but she seemed almost dejected.

'Are you?'

"Am I what?"

'Scared of me.'

She cocked her head curiously. The suggestion of that long coat in the shadows was easier to see now that she was right-side-up and, as intimidating as she had seemed before, and as terrified as Wally had been a moment ago, for some reason it just wasn't as crippling now.

It was more fascinating.

"Can . . . I mean, will you come a little closer?" Wally stepped back to make room between her and the containment unit.

The apparition raised a single eyebrow, a curiously normal expression on such an objectively horrifying face, then her form flickered like static and she was suddenly less than a foot from Wally's face, prompting a startled squeak. Forcing herself to swallow back her apprehension, Wally willed herself to look the woman in the eyes. Her gaze was intense, and not just because of the unearthly blue fire in her eyes. It was something in the directness of it and in the unwavering force of her expression.

"What's your name?" Wally asked shakily.

The daemon crossed her arms, and the corner of her mouth quirked up in a charmingly lopsided smile that made Wally's heart do an incredibly unusual flip. Alright, daemon-faced or not, that was something she was apparently into. She was going to unpack that *later*.

"Veszha," she said—actually speaking aloud, finally. "My name is Veszha Gibson, but you can call me Vess."

"Vess." Wally rolled the name over in her mind. It was a sharp name. A name like a hand-and-a-half blade leveled squarely at an enemy. It was a name that sounded almost like a challenge.

It fit her, Wally decided, and she drew in a shaky breath as she forced herself to keep looking squarely at Vess. Her face was . . . not quite as inhuman as it had looked when she'd been on the ceiling, but Wally couldn't be sure that that wasn't on purpose, or if terror had warped her perception. Now, though, her face seemed almost normal. Or at least, normally *shaped*. Her skin was still a ruddy, inhuman shade of red, and her veins still carved with rivers and tributaries of neon blue beneath it. If Wally tried, she could ignore the fangs and the hooked fingers, and unnaturally queasy energy that Vess exuded, and see an odd kind of beauty to her. Very different from the beauty of her physical body, true, but beauty for all of that. Like a wolf in the wild. Dangerous, sure, but majestic.

She still wasn't even sure how Vess was standing there, nearly solid. Some kind of astral projection? Without thinking, Wally brought up her hands to the Vess' face—

—and Vess *flinched.*

A pregnant silence welled up between them, and both Wally and Vess' eyes slowly widened as they each realized what had just happened.

"What . . . What are you doing?" Vess asked, the airy confidence of her voice cracking for the first time.

Wally jerked her hand back, mortified. She'd just tried to *touch* Vess! For no reason! Without even asking! "Sorry, I'm sorry!" she stammered. "I just . . . I wasn't sure how you were staying solid, that's all!"

Vess just stared at her, and for a heartbeat, Wally actually thought she was about to lash out. Reflector or not, those claws could leave her dead on the floor in seconds.

She didn't.

Instead, Vess slowly reached out a hand, and the pads of her clawed fingers brushed Wally's knuckles. Her touch was feverish; like there was a furnace burning just underneath her skin. When Wally didn't pull back, Vess gingerly took hold of the smaller woman's hand and drew it back up to her cheek, all the while holding Wally's gaze.

Wally swallowed back a dozen different questions. She just stood and watched and waited. Vess' cheek was so warm. Hot, really. Definitely hot. It was like touching the handle of a cast-iron pan just as it was becoming unbearable to grip without a mitt.

And then she was gone.

There was no sound or fanfare. One moment Vess was standing there, letting Wally touch her, however gently, and the next it was just empty air. The faint clicking noise of the containment unit's covering plate rattled quietly as it returned to its place over the viewing window of the cylinder.

Wally turned and looked around, trying to spy the daemonic shadow in some corner or alcove, but there was nothing. She was just gone. Returned to her body.

Had she done something wrong? Said something?

"Vess?" Wally called weakly. "Vess, I . . . I'm sorry if I . . . if I did something wrong!"

Her voice echoed off the carved metal walls, bounced back like curses from the eyes of aversion.

"Vess!"

Nothing.

She wasn't going to cry. That was stupid. Vess hadn't gotten angry, or yelled, or said anything . . . maybe she was just tired. Wally hoped she was just tired.

"Okay I . . . I'm going to go," Wally said quietly, trying to bite back the tremor in her jaw.

She edged back towards the door, part of her still wary of Vess jumping out at her, while at the same time almost hoping she would despite how much Wally hated being frightened. There were no jump scares, though. No airy, confident laughter. Nothing but silence followed Wally as she reached the door, rapped her knuckles against it, and waited the few seconds it took Mizer to crank the door open.

"So?" Mizer asked, looking hopeful.

He glanced over her shoulder, clearly looking for the room's owner, and frowned when he didn't see her.

"Where is she?"

"I think I did something wrong."

She hung her head, her ears drooped, and her hair fell across her eyes like a veil. There was an uncomfortable ache in her chest that she couldn't put a finger on, and wasn't sure she wanted to. Especially not now that she'd probably blown her chances.

All because she couldn't keep her hands to herself.

Stupid. Why was she always so *stupid*.

"I'm sure you didn't," Mizer said, patting her shoulder gently. "I'll talk to her and we'll see how she feels about you being her reflector, alright?"

Wally felt a little lighter at that. Maybe if Mizer talked to her, Vess would give her another chance. She got the impression they respected one another. She'd be very grateful if that were the case, even though she knew Mizer would probably only be doing it because of how badly they needed a reflector on their staff.

"Okay," she said, forcing a slightly wider smile than she felt was honest as she looked up at Mizer and nodded. "I'll uhm, I'll go home and wait then, and Mizer?"

"Mhm?"

"When you talk to her? Can you tell Vess I'm sorry for whatever I did?"

Mizer's jaw clicked open and he stared at Wally like she'd just grown a second head. The look went on long enough that Wally was starting to feel a little self-conscious when Mizer finally blinked and snapped himself out of it, offered a slightly shakier smile than he had been wearing a moment ago, and nodded.

"Yeah, no . . . no problem, I'm sure it's nothing."

Wally blew out a relieved sigh.

"I really hope so," she said. "Thank you."

"I'll go chat with her now, okay? Have Polly walk you out," Mizer said, gesturing down the hall. "Can't have you wandering the precinct on your own yet, I'm afraid."

"I completely understand, and thank you again," she bobbed her head in a short bow, "for both the interview and for talking to Vess for me."

"Of course, have a safe trip home." Mizer looked almost uneasy again for a moment, then the look was gone and he was wearing that same, endearingly boyish smile.

Wally gave another stilted bow then turned on her heel and began walking down the hall as Mizer cracked open the door to Vess' chamber and slipped inside. If anyone could sweep up whatever it was Wally had done, she had a feeling Mizer would be the one to do it.

Idiot.

Idiot.

What had she been *thinking?!*

"Vess?"

Vess Gibson snapped herself out of her mental self-flagellation and cast her senses outward towards the familiar voice. Light, or something very like light, flood her perceptions. and the world came alive with skeins of magical energy. The room was saturated in a soupy mixture of grey shadow and purplish miasma—the by-products of her own twisted soul—and from that mist a bulwark of elemental light was pushing its way toward her.

'*Mizer.*'

Vess pulled herself together enough to cast her thoughts and senses out, and Mizer's left eye twitched faintly as she tickled his frontal cortex before slipping around his occipital lobe and settling in to begin communication. It was an uncomfortable process for most people, but that girl, Wally . . . she hadn't even noticed Vess doing it. Hell, *Vess* had hardly noticed she'd done it. It had happened as easily as if they'd been doing it for years. Wally had walked in and Vess had simply rolled in and settled into the rear quarters of the girl's mind without so much as a hiccup.

"Can I ask what happened?"

Mizer was upset, she could feel the turmoil in him.

'Hire her.'

"No shit, of course I'm gonna hire her. I'm asking what happened," Mizer replied a little more sharply. "She walked out looking like a kicked puppy!"

'I . . . I didn't mean for that to happen.'

"Gods' hooks, for *what* to happen?!" Mizer squared his shoulders, the force of his personality—and his magic—driving her cursed energy away from him before it could root in his aura.

Vess didn't answer, but Mizer wasn't letting it go.

"You told her your name, Vess!" he continued sharply. "You made Dolin call you 'Boss' for eight months before you told him your name, and you threatened to skin-walk Polly out a window if she told him on the sly!"

'It's not my fault I like messing with people.'

"Actually, yeah, it's entirely your fault, in fact," Mizer said flatly.

'Shut up, Mizer.'

The stubborn bastard wouldn't let it go. He crossed his arms and set his jaw, and Vess could feel him laying down roots into the bones of the earth even as the air anchored him to space itself. He was powerful. Not as powerful as Vess. Not by main magical force, anyway. But he was practiced, sharp, keen-eyed, and smart, and he knew exactly how to use what he had to its maximum effect.

"What. Happened?"

'She made me flinch, alright?'

Vess snapped out the answer and buried herself back into her hindbrain. That had *not* been her finest moment. Why had she done that? She literally couldn't remember the last time she'd flinched.

Surprise rippled through Mizer's mind.

"You're serious?"

'No, I'm fucking with yo—Yes I'm fucking serious, do you think I'd just say something like that?!'

Mizer winced at the anger in her tone, and his eye twitched. The cursed energy hissed and snapped like an angry cat all around him, but he hedged it out and rallied. Vess reeled herself in a little and sent a soothing wave of cool relaxation over him by way of apology.

'Sorry.'

"It's fine," Mizer waved it off, "so how'd she do it?"

'She tried to touch me,' she replied, and Mizer's eyebrows inched upward.

"Did you do the ceiling thing?" he asked with a wry laugh.

'Yeah.'

"Dolin damn near shit himself when you pulled that on him."

'She stood her ground. Even slapped herself to make sure I wasn't nicking around with her neocortex and taking her perceptions for a spin.'

"She's got iron in her spine, that one," Mizer replied. "She survived Bressig, you know."

Vess cursed. Bressig? Shit. If she'd known that she might've gone a little easier on the girl. There weren't a lot of things that could make her want to pull punches but nobody deserved the full force of her rancid personality after surviving something like Bressig no matter how long ago it was. She knew better than anyone the sorts of scars those experiences left behind.

'She must've been what . . . seven? Eight?'

"Nine."

'Nine. Shit.'

"She miraculously still wants the job," Mizer said. "She was actually worried she'd done something wrong and offended *you* and asked me to apologize for her for whatever she thought she did."

And she was also apparently a saint. Great. As if Vess needed more of a reason to feel like the biggest asshole of the century.

"So she tried to touch you, huh?" Mizer asked, bringing the conversation annoyingly back around.

'It's like she wasn't scared of me at all, it . . . it caught me off-guard,

that's all.'

"Did you let her?"

Vess didn't dignify that with an answer, which, she supposed, was probably all the answer that Mizer needed.

'Wipe that smug look off your face.'

"I have no idea what you're talking about."

Of course he didn't. Smug, self-satisfied, meddling little—

"How long has it been?"

Despite not being fully anchored to her body, and despite her body being alive only by the loosest and most technical definitions of the word, Vess' stomach dropped.

'A long, long time,' Vess answered, and even her mindspeak was subdued. *'Not since before Geddenheim.'*

"Not even Jemma?"

Vess snorted, although the sound translated a little strangely through the mindspeak medium she was sharing with Mizer. He got the gist though, he knew her habits and her little idiosyncrasies better than anyone else.

'No. Jemma loves me, but less so than she fears me. For all that she would deny it, I don't think Jemma could ever bring herself to get that close unless I ordered her to.'

"Are you sure you'll be comfortable with Wally?" Mizer asked, his tone taking on a more paternal tone.

Vess exerted some pressure on him, the equivalent of a glare, and a stiff reproval. *'The problem is that I might be too comfortable with her, I'm more worried about that.'*

"Why?"

If only he could see her shaking her head in dismay at his lack of imagination. It wasn't that Mizer was stupid. He was a good man, one of the very few that Vess had ever met, but he was a bit naive, especially for a man nearing forty. Despite the horrors in his past and the darkness he'd faced—that he continued to face even now—he was still, somehow, an idealist.

Vess' ideals had died a long time ago.

'There are far too many answers to that question for me to choose just one,' is what she finally decided to say.

Mizer sighed.

"Vess, you're more than just a corpse waiting to die, you know," he said quietly. "You're allowed to have a bit of life and we're willing to help make that happen."

But did she deserve it? That was the bigger question.

The quick, dirty, and brutally honest answer was 'no'. By no logical, ethical, or legal definition did she deserve to have a life. She earned a death sentence a hundred times over. Commuting it to self-imposed imprisonment in stasis doing whatever bits of good she could in the meantime was what she deserved.

'Just hire the damn girl, Mizer.'

He was silent for a long stretch, then his lips flattened to a hard line and he crossed his arms.

"On one condition."

'Seriously?! You were just raving about her!'

"One. Condition."

'Bullshit.'

Mizer narrowed his eyes at her, and once again Vess' stomach sank. He really was that stubborn, wasn't he? Damn that bastard shaman.

'Fine, what?'

"You take a walk," he replied, relaxing and letting his arms fall to his sides. "I'll flood your tank with holy water and drop in a purification tab, Gods know you need a bath anyway."

'Fuck you, Mizer.'

"Deal?"

Vess' mental grumbling turned the psychic landscape of the room into the mental equivalent of gravel briefly before she relented, sighed, and said:

'Fine.'

CHAPTER 5

Colvus was a cold city. The Colver River flowed down from the Ulverike to carve both around and through Colvus, carrying the wolf-winter through the city via three immense, man-made canals at their associated waterway networks, the largest of which cut through the heart of Colvus. Heretic dredgers working off some odd blasphemy or other drifted along the canals in two's and three's on their skiffs, fishing out litter and keeping the waterways clean, while mighty airships moved ponderously overhead. Their shadows crossed Wally now and again, moving slowly to or from the aerial tower berths as they moved through sovereign elemental airspace. Once they reached the city limits they would engage their spark engines and reach speed, most making for the Arka Menais and its twin harbors.

Once, Wally had imagined herself serving aboard one of those vessels. Nothing grand. She didn't think she had the stomach for any sort of responsibility. The idea more than any specific job had been enticing; go wherever the wind takes you, never having to lay down roots. Never having to feel guilty about her solitary life.

Like, most things in Wally's life, though, she'd never gone anywhere with the idea. It hadn't been any great failing or anything like that. The dream had died like most dreams did—from quiet, apathetic disinterest.

Maybe, if things didn't work out with the precinct, she would give the idea another look. She didn't want to give up quite yet, though. Not this time. She would wait, and while she waited Wally walked alongside one of the many tributary canals towards a particular cafe not far from the precinct in the older part of the Sixth District which was colloquially called 'The East End'. It was among the poorest areas of the city, so it was the destitute and unlucky would always 'end' up.

If she followed the street and its adjoining canal far enough, though, she would reach the primary canal and all its wealth, and from there the great water temple of Jiani'Kai would be in sight, although these days it was less of a temple and more of a hospital. At eighteen stories high, it served as the largest and most notable medical facility in almost two hundred miles. It would be busy now what with the Colver, swollen with spring snowmelt, marking that time of prosperity and health according to the Jiani faith. People of all walks would be flocking to the priests and priestesses of the great water spirit for healing for the next few months since Jiani doctrine required them to offer alms during this time of year.

That, Wally reflected, was probably why the street was so packed with people at that moment, and she huddled in on herself to keep from being carried along by the swell of bodies.

She didn't do well in crowded spaces.

The streets weren't so bad, mostly because everyone was going somewhere and no one had the time to pay attention to her, but that didn't necessarily mean she *liked* being crammed in between half a dozen people who smelled vaguely of socks and corn chips. All of these people, many of them she could tell were ill, would be crowding the great hall of the temple in a few hours' time, but for now, she was trapped with them and that made her skin crawl.

Swiveling her head around, Wally scanned for any kind of escape. She didn't really have the money to pay for a ferry—the elementalists would be charging through the nose at this time of day—and she was almost there anyway. Wally grit her teeth, braced herself for unwanted human contact, and shouldered off the walkway toward the wall of businesses lining the street and down to a little stairwell of five steep concrete steps leading to a simple wooden door. No name adorned any part of the stairs, threshold, or door, and only a small sign hanging from a wrought iron arm gave any hint as to its nature. The sign, also devoid of words, showed a minimalistic, wide-mouthed teacup with three squiggles of steam rising up from it.

Wally pulled the deceptively heavy door open and the smell of rich coffee and baked goods wafted out. She breathed deeply of it as she stepped in and a calm settled over her that went a long way towards soothing her frayed nerves from the day's ordeals as the low chatter of the hidden cafe filtered past her, and she pulled the door closed behind her gently.

A young woman was working the coffee bar behind the register with quick, efficient movements that spoke of long practice. Her skin was the color of coal and her hair was even darker, though the thin plaits it had been braided into were adorned with dozens of colorful beads. Her broad, warm smile matched her dark, glittering eyes, and it grew a fraction wider as Wally stepped up to the counter.

"Welcome back, baby, how you doin'?"

Niabi Jesk was more of a fixture of the East End than some of the actual fixtures, although most of the locals knew her solely by the pseudonym of the little cafe she ran.

"Hi, Cuppa, I'm okay."

Wally wove her way between the tight cram of low tables and mismatched, cushioned chairs towards the front counter.

"Can I get a wayleaf tea?"

Cuppa's smile softened as she nodded. "Sure thing, baby . . . you wanna shot of anything in it? Glee? Maybe a dash'a hope? Seems like you could use a little pick-me-up."

Her hands, all longer-fingered grace and easy motions, operated the little copper heating apparatus at the bar with simple rote efficiency.

"Uhm, no thanks." Wally's smile faltered. "I uh . . . I think I flubbed my interview at the dispersal precinct, so the cognitive dissonance would probably just give me the jitters, can I get a shot of nostalgia, though?"

"Sure can, but mind not having too much of that in a week," she worked the pump as she spoke. "Liable to stop appreciating the 'now' if you're stuck in the 'then', y'hear?"

"I know."

Right now it was the most she could afford. Her meals were spartan by necessity until she got a solid job, and there weren't many calls for someone with little-to-no magical talent beyond reflecting, so she couldn't buy many groceries. Most of her funds came from a university stipend that would expire in a couple of months whether she found a job or not.

Maybe she could go back to school and get a teaching degree or something. There couldn't be *that* many Theoretical Necro instructors.

"You sure you're alright, baby?"

Wally looked up to find Cuppa staring at her with concern. Her wayleaf tea was steaming in front of her, and she'd completely spaced out.

"Yeah," Wally said as she took up her tea, "I just had a really long, loud day."

"I hear that."

That got a laugh out of her. A little one. It was better than nothing though. Today hadn't gone well but it could have gone worse. Mizer had promised to talk to Vess and if that went well then maybe she still had a shot at getting the job.

Retreating from the register with her drink in hand, Wally sidled between tables toward an isolated corner. Cuppa's was the sort of place you could lose a lot of time in if you brought a book, and it had been where Wally had done most of her coursework during her years at university. She didn't really have any friends beyond the occasional passing acquaintance from class that she got along well enough with to share conversation with, but those had never lasted past the end of the semester itself.

Wally sipped at her tea.

No, if she were being honest, her social life was defined largely by its absence. She was twenty-four and had no friends, no relationship, no career, and no real prospects if this precinct job didn't work out. In fact, the person she spent the most time with on a consistent basis was Cuppa, which was extra depressing since that was only due to her needing a daily tea fix. The wayleaf tea she made at home out of the cheap, store-bought baggies just wasn't the same.

Another sip.

Wally stared down into the steaming surface of her mug and breathed deeply, letting the sense of ease wash over her as the nostalgia settled in, and for a moment she felt comfortable. Just a moment. That feeling never lasted long, but it was nice while it did.

The emotional warmth started to fade with the heat of the drink as Wally got down to the dregs, but the herbal and slightly savory flavor of the tea was still as good as ever, and she dragged out every bit of it that she could. A part of her wanted to order a refill, but her budget was staring unpleasantly at the back of her neck. If she got the job at the precinct it wouldn't matter, but a quick glance at her phone showed no new messages, and her e-mail displayed the same which didn't bode well, but maybe there was some kind of company meeting that had to happen before a new hire could be agreed on? Mizer seemed like the kind of person who would take everyone's opinion into account.

Including Jemma's.

But Polly liked her, at least! And Mizer seemed to, as well.

So that was one vote against, two votes (probably) for, which would mean that . . . that Vess would be the tiebreaker assuming it was a democratic sort of thing.

Either way, it all came down to Vess.

She'd been so stupid. Why had she done that? Just reached out and . . . but then Vess had let her do it anyway. She'd taken Wally's hand and put it on her cheek herself.

That was good, right?

Sip.

Wally grimaced. Her tea had gone cool. Wayleaf was still good tea no matter what, and it was perfectly good to drink cold in the summer, but in the chilly spring air it was a little disappointing.

"Guess we have that in common now, huh?" Wally said to the bottom fifth of her tea which, predictably, had nothing helpful to add to the conversation.

"Have what in common?"

The puffy chair at the other side of the table Wally was occupying slid out with a dull scrape, and a dull thump of someone dropping into the seat followed it, and Wally looked up with a frown and a request for solitude on her lips.

The request, along with most of her coherent thoughts, blinked out of existence at the sight in front of her.

Fiery auburn hair fell in waves over warm sun-kissed skin and in front of eyes like gleaming skies. A full mouth was curved into a crooked, confidant—some might say arrogant—smile, that made Wally's heart do another awkward backflip that it didn't quite stick the landing on, leaving her red-faced.

Vess Gibson settled into the chair, a steaming mug in one hand a wide-mouthed cup of tea that smelled suspiciously of wayleaf in the other, and her grin widened just slightly.

"Hey cutie."

The sensation of drowning was brief but all-encompassing for the split second it lasted before the soothing chill of sanctified magic sluiced through her soul. There was a faint burn as it purged away the patina of miasma that had caked on, as there always was, but the pain was both a distant and a familiar thing. A moment later, the little fizzing purification tablet was slotted in and deposited into the holy water where it began fizzing away. It was a mixture of alka-seltzer, blessed silver shavings, ash from an Aighiran brazier-altar, and a single drop of liquid grace.

Vess had to go through one of them every month or so at least in order to keep the miasma she exuded from building up too thickly. Interacting with her was dangerous at the best of times, but doing so after she'd been marinating in her own spite for six months straight was straight up suicidal.

She never got used to the drowning sensation though.

What came after was far more tolerable. More than tolerable, it was downright enjoyable. It never lasted long, a few days at the most depending on how excessively she was forced to use her powers, but, for a little while, after the miniaturized purification ritual was performed, Vess almost felt normal. Not normal enough to physically leave her containment unit, of course—her body would never quite work the way it used to—but normal enough to project without dragging a trail of curses behind her like a milky fart so long as she left most of her power at home.

Focusing, Vess carefully stitched her astral form together. She separated out her talents and her magic inasmuch as she could, wove her mind into the facsimile of her soul, and then projected it out into the arming room of the precinct.

Her eyes snapped open, and the world flooded with color that, for the first time in a month, wasn't from behind a wall of glass.

"Vess!"

Polly's bright voice chimed behind her, and Vess turned. Her coal greatcoat wavering into existence as she solidified herself fully.

"Hey, Pols," Vess opened her arms, "how's my favorite immortal towhead?"

Polly stuck out her tongue but walked into the hug anyway, wrapped her arms around Vess' middle, and squeezed as Vess tousled her flaxen blonde hair.

"I'm fine," she mumbled into Vess's button-down before pulling away and looking up at her. "You're looking sharp today."

Vess' cheeks colored as Polly reached out and adjusted the crimson tie she'd chosen to construct, and flattened some of the wrinkles she'd made of her shirt before tugging the coat straight.

"Hot date?"

"Don't start with me," Vess replied archly. "I haven't been out of the tank in three and a half weeks. I'm taking a walk and I'm allowed to look good doing it."

"Mhm . . . just a walk?"

Polly flashed a vulpine grin that Vess blocked off with a hand over her face.

"*Just* a walk."

"I'm just saying, the last time you 'took a walk' you made it all the way to the kitchen and then binged on ice cream and watched dwarven soap operas for six hours."

She wasn't wrong, but in her defense she hadn't been out of the Precinct *at all* since her last 'walk' prior because Dolin had been gone for better than five months by that point and she hadn't been handling it well.

"I'm only joking, Gibs, go have fun." Polly pushed her, and Vess chuckled and nodded.

"Yeah, yeah, hey, you try living without tasting anything for a month and see how easy it is to resist ice cream, okay?" Vess replied as she tugged at the corners of her greatcoat perhaps a bit harder than necessary.

Polly gave Vess a good-natured shove.

"Okay well, *you* don't need a pill to be able to digest it without sacrificing your next day and a half, along with the integrity of your asshole, to the porcelain throne."

"Mmm. Gross. Thanks for that." Vess flicked Polly across the forehead. "Now, if you're done regaling me on the finer details of your personal inner plumbing, I'm going to go take that walk."

She moved past Polly, her booted feet clicking on the hard concrete floor. Vess flicked her finger, barely a twitch of motion, and the stubborn basement door swung open without a word of complaint. As she was ascending the steps, Polly called out to her from her desk.

"Vess?"

She paused in the doorway and looked over her shoulder at what anyone else would see as a young woman.

"Yeah?"

"When you see her, make sure to tell her she didn't do anything wrong." Polly wore a wan smile, and Vess' cheeks colored. "She was really beating herself up over it on the way out, Gibs," Polly said, a touch more seriously.

Vess didn't answer her, but this time it was because there was a stone in her throat she couldn't seem to dislodge. Polly didn't raise the subject again before Vess made her way up and out.

Once that she was outside though . . .

"Fuck you, Polly, I owe her an apology, that's *all*," Vess muttered

Shutting her eyes, Vess rewove the perceptions of her astral form and tuned herself to the echoes of the souls around her. Normally, this would be seriously hit or miss because, contrary to popular belief, soulstuff is pretty interchangeable.

Reflectors were the exception that proved the rule, though.

Their souls had a glassy, mirror quality to them; a side-effect of their exposure to, and survival of, powerful necrotic miasma in their youth. Usually, that made them a bitch to track, but only if you were trying to anchor a locator spell on them.

This wasn't the first time she'd had to track a reflector, though, and she found the best way to go about it was to just sniff them out.

She had to stop somewhere eventually.

Opening her eyes, Vess scanned the parking lot of the Sixth Precinct. Everything had an odd, violet overwash to it, a side-effect of messing with her vision, and Vess tracked the vapor trails of the souls that passed to and fro in front of it. Most were just soulstuff like any other, leaving behind a trail of vague, emotional material behind in its wake.

But there!

A flash of silver threaded through the morass of violet-washed wakes. A weaving trail that tasted faintly of springberries and elven wayleaves.

Vess licked her lips.

It was Wally's trail. She would stake her life on it.

In fact, she was so sure, she might even stake something on it of actual value. Now, like in her room, something about Wally tickled at the edges of her memory. It was like deja vu in reverse—or a dream, or a memory that wasn't quite in reach. Something about Wally scratched at Vess' hindbrain and it was driving her nuts. What was it about her that was so familiar?

Whatever, she'd find out eventually. She always did.

Tugging her greatcoat straight again, Vess began walking, following the silver-light trail down the street, around the corner, and onto the main thoroughfare of Canal street.

Hundreds of people were crammed shoulder to shoulder, most moving downriver towards the temple to beg the priests for alms, or, more likely, for a cure to their groin-pox before their husbands or wives took notice. Vess' lips curled back in a sneer. So many people and so little worthwhile. Even here in prosperous Colvus the poor still clung to the shadows and eked out a living from bare stone where they could, lucky to scrape up a few ducar to pay for a hot meal, to say nothing of a place to sleep. She bristled as she passed a pair of jeering youths, eighteen or nineteen maybe, poking fun at an older half-elf woman curled up in an alleyway off the main drag, and in an instant, Vess' blood *boiled*.

"People really never change, do they?" She muttered, flicking her finger through the shapes of a rune. "Even after so many years, nothing *really* changes . . . misery begets misery, bad fortune begets yet more bad fortune, well," she hissed a word that as much a sound as it was a name as it was a statement of intent, "let's see how *you two* like a little bad luck."

She didn't wait to see the shiver roll down the spines of the boys. Let them come to understand the weight of a grudge, and how, when you do ill unto others, it's not so strange to find ill wished upon you. The moment her hand was back in her pocket, though, she regretted it. Her stomach twisted unpleasantly as she tried to push the thing she'd just done out of her mind. It wasn't . . . wrong. Nothing she did was wrong. Those boys would only suffer consequences if they continued to be cruel. That cruelty would be visited back on them! It . . .

"It's not my fault." Vess tightened her hand into a fist in her pocket. "People . . . they never change, not really."

Vess hung her head and reached up to lay a hand over the weight hanging around her neck. Mizer would be so disappointed in her. He believed she could be better. Polly, too. And yet here she was, spreading more misery, just like always.

"Misery . . ." she snorted sharply. "Who does misery love?"

Forcing herself to ignore her gnawing conscience, Vess sharpened her eyes back on the trail of silver. It led her a long way down the street, deeper into the East End. The trail stopped and veered off right about where the neighborhood started getting *really* grungy, and a few blocks before the gentrification. Frowning, Vess scanned the street, trying to pick up the trail again. There were so many people that even the distinct silver color was getting mashed up in the ambient soul-noise. People elbowed past her, earning a few muttered oaths, and her temper prickled.

She held onto it this time, and focused.

There.

Turning off from the street to the businesses lining the row, Vess picked up the thread of silver as it spun away and down a stairwell to a little nondescript wooden door. She followed it down cautiously, eyeing the minimal sign that hung from it.

"A cafe?" Vess tapped her chin and smiled. "I could go for a drink."

She reached out for the handle on the door and—

. . .

Vess drew her hand back slowly as if the handle were some kind of venomous serpent she'd very nearly grabbed onto.

It was blessed.

More than blessed; the door and the grounds beyond it were sacrosanct. Someone had worked some old, deep magic when they'd settled in here. It was more than just a shop, it was someone's home, and being almost entirely *spirit* that made her getting in a little more . . . complicated.

"Shit." Vess lowered her hand and scowled at the door.

Alright, think. This was just a spell. *Everything* was a spell. Spells had rules. Rules had exceptions. Read the rules, know the exceptions. Vess scanned the structure of the spellwork. It was hard. So much of it had sunk into the bones of the building— into the foundation stones and the woodgrain and the very soul of the place. The protection and the protectee were almost one being at this point.

Damn. That was the problem with magic that lasted a really long time. The longer it stuck around, the harder it was to pry up.

Thankfully, no one had come in or out, so she didn't look

like a complete idiot as she flickered through a half-dozen scanner spells, giving her the lay of the spell's topography, the wavelength, the harmonic frequency, and the arcane syntax.

That was where she found her answer.

"Horseshit," Vess laughed as she lowered her hand and stared in disbelief at the door. "You're *joking*. It's that one? Oldie but a goodie, I guess."

Raising a hand, she curled her fingers into the elven rune for 'peace' and said in sibilant Oreliaun: "I come bearing neither weapon nor grudge, to partake of hospitality and be hospitable in return, and may my oath return to me tenfold should I break it."

A weight settled around Vess' soul as the protection on the little shop that had, moments ago, been as unassailable as a thirty-foot-high stone wall, became as soft as gossamer.

Putting a hand carefully on the door handle, Vess smirked, pushed open the door, and stepped inside. Now she just had to make sure she kept her magic to herself while she was inside unless she wanted the oath she'd just given to blow both of her femurs out through her nostrils.

No problem.

There were far fewer threads of soulstuff in here, and it was noticeably calmer. Vess couldn't help but wonder if anyone here knew the reason it felt so calm was that there was a literal blessing on the place. And a strong one at that.

She spied her quarry easily enough. The bob and curl of brown and green hair stuck out in a lonely corner of the cafe where Wally sipped at her drink.

Wayleaf tea.

What an elf.

Well, Vess couldn't exactly blame her. If there was one thing the elves could do right, it was a damn good cup of tea.

"Hey, sugar, new here?"

Vess looked up and over at the front counter where, she assumed, the proprietor was waving at her. With her dark hair, dark eyes, and easy smile, she was fetching in a lot of different ways, but the most obvious one wasn't obvious to anyone but

Vess.

"I suppose I am," Vess replied as she closed the distance and tugged a billfold from her pocket.

"Well, welcome to Cuppa's," she said brightly. "What can I get for ya?"

"One caff, a dark dwarven roast if you've got it, and a cup of wayleaf tea."

The price total rounded itself out on the surface of Cuppa's mind, and she had just started to recite the number when Vess held out a crisp black-and-gold twenty-ducar bill. Enough to cover the drinks, plus a generous tip.

Cuppa raised an eyebrow, then took the bill and rang it through the register. The change went into the tip jar as Cuppa began making the drinks.

"Can I ask a personal question, Miss Cuppa?"

The proprietor looked up at her curiously as the smell of rich dark caff filled the air. "Sure thing, sugar, what's on ya mind?" she replied as she pushed the ceramic mug towards Vess just as the wayleaf finished steeping.

"You know Wally, right?" She asked.

The woman narrowed her eyes protectively. Good. Cuppa clearly saw Wally as more than just a patron. That was the response that Vess had been hoping for.

Vess held up a hand. "Relax, I'm just asking because I'm going to be hiring her to work at a dispersal precinct, and I was wondering what she took in her tea."

The apprehension melted from Cuppa's features, and a broader grin bloomed on her face.

"Oh, she'll be over both moons about that," Cuppa said with a chuckle. "She usually takes nostalgia, but she's had a bit too much of that in my opinion, maybe . . ." she trailed off, then took up the teacup and dropped a pump of something faintly gold into it, "how's a little delight sound, Miss—?"

Vess took the cup from her and picked up her own mug of caff, and smiled toothily.

"Call me Vess."

CHAPTER 6

"THIS CAFF IS SHOCKINGLY good."

Vess took another sip of her brew as Wally watched, both perplexed and panicked at the sight of the woman who'd lately been in a stasis sarcophagus suddenly sitting across the table from her whole and hale. If Wally hadn't noticed how stunning Vess was before, she definitely did now. Not to knock against Vess' natural beauty. It was only that, when she'd been in the tank, she'd seemed almost waifish—leaner, smaller, and more ethereal than a normal person.

Not anymore.

Now she was alive.

Gods, she was so alive. Her eyes sparkled with humor and brilliance rather than blue fire, and her full cheeks softened the sharp definition of the high bones beneath. Her hair, which Wally had thought seemed almost crimson beneath the auburn sheen, was now the color of a forest fire in autumn.

"How?" The word left Wally's lips dully as Vess pushed the new cup in front of her.

"I assume she has a supplier, but I suppose I could be wrong," Vess quipped as she took another sip.

Wally snorted and Vess smiled. It was a small, smug little expression, but it did pleasant things to her lips, and a weak laugh escaped Wally on the heels of her undignified snort.

"N-No, I mean," Wally gestured up and down at her, "how are you here? You're outside! I thought you needed a reflector!"

"Ninety-nine percent of the time, I do," Vess replied. "And to answer your question, I'm not here . . . not really. You can see me, and hear me, and we can talk, and I can—" Vess reached out and brushed a strand of green from Wally's face leaving behind a depth of color in her cheeks— "touch, but in the end, I'll just snap back to my body where I'm sleeping."

Wally's eyes widened.

"Projection?"

"Mhm."

Vess nodded and smiled over her mug of caff and took a much deeper draught of it, humming appreciatively at the flavor before lowering it and nodding down to Wally's own cup of tea.

"You should drink, it'll get cold otherwise."

Wally looked down at the new mug, then nodded and took it up, sipping tentatively at it before looking back up at Vess.

"How are you solid? Astral projection . . . it doesn't do that."

Vess huffed against her mug, scattering the steam, and shook her head.

"What is astral projection but the projection of the senses?" Vess asked. "The sense of sight and sound, sure, but why not smell, taste, and touch too? And why should it be different to project that same sense to others?" Vess' expression curved into a grin, and Wally's heart did a little flip at the excitement that suddenly rose into her voice. "It's not that hard, you know. A little telepathy, some empathy, a touch of kinetic facsimile, mix it all together, add water, bake at three-fifty for an hour and a half, and bam!"

Her smile showed pearl-white teeth and Wally couldn't help but laugh. This was nothing like how she imagined Vess would be. She was so dynamic. So sharp-eyed and talkative! It wasn't that she'd thought Vess was dim or anything, obviously, but she'd never imagined *this*.

"You just rattled off five different magical disciplines and said it's 'not that hard'?" Wally gawked at her for a moment before shaking her head in disbelief.

"It's not hard for *me*," Vess clarified. "But then, I'm a genius, so . . ." She gave a nonchalant wave of her caff mug before taking another sip.

"And humble," Wally added.

"Humble as *fuck.*"

Wally snorted and laughed again. Gods, should it be this easy? Why was it so easy to just sit here and talk to her? Wally had never in her life been able to just sit down and talk to someone like this. But the moment Vess was in front of her she became the sun and Wally's world started to orbit her like it was the most natural thing in the world, and it was just . . . easy.

Sipping at her tea, Wally struggled for something else to say, anything to keep the moment from fading.

"It's called Bi-location, by the way," Vess added as she lowered her mug. "This spell, I mean."

"O-Oh, it's amazing," Wally said, desperately grateful she didn't have to carry the conversation. "I've never even heard of it."

"You wouldn't have, it's not something most would bother to learn and even fewer could perform the spell if they knew the how of it, you know?" Vess said.

"I guess so."

"Simply put, astral projection is simpler, easier, and more energy-efficient," Vess continued.

Wally raised an eyebrow.

"So why did you . . . bi-locate?" That sounded like the right way to say it but Wally couldn't be sure.

Either it was or Vess didn't care because she didn't comment on the wording. Instead, she just smiled again, reached out, and brushed another strand of green from Wally's face.

"No reason."

Wally matched her smile and she didn't even need to try. For once it felt natural and comfortable to smile and she wondered, passingly, if this is what having a friend felt like.

Just comfortable.

"You're shameless, huh?" Wally asked softly as she took

another sip of her tea.

"Pretty much," Vess agreed.

"What about the, uhm, the reflector thing?"

Vess shrugged.

"I undergo purification once a month to ensure I don't lose any more of my soul to necrosis, right after it's done the curse on me is subdued enough for me to go walkabout for a little while, a day or two at most, but to be safe we limit my walks to eight hours at a time."

"Did you say . . . more?"

More of her soul? Which naturally begged the question of how much of it was even left intact? Or how she was even sane with her soul partially necrotized. Wally hadn't even heard of someone stopping the process partway through. Necrosis was supposed to be inevitable once it started.

"Yeah," Vess said quietly, her humor faded. "More."

"That's why you're in the sarcophagus?"

"Among other reasons, yeah," Vess replied.

"How did it . . . no, I'm sorry, you don't have to—"

"I betrayed someone dear to me," Vess said before Wally could finish backpedaling. Her eyes, so blue and vibrant before, were suddenly hard and vicious. "I killed her in the most nightmarish way possible and on her way out she made sure I would never forget what I'd done."

That didn't so much puncture the mood as impale it and leave it bleeding out on the floor of its childhood bedroom. Wally stared over the table at Vess. There was a hardness there beneath the humor and the sass and the brilliant raconteur that was Vess Gibson, and it wasn't even that far down.

She barely bothered to hide it and clearly wasn't ashamed.

"Why?"

"I told you," Vess said flatly. "I'm a bad star, and I figure you should know at least a little about what kind of person you're going to be working with."

"A bad . . . wait, working with?!" Wally's head shot up and she stared at Vess, who blinked in confusion for a moment.

Then she started laughing.

Gods, what a laugh. It was rich, warm, and husky, and it started somewhere deep inside her chest only to bubble up and out, and it warmed Wally from the inside, leaving her with a smile plastered inexorably back on her face. This conversation was going to give her whiplash if she wasn't careful.

"Yes, Wally, 'working with', why did you think I came out here?" Vess asked.

"Pity?"

"Well that's depressing, but no, I came to . . ." Vess trailed off as she chewed on her words, then said, "To tell you you're hired and to . . . apologize for how our last conversation ended, you caught me off guard and I got defensive, that's all."

Wally lowered her head and chuckled weakly as she took a long draught of her tea. "I thought I'd done something, or said something, and messed up."

"No, you didn't, I'm just kind of a bitch sometimes and if you do accept the job you'll have to get used to that side of me, sorry about that in advance," Vess said.

"Mm, no, it's . . . it's okay," Wally said softly. "I like talking to you."

"What about what I just told you?" Vess asked. "I wasn't lying about what I'd done."

"I didn't think you were," Wally said.

Vess frowned. For all of her odd mannerisms, and Vess had more than a few, she hadn't struck Wally as a liar. Vess, for whatever it said about her actual personality, seemed like far too proud and brash of a person to bother with lying. People like her wore their decisions like badges of honor, the good and the bad. The good to prove she was *able*, and the bad to prove she was *capable*. It hadn't even occurred to Wally that Vess might be lying, but maybe that said more about Wally than it did about Vess.

"If you don't think I'm lying, then are you saying my betrayal doesn't bother you?" Vess asked, her voice growing grim.

Wally shook her head. "No it's . . . it's more that I just think that, whatever happened, you probably had a good reason for it."

Whatever Vess had been expecting Wally to say, that obviously wasn't it. Her eyes widened as, for a moment, Vess' bi-located form flickered like a hazy television transmission. Wally couldn't help but stare. It was one thing *hearing* that Vess was projecting a, for all intents and purposes, fully physical body from her sarcophagus in the precinct, but to actually see the proof was something else entirely.

"Sorry," Vess said hollowly. "I just . . . you surprised me again, that's all."

"It's okay," Wally said with a weak laugh. "Uhm, I mean, is it strange that I trust you? If we're going to be working together I kind of have to, don't I?"

"Less than you'd think," Vess replied quietly.

Some strange combination of emotions flashed across Vess' noble features too quickly for Wally to pin any one of them down. A moment later Vess had schooled it all back beneath the cool air of confidence that she wore like a cloak.

"So you trust me?" she asked.

"Should I not?"

Vess looked perplexed for a moment, then laughed.

"Would it bother you if I said that I wasn't sure?"

Wally shook her head, still smiling faintly as she drank down the last of her tea. Vess finished her caff at the same time, set down the mug, and leaned back in her chair.

"Are you going home after this?" Vess asked.

"I guess so," Wally replied.

Originally she'd been looking forward to it. She'd been looking forward to going home and wallowing in her probable failure to become gainfully employed while tending to her plants and then capping off her day by depression-snuggling with her cat.

Well, maybe 'looking forward to' wasn't quite the right word.

That changed when Vess had sat down and became the sun, because going home would mean that the moment would end.

"Can I walk you home?" Vess asked softly.

Or maybe not.

Wally looked up hopefully. Vess had a smile on her face, but it wasn't the broad, confident smirk she'd been wearing before. If anything, she looked hopeful, too.

For once, Wally decided *not* to question her apparent stroke of good fortune and just said 'yes'.

Polly set the phone down on the cradle with a muted click and scanned over the notes she'd just taken from the call. It wasn't the most profitable job, but it wasn't far or difficult either. It would be a few hours of work at most, and it would pay a few bills.

'Eastland Burroughs. Eighth floor. Apartment H-twelve.

She underlined the address and copied them over to another piece of paper for Jemma.

Not for the first time, Polly considered asking Mizer to invest in an answering service or some kind of secretary but she set the notion aside just as she had every other time. The fact was that she didn't trust anyone else to ask the right questions or to understand the right answers even if they were given. It was her job to know what the team was going to be walking into and that meant that something as menial as taking calls for dispersal requests couldn't just be fobbed off. It wasn't glamorous, but the thought of her people walking into a job with the wrong equipment and getting seriously injured because she hadn't wanted to field a call was a sobering one.

That sort of thing was *already* a danger since your average homeowner or renter with a haunting in Colvus could rarely tell their head from their asshole to say nothing of differentiating between a Class Four spectral 'repeater' and an actual poltergeist. Likewise, she didn't trust some egg-sucking rando off the street to be able to identify the markers of a ghoul versus a particularly aggressive shambler, so knowing what questions to ask and how to phrase them was crucial.

It was tedious, though.

Reaching across her desk, she pressed the beige button that connected the receiver to the P.A. system of the lower level and lifted the phone.

"Jemma, call-in from the East End, prep your gear."

Her voice rang tinnily and echoed through the halls, and Mizer emerged from his office with a small smile.

"Should I gear up?" He asked.

Polly shook her head.

"Nah, Jemma and I can handle this one," Polly replied. "It's a repeater, and a Class Three at worst."

He looked almost disappointed, but Polly gave him an even look. "Bringing you for a repeater would be like sandblasting a soup cracker. It's *fine*. Jemma could probably do it solo."

"No solo work," Mizer said flatly.

"I know," she replied. "I'm not arguing the 'no one alone' rule, I was just making a point."

Mizer massaged his temples, then nodded.

"Right, I know that I just—"

"Hey," Polly put a hand on Mizer's arm. "I know, but you don't have to babysit."

He chuckled and waved her off, carding his fingers through his hair as he did. It was a bad habit and always left his hair messy and a little greasy no matter what he did. He was still a good-looking man, of course. And a good man.

"Babysitting is what 'mom' is for," Polly said, sticking her thumb to her collar.

Mizer snorted. "Please, you're the 'dad' of this operation and you know it," he said as he nudged her shoulder. "I think I'm getting softer the older I get."

Laughing, Polly gave his stomach a light, open-palmed slap. There was a little more softness than there had been ten years ago, but less than most men. Mizer kept himself reasonably fit.

"No dad bod yet, old man," Polly replied with a grin.

"That's not what I meant," he replied.

"I know," Polly leaned against him, indulging herself a little as she rested her head on his broad chest. "But to be honest, I prefer you like this, you were made to be kind."

Mizer settled his hand on Polly's shoulder and gripped gently, and Polly felt a pang of regret in that moment. Not of anything she had done. Or even anything *really* particular. Just regret. Formless and aimless regret.

It would have been nice, being with Mizer.

In a different life, maybe. In a different age or a different set of circumstances, she occasionally imagined that they would have been good together. They already *were* good together, truthfully. A good team. A good pair. They knew each other, trusted each other. Even loved each other after a fashion. She'd known Mizer too damn long not to love him because he was too damn nice not to love. He loved her too. He'd told her that nineteen years ago, after Geddenheim and a bottle of wine too many and she'd never forgotten it, especially not after he'd belched deafeningly and passed out, and Polly realized that she'd found it endearing.

"I'll keep an eye on things here, then," Mizer said briskly. "Call if things go south, yeah?"

"Always do," Polly replied.

The door at the other side of the arming room creaked as Jemma entered. She bore the strap of a heavy kitbag slung over her shoulder and a scowl on her face that made Polly frown.

"She's going to be in a mood today," Polly said under her breath.

Mizer nodded but, perhaps wisely, didn't comment. Instead, he gave Polly another pat on the back and turned to Jemma.

"Be safe, kid," Mizer said with a smile, and Jemma's scowl lightened a touch.

Even Jemma had a hard time being truly angry around Mizer despite being an angry person by nature. He was the closest thing to a real father figure she'd ever had, and, truthfully, was a bit of a daddy's girl about it. That was probably one reason why she'd reacted so negatively to Wally's presence now that Polly thought about it.

"Yeah, sure." Jemma adjusted the strap and kicked open the door to make her way up the stairs.

As soon as the door swung shut, Polly sighed. The other reason for her attitude was even more obvious.

"I swear," she muttered. "The moment Vess gives anyone else the smallest bit of attention Jemma acts like she's been abandoned on the side of the road in the rain."

"She'll get over it," Mizer said, waving a hand. "She's a strong girl."

"And we'll endure the pining until she does," Polly remarked.

• • •

Like most dispersal precincts, the Sixth had a company vehicle. *Un*like most, which generally made use of more common high-top vans or, in the case of the precincts in the more fashionable parts of the city, sleek, long-bodied sedans, the main vehicle of the Sixth was an old surplus armored military vehicle.

Specifically, the K-T Twelve-Fifty Hideback.

Polly *hated* Hidebacks.

She hated them for two major reasons and the fuel mileage was one of them. Hidebacks had inbuilt spark reactors that either needed a refuel at a charging main every forty miles or else a manual recharge from someone's personal reserves. The idea during its manufacture was that the loss of efficiency was made up for by being able to be recharged in the field. That was fine in theory but shit in practice for the soldier that drew the short stick because the power draw put them permanently out of commission since they'd spend every day of travel laid up in the back of the cab recovering from refueling the damn Hideback only to be roused at the end of the run to refuel the *fuck damned Hideback* in an unrelenting cycle more consistent the *fuck-mothering dawn*.

The other reason was its complete lack of suspension.

Drivers and riders alike could feel every notch and pothole in the damn road no matter how much you babied the old thing along, which was why she generally opted to drive it like a bat out of hell just to get it over with. This particular Hideback, though, she reserved a special hatred for. Mizer had brought her back with them because he considered her to be a good luck charm *for some reason.* He even named it. Katee, naturally. Never mind that their old military unit had nicknamed the old bitch the 'Rolling Tomb'.

By Polly's reckoning, Katee had run over more Sunfall-Cult IED's than it had cobblestones in the time she'd ridden in it and despite all of the times the bitch had flipped its top and given her and Mizer concussions or boxed them in—they'd been stranded in her back compartment for two days once—it never stopped running!

Katee, miserable hag that she was, just wouldn't die.

She handled like a blind nag on painkillers, too.

"Gods, Pols, ease up the lead foot, will you?!"

Jemma swore viciously as Polly put her foot down extra hard, overtaking a little coupe whose elven owner looked liable to shit himself in the split-second Polly saw his face.

"Am I driving?" Polly asked flatly.

"That's a *word* for what you're doing, sure!"

"Then shut up."

Another stream of invectives left Jemma's lips as she clung to the door handle for dear life while Polly pulled a few more death-defying swerves to get them into the far lane of the freeway and onto the exit ramp in time to slide down into the East End. Even by downtown Colvus standards, the East End was a crapstain of a neighborhood consisting as it did mostly of half-built housing projects, drug dens, other drug dens that were poorly disguised as nightclubs, and the odd twenty-four-hour diner that served the working poor unfortunate enough to make the place their home.

It was also where a lot of dispersal calls came from.

Hauntings occurred most often in places of emotional turmoil, stress, and violence, and since the colloquial 'East End Alarm Clock' was a reference to the sound of emergency sirens, that meant this place got its fair share of all three.

"What's the target?" Jemma asked.

She'd settled back into her seat with an audible sigh of relief as Polly pulled onto the markedly lower-speed streets of downtown and began fishing through her kitbag for her prep materials.

"Repeater," Polly replied. "Probably a Class Four, but it's tough to tell."

"Sitch?"

Polly shrugged. "Some poor bastard's nanna went to sleep last night and when she got up in the morning she did it without moving her body. He only realized it when he got home from backshift, saw her watching T.V., then went upstairs to make her bed, and there she was."

"That's rough," Jemma said as she popped open a metal tin containing handmade grey grease paint.

Dipping her fingers into the mixture, Jemma caked on a good amount of it before pulling her hand out of the tin, pressing her fingers to her face at her temples and forehead, and dragging her fingers down, leaving streaks of grey on her dark skin in a crude facsimile reminiscent of a skull.

It was evening, by the time they pulled up to the sidewalk parking space alongside the tenement their client occupied.

Well, technically the 'client' was the slumlord who owned the place but a haunting was one of those things you couldn't just brush under a rug. Undispersed hauntings functioned a bit like cockroach infestations if the cockroaches looked like your dead loved ones, could move through walls, and were somehow infinitely worse than even *that* description. Hauntings caused tragedy, pain, and turmoil, and tended to increase in severity exponentially.

One day you've got a repeater, then you've got a poltergeist, and the next thing you know a full-blown dreadnought is knocking new holes in your walls, so it never paid to dawdle.

"Ready?" Polly looked over to Jemma who was sitting cross-legged in the passenger seat.

Her eyes were thickly rimmed with kohl, and her face was painted with a ghoulish death's-head. Ashes were mixed into her dark hair, and softly muttered words spilled from her lips in the elven tongue. It was the old Oreliaun dialect; rarely used since their empire fell during the Sunfall Queen's Rebellion more than a century back. Polly only knew the tongue because she'd fought remnants of the rebellion. Those throwbacks that were holding out in cult cells even after all a hundred and fifty years, still convinced that their savior queen and her ephorate would spontaneously rise from the dead to lead them to victory.

"Conflict is the forge of convictions," Jemma murmured as she laced her fingers. "By convictions our flesh is tested, and as so unyielding are those conviction so too shall I never yield, for the strong never yield and my strength shall be legion, for legion is the strength of my convictions."

Her eyes opened and, Gods, they were cold things. Jemma's faith was a dark one, but it was strong and Jemma was stronger, still, and she wielded it well. She was a cut above the average exorcist. Jemma could put down a spectral faster than almost anyone she'd ever seen. Even Chaplain Kulon from her and Mizer's old unit wasn't as good, but then, Kulon's method of exorcism wasn't to challenge the ghost to the spiritual equivalent of a shin-kicking contest.

"Ready to put nanna to bed?" Polly smirked.

Jemma's shoulders slumped for a moment before she rolled her neck to the tune of a few cracks and pops, then nodded. "Yeah, alright," she muttered. "Let's go knock some dentures in."

Polly snorted and set her palms on the hilts of her blades. Hopefully, they wouldn't be needed but she wasn't going to be caught with her panties 'round her ankles on the off-chance this spectral *was* higher than a Class Three.

Time to go to work.

CHAPTER 7

Insofar as downtown housing projects went, the Commonplace was one of the nicer ones. For certain definitions of the word. The apartments were more than just glorified closets with a toilet and a fold-out bed, at least, and there was a proper kitchenette with a sigil-heated stovetop, and the icebox was decent even if the chill-rune tended to fritz out during the summer.

With that said, Wally wasn't entirely thrilled that she ended up on the sixth floor but beggars could not, as they say, be choosers, and Wally was not in a position to be choosy.

It wasn't the cleanest place, but nowhere so close to the East End of Colvus could really claim to be all that tidy. Tenements were kept up on a shoestring budget, so Wally adjusted her expectations to that. It didn't make entertaining anyone any less embarrassing, but Wally hadn't given much thought to Vess seeing where she lived until they actually got there. She was far more enamored with the fact that she was being walked home by what might be the most beautiful woman to ever give her the time of day, to say nothing of one who would actually hold a conversation with her.

". . . so the theory of necrosis really does have a lot of holes in it, you know?" Wally continued. At some point, she'd started talking and, uncharacteristically for her, actually *kept* talking.

"We call it necrosis as if it's the death of the soul, but that's not really what necrosis is, is it?"

"I'm not sure I follow," Vess admitted. "And that's kind of novel for me." She shrugged, smiled, and waited for Wally to keep talking, and to her own surprise if no one else's, she did.

"Well it's just decay isn't it?" Wally asked.

"Which is what dead things do," Vess added.

Surprisingly, Wally found herself shaking her head. Now she was *disagreeing* with Vess but it didn't balk her like it used to at University. Anytime someone would talk over her or challenge her or bring up a counterpoint, she would always swallow back her retort and fold up.

But not with Vess.

The way Vess smiled and watched her as they walked down the sidewalk towards her grungy apartment, the way she never took those painfully blue eyes off of Wally. The way she just . . . listened made her want to keep talking.

"It's what people do," Wally corrected. "It's what plants do, and animals, but decay isn't death. People die, but that's just the process of consciousness slipping away! It's the soul moving back into the cycle of rebirth! Decay has nothing to do with it. Decay, that is necrosis, does a different job!"

Vess tapped her lip with a finger in a graceful motion that captured Wally's eye as Vess smiled. "That's morbid but I like it," she said. "Decay not as death but as life in extent."

"Exactly!" Wally beamed.

And Vess continued to smile back at her. If anything, her smile only broadened, and a laugh carried out of her on its heels.

Everything about Vess was just so . . . cool, for lack of a better term. Vess was just really *cool*, with her high-collared greatcoat, easy smile, and the way her eyes fairly glittered like she had a secret she was *dying* to tell you. She had that kind of effortless confidence that drew everyone's eye—the kind that commanded attention rather than demanding it.

Even just walking down the street, side-by-side, Vess turned heads, and the weirdest part was that Wally wasn't even sure that Vess noticed because she almost never looked away from Wally.

"You should do that more often," Vess said

"Huh?" Wally blinked owlishly. "Do what?"

"That." Vess reached out and tapped Wally's cheek, and she realized she was still beaming. "That smile. You've got a pretty smile, Wally Willowbark."

Oh.

Oh *wow*.

Before that point it hadn't occurred to her that she could like the sound of her own name so much, but coming from Vess she definitely did. Well, now she definitely wasn't going to stop smiling for a while, although the breadth of her smile did take a small hit when they reached her apartment building. There was no hiding the grunge from any angle. It looked about as bad on the outside as it did on the inside which was, at least, decently honest of it.

"Nice," Vess said, looking up at the ugly, towering brick of dirty concrete. "Looks like it has plumbing at least."

Wally raised an eyebrow as she pressed her thumb to the identification rune by the door. There was a faint snap of static discharge and the lock-ward released, letting her pull the door open with a bit of effort since it didn't quite fit the frame.

"It's uhm . . . it's okay," Wally said, not sure what to make of her comment.

"Oh I wasn't cracking wise," Vess said as she followed Wally inside. "I've lived in some real shitholes, including an actual shithole once! Latrines are a lot of things but they're at least semi-warm in the winter."

For a moment, Wally just stared up at Vess with her jaw hanging slightly open as she prodded the call button for the lobby elevator. There was a downside, it seemed, to Vess' unswervingly confident face and that was that Wally could not, for the life of her, tell if Vess was fucking with her.

"I . . . beg pardon?"

Vess just flashed that insouciant grin of hers then reached out with a finger and pushed Wally's jaw shut.

Ding

The doors to the elevator slid open with a barely audible hiss and Vess turned and cut an exaggerated bow.

"Ladies first?"

Wally blinked again. "Uhm, we're both ladies."

That grin widened fractionally.

"Capital letters, Wally, you're a Lady, while I'm really more of a Rake."

She couldn't help it. Wally started laughing. It was just so over the top that she couldn't help it! One moment she was staring at Vess, trying to decide if she was serious about *anything* or not, and the next she was practically falling over laughing! But she did, at least, manage to stumble into the elevator before the doors closed on automatic with Vess right behind her looking impossibly smug.

"How can you say any of that with a straight face?!" Wally gasped out between swells of laughter that threatened to steal the breath from her lungs.

A huff of exaggerated offense left Vess as she bristled playfully.

"Well, first of all, how dare you assume anything I do is straight, and second of all, it's a lot easier when I'm making a pretty girl laugh."

Already breathless, Wally doubled over in paroxysms of laughter until she was red in the face and tears were streaming from her eyes. She was still laughing when the elevator reached the sixth floor and let out a tinny *ding* as the doors hissed open, and a pair of men were left staring at a tall, bemused young woman who was holding up another, shorter one, who could barely stand.

"Y-You . . . are a *louse* . . . Vess Gibson," Wally gasped out as Vess let her take a sort of half-lead into the hall.

"So I've been told," she replied dryly.

Wally's lungs burned but it was a good pain. It was good because, so long as she was laboring for breath and footing, Vess would have a reason to keep her arm around Wally's waist, and Wally would have a reason to keep leaning on her. Eventually, though, they reached the door to Wally's apartment, and she was forced to begrudgingly detach herself to unlock it. She fitted the key, and as she did so she admitted silently that she'd gotten her breath back about a minute ago. She was also certain Vess knew that but was too polite to say anything.

"You know," Wally started, "I can't really tell what's going on if I'm being totally honest."

"How's that?" Vess asked as she followed Wally into her cramped little apartment.

"I can't—*oh!*"

A little black cat with a speckle of white across its back darted at Wally, giving her an affectionate if lopsided rub that was more of a controlled collapse than anything. Wally laughed lightly as she knelt and picked up the little black rumble factory that had attacked her.

"Hello Tipsy, did you have a good day?" Wally cooed.

"Is that—" Vess leaned in and around Wally's cat with a look of astonishment. "That's a three-legged cat."

"Excuse you, she's . . . differently legged," Wally said primly. "And she's my ESA, so be nice."

"ESA?"

Vess asked the question with such genuine confusion that it caught Wally off guard.

"Emotional Support Animal? ESA?" Wally clarified, and Vess just smiled and shrugged. "Really? You've never heard of an ESA?"

"Can't say as I have," she replied. "But I do live in a metal tube, so . . ."

"Well you couldn't have been in there your whole life!" Wally countered.

The good humor on Vess' face flickered for a moment and a surge of regret hit Wally in the stomach as Vess moved past her, shrugging off her greatcoat as she did and hanging from the coat rack by the door—the coat which vanished the moment it left her fingers—before wandering into the kitchenette. Her fingers traced along the piles of discarded mail, the topmost one of which caught her eye, which she picked up and scanned.

"Huh, I didn't realize Mizer was desperate enough to use a mailing service," Vess muttered, turning back to Wally as she did and turning the paper around. "I guess that's how you heard about the job?"

It was a printed job posting from the dispersal precinct, and on the requirements section, in bolded and underlined black letters it said: **Reflector Talent.**

"I . . . yeah," Wally replied, wrong-footed by the sudden change of subject. "It worked, though, didn't it?"

"I suppose it did," Vess agreed, lowering the page. "As to your question . . . no, I haven't been confined to the containment unit my whole life, just the past fifteen years-ish."

Wally's mouth dried up.

Fifteen years?

"I'm sorry," Wally said weakly.

"You didn't know."

Vess tidied up the pile of papers she'd been messing with while Wally buried her face in Tipsy's scruff for a moment before sighing and steeling herself. She just had to go and open her big mouth, didn't she? Vess was being patient with her, which was more than she deserved, so she . . . she needed to do better.

Lowering Tipsy to the ground, the black cat wobbled away, and Wally went to the little living area to start her evening routine. One of the few things that made her apartment liveable, at least in her opinion, were her plants—her flowers. It was nice because they were relatively cheap to pick up and take care of so long as she kept up with them. That was why Wally kept a little spray bottle filled with a mixture of water and a cheap, simple nutrient booster, on the coffee table.

Taking up the bottle, Wally went around to her plants, giving each one a gentle spray. She wet the leaves and the petals of some, and others just the base. Each one had slightly different needs, but they were simple needs. Like Tipsy, the plants were relatively self-sufficient, they just needed a bit of looking after now and then.

When she got to her last and favorite flower, Wally took her time. She checked over the leaves and the stem and poked at the petals, making sure there wasn't any withering or disease and that it hadn't picked up any insects that might be bothering it. Satisfied, Wally gave it a couple of gentle sprays, then turned to set the spray bottle back down where it belonged only to find Vess standing a few feet away, staring past her with an unreadable expression on her face.

Wally frowned as she looked between Vess and the flower she was apparently entranced with.

"Vess?"

"That's a Dwarven Helion," Vess said quietly.

Before Wally could comment, Vess stepped closer and reached past her, brushing her fingers along the slender, red-orange petals, then over the bright yellow center, and she looked so very far away for a moment.

"It's uhm . . . they're my favorite," Wally said weakly. "They're beautiful, and uhm, stubborn, too. They can grow almost anywhere, so long as there's a little sunlight."

"I know," Vess replied softly. "I hate them."

Wally's heart plunged into ice water at the sharp tone of Vess' voice. She'd never heard that tone from Vess before. Admittedly, she'd only had a couple of conversations with Vess, but it still took her by surprise. Every time Wally thought she had a grasp of the kind of person Vess was, something would happen or be said, and everything she thought she knew would be thrown out the window.

"O-Oh."

"Sorry, it's just . . . my childhood home had a huge garden of the things," Vess said quietly as she walked away from the flower, around the coffee table, and dropped down onto Wally's lumpy couch.

She tugged at her tie and the collar of her button-down, loosening them, and sighed.

"They were fucking *everywhere*."

Uncertain of what to add to that, Wally just shuffled her feet nervously. Vess gave a wan chuckle and patted the seat beside her.

"Yeah I . . . sorry, c'mere," she said softly.

Well, Wally wasn't exactly going to turn her down, even if it was a little silly to be invited to sit down on her own couch. That said, she'd apparently needed the invitation which was even sillier.

The couch wasn't large, more of a loveseat really, and Wally tried to put some space between her and Vess.

Vess was having none of that. She put an arm brazenly over Wally's shoulders the moment she started to lean away and pulled her in until Wally's head was resting against Vess' shoulder, and her cheeks were absolutely *burning*.

"Is this okay?" Vess asked.

Not trusting her vocal cords quite yet, Wally just nodded.

"Okay."

Vess leaned her head to the side and rested her cheek on the crown of Wally's head, and they sat in silence. Vess kicked her boots off, which vanished just like her coat had, and propped her feet up on the table, while Wally curled her legs up and tucked them beneath her.

This was . . . impossibly comfortable.

Whatever was happening. Whatever this was? Wally could honestly say, at least in that moment, that she hoped it never stopped.

"I'm sure you probably think I'm an absolutely shameless flirt, huh?" Vess started, apropos of nothing.

Wally cleared her throat and gave a weak chuckle.

"Maybe a little."

"Fair, but I'm . . . okay, I kind of am, but I'm not . . . not doing that with you," Vess said, then sighed softly. "I do like you. I like you a lot, Wally. You're charming and honest, and braver than I think you credit yourself for. I can count on one hand the number of people who have made me flinch in my whole life."

"You've only just met me," Wally said quietly.

Vess shook her head and squeezed Wally a little closer in a gentle hug that didn't last nearly long enough for Wally's liking. It occurred to Wally as that happened, that pointing out the extremely short time Vess had known her was hilariously hypocritical given how unreasonably attached to the woman she herself was becoming.

"I always was a sentimental idiot," Vess admitted. "And anyway, I'm not saying we ought to throw caution to the wind and get hitched, I'm saying I like you, and I'd . . . I'd like to get to know you and see where this goes which should be easy since, with you being my proxy, we'll be spending a lot of time together anyway. I just want to be up front about everything."

That didn't sound too bad at all.

Moving a little fast, then a little slow, then who knows? It would be strange, certainly. Vess being confined to her sarcophagus most of the time would make for an odd relationship, but it wouldn't be terribly different from, say, a long-distance one. Except Wally would be able to see Vess in person and talk to her whenever she wanted, so it was a little better.

"I think I'd like that," Wally said quietly as she finally let herself relax against Vess. "How uhm, how much longer do you have on your 'walk'?"

Vess blew out a slow breath.

"Three hours, maybe a bit more," she replied.

"Can I ask about you? A little, I mean?" Wally ventured.

"Shoot."

Wally laughed quietly and allowed herself to nestle a little closer. Despite knowing that Vess' body was just a projection—a bi-location—the woman beside her was surprisingly warm.

"How old are you?"

Wally felt a laugh rumble up from Vess' chest.

"Starting off strong, huh?" Vess asked. "That's . . . a complicated question, given that my body doesn't age and I only spend about an hour or two every day conscious on average, but, biologically?" she gave a thoughtful hum, then said, "about twenty-nine or thirty, I think."

So not *too* much older than her. That wasn't so bad. It wasn't really accounting for two decades in stasis, but, as Vess had said, she didn't spend much of that awake. Wally could work with that.

"My turn," Vess said. "Why Theoretical Necromancy?"

That was a common question and Wally was used to it. With that said, she also tended to brush it off or give a noncommittal answer and Vess deserved better than that, especially since they were trying to get to know each other.

"I . . . I wanted to understand what happened at Bressig," Wally said, and Tipsy chose that moment to hop up onto the couch between them and curl up, and Vess chuckled as she began scratching the black cat between the ears. "The whole town was swallowed in a minor exclusion zone generated by a powerful spectral . . ." Wally trailed off, then said, "sorry, an exclusion zone—"

"—is a place where a curse has become so powerful that reality and its laws, both physical and magical, have ceased to have meaning," Vess recited quietly, "I am a disperser, remember?"

She turned her head just slightly. Just enough to meet Wally's gaze with a strange look in her eyes. "Sorry, please continue."

"R-Right," Wally stammered. "Well, the spectral, it was a daemon, a real one, I mean, not like—" she paused again, choking on her words, but the husky chuckle from Vess told her she wasn't going to say anything new, so Wally plucked up her courage and said it. "Not like I thought you were, but a real one, a soul so warped by necrosis that it wasn't human anymore . . . not really."

"And that's what you wanted to understand?"

Wally nodded. She wasn't sure how else to say it. Where were the words for that sort of obsession? For that sort of experience, even? She had seen something as a child. A monster like nothing she'd ever imagined. No childhood nightmare could ever be compared to that thing.

"I don't even remember what it looked like," Wally admitted. The theurgists who treated me said I probably blocked it out."

"Your mind was protecting itself, that's all," Vess said.

That was probably true. There were more mundane horrors that got the same treatment. People often found themselves unable to recall traumatic events in proper objective detail, or even at all in some cases. Of course, the flipside of that coin were the people who could recall those events with perfect clarity. The moment etched so indelibly onto their mind that every second was accounted for.

Despite her curiosity, Wally was glad that wasn't the case with her. She had enough damage as it was.

"I do dream about it, sometimes," Wally said quietly. "About Bressig, but they're just dreams." She leaned in, indulging herself a little by nuzzling against Vess. "I think they're just more pieces of my mind trying to defend itself, distorting the events . . . making things up."

Vess raised an eyebrow. "Why do you say that?"

"Because in my dreams there are *two* monsters, and they're killing each other," Wally said with a brittle laugh. "Which I guess is about as close to a good dream as that kind of thing gets, right?"

Vess nodded silently, still resting her cheek on Wally's head.

"I think it's like, my little kid brain saw this inconceivable monster, and did that thing kid-brains do . . ."

"It made up a bigger, badder, uglier monster?" Vess asked wryly, and Wally thought it sounded a little strained.

"Pretty much." Wally laughed as she curled up a little closer to Vess. Fuck propriety, she was going to enjoy this. "So uhm, can I ask why you hate Dwarven Helions?"

"Because I loathe my parents," Vess replied flatly, and Wally winced.

Sighing, Vess let out a quiet huff and muttered apology. Wally shrugged, trying to salvage something of the conversation, but Vess picked it up as if it had never been dropped or broken.

"No, sorry, that's just me being defensive again," Vess said. "Those stunted Helions were everywhere when I was growing up and they remind me of my childhood home."

"Was it bad?"

A bit of Wally regretted asking but another part of her was almost recklessly curious. Vess was this weird conglomeration of sass, snark, and vicious cutting wit, and yet beneath that she was so gentle, and then, again, beneath all of *that*, there was pain.

Old, bitter pain.

Maybe it was selfish of Wally but she wanted to see it. She was desperate to know what could hurt someone like Vess. Desperate to know and maybe just as desperate to take some of it away if she could, but that was probably going too far. But she wanted to know.

"My family was old money, not that you'd know it since most of it was gone by the time I was born," Vess began. "I'm pretty sure the only reason I made it out of infancy was because mom and dad had me nannied til I was six, because Gods knew they weren't going to interrupt their parties, binge-drinking, and hedonism to raise me themselves.

"I was on my own most of my childhood. Mom was on a different drug every week while Dad was drunk nine days out of ten and hungover on the last one, at least, that was the case up until I was seven."

"Did he get sober?" Wally asked.

An ugly laugh rattled out of Vess.

"Fuck no, he hung himself in the foyer."

Wally's jaw clicked open and she stared, dumbstruck and wide-eyed, while Vess fixed onto some unseen point in the out the window that was across from them over the small shelf of flowers that rested beneath it. Her eyes had that haunted look again.

"I remember finding him just . . . just hanging there, swinging like a pendulum," Vess said hollowly. "There was this sort of creaking sound from his weight being borne by the old timbers of the house." She blinked rapidly a few times and shook her head gently. "Anyway, mom spent the rest of her life, all two years of it, in a narcotic haze before dying in a pool of sick in her bed and leaving me with a mountain of debt, an empty bank account, and a crumbling old house surrounded by flowers."

She turned her head and smiled a wide, humorless grin, her eyes glacial and hard. "So yeah," she finished. "Dwarven Helions? Not my favorite."

Unable to think of anything else to do, Wally sat up, dislodging Vess as she straightened, then wrapped her arms around Vess and pulled her head down until it was resting in the curve of Wally's neck, neatly reversing their positions.

"I'm sorry." Wally whispered as she buried her face in the tumbling locks of auburn. "That's . . . horrific."

Vess went stiff, and for a moment Wally wondered if she was about to bolt. It wouldn't be hard for her. She could probably pull the string on her projection any time and just snap back to her body. She could leave Wally behind easily if she wanted to.

She didn't.

Instead, Vess let out a shaky breath, laughed, and nodded.

"Yeah, actually," she replied. "It kind of was."

"I can get rid of the uhm, the Helion, if you want."

Vess shook her head. "Keep it, if you like it then maybe there's something to them after all."

That was more than Wally had expected. A lot more, actually. Vess hadn't seemed like the type to bend. Then again, the one consistent thing about Vess was that she continued to go against what Wally expected her to do. In a way, though, Vess had admitted to Wally doing much the same to her. Perhaps it was a matter of them both surprising each other.

They didn't know each other very well, that much they agreed on for sure, but Wally was very much looking forward to changing that, and she hoped Vess was too. As it was, Wally didn't really feel like asking anything else after hearing how Vess had grown up, and Vess clearly didn't feel much like talking. Instead, they spent the last tapering hours of Vess' 'walk' in silence, watching the occasional patter of rain come down from the darkening evening sky above Colvus while Tipsy rumbled between them.

When the time finally did come for Vess to go home it was far too soon. There was no fanfare or announcement. Vess just slowly roused herself, sat up, and took a long, deep breath through her nose as she tipped her head back and closed her eyes.

"What are you doing?"

Vess opened her eyes and looked down at Wally with a small smile.

"Memorizing," she replied. "I'm not going to be able to experience this again for at least a month, remember?"

"Oh, right." Wally's good mood deflated a little at that.

The downsides of her condition, such as they were.

Still, Wally didn't have any regrets, so instead she scooped up Tipsy and stood, letting Vess rise from the couch on her own.

"I swear, every time we sit down I forget how tall you are,"

Wally said with a small laugh.

Vess had more than a half-foot over Wally, which objectively didn't make her all *that* tall. Wally was just short. Which was fine. She would probably never admit it out loud, at least not without suffering an embarrassment-induced major coronary event, but she liked the way Vess looked down at her.

Grinning, Vess knocked her heels against the couch, first one, then the other, conjuring her boots back onto her feet, then made an odd tugging motion in the air above her button-down collar, and her coal greatcoat flickered into existence.

"Did you need to do all that?" Wally asked.

"No," Vess replied, "but it looked good, didn't it?"

"You're ridiculous."

By way of reply, Vess wiggled her nose.

Vess could wiggle her nose like a bunny. One person should not be permitted to have that many charming qualities. It really wasn't fair to everyone else.

"See you at work, tomorrow?" Vess asked, and Wally dared to believe there was an air of hope in her voice.

"Definitely," Wally said with a grin that went ear-to-ear.

"Then sleep sweet, Wally Willowbark."

And then she was gone.

There was no flash of light or folding of space. No sparks or crackles of otherworldly magic. One moment, Vess Gibson was standing in her little den, and the next, she was gone.

"Hey Tipsy?" Wally said a little woodenly.

"*Mrrow?*"

"I think I'm in love."

Tipsy, like most cats, didn't have much of an opinion, or if she did she didn't share it which, Wally reflected, was just more proof that cats were both wiser and better than people.

CHAPTER 8

Jemma's breath was misting in front of her before she'd even gotten onto the eighth-floor landing. Frowning, she looked back at Polly whose brow had a petulant crease that was less a sign of immaturity and more a by-product of her terminal case of baby-face.

"Temp-drop," Jemma said, a bit pointlessly. "There's no way that's right . . ."

"No," Polly said quietly as she followed Jemma up the stairs and out into the hallway. "We're not close enough to the client's apartment. Hells, it's a repeater, it should barely be strong enough to drop the temperature inside the *apartment*."

This was at least a ten-degree drop. Heat diffusion was the purview of powerful corpses and spectrals, or else the sign of a major infestation. Jemma's hands tightened into fists as fear crept up her spine. No matter what the cause was, whatever was in here was way more than some numpty Class Four. It definitely wasn't just a repeater. Even if the temp-drop was being caused by a mass infestation, there would have to be a triggering event!

"Jemma, nail down the entrance with iron, then call Mizer!" Polly said as she stepped quickly into the hallway. "I'm going to start evacuating the residents!"

"Wait! Why am I—?"

"I gave you an order, Jemma!" she snapped, and the fiery young woman bristled, but before she could bring her temper to bear, Polly overrode her. "If this floor gets excluded we need our exit secured! Now, Nail. That. Fucking. Door!"

She punctuated the last four words with light jabs from her machete as Jemma's eyes grew wide.

"E-Excluded?" Jemma breathed. "You don't really think it's that bad do you?"

"You wanna find out the hard way?" Polly asked dryly.

Jemma shook her head violently, sending her dark hair tumbling around her face.

"Me neither."

Then Polly was gone, running down the halls and slamming her fists against doors shouting *'Dispersal Six! Evacuate the premises, this is not a drill!'* at the top of her lungs.

While she did that, Jemma stumbled out into the hallway, turned to face the door, dropped her kitbag to her feet, then knelt and began rifling through it. She found her prize after a moment; a wooden box etched with blessings of cleansing to ensure the contents remained magically sterile.

Breaking the seal, Jemma pulled the sliding top of the box open and pulled out seven inch-and-a-half-long spikes of cold iron, hammered into tapered points and etched with gods of aversion.

"Shit!"

Jemma spat the curse as she grabbed her hammer from out of the bag, put the first nail to the threshold of the door, and began hammering.

Vess reconstituted her astral body in the precinct arming room. The split-second journey here from Wally's apartment hadn't done a damn thing to soothe her nerves. Her mind was a storm of chaos. If she had a physical body she'd be sweating bullets and on the verge of panic-vomiting herself inside out.

"Polly!" Vess called as she turned on her heel, only to find Polly's desk empty.

Frowning, Vess moved over to it and swept up a steno pad,

one of the cheap yellow ones, covered in Polly's tight, crabbed script. It had notes on a haunting, an address, and a variety of unknown variables to watch out for along with a list of equipment to counteract said potential threats.

She was as fastidious as ever.

"Damn it." Vess dropped the paper and stormed over to Mizer's office door.

Hopefully, he hadn't gone, too. Something was going on. Something that Vess did *not* like the smell of.

"Mizer!"

She didn't bother opening the door, opting instead to simply flicker inside the office.

"GODS' HOOKS!" Mizer practically fell out of his chair as Vess appeared a foot from his desk. "Damn it, Vess! Shave years off Pols' life, not mine! She's got spares!"

"It's her."

"What?!"

Vess slammed her fist into the desk, rocking it on its mismatched legs, and roared, *"It's her!"*

Her heart was better than two hundred feet away through several yards of concrete but Vess could swear that there was thunder in her chest and in her ears. Her blood was boiling in her non-existent veins.

"Vess," Mizer said slowly as he held up a placating hand. "I'm gonna need you to calm down, and tell me what's going on, okay?"

Despite not needing to breathe, Vess was panting. Her astral form was flickering in and out of existence. Damn him. Damn this! And damn her own snap-fucking-temper!

"The girl from Bressig," Vess hissed. "The exclusion event! The wraith! Remember?! The girl! That's Wally! I fucking *knew* she looked familiar, but I couldn't put my finger on it until she told me about her dream!"

Mizer lowered his hand, shaking his head all the while.

"Vess, we've been over this, I did everything you asked me to, I chased down every lead after the event, and that girl? She *died!*" Mizer said sharply. "And it was *not* your fault! The AAR said she died of necrotic shock, just like damn near everyone else in that town."

"I'm telling you, it's her! No one else was close enough to see me fighting the daemon! No one else knew I was there!" Vess insisted, and she knew how desperate she sounded.

Vess knew she was being irrational too, but, dammit, she'd tried so fucking hard to save that girl! Finding out she'd just gone and carked it anyway, and that necrotic shock from exposure had been the cause, had almost destroyed her.

"No one we *knew of,* Vess, please," Mizer said quietly. "There were dozens of children who survived Bressig. Hells, I'd wager half of the local reflectors in the Colvus metro area originated in Bressig! You're grasping at straws!"

"Didn't you hear me?! Wally remembers me fighting the wraith! Can't you look up the name, at least?!" Vess begged. "Please! Didn't the report have the name of the . . . the deceased?"

Mizer shook his head.

"It was redacted, like every other piece of personal information on the Bressig survivors, you know that," Mizer said calmly. "Those people suffered enough, they don't need the stigma of having been involved in an exclusion event hanging around their personal files." He leaned forward on his elbows and buried his face in his hands, breathing out slowly as he did.

"Mizer, c'mon," Vess said quietly. "I . . . It's her."

"Don't do this to yourself, Vess," Mizer said, reaching out a hand to take hers. "They recovered her body. It was right where you told them she'd be. We both saw the report. The Jiani pronounced her dead on arrival of massive organ failure, and even getting that much released almost cost me my rank."

Vess backed up until she cracked against the wall of Mizer's office, wrapped her arms around herself, and slid down the wall until she was sitting in a miserable ball on the floor. Her hair hung over her face as her shoulders shook.

"She . . . She was just a little girl," Vess sobbed. "Gods, she was just a *kid.*"

Mizer stood and walked over to her, turned, sat down, and put an arm over her shoulder.

"I know, Gibs, and you did your damndest," Mizer said. "You took down the first manifested daemon since the Sunfall Rebellion, and it was a wraith to boot." He squeezed her shoulders gently, and Vess let out a quiet, wracking sob. "You did your best and you brought down the exclusion zone. Everyone who got out of that hellhole owes you their life, even if they don't know it."

"I didn't want to save them," Vess said in a raw croak. "I wanted to save that little girl!"

Pulling her closer, Mizer gripped Vess' shoulder tight as she shook through dry sobs.

"You know one of those people you saved was Wally, right?" Mizer said. *"Everyone* who got out of there was someone you saved, and Wally was one of them."

Some tension bled out of Vess' shoulders at that thought.

Mizer was right. As usual. The weight, though—the memory of that little girl's terrified face and her screams as Vess fought that damned wraith, hammering at it even as it bloated itself on the power of thousands of necrotized souls . . . Vess didn't dream anymore thanks to the half-sleep induced by her sarcophagus. She couldn't afford to. Couldn't be allowed to because of her curse. Maybe that was a blessing. If she could dream, she was sure she would dream of that night. Of Bressig, and of other, worse memories.

"Don't tell her," Vess said quietly.

"If you say so," Mizer replied, as he squeezed her shoulder again. "Mind if I ask why, though?"

"I just don't want her thinking she owes me anything, okay?"

Mizer chuckled.

"She really charmed you, didn't she?"

A weak chuckle escaped Vess' lips, and she reached past her collar to the chain around her neck and drew it out. A ring of singular beauty hung from the fine chain. The shank and bridge were crafted from impossibly rare red gold, and the setting was shaped to resemble the flared wings of a bird of prey with a gleaming crimson stone in the center.

Vess ran her fingers over the stone, feeling the familiar planes and facets with the pad of her thumb as she stared at it. "She used to say that I fell in love far too easily, you know."

Perhaps wisely, Mizer said nothing about that. Thinking about that woman never did Vess any good, but she still did it. What happened in the past had happened and Vess was doing what she could to atone for it. She intended to keep doing it until her dying breath because no matter how much she did, it would never, ever be enough.

Not for her.

"I know it's all but impossible, but . . . what if the reports were wrong? What if Wally *is* that girl, Mizer?" Vess asked.

"Then they were wrong," Mizer replied, and Vess could tell he didn't buy it. That was fair. Vess wasn't sure she bought it either.

But Gods, what if?

What if?

Vess didn't believe in coincidences. Not with the power she used to wield. If Wally was the girl from Bressig then the odds of their paths crossing again was *astronomical*. If it was a chance then it was one hells of a chance and if it wasn't then that begged the question: why? Why was she listed as dead? What happened?

And why did she suddenly appear on the doorstep of the Sixth?

As much as Vess hated herself for thinking it, it would be easier if the girl really had died. It would be simpler and better if Wally was just one of the survivors of Bressig who'd walked away with more than just a traumatic memory.

But . . . damn it . . .

The phone rang on the heels of that morbid thought, and Mizer pushed himself to his feet to stumble back over to his desk and pick up the receiver.

"Mizer," he said in his more clipped, professional voice. "Jemma? Wait, hold—no, slow down, and say it again," then, "Gods' hooks, how bad is the infestation?"

Vess sat bolt upright. Infestation? The notes on Polly's desk suggested nothing worse than a single repeater! Class Three at the *very* worst! Infestations were their own gods-damned classification system! Clearing an infestation required a full dispersal team, including their fumigation specialists which meant Siobhan and herself! That was why they hadn't taken on any infestations since Dolin left. Without herself at full steam Siobhan was left with only Polly for backup and, as good as they were, two people couldn't protect Jemma while she conducted an exorcism, there just weren't enough hands in enough places.

"Damn it. Clear out of there! Both of you!"

Vess could hear Jemma's voice sound frantic over the phone in reply, but couldn't make out the words, and she couldn't focus enough to skim Mizer's mind and listen in.

"Okay, okay, I'm sending in Siobhan but this is an *extraction*, Jem! We don't have the resources to cleanse an infestation yet!"

Mizer slammed the receiver down onto the cradle and carded his fingers through his hair. He looked pale and shaken.

"Shit," he muttered. "That job went gonads up like nobody's business, Gibs, the whole damn floor is infested and on the verge of exclusion."

Vess' eyes went wide.

"Siobhan won't be enough for that," she said sharply. "You have to send me in!"

"Vess, look at me," Mizer pointed sharply at his own eyes. "If I send you into that shitstorm without a proxy, you will *fucking die.*"

"I just underwent purge, Mizer, I can run unassisted for a few minutes at least. Longer if I don't push myself."

That was a long shot, and she knew it. There was also a good chance she was overestimating her abilities. If it had happened right at the start of her eight hours that might be something but it was at the tail end. Still, she wasn't going to leave Polly and Jemma and gods only knew how many innocent people trapped in a building full of corpses and spectrals.

"I'll let Siobhan go in first," she offered. "But they'll need me!"

Mizer pressed his lips to a thin line. It was riding the ragged edge of risk but they both knew that neither Polly nor Jemma were going to leave an entire floor's worth of civilians to become corpse-feed without a fight. Mizer could order them out until he was blue in the face but Polly, at least, didn't have that kind of cruelty in her. Jemma, maybe. Jemma had no love for the people of Colvus, but as bitter as she could be she loved Polly like a mother. If Polly stayed then Jemma would tell Mizer precisely where he could shove his evac order. All of that flickered through Vess' mind in a split-second and she could see the same thoughts cross Mizer's.

"Okay," he said quietly. "Go get Siobhan and have her prep the Invocation on your sarcophagus, then load it onto the hearse. The less distance you have to project, the safer it'll be."

Vess nodded. Without a proxy and with all of her restraints running hot, it wouldn't leave her with a lot of power. It would be enough to deal with shamblers and a few angry stalkers, though.

Hopefully, that's all she'd *have* to deal with.

Focusing her mind, she scanned the layout of the precinct, located Siobhan's turbulent mind, and flickered in that direction.

Mizer watched Vess vanish and swore under his breath. This was the worst-case scenario but it was bound to happen eventually. Dispersal was a risky business, which was why Polly always went in loaded for bear.

According to Jemma, their line of egress was nailed down, but there were too many people and too many threats. Over a hundred people lived on that floor alone, enough that it was well past the limits of both fire and dispersal safety code, and that was going to make their job a nightmare.

His eyes lingered on the phone.

He had an idea but it was an objectively awful one. It was unfair in the extreme and absolutely more dangerous than the poor girl had signed up for. Hells, she hadn't even signed up yet at all!

But Polly and Jemma were in danger. She could probably walk out of almost anything if need be, but if Jemma died? Gods, Polly would never get over that. Neither would he for that matter—Jemma was young, dumb, angry, and the closest thing to a daughter Mizer would ever have, and Vess might not say it but she always went out of her way to talk to her, help her polish her skills, or even just listen.

If Jemma died and Mizer could have done something . . .

"Shit." Mizer picked up the phone and dialed the number that was still on his desk from that morning. The line connected after only a ring and a half.

//*Hello?*//

"Hey, it's Mizer."

//*Oh, hi Mist—uhm, I mean, Mizer . . . sorry.*//

"No it's uh, it's fine, look, Wally, I know today was a mess but it just got a lot messier, and I have a huge favor to ask . . ."

It was fair to say that Paulina Truelight had been in some relatively rough situations. On the scale of her worst operations back in the Union Legionaries, this mess didn't really compare.

Her unit within the Legions had entered some of the most hostile exclusion zones around the Elemental Union. She'd gone up against cells of Sunfall cult insurgents who had no compunctions about anchoring miasma to dead bodies to create corpses or riling up spectrals and pointing them in the direction of civilians to make chaos. If she could deal with a bunch of crazy, death-worshipping, xenophobic elves along with their various confederates then she could deal with a damn infestation.

Of course, back then she'd had a little more backup.

The runes of sharpening on Polly's machete flashed as she sheared through the arm of a shambler and the bloodless limb thumped to the floor. Its owner, unperturbed by the loss, continued to stumble towards her with jerky, marionette movements. It was driven by formless malice; all it knew was that the warmth of life had been taken from it and that Polly was alive, and that was the only reason it needed to hate her.

"Damn it," Polly cussed as she dove inside its one-armed reach, ducked beneath a wild swing, and swung both machetes hard in a cross-stroke, bisecting its left leg and dropping it to the ground.

Bastard things were more durable than a dead body had any right to be.

"Uuuurrrrrhhhggg~"

"Yes, brains good, much eat, I get it," Polly snapped as she turned her machete point down and buried it through the back of the thing's skull.

More runes along the body of the blade flared and the hallway filled with the acrid smell of cooked meat. The corpse went limp as the motive apparatus that was driving it was scorched into ash. Corpse or not, it still needed most of a brain to guide its movement.

"One down," Polly muttered as she looked up from her kill at the milling enemies down the hall, " and about . . . three dozen to go."

This was getting out of hand.

"Pols, help is on the way!" Jemma called from the far end of the hall where she was slowly funneling the few surviving residents who weren't too terrified to make a run for freedom out the door.

The young exorcist's hand was raised above her head and a sickly violet light spilled from it. Several dead shamblers and the ashes of what was either a particularly brave or stupid repeater were collected around her from where she'd abjured them.

Of course, the problem there was that she couldn't *move*. Not without leaving their extraction point vulnerable. If the nails were pulled out or the exit was somehow broken then they were screwed. Doubly so if the floor ended up getting excluded.

If that happened then it might not matter how many reinforcements Mizer could muster before the two of them were overwhelmed.

"How many more?" Jemma yelled.

"I have no fucking idea!" Polly spat. "There could be fifty live ones or everyone could be dead! Without Vess doing mindscans, we can't tell!"

A stream of Oreliaun curses flowed from Jemma's lips as she planted her feet and thrust her hand out towards an advancing shambler. Violet energy flared deep and dark, and the shambler began convulsing. Its mindless hate drove it forward even as its flesh began to wither and its bones turned brittle, and before it made two more steps forward it collapsed to the ground at Jemma's feet, aged beyond recognition.

Jemma let out a breath and looked up at Polly, her lips parting to say something. The words died stillborn as her eyes went wide and she screamed.

"Polly!"

A chill went up Polly's spine at the same moment Jemma cried out her name, and she whipped around, flourishing her machetes in hacking arcs. In the flare of light from her blade-runes, she glimpsed it; a skeletal shadow, emaciated, hideous, and utterly silent. Even as her blades hacked one of its cruelly bladed limbs off at its grotesquely double-jointed elbow, it made no sound.

S'a fuck-damned stalker! Polly had time for that single thought before the stalker's other limb carved through the gap in her defenses.

There was a sound like ripping leather, and Polly bit back a scream as one of the stalker's serrated limb-blades tore through flesh and bone. Warm blood splattered against Polly's face as she staggered backward, half-blind, weaving a net of deadly slashes in front of herself.

It was less effective than it could have been, Polly thought bitterly through the shock and agony, given that she now only had one machete. The other was still gripped in her right hand which itself was attached to the arm that was lying four feet away, severed just beneath the shoulder, on the ground beneath the arachnoid stalker. The corpse ambusher chittered with an ugly, insectile noise as it jabbed the severed arm with the tip of its blade and lifted it like a speared sausage. Even the weakest stalkers were Class Two corpses at least. The remains of murderers, usually, and possessed of an insatiable need to inflict pain and death. This one was big; ten feet long and built like a centipede fucked a black widow, with eight mismatched, bony limbs that bled noxious shadows which muted almost all of the sound it made. Its head was a malformed skull with a hangdog leer to it, and its twisted, fanged jaw clattered open to bite deep into her arm.

"Oh c'mon!" Polly snapped. "At least wait until I'm *dead* to eat me!"

Pain was gnawing at the edges of her mind. She couldn't fight like this.

"Fine, you wanna go—?!" Polly bellowed as white and green light effervesced around her, flashing across her skin and sinking into the grievous wound she'd just suffered.

Dust, grime, and the remains of her prior kills lashed around her as magic flooded the air, whipping her flaxen hair around her face. The sickening sound of bone snapping wetly filled the hallway as Polly's ruined shoulder and rotator spontaneously repaired itself. A moment later, her humerus reconstructed, followed by the radius, ulna, and all the bones and joints of her hand. The meat followed; muscle, tendon, fat, then skin.

Polly bared her teeth in a snarl as her biomantic regeneration engaged at full chat.

"*Then let's fucking go!*"

CHAPTER 9

"AKUR, MASTER OF DAEMONS, turn your eyes upon me." Jemma spoke the prayer through chapped lips as she stood her ground and repelled another pair of shamblers.

The halls were filled with the acrid stink of dispersed flesh and spectral remains, mixed with the hot tang of blood and sweat. Down the hall, Jemma could hear the crashing clangor of Polly fighting her war of attrition. Against this many undead, it was an even match; the unstoppable force of dozens of murderous corpses marching inexorably against the immovable object of Paulina '*Nine-Lives*' Truelight.

That stretch of the hall where Polly was fighting was a truly gruesome sight. When she was in the throes of her regeneration, Polly fought like a berserker, sacrificing blood, flesh, and even whole limbs to bring down her target only to heal the damage within moments as she moved on. She was easily one of the most powerful Biomantics in a generation, at least in Colvus.

Jemma had certainly never seen anyone regenerate as fast as Polly, who referred to herself as a freak of nature with good reason. At the rate she was going, the guy who owned this building was gonna need a power washer to get all of Polly's blood off the walls to say nothing of the assorted limb disposal.

As for Jemma . . .

"Akur take you all!" Jemma spat, swung her hammer, using it as a focus to project her will forward to crash amongst an advancing cluster of the dead.

The Master of Daemons helped those who helped themselves. He had no interest in those who pleaded for power, only in those who stood at the front lines and demonstrated their strength, and that appealed to Jemma.

Her faith was a complicated one, both spiritually and politically. On the one hand, Fah'Akur wasn't considered one of the Dark Ones; his doctrine espoused personal strength of body, mind, and will. It demanded that its adherents hold strong convictions and brandish those convictions against challengers. But, on the other hand, the Daemon-King was still just that: A daemon. He was an ancient and powerful necrotic entity birthed at the height of the First War between the Divine Realms and the Descent of Hells. Legend held that Akur didn't fight for any one side but would simply appear in the midst of pitched battles attacking whomever he saw as the strongest.

The temples of the Union cast Fah'Akur in the role of the chaosbringer; the disruptor of order and the unknown variable. The faithful, like Jemma, knew that the Daemon-King was far from a force of chaos.

Jemma gritted her teeth, planted her feet, and drew from her well of faith in the Master of Daemons. "Mine is the strength of legions," she recited in a breathless rasp, "for legion is the strength of my convictions!"

She raised her chisel like a great nail, brandishing it at another, larger shambler that was charging down the hall at her. Once, twice, thrice, she struck the head of the chisel, and the massive corpse slowed with every step it took closer to Jemma, its body hampered by ephemeral nails of Jemma's will that she pounded into it. They were her conviction made manifest and pitted against the mindless fury of the shambler. If it wanted her dead, it would have to prove that it wanted to kill her more than Jemma wanted to live, and so far Jemma's will to live was stronger.

Two more shamblers broke through previously shut apartment doors behind the ensnared one, and Jemma cussed viciously as they bore down on her and she dropped to a knee, slamming the chisel into the floor and beating it into place with her hammer. The air around her lit with coruscating violet energy, catching the two corpses on either side of the shambler she'd already caught.

Their combined hate and need to kill struck Jemma's mental fortress like a hammer blow to the skull, and she rocked back on her heels, but she didn't move.

"Damn you!" Jemma spat blood as the strain of holding them back inflicted sympathetic damage to her body. "I reject you! I abjure you!" Jemma stood haltingly. "You are nothing! *NOTHING!*"

She screamed the last word as she closed her hand into a fist and punched forward, staggering them backward for a moment. In the brief lull as the shamblers found their feet again, Jemma swept up her chisel and began striking the air in front of her with it, beating the head of it with her hammer at specific points of her movement. The motions left a burning rune hanging in front of her that invoked the will of Fah'Akur directly.

"Your convictions are dead! They cannot match mine!" Jemma declaimed as she cast her arms wide in challenge.

The rune, the first syllable of the King's name, flashed, and Jemma's soul projected violently from her body, propelled through the force of the rune directly at the shamblers. Their renewed charged met with the meteoric conviction of Jemma Corsivo, and her spectral form tore through them. Where it touched, she gripped and *wrenched* their animating force directly from their bodies, shattering them against herself. The shamblers crumpled like masterless puppets as Jemma pulled the spiritual ripcord of her spell and slammed back into her body.

Bruising and abrasions appeared like shadows on Jemma's dark skin. It was the cost of throwing the entirety of her will at beings made up of little more than mindless hate. She broke them, but they got their licks in.

"Bastards," Jemma rasped as she dragged in deep gulps of hot, bloody air. "Akur take every single one of you."

Silent alarms screamed in the back of Jemma's mind as the

warding circle surrounding herself and the door she was guarding was pierced from the direction Polly had been fighting in.

"SHIT!" Jemma spun her heel, a rapid warding imprecation already spilling from her lips as she thrust her hand out.

Her spell stopped the killing stroke of a stalker's bone-bladed limb less than an inch from her open palm. Jemma spat blood as the sympathetic strain of holding back the sheer killing intent of the Class Two corpse slammed into her.

Fuck getting impaled, if she had to hold this thing off for more than a minute her own magic was going to put half her insides onto her outsides!

"Akur take your head and fuck your neck you bony shit!" Jemma spat.

The stalker's blade inched closer and Jemma's vision washed red as a blood vessel popped in her left eye. The tip of the blade split into the skin of her palm with agonizing slowness, and Jemma swore she could hear the bone-rattle of the stalker chuckling.

The rattle cut off with a dull crackle that originated somewhere in the stalker's chest, and a moment later the pressure on Jemma's soul let up as the stalker arched back and let out a keening wail. Its shadow-wrapped chest bulged and twisted sickeningly in the shape of fingers, and Jemma dropped to her knees in relief as she grinned around bloody teeth.

Claws attached to ruddy red fingers tore through the stalker's ectoplasmic flesh, followed by a black-clad arm that reached out and up from the snarled and half-fused ribcage to grab the malformed skull of the stalker. The claws dug deep into the bone, cracking it with its grip only to drag it down. Vertebrae snapped as the skull bent past the limit of its neck before separating completely and being dragged into the hollow of its own chest.

The stalker collapsed and a husky chuckle echoed out from inside the shell of its body as a figure rose up from the dissipating flesh.

Vess Gibson, in all her wicked glory, shrugged off the melting, ectoplasmic matter from herself before rolling her shoulders and popping her neck with a satisfied 'ah!'.

"And that's the last time I fly coach."

Shadows clung to Vess in the suggestion of her greatcoat, and the icy blue of her veins stood out starkly against the red of her skin as she flashed a wide, shark-toothed grin. Jemma's soul sang at the sight. Vess was as beautiful as she was terrifying, and Jemma didn't want to look away. Never. Not from Vess.

Then a thought pierced the cloudy veil of exhaustion wrapping her mind.

"Wait," Jemma gasped. "How are you projecting?!"

Vess' grin weakened a little.

"I may or may not be going commando on this one, so let's wrap it up post-haste, how about?" Vess replied.

Shit.

"R-Right!" Jemma scrambled to her feet. "Where am I heading?"

Vess closed her eyes, and Jemma felt the tell-tale spiritual shiver of Vess casting her mind out and scanning the eighth floor. Even as she did that, Jemma could see Vess' blue veins starting to cloud and darken. Her unshielded power had already begun the process of killing her, and every second that ticked by put Vess in more danger.

Damn Dolin, that spineless coward! If only he hadn't quit!

"Apartment H-Twelve, thataway," Vess jerked her thumb in the direction the shamblers had come from. "I'll go first and open a path, you grab your gear and follow up."

Jemma frowned. "H-Twelve? You're sure?" That had been where the first call had come from. The repeater.

"Sure I'm sure," Vess replied, "now can we maybe get the lead out?"

"Right, sorry." Jemma gathered up her things and took off.

So the kid had misread the signs and given the wrong details. Maybe the spectral hadn't been aggressive at first. It wouldn't be the first time. What mattered was putting the old lady down and this was going to be an exorcism for the speedrun record books if Jemma had anything to say about it.

Mizer rested his back against the rear door of the hearse. It was a grim name, but accurate. It served as a specialized vehicle for transporting Vess on those occasions that they needed to ensure she had the maximum possible time available to her. The further she projected herself from her body, the more power it took, and that power consumption increased exponentially while she was fighting, so bringing her to the scene of a dispersal meant she could bend more of her fearsome magic to the actual fight.

Siobhan had already gone ahead, but unlike Vess, she'd had to take the stairs, so it would take her a bit of time to get up there. Vess, true to form, had projected ahead of her to buy them a little more time, despite offering to wait.

Fifteen minutes.

Even that was an almost unconscionable risk.

Five minutes was a risk.

Even now, Vess was dying. Her own magic was dismantling her body bit by bit, eating away at her thanks to the combination of the curse on her and the damage she'd taken back during the Bressig exclusion which she had never, and would never, recover from.

But this was her family. Jemma, Mizer, Polly, and Siobhan were her *family*, and Mizer knew that. Even Dolin had been treated like a bratty younger brother by Vess until he'd left. Vess would never admit it, but his leaving had hurt her, and not just because it had left her benched. She was a lot more sensitive than she let on, and she blamed herself for being too hard on him. Vess was willing to lay her life on the line for any one of them, and they all knew it, and any of them would do the same for her. There was something about Vess that provoked that kind of loyalty. She had a certain magnetism to her, a dynamism that made people want to follow her into hell, regardless of if they thought they would make it back.

It was the quality of a hero, Mizer had often thought, which was ironic given her chequered past.

"Mizer!"

He looked up sharply. Running down the sidewalk toward him, red-faced and out of breath, was Wally Willowbark. She came to a staggering stop by his side and hunched over, one hand on her knees and the other raised with a finger up to beg a pause as she caught her breath. Apparently, she hadn't been joking about her terrible physical assessment scores. That was fine. That wasn't a requirement for what she was doing. Besides, that sort of thing could be improved with good old-fashioned exercise.

"W-Where . . . Where's Vess?" Wally gasped.

"Physically?" Mizer nodded back to the hearse's rear hold. "But more accurately, she's up there," he pointed to the eighth floor of the housing project, "and right now, she's fighting without a proxy to buffer her."

"Then hook me up, or whatever it is you need to do!" Wally didn't even hesitate, and Mizer couldn't help but admire that. She had iron in her spine.

Mizer checked his watch. Vess had been up there for just over a minute and a half. As much as he wanted to protect her, Mizer couldn't just let Wally proxy for Vess without at least a basic understanding of what she was walking into.

"Before you do that, you need to know what I'm going to be doing to you," Mizer said, putting a hand up.

"But she's—!"

"Either you listen or you leave!" Mizer's voice dropped low and hardened into granite, stopping Wally cold.

She swallowed audibly, then nodded.

Foregoing any fanfare, Mizer launched into the meat of it. "Have you ever been cursed before? With intent, I mean." He asked, and unsurprisingly Wally shook her head.

"The uhm, the only curses I've reflected that I know of are the ones that the examiners used to grade me," Wally admitted.

Mizer had expected that. Curses were powerful malefic spells. The most common form of a curse was embodied in a spectral, and even those weren't something that just anyone would encounter day-to-day.

"That's okay, but you have to understand something." Mizer patted the rear doors of the hearse. "When you proxy for Vess, you'll be taking the brunt of the curse she's under. It's powerful enough that part of the prep for it is attaching a pair of warding bracelets to your arms and affixing an IV drip of saline blessed by Jiani priests, and even then you're only going to survive it because you're a reflector."

Wally's eyes widened.

"The person who cursed her . . ." Mizer continued, then trailed off, this wasn't his story to tell and even if it was they didn't have time. "Look, Wally, the power of a curse is determined by three things—the curser's main magical strength, their skill, and how much they hate their target." He blew out a slow breath. "Vess was cursed by someone with a full S-Grade in the first two categories, and there wasn't a being alive who hated Vess more than that person when the curse was spoken."

"How did she survive it?" Wally breathed.

That was the million-ducar question, and one that Mizer had never had the stones to ask. With that said, though, he had his suspicions.

"I can't say for sure, but I can tell you my theory."

Vess had no official power grading on file, but after years of working with the strange woman Mizer came to the conclusion that the reason was probably the simplest one of all.

"My theory," Mizer began as Wally leaned in, "is that Vess survived because she was just stronger than the person who cursed her."

And that was an absolutely *staggering* concept, made worse by the fact that Mizer knew full well who had spoken the curse. The idea that Vess eclipsed that woman enough to be able to endure a curse of that magnitude was existentially terrifying.

Wally looked equally shaken but rallied surprisingly quickly.

"And she's suffering from it right now?" she asked.

"Every moment of every day," Mizer replied. "And you'll know what it is she endures if I proxy you to her, so I'm asking you again, *are you sure?*"

"Absolutely."

There wasn't even a heartbeat of hesitation.

The shyness was gone from Wally's eyes, and in its place was a kind of hardened resolve that put Mizer back on his heels. When he'd first spoken to Wally, she'd seemed almost fragile. Seeing her here, now, with her shoulders squared and her chin up, it was hard to reconcile the two images.

She was all but a different person.

"Okay," Mizer said quietly. "Follow me."

He led her around to the passenger side door of the hearse and opened it. Inside, the seat had been replaced with a kind of compact reclining hospital bed, which was somewhat crumpled from having endured Siobhan being seated in it for the ride over.

"Lie down," Mizer said.

Wally, to her credit, didn't question the order. She clambered into the cab and settled in. The warding bracelets were attached to the arms of the gurney and looked more like restraint cuffs than anything. Wally slipped her hands into them, palms up, without even asking, and waited as Mizer secured them. Then, Mizer reached down below her leg and pulled up a notched strap of leather.

"I'm going to belt you down, okay?"

"Why?" Wally asked.

"In case you seize."

It was a serious concern. Enduring Vess' curse by proxy was a nightmarish experience. Dolin had never wanted to talk about it. He had heard bits and pieces from Nella, the reflector that had been with them prior to Dolin, Gods rest her, and that had been bad enough. Her loss had been a hard day for everyone, but for Vess most of all.

Mizer pulled the last strap secure on Wally. Her legs, waist, and arms were all held down, and after one last test, he turned to begin rolling up the sleeve on her arm.

Wally jerked in his grip, and he pulled his hands back.

"What's wrong?" Mizer asked, a knot of worry forming in his chest. Wally looked . . . terrified.

Her eyes were wide and her breathing had turned shallow, and she had to swallow several times before answering.

"N-Nothing, just . . ." she trailed off. "Just . . . I'm not that person anymore, okay?"

"What do you mean?" Mizer asked quietly.

She shook her head, then nodded down to her arm.

"Don't tell Vess, please?" Wally's voice quavered as she visibly forced herself to relax.

Mizer swallowed back another question. They didn't have time for that, and neither did Vess, so instead, he just said 'I promise', and rolled up her sleeve.

A scar, long and pale with age, ran down the length of her forearm. The skin around it bore the shadows of other, smaller scars, but the one in the center was one that froze Mizer solid. It was an ugly thing. An ugly death. It had been laid into Wally's tawny flesh with nothing short of total intent.

"I'm not that person anymore," Wally said in a shaky voice. "I'm better."

Mizer nodded. That would probably have to be a conversation at some point, if for no other reason than for his own peace of mind considering he was going to be throwing her into the arms of the worst curse he'd ever seen over and over. Dutifully avoiding the scar tissue, Mizer forced his hands to remain still with every iota of willpower he possessed, tied off the rubber tourniquet above Wally's elbow, and attached the IV line with practiced efficiency, finding a vein with ease. The drip started and with a pass of his hands, Mizer engaged the warding bracelets.

"Remember, you promised," Wally said as she swallowed thickly.

"I remember, now I'm going to invoke the proxy, okay?" Mizer said quietly.

Wally nodded, and Mizer wove his fingers together, knelt, and began to commune with the spirits beneath him.

He didn't have a daemonic entity backing him, like Jemma, or a freakish regeneration factor, like Polly. Mizer, if anything, was more of a generalist. He was a shaman, a spirit-talker. His family, and his people, had lived on the border of Colvus and Ulverike before the Elemental Accord writ the Union into existence. He had been trained in the old ways of magic.

His was not the spirit-worship of the temples. His was a communion.

Air was the spirit of memory, it recalled every breath and every spoken word. It knew every heartbeat as it wove through every body. Water was the universal medium. It connected all things in all ways, from the veins of the body to the veins of the world itself. Mizer called upon spirits of water and air, invoking their names in his mind as he drew them into himself. He felt the spirit in the breath he held in his lungs. He felt it in the way his blood pounded in his ears.

Reaching out, Mizer laid one hand on Wally's forehead, and with the other, he reached into the back and laid his hand on the seal-covered containment sarcophagus that held Vess' earthly body.

"By air, I bind thy minds, by water, I bind thy spirits, together as one."

It was a simple spell, but the moment it took hold, Wally began to scream.

CHAPTER 10

No matter how skilled or how powerful you were, a curse would always be measured by your hate. To cast a curse, you had to feel true hatred, and, even worse, you had to believe in the heart of your heart that your hatred was *right*.

But what defined hate, exactly?

Wally couldn't help but wonder that as she floated in a whiteout haze of agony.

Magic could be born from so many places. From spirits of the land and sky to be used by shamans, spiritualists, and planar mediums. It could spring forth from the divine flames of Aighira the Lion and the everflowing waters of Jiana'kai, the Serpent of Rebirth. Magic could be born from the mingling of bloodlines with those whose natures aren't fully mortal, and some magic could even be born from the mortal soul itself.

So what, in that context, defined hate?

What was it about hate that put it on par with spirits and gods?

Wally's veins were filled with venom. Her soul ached. Every inch of her burned as if something were trying to sear its way out from the deepest quarters of her body.

Hate.

This was *hate*.

Someone had hated Vess so deeply that they had spoken that hatred into the world and cast it inside of her in the form of a curse. It was irrational to the point of madness. This kind of hate had no basis in reality! It couldn't possibly! It was like someone had struck a match and lit Vess' marrow on fire!

Was this . . . was this what her life was like? This pain? Was it always there?

Wally's stomach clenched and nausea rolled through her. The idea of being in this kind of pain all the time was insane. This curse was insane! What kind of person could hate with such unreasonable intensity? Maybe that was it. The answer to her question; what was hate? Wally couldn't help but wonder if the answer to that was simply: madness.

That had to be it. Madness. It had to be madness. They would have had to be mad to hate someone as beautiful as Vess.

Wally focused past the pain and forced herself to concentrate. It was a vertiginous feeling, being linked to Vess; a feeling of being both here and there at the same time. The feeling of dislocation and disassociation made her stomach flip every time she tried to orient herself as her brain tried to process two sets of physical reference points and two sets of proprioception. She was aware of Vess' body—of her pain—and in that very same way Wally was aware of herself. She was aware of the cold sweat clinging to her face, neck, and back, and of the way she had to force herself to breathe past the agony. Wally was aware of how her fingernails were digging into her palms and how tightly her jaw was clenched.

She could see the ceiling of the hearse above her from where she was reclined in the passenger gurney. She could hear Mizer's soft, baritone chant, imploring the spirits to ease her. She could see a curved crystalline surface above her in a lightless container. The inside of Vess' stasis sarcophagus—her prison.

Another breath, in, then out.

Gods, there was so much pain. Vess was in pain! She was burning up! The curse and her own unimaginable power were destroying her body, and yet she was fighting anyway! Wally could feel it. She could feel Vess fighting in the building above her, and feel her face stretched in a manic grin as she cut and slashed through shamblers, denying and defying the searing pain with every breath she took.

Never again.

Wally swore an oath to herself in that moment: *never again. No one would ever hurt Vess again!*

"Thread synchronized."

Mizer's voice was the last thing Wally heard before silver fire flashed around her, and the pain vanished like a match dropped into ice water.

It started with a feeling like being squeezed from all directions. Not unpleasant or painful, just an odd, omnidirectional pressure that took Wally several moments to tentatively identify as her own reflector nature being utilized to a degree it had never been forced to before, like a dense but untoned muscle.

'WALLY?!'

Wally's eyes—or her spiritual approximation of them—snapped open, and immediately she was assaulted by vertigo as the world heaved around her.

No, not heaved.

She was moving.

A spectral horror appeared in her vision; it was long, spindly, and almost arachnoid if it weren't clearly fashioned from mutated bones and necrotic shadowflesh. A *stalker.* Terror lurched in Wally's stomach as the stalker rounded on her, surged forward and another wave of vertigo hit her as the world dissolved and reformed, and she was suddenly behind the corpse digging wickedly sharp blades protruding from ruddy red fingers whose veins were streaked an unhealthy blue into its back, flaying it apart and dispersing its energy back into the world.

Then it clicked.

This wasn't her body. The vertigo wasn't from *her* moving. It was Vess. She was riding Vess' perceptions!

'Wally what the hells are you doing?!' Vess snarled across their mental thread.

'I'm . . . I'm your proxy, remember? I'm right where I'm supposed to be.'

A stream of invectives skittered through Vess' mind, tickling the edges of Wally's consciousness. *'You aren't even officially hired yet!'*

'And you're not supposed to be projecting without a proxy!'

'Cut the thread! RIGHT NOW!'

A ringing clap of mental pressure blew through Wally, shaking her resolve and a faint pressure and a tang of copper invaded her senses. It was the force of Vess' displeasure that she was feeling, and Wally hated that she'd made Vess mad but . . . but no, she had to stand her ground.

Wally mentally planted herself and pushed back against the intruding force of Vess' personality. Her body was clenching its teeth, and she thought that she'd bitten her cheek, or maybe her tongue, but she couldn't tell. There wasn't enough feedback. It was like, by proxying for Vess, she'd become one step removed from herself. It didn't matter though, what mattered was not budging, so she didn't budge. Wally dug in, focusing on hardening that thread that connected them so Vess couldn't cut it, and met the burning pair of cerulean embers that were boring a hole in her mind's eye with two words.

'Make me.'

The eighth floor of the housing project rang with a deafening stream of vicious expletives that crossed enough languages that Wally lost track of them as Vess went berserk. She lashed out, spearing a shambler through its rotten skull with her clawed hand in a swelter of rot and gore before turning on another and tearing its arm from its socket. Every torrid oath and curse from her lips was punctuated by a savage beating meted out with the shattered limb as Vess raged through the hallway, leaving a trail of broken shamblers behind her.

Vess stomped through the hall dragging her brutalized weapon behind her. Wally could feel Vess' fanged teeth grinding against one another, and the furious tension in her projected musculature.

Briefly, Wally took a moment to marvel at the complexity of Vess' projected body. It wasn't just a crude soul-shape. Vess had managed to create a facsimile of actual bone structure, muscle, and tendons, all many times stronger than a normal person could possibly be. If Wally had to guess, she would say Vess's form probably had physical attributes comparable to a high-grade dreadnought. Riding shotgun in Vess' mind was as terrifying as it was exhilarating, but she had to be careful because, as Vess proved when she'd vented her anger, the proxy spell didn't insulate Wally completely. There was no telling yet how much mental shock she could sustain before the link broke.

'We are going to have a fucking conversation when I get back in my body, Willowbark.'

Wally winced at the harsh use of her surname. There wasn't even a hint of the softness or warmth that had been in Vess' voice back in her apartment.

She was really angry.

'That's fine,' Wally replied quietly. *'So long as you're alive to have it with me.'*

Vess clicked her tongue audibly, then tensed as a sudden wind kicked up around her. Wally braced herself in the back of Vess' mind as a storm of rubble and broken bodies was kicked up, and something hurtled the gruesome debris at Vess with back-breaking force.

"A poltergeist?!" Vess snarled as she put her arms up and hunched in on herself, taking the hits and rolling with them like a boxer. "This just keeps getting better and better!"

That gut-wrenching sense of discorporation assaulted Wally's senses again, rattling her as Vess briefly dispersed her body and reconstituted it on the other side of the storm midway through the motion of a loping run. Her booted foot hit the ground and she pounded forward. Wally experienced another heave of nausea as Vess' modulated her vision, and the world instantly became a chaotic spray of virulent color. It was some flavor of soul-sight, Wally knew that much, but it was sickening.

Vess clearly had no issue with it, and instantly oriented on a particular noisome shade of puce hovering near a corner. She warped again, and Wally barely held on as Vess landed directly in front of the poltergeist with her fist out and clenched tight inside of its invisible and ephemeral form.

Normally, an exorcist was required to disperse a spectral, especially one as strong as a poltergeist, but Vess clearly had her own methods of dealing with them.

"*Thanks for the meal~*" Vess hissed through her teeth.

And her jaw unhinged.

Never before had Wally more desperately wished to look away, but—close her eyes as tight as she might—the proxy spell ensured that she was *agonizingly* aware of Vess' every action as the sorceress distorted herself malignantly in order to consume the spectral she had a hold of like some kind of daemonic python.

Her jaw moved with foul, liquid motions, dragging the spectral deeper into her craw until it was gone, and Vess' jaw wrenched shut with a sickening *click*. Vess pointedly licked her lips while Wally stared into space, desperately trying to forget what she'd just witnessed.

'Was . . . Was that really necessary?' She asked hollowly.

'*No.*'

Wally fought back a dry-heave.

'*You can always cut the thread.*'

Forcing herself to take a deep breath—or at least go through the mental motions of it since she wasn't sure how much of what she did here translated back to her physical body—Wally shook her head.

'*You know I'm not going to do that.*'

'*Suit yourself.*'

For a long moment, Wally was silent as Vess went looking for another fight, until finally . . . '*You're a louse, Vess Gibson.*'

Apartment H-Twelve was, in all respects, identical to all of the other doors that Jemma passed in her sprint to the source of the infestation.

Behind her, Vess was cursing up a storm—only in the linguistic sense, thankfully—and keeping the rapidly manifesting corpses off of her back. They were mostly shamblers, anyway, but those were bad enough in numbers, and numbers were what they had. Jemma's more pressing concern was that if this many and varied grades of corpses, and even the odd spectral, were manifesting in this infestation, then what the *hells* kind of monster was causing it?

"Vess! I'm breaching the core!" Jemma called out and got a roughly affirmative snarl back from the ill-tempered sorceress.

That would have to do.

"Okay, let's see what's behind all this." Jemma rolled her shoulders as she raised her hammer and chisel to the ready, then leaned in and solidly elbowed the apartment door open.

Nothing.

She'd half-expected a poltergeist or a skin-rider or some other equally horrifying spectral to come rushing out on a tempest of rage to wrap itself around her, but there was only silence, which, in Jemma's opinion, was almost worse.

The floorboards creaked beneath her feet as she stepped into the small apartment. Polly said the guy who called it in had described a repeater, but repeaters didn't trigger mass infestations. They couldn't. It took a hell of a lot of miasma to animate this many necrotics and repeaters were the lowest of the low. They barely had enough in them to keep *themselves* going.

'Jem, status?'

Jemma flinched as Vess' mind synced with hers. The snap of connection was cold and painful for a heartbeat, exacerbated by her bad mood no doubt.

'No movement,' she sent back. *'Air quality is fine, too . . . no more stagnant than the hall.'*

'Odd . . . can you augur for miasma?'

'You don't have that kind of time, do you?' Jemma replied worriedly. *'We need to get you back into stasis ASAP.'*

'Oh, right, no I—shut it, Willowbark, I'm aware that you—ugh, sorry that was . . . just . . . I'm fine, Jem, I've got . . . plenty of time.'

'Willowb—?' Jemma stood up sharply and looked back over her shoulder, even knowing Vess wasn't actually there looking over her shoulder. *'Vess . . . are you proxied?!'*

There was silence for a long moment before Vess' reply finally came and when it did it was tight with poorly controlled anger.

'Just augur the damn room, Jem.'

A chill went down Jemma's spine. She wanted to argue but

couldn't find it in her to do so. Vess tended to have that effect on her. She answered with a silent affirmative pulse over their mental connection, and Vess cut the line. The moment she did, Jemma let out a breath of relief. The pressure of having Vess' mind bearing down on hers was immense. It was like a migraine but distant and removed, or an intense pressure just subtle enough to be impossible to pinpoint its source.

Swallowing back her gorge, Jemma knelt, set her chisel to the floorboard, and beat it two inches deep with her hammer. Taking a deep breath, she focused and attuned herself to the resonance of the room and the astral space that lay just beyond it. She could feel the miasma permeating this whole building, but strangely it wasn't considerably more concentrated here than anywhere else. A bit more than the halls, but . . . barely.

"Show me where you are . . ." Jemma tapped the top of the chisel lightly, and the tinny ring of metal on metal echoed out around the apartment.

Woe. There had been death in this household before the infestation. That would have been the grandmother.

Tap.

Another ringing echo picked up yet more woe, more death, and Jemma furrowed her brow as she followed it to . . .

Snapping her eyes open, Jemma moved cautiously into the small den. A television set buzzed with static white noise on a short stand at the wall in front of a recliner and an easy chair. Both showed their respective owner's preferences—the recliner was small and plumped with cushions, perfect for an old woman, while the chair had smears and stains from having regular meals taken in it.

She moved past those to the door just beyond. The bathroom.

Jemma smelled the death past the door before she opened it. It smelled of rot and blood, piss and sweat. Swallowing thickly, Jemma took a few shallow breaths through her mouth as she kicked the door open.

"Akur look down," Jemma cursed as she staggered back, throwing an arm across her nose.

By some miracle, the grandson hadn't reanimated but that

was the extent of his luck. He was curled up in the bathtub, eyes bulging and jaw hanging slack. In his right hand, he had a kitchen knife in a death grip, the tip of it was still partially buried in his left forearm. He'd been mutilating himself. Carving into his own skin. Was it a skin-rider after all? Maybe worse. Certain spectrals could drive you mad.

"Why, though?" Jemma knelt, careful not to disturb the body overmuch. "What were you . . ."

Edging a little closer, she started to pick out a pattern in his wounds. They weren't just random cuts. They were letters. Words. A last message maybe?

"M . . . I . . . S" Jemma mouthed the letters. "Misery . . ."

Misery?

Shaking her head, Jemma stood and backed away from the body to head towards the cramped staircase. She took the steps two at a time, keeping her chisel and hammer raised and a deep breath in her lungs to call for Vess if something jumped her.

Turns out, she needn't have bothered.

As she stepped into the hallway, the soft sound of weeping reached Jemma's ears. It was a familiar noise that any practiced disperser would recognize. What surprised Jemma was hearing it *here* of all places.

The grandmother's room was at the end of the hall, right where the weeping was coming from. Keeping her guard up, Jemma approached the door and tasted the air. Salt and water. Tears. The air was still clean-ish. Still no stagnation.

"You're joking," Jemma muttered as she lowered her chisel and hammer, and kicked the door open.

Sitting on the edge of the bed, her body pale and opaque, was the shade of an old elven woman. Her shoulders were hunched and shook with sorrow, and lean, bony hands covered her face like a mourning veil as tears dripped from between her fingers.

"This is it?" Jemma looked around, expecting something—anything—else to be in the room with her. There was nothing. Just an old woman lamenting the end of her line.

Shaking her head, Jemma approached the woman, knelt, and began etching out runes of dispersal in front of the spectral.

Akur's maw, closed, for the Master of Daemons had no taste for those who died in bed. Akur's claw, its six fingers splayed to deny its target their power. The crumbling tower, the sign of defeat, the inevitable end of all who stand before the Master. The blind seers slipknot to choke off their strength.

"Akur commands your ears, oh shadow," Jemma intoned softly, and the weeping quieted, then ended as the shade raised her head. "You have lingered in this place," she continued, "yet death calls your name. You remain when your end has already been claimed."

Her eyes struck Jemma for a moment. They were so old and so . . . sad. There was pain in this woman's life. Powerful, bitter pain.

"Go now," Jemma commanded, raising her voice, and the spectral woman's body shimmered hazily. "Your battle is done. Your defeat is written. So Akur demands of you . . . *go!*"

And she was gone.

One moment she was there, then she wasn't as Akur's power devoured the threads of miasma that kept her coherent. Her spirit would speed along to wherever it was destined. Behind her, the sounds of battle faded and grew quiet. With the cleansing of the infestation's center-point, the miasma would thin rapidly and disperse into the atmosphere. Still, none of it made a damn bit of sense, and it rankled.

"Done?"

Jemma turned to find Vess standing in the doorway. She looked every inch the terrible phantom. Had something like *her* been waiting for Jemma here in the middle of all of this, she would probably have been more sanguine about it all.

"Yeah, I'm done," Jemma said.

"What was it?" Vess entered the room and looked around, her keen eyes taking everything as she walked around the bed, finally stopped at the side where a misshapen lump lay under the covers.

"It was nothing . . . just an old lady." Jemma reached over the bed and pulled the covers away, revealing an elderly elven woman, thin and willowy beneath them. "A weeping woman, barely a step above a repeater."

Vess made a quiet sound in the back of her throat as she covered the woman back up.

"Well, it's done now," she said, "gather up the body and bring it with us, we'll do an autopsy and see if something's going on under the hood."

Jemma nodded and dropped her satchel to start pulling out the requisite materials, including a miniaturized bodybag. As she did, a thought occurred to her.

"Hey, Vess?" She pulled out the bag and began scrubbing away the diminution runes scrawled on them, and it started to slowly expand.

"Yeah?"

"Does the word 'Misery' mean anything to you?"

The temperature in the room dropped five degrees *at least*, and Jemma froze as a sudden, animal terror carved down her spine and settled into her gut. Shadows loomed over her, swallowing her, and from behind her a voice like nails on a chalkboard, said, "Misery?"

Jemma swallowed hard, her breath misting in front of her, and for a brief moment, she was almost *certain* that she was about to die. It was nothing rational. In her heart, she knew that Vess would never hurt her, but still . . .

Then the cold and shadows faded, and the fear went with it, as Vess answered again in a slightly more raw voice.

"Yeah, in a sense," she said quietly. "But then, this is the East End. Misery is all some of these people have left to them."

Turning her head slowly, Jemma stared over her shoulder at Vess who was standing in the doorway with an inscrutable expression on her face.

"Bag it and tag it, Jem, and let's get out of here," she continued. "I have a bone to pick with a shaman."

CHAPTER 11

All told, it took Vess, Polly, and Siobhan another hour to clear the upper level, something Vess pointedly had made no comment on regarding the fact that her participation in that action would have been impossible without Wally.

Wally had graciously chosen not to point that out either. Vess was already in a foul enough mood as it was.

Halfway through clean-up, an exhausted Jemma had been extracted back to street level by Polly after doing a full cleanse on the core of the infestation where she had dispersed the old elven woman. It still needled at Wally—the idea that something as relatively harmless as a weeping woman could be a center of an infestation of that grade. Weeping women were, by all reports, mostly passive unless you disturbed them, and even that took some doing because you had to get them to notice you through their grief. Maybe more troubling, though, was Vess' reaction to the word 'Misery'.

The moment Jemma had said it, Vess had gone so cold that Wally had nearly lost the thread of the proxy from shock. She hadn't had the nerve to ask about it, their fledging relationship was already strained enough as it was.

By the time Jemma was extracted, Vess had lapsed into a sullen silence punctuated by bursts of rage and terrible violence, and Wally hadn't found any more words to dredge up that weren't just repetitions of their argument. She knew that Vess was still mad at her, that much was obvious, but what Wally *hated* was the silent treatment.

She rode along quietly through the last half of the clean-up all the same, which proved to be just as gut-wrenching as the first half. It was during that fight, though, that Wally finally witnessed Siobhan in action. The enormous dreadnought fought like a machine. She gripped her wood-axe and swung it in patterns that were more agricultural or mechanical than they were martial, and Wally witnessed her bring down no less than two stalkers simultaneously at one point.

When it was finally over, rather than discorporating out of the building, Vess conjured up a shadowy hood, threw it over her head, and walked out of the Burroughs at Siobhan's side. It took Wally a moment to realize it was a show of solidarity, not making their lone necrotic employee walk out alone.

The moment they were away from the housing project, Vess scanned the area, then fixed Mizer with a glare of incandescent rage. "Mizer, you *rat bastard!*" she snarled. "Break the proxy or so help me I will do it myself and it'll be a lot less pleasant!"

Suddenly, the full-body pressure Wally had been feeling—and had all but stopped noticing—faded, and with it went her awareness of Vess. For a moment, Wally experienced a brief surge of irrational panic at the loss of Vess' presence. It had felt as natural as breathing to be so aware of Vess that the loss of it was like losing a sense altogether, and she had to tamp down the surge of anxiety that followed.

The sensations of her body came back in calming waves, no doubt helped along by the spirits Mizer had called up to invoke the proxy in the first place. Wally's first and overriding sense of herself was of pain. Not agony. just . . . pain; like every inch of her skin was covered in a light bruise, combined with coming down off of the worst kind of surgical anaesthesia. Her eyelids felt gummy, her mouth was achingly dry, and Wally could swear that her *bones hurt.*

"Ow."

It took an effort to pry her eyes open, but when she finally did she had another moment of panic as she thought she'd gone blind. No, it was just dark. How had she not noticed how dark it had gotten? It had well after sunset, so objectively Wally knew it had to be quite late. Of course it would be dark, but up until now . . . no, it was Vess. She must have done something to her own eyes; modulated them to perceive light more intricately so she could see in the dark. She really was incredible. The thought stuck fast in Wally's mind as Mizer unhooked her right arm from the gurney. There was a blanket over her, serving the dual purpose of warding away the chill and covering up her arms, and Wally was deeply grateful for it as she tugged her sleeves back down.

"Did it go alright?" Mizer asked as he reached over her to her left arm.

"Mm, I think so," Wally replied. "Did everyone get away?"

Mizer nodded. "The building finished evacuating a few minutes ago, and justicars cordoned off the block in case of any bleed-over from the infestation," he gestured around at the empty street. "Everyone did great, and we're—"

"MIZER!"

"Shit, here we go."

Mizer sighed, and stood up as a furious Vess rounded the corner of the hearse. Shadows leaked from her like falling ashes, and from beneath her conjured hood, two eyes like dead blue stars glared out.

Crossing his arms, Mizer faced Vess squarely and nodded. "Gibs."

"Don't you fucking 'Gibs' me, Mizer, you proxied Wally with zero training and half the precautions!" Vess jabbed a finger at his chest.

"If I hadn't been completely certain she would be safe I wouldn't have tried it, you know that," Mizer countered.

"EXCEPT YOU COULDN'T KNOW!"

Wally jumped and even Mizer rocked back on his heels at the manifold fury in Vess' tone, and with a sudden, sharp snap of movement, she had Mizer by the collar and off of his feet. The

Vess that Wally had sat with back in her apartment was only five foot and ten, but this Vess, true to her modular form, suddenly towered almost a head over Mizer's impressive six and five.

Still half-strapped to the gurney, Wally struggled to sit up. Her body was protesting loudly, but she couldn't just watch. Polly and Jemma both kept to the side of their modified ATV while Vess raged at Mizer, while Siobhan remained opposite them, the length of her wood-axe resting across her shoulders with phlegmatic ease, seemingly unbothered by what was happening.

"Tell me, Mizer, did Wally scrub down with holy water before she proxied?" Vess snarled. "Did Jemma paint gods of aversion across her lambda junctions? Or did you just cherry-pick my spell precautions and then boost her into my astral form?"

Wally hadn't followed most of that, but whatever Vess was talking about left Mizer looking abashed.

"After what happened to Nella, I should kill you for this," Vess hissed.

Somewhere deep in Wally's chest, a cube of ice froze over solid. That wasn't rage in Vess' voice. That wasn't even really *anger*.

It was cold murder.

"Vess, your miasma . . . you're not proxied," Mizer rasped.

"Maybe I don't care," Vess replied. *"You* sure as fuck didn't."

Polly approached, a hand stretched cautiously out even as the tremble to it betrayed her fear. Wally had gotten the impression that very little could shake Paulina Truelight. Despite her youthful features, she had a hard-bitten quality that spoke of years of weary resignation. Seeing her like this—actually scared—shook something loose in Wally.

"Hey, Vess, c'mon," Polly pleaded. "It was an emergency."

Vess turned her cowled head down to Polly, and Wally's jaw dropped as the powerful Biomantic's eyes crossed and her hands flew up to her neck as she began struggling to breathe. She staggered away, only finally getting a gulp of air once she was back by Jemma.

"Don't tell me what it was!" Her voice barely sounded human. It was a wet, monstrous thing somewhere between an ursine snarl and a serpentine hiss.

Finally, Wally got herself free of the gurney and all but rolled off of it. Her legs were like jelly and her stomach was still loudly informing her that all of the warping around and vertigo was going to have to be dealt with eventually. Later, though.

"Vess!"

"Don't, Wally!" Vess rasped, her voice warping hideously.

Suddenly, Wally was deeply grateful she couldn't see Vess' face underneath that cowl.

"You have no idea how dangerous what you just did is, so I don't hold it against you, but this bastard—" Vess shook Mizer like a ragdoll— "knows *exactly* what he did!"

"It was a *proxy*, Vess! Gods' hooks! It's not like you were wearing her!" Mizer spat as he took a hard grip on one of her wrists. "Besides! Wally is a stronger reflector than Nella and Dolin combined!"

"I. Don't. Care." Vess lifted him another few inches, and Mizer's throat bobbed as he swallowed thickly. "If you *ever* put Wally in that kind of danger again—!"

"Enough!"

Wally lunged in and grabbed Vess by her arm and silver fire flashed where they touched. Vess howled as she was sent reeling backward, dropping Mizer onto the street in a sprawled pile. Wally stared at the noxious smoke rising from Vess' left arm as her towering form shrank back down to her native height.

Vess glowered at Wally, although it was almost a relief because her face, while daemonic and streaked with ice-blue veins, was still mostly human.

"Wally . . ." Vess growled.

"No!" Wally stepped past Mizer, stood her ground, and matched Vess' glare. "You don't get to tell me what I'm willing to do! I knew I was taking a risk! I'm not a *child!* Even if I didn't know everything about what I was getting into, it was still my choice!"

Vess bared her teeth like an animal.

"You could have suffered permanent damage!"

"I don't care!" Wally shouted.

Like every other time she got angry, tears sprang up in Wally's eyes. Wally *hated* arguing. She hated yelling and she hated getting mad most of all because every time she did she started crying. Some people could cry and look okay doing it; there were women who could cry and still look beautiful, and men who could do it and look dignified.

Wally just looked damp and snotty.

"Even if I knew for a fact that I would be risking my life, I still would have done it!" She made a sharp slashing motion with her hand as she advanced on Vess. "You can't fight without a proxy! That's the whole reason I'm here! So don't tell me not to do my job! You're not the only one who gets to be reckless!"

Vess' body swelled monstrously again, and she loomed over Wally. Those blue-flame eyes became deadlight blue pins and her mouth split into an ugly snarl.

"The bi-location is *my* spell," Vess said, and her voice seemed to chill the air around them. "The proxy too! Every safeguard and precaution is a part of it." She lifted a single clawed finger to hover beneath Wally's nose. "It's all my spell!" she bellowed. "And if you're going to make use of it then you'll *do as I say!*"

Wally didn't look away. She didn't flinch.

"I'll do whatever I have to!" Wally replied through a throat that was tight with emotion. "Because I think you're worth it even when you're being a bully!"

The wind went out of Vess in an instant. The unearthly lights of her eyes shivered and the warp and weft of her body collapsed back down to her common, red-skinned combat form as she worked her jaw soundlessly at Wally.

"A . . . you . . . you *dare~*"

Wally stomped up the last few feet and got in Vess' face, scowling all the while, keeping her eyes fixed on Vess' the whole while.

"You can't bully me, Vess," Wally said flatly. "I'm not scared of you."

That was true. She wasn't scared of Vess. Wally *was* scared. She was scared of how unhinged Vess seemed. She was scared of how unstable the put-together sorceress had become at seemingly the drop of a hat. But she wasn't scared of *Vess*.

Wally wasn't sure she *could* be scared of Vess, although, for the life of her, she couldn't say why. Something deep inside her just . . . wasn't.

'I'll protect you.'

For a moment, Wally could have sworn she heard Vess' voice in her head. The mind-speak voice. The calm, cool, sardonic voice of Vess Gibson, but it wasn't her, was it? It couldn't be. The Vess in front of her was anything *but* calm, so where . . . ?

Wally's train of thought was derailed by an inchoate scream of rage as Vess spat a wicked Oreliaun epithet, then vanished, taking the oppressive miasma of her magic with her.

"Really?!" Wally spun on her heel and stomped back towards the hearse, stepping over a stunned-looking Mizer as she did. "Did you *really* just do that?!"

Wally slammed open the rear door of the hearse and glared at Vess' sarcophagus.

"VESZHA GIBSON GET BACK OUT HERE!"

There was no response. The mobile power supply of the unit just hummed quietly. Wally narrowed her eyes. She *knew* Vess could hear her. She was fucking *telepathic*.

"VESS!" Wally shouted, lashing out a kick at the bottom of the sarcophagus with a dull *clang*. "Oh you are such a—well, *fine!* Go ahead! Sit in your soup can and *sulk!* You're a complete child, you know that!? You're so—UGH!"

She kicked the sarcophagus again.

"I know you can hear me, Vess!" Wally raged at the silent unit, slamming a fist down on the armored cover.

There was no response, and Wally huffed angrily, then sighed. The anger drained out of her visibly as her shoulder slumped and, and after a moment she reached out and laid her palm on the cool metal.

"You're a louse, Vess Gibson," Wally said quietly, "but I'm not going anywhere and you can't sit in there forever. You'll have to talk to me eventually, and besides," she ran her hand down the metal frame, "you promised . . . didn't you?"

Hadn't she?

For some reason, Wally had a crystal clear memory of Vess promising to protect her, but she couldn't put a finger on when it had happened. Was it back at her apartment? At Cuppa's? When had she made that promise?

"Didn't you promise to protect me?"

Vess had, Wally was sure of it.

Wasn't she?

CHAPTER 12

EVERYTHING HURT.

Every muscle, all the way down to her bones, hurt. It wasn't agonizing, it was just a constant ache that clung to Wally like chilled molasses.

As much as she hated to admit it, Vess might have had a point. Proxying for her without the proper precautions had left her feeling absolutely miserable. At no point during the proxy had Wally felt as though her life were in danger, though, so she still thought Vess had been overreacting, but still . . . she was definitely miserable.

"*Mrrow?*"

"Morning, Tipsy," Wally groaned as she rolled over in her bed. "Can you get mommy some painkillers?"

"*Mrow.*"

"Well, a fat lot of good you are."

Wally forced herself to sit up. Her mouth was dry and gummy, and she smacked her lips to try and work some moisture back into it. Her eyes felt sunken in, and her skin papery. It was like the worst kind of everyday illness. Not enough to warrant a visit to the temple, but definitely enough to ruin her week.

Vaguely, Wally had the thought to call Mizer. He'd mentioned side-effects and had certainly taken Vess at least semi-seriously when the two of them had been arguing. She fished around for her phone as she followed that line of thought. Maybe Mizer had some remedy ideas.

"What time is—*ah!*"

Wally's eyes flew wide as she stared at the time and date.

She'd been asleep for almost a full day!

Rolling out of bed with a dull thump, Wally paused for a moment to fill poor Tipsy's food and water bowls, and give her a good snuggling by way of apology for missing her breakfast and being so late with dinner. Her plants got their water, and she had to be careful not to overdo it. Making up for the missed watering wouldn't do them any good if she drowned them.

At least she didn't have to worry about work. Mizer had been clear when he'd dropped her off at home that he didn't expect her to be back at the precinct for at least a couple of days. It wasn't just her, either. Everyone needed a break. They wouldn't be taking any more dispersal calls until Jemma had gotten a good long rest, and even Polly had been burnt out by the combat.

Siobhan, by contrast, seemed entirely unphased.

Of course, that didn't make Wally want to visit the precinct any less, and not because of work. She wanted to see Vess. They had a conversation to finish. To be honest, Wally wasn't even sure she wanted an apology, and she certainly didn't owe Vess one after how the woman had acted. What she really wanted to know was *why*.

Why had Vess reacted so viscerally to the proxy? Sure, it hadn't been ideal, but . . .

Wally dragged her phone out of her pocket and shot a message to Mizer, asking after everyone and following up with a small request for any thoughts on how to alleviate the post-proxy misery.

//Mizer: Polly will bring something by in an hour or so. Other than that? Just rest.//

Wally smiled at the reply. They were good people. Even Jemma didn't seem *bad*. Just bristly. Sort of like Tipsy had been before she'd gotten used to Wally, and now the little black ball of rumbles wouldn't leave her alone. Not that Wally wanted her to.

Retreating back to her bed, she dragged the comforter off of it and stumbled over to the couch to curl up before flicking on the television. Late-night T.V. wasn't her favorite, but it was more about white noise than anything else at this point. She was too tired to move and too sick to sleep, and Wally didn't particularly fancy lying in the middle of her apartment in dead silence.

She was about halfway through a rerun episode of the Great Elven Bake-Off when a knock came at her door, and Wally let out another quiet groan as she untangled herself from her blanket, stood, and trudged over towards the insistent noise.

Wally cracked the door open, peeked out, and smiled at the grinning blonde on the other side.

"Hey kiddo." Polly held up a ceramic bottle and gave it a shake, "Heard you were under the weather."

Wally opened the door the rest of the way and stood back.

"Thanks, Polly, I really appreciate it," Wally said softly.

Polly shook her head. "Don't sweat it, you're not the first one I've had to bring some of this out to." She held out the bottle as she passed, and Wally took it gratefully. "Mind you, it tastes like dumpster juice but I'll guarantee it does the trick assuming you don't yak it up right away."

Grimacing, Wally took another tentative look at the bottle and gave it a shake. The contents did sound a little more viscous than she thought a proper liquid should.

"So, now that your first proxy is done with how are you feeling?" Polly asked.

Wally briefly considered putting on a brave face, but, frankly, she just didn't have the energy. That and she had no doubt that she looked exactly as bad as she felt, if not worse.

"Rough," Wally said as she trudged back to the couch and sat down. "Like an old rag that's been wrung out too many times."

"Yeah, that tracks . . . Mizer was right, you were always going to be fine, but there's a reason we have so much prep that goes into proxying." Polly dragged one of the kitchen chairs over to the den and sat down on it backward, leaning forward as she rested her chin on her arms, and turned to watch the T.V. while Wally got herself settled again. "Ooh, this is the episode where

Nelphas fucks up his macaroons!" she kipped up from the chair and dropped down on the couch beside Wally with a grin. "He was so smug in the first episode. I wanted to punch his stupid face in!"

"He's actually pretty talented, though," Wally pointed out.

"That made his attitude even worse," Polly replied grumpily.

Wally didn't necessarily disagree.

"Speaking of competent assholes, Vess still hasn't emerged from her—what did you call it? Her soup can?" Polly snorted and started laughing. "I'm calling it that from now on, by the way."

"Still?"

"Don't agonize over it, Vess is probably more exhausted than any of us," Polly said, waving a hand dismissively.

"Was it that strenuous for her?"

Polly nodded and leaned back against the couch, kicking her feet up on the table in much the same way as Vess had. Apparently, everyone in the sixth precinct had been raised in a barn.

"Even though she didn't have to project herself very far, she was still fighting full-tilt for over an hour on five restraints, so yeah, I'd imagine it was."

"Restraints?"

"Damn, Mizer told you jack shit, huh?" Polly said with a dry laugh. "Maybe Vess was right to crawl up his ass about the proxy."

"There was no time, and he told me I'd be safe," Wally protested weakly.

That sounded a little lame even to Wally. She'd known Mizer for what? Less than a day? Still, she felt like she was a semi-decent judge of character and Mizer had struck her as a fundamentally honest sort of person.

"I mean, he was right," Polly allowed. "Honestly, you're a hell of a reflector, kid, but still . . ." she trailed off and tapped her lip thoughtfully. "The next time you're in Vess' chamber, check beneath her soup can and you'll find five cylinders set into alcoves, those are her restraints. They're throttles on her power to make sure she can't overburn herself *or* her proxy, so, for reference—"

Polly held up four fingers at Wally with a wan grin— "imagine how bad you'd feel if you'd proxied for Vess at four restraints?"

Wally grimaced. She was already miserable enough and that was the side-effects of proxying for Vess while she was completely restrained?

"The first time Dolin tried to proxy for her at three, he ended up confined to the Jiani temple for a week," Polly continued, her tone growing more subdued. "We were up against a dreadnought, a big one. Jemma couldn't get close enough to abjure it. I'd been bisected twice, and even Siobhan was struggling, so Dolin removed the limiter without asking. Vess was livid."

Without asking? Even to Wally that seemed like too much. "Why would he do that?"

Polly shook her head, sending her flaxen locks tumbling around her face. "That was their relationship," she replied. "It was a kind of younger-brother, older-sister dynamic. Dolin desperately wanted Vess to acknowledge him, and she's . . ." Polly sighed and let out a weak chuckle. "Well, she's a hard woman to please, and Dolin, being young and reckless, kept trying to prove himself even though, objectively, he was pretty weak."

Although she'd never met him, Wally felt for Dolin. He wanted desperately to be noticed and seen as competent, and he wanted to impress. It was hard being hungry for something you could never have.

"He left not long after he was released from the temple," Polly continued. "I think he got spooked. Proxying had never hurt him that badly before so we didn't blame him, but Vess took it hard. She blamed herself for going off on him after the proxy, but we all knew it was because she was worried about him."

Ah, there it was. Wally understood, now, why Polly had come over, and it wasn't just to give her to remedy, obviously. It was to explain Vess' behavior in a way Vess wouldn't, or maybe couldn't. Of the many impressions Vess had left over the past forty-eight hours, one of the most overriding ones was of an incredibly proud woman. Part of Wally wanted to say Vess was brave, but she wasn't sure that was accurate. Wally wasn't sure she was brave so much as she was *reckless*. But she was only reckless with herself, and, in fact, seemed to take it personally when other people did the same thing which either meant she was a hypocrite or . . .

"Vess doesn't value her own life very much, does she?" Wally asked. The notion put a pit of sorrow in her.

"She's got a lot of baggage," Polly replied quietly. "And a lot of pain."

Now that, Wally could relate to. She turned the odd bottle over in her hand a few times, considering it. Something told her it would probably be even less pleasant to drink than Polly had made it sound, which was sort of impressive in its own way.

"Hey, Polly?" Wally started, looking up from the bottle.

"Hm?"

"Back on the street, Vess mentioned someone named Nella?"

Polly's expression darkened considerably, and she carded her fingers through the fine strands of her hair in a manner that reminded Wally of Mizer more than anything.

"Nella." Polly blew out a hard breath. "Yeah, she . . . she was Vess' reflector for almost . . . shit, eight years? She was the one that Dolin took over for."

"What happened?"

For a long moment, there was no answer. There was strain on Polly's face, though. An expression that said she was consider her words carefully. She was also, Wally thought, struggling to even put the words together. The lines on her face cut deeper than they should have on someone who looked so young, betraying her true age somewhere.

"That's a simple question with a complicated answer, Wally, but the short of it is that Nella is the reason that Vess is so sensitive about this, and why she's so mad at Mizer." Polly massaged the bridge of her nose and closed her eyes.

"She died?" Wally ventured.

"Polly let out a bitter huff of a laugh.

"Yeah, she did," Polly replied. "Nella died, and, in more ways than one, Vess is the one who killed her."

Vess Gibson's mind was a dark place where sleep came only in half-measures, and it was never quite what one would call restful. Vess couldn't even recall the last time she'd truly slept. Back when she'd been properly human, she supposed.

Certainly not since she'd been permanently confined to her sarcophagus.

The fumigation of the housing project had been three days ago and it had been strenuous enough that she'd spent all of her time resting since she'd returned—*Call what it is you coward*—retreated back to her sarcophagus.

She had 'retreated' after losing her temper with Mizer and, worse, with Wally. Since then, she'd been floating in the nonspace of her convalescent state. During that time, while her mind was recovering from the strain of combat, Vess found herself unconscionably grateful that she couldn't dream. She had the distinct impression that any dreams she had would be unpleasant in the extreme.

'*You promised . . . didn't you?*' Inside of her sarcophagus, Vess' mortal hand curled into a weak fist, despite the stasis spell on it. '*Didn't you promise to protect me?*'

The last time that Vess had wished that she was weak enough for a stasis spell to fully affect her had been in the months after Nella's death. During that time, she'd wanted nothing more than to just not exist. To not have to deal with the pain of losing someone like that. This time, it wasn't the pain of loss. It was shame.

Gods, she was so *ashamed*.

Wally had done nothing to deserve her ire, but Vess had taken it out on her anyway. Thinking about the way she'd shouted at Wally made Vess sick to her stomach. All she wanted to do was sink into her sarcophagus and never, ever come out.

What a mess.

A soft knocking sounded from somewhere on the edges of Vess' perception, and with it came the faint awareness of a seething mass of necrotic energy. It was standing over her sarcophagus, and in most situations that would be a bad thing but in this case Vess knew precisely who had come to see her. The one person other than a reflector who could stand in her presence without suffering any deleterious side effects. After all, you can't curse the dead.

Another faint knocking sounded, and Vess briefly considered ignoring it. That hadn't worked out incredibly well for her so far though and, as Wally had so deftly pointed out after she'd gotten done kicking the base of Vess' sarcophagus, she *would* have to come out eventually.

Might as well ease into it.

Vess focused and began counting upwards, raising herself up through the planes of conscious thought, out of the murk and mire of her stasis-enforced half-sleep and finally . . . *out.*

Vess opened her eyes as her astral form coalesced on the side of her sarcophagus opposite her visitor, and immediately sagged.

"Gods, I feel like shit," Vess grumbled.

"Good."

"A little moral support would be nice, Vonnie."

Siobhan raised an eyebrow that disappeared under her matted, off-red hair. Her eyes were the one aspect of her that had survived her death. Striking irises that were a singular shade of steel-gray, and reminded Vess of nothing so much as a stark winter sky.

"My morals are kinda questionable for that," Siobhan replied with a shrug.

Then she grinned, which was a deeply disturbing expression. Her undead features were warped by her transformation, stealing any softness she may once have had. Her cheeks were hard, sunken things, and her mouth was a too-wide rictus filled with crooked fangs—a look that Vess had cribbed for her own astral form for the intimidation factor.

It was just a mockery, though. Siobhan was the real deal.

Siobhan was a dreadnought; her kind were amongst the most physically powerful corpses, and she was an older one by their standards. Not even Siobhan herself was sure why she'd held together this long. Most corpses and spectrals only held up so long as they stuck near wherever it was they were haunting, drawing from the memories of the land to sustain themselves. Normally, even the sanctioned couldn't stray far from where they'd risen before they started falling apart. Siobhan wasn't beholden to that rule, and no one was entirely sure why that was.

"So, just out of curiosity, did you come here for a reason? Or just to shit talk me to my face?" Vess asked.

Siobhan shrugged. "You say that like shit talking you to your face can't be the reason I came in here," she replied.

Vess gave her a flat look, then rolled her eyes and nodded. "Fair."

"So, you gonna apologize to the kid?"

Vess lowered her head, staring pointedly at the ground.

"She's got guts," Siobhan rasped. Her voice had a naturally harsh quality to it, although Vess wasn't sure if that was from her death or if it was a leftover from her life.

"What she did was stupid," Vess said quietly.

"That's rich, coming from you."

Vess looked up with narrowed eyes. "It's not the same, Wally had no idea what she was getting into, no clue what she was doing, and should never have been put in a situation where she felt obligated to do it!"

"Seemed like she did fine to me," Siobhan said calmly.

"She—!" Vess bit back a response.

The annoying thing was that Siobhan was right. Wally had done just fine. She'd been *just fine*. The only one losing her shit about it was Vess herself. She was being irrational and she knew it, but for some reason she just couldn't get a handle on herself.

No, not for 'some' reason. Vess knew damn well why she was getting so worked up.

"I just . . . I didn't want to start it off like that," Vess said, reaching past her neckline to pluck out the slim chain that hung around her neck to toy with the ring that hung from it, rolling the smooth, ornate metal between her fingers. "I wanted it to be easier . . . gentler."

Siobhan cocked her head curiously, and Vess blew out an angry breath.

"I didn't want to hurt her, okay?!" Vess snapped, and the ring dropped down to hang heavily at her chest.

"Well good job on that one, chief."

Her tone was so dry that Vess swore her physical body just lost water weight, but she wasn't wrong. She'd taken a less-than-ideal situation, lost her temper, and, per usual, made it worse.

"Yes, thank you, I was unaware I'd *fucked myself* up until now." Vess dragged a hand down her face and sighed. "And the day had gone . . . not so bad, prior to all of that."

"She'll be back," Siobhan said without inflection.

"Bold claim, Vonnie."

"Not really."

This time it was Vess' turn to raise an eyebrow. The expression only lasted a moment before she caught on and groaned. A quick mental scan of the lower level, even given the dulling effects of the apotropaic eyes carved across the walls, showed Jemma in her room, Mizer in his office, Polly at her desk, and outside Vess' chamber door . . .

"How long has she been here?"

"Mizer asked her to come by yesterday to talk t'you, but you kinda shut her down in your sleep," Siobhan replied with a smirk, and Vess winced. "She shook it off, though, and came back today to try again. Not gonna lie, the kid looks rough but, like I said, she's got guts."

Vess gave a stiff nod. She wasn't wrong about that. It took some real brass to look someone like Vess in the eye while she was properly raging and call her a bully. It had been so brazen that it had shocked her even more than when Wally had touched Vess' arm and reflected her own miasma back at her.

"So I guess you *did* come in here for a reason," Vess said, finally.

Siobhan shrugged. "Figured I was the only one you wouldn't snap at, plus the kid seems nice. A little skittish, but nice."

Vess snorted quietly and nodded.

"So want I should send'er in? Or away?"

"It's fine." Vess waved dismissively. "She's probably just here to chew me out again."

A dry, rhythmic hacking noise came from Siobhan, and Vess frowned as she looked back up at the towering dreadnought. The noise was sickly, ashen, and sounded almost painful, and it took Vess several seconds to realize that that was the sound of Siobhan *laughing*.

It had been so long since she'd heard it that she'd forgotten the sound.

"*Wow.*" Siobhan clapped a hand on Vess' shoulder. "You haven't even worked with her for a whole day and you already whipped? Send'er my way when you're done kissing her ass, I wanna know how she did it!"

Prior to this, Vess had never had cause to be thankful that her astral form couldn't blush.

"I'm not whipped," Vess hissed, and her hand went reflexively to the metal loop at her chest.

"Really? Because the way I remember it, all it took was her getting in your face and calling you a bully to put your tail between your legs."

Siobhan was wearing a shit-eating, ear-to-ear grin, and her steel eyes fairly glittered with humor while Vess bristled and ground her teeth as she struggled not to say something she would regret. Her temper had bought her enough trouble.

"Just . . . tell her she can come in," Vess bit out.

"Right, yeah, sure thing, chief."

It occurred too late to Vess that Siobhan had agreed to that far too easily, and all she could do was listen in horror as the dreadnought opened the door, then opened her mouth, and said:

"Hey, y'wife's done sulking."

CHAPTER 13

WALLY SAT RESTLESSLY in the waiting room of the sixth precinct's upper level. She wasn't feeling a hundred percent, but she was better than when Polly had visited.

That conversation still hung over her like a cloud. It was only exhaustion that allowed her to sleep despite it and Wally still wasn't sure if she'd rather nothing had been said at all. In the end, it didn't matter. If Vess wanted to confide in her, she would, if not then . . . well, Wally would burn that bridge if and when she came to it. Until then, she was left sitting in the waiting room, and it still didn't smell any better than it had on her first time here. Mizer had sent her a message asking her to meet him as soon as she felt up to it, so she'd come almost immediately. He'd been insistent that it wasn't *that* urgent, but Wally had been looking for an excuse anyway.

Now, though, she kind of wished she'd waited. At least she could have been cooling her heels at home with Tipsy instead of in this grungy waiting room. She'd tried to start a conversation with the desk clark who had checked her in during her interview but his response had been soft and monosyllabic, never inviting more conversation, and he'd always gone back to reading his novel until she had felt it was too awkward to try again.

In the end, all she could do was wait for Mizer and hope

that Vess was in a better mood than she'd been back at the Burroughs. As it happened, she'd just barely given up trying to converse when Mizer emerged from the hallway left of the clark's desk with a weary smile on his face and waved her over. Despite herself, Wally smiled as she stood, tugged her slacks and blouse straight, and made her way over.

"Wally, it's good to see you." Mizer put a hand on Wally's shoulder and gripped gently. It was a reassuring pressure. He nodded back towards the hall as he stepped to the side. "Sorry for the delay, I—"

A door behind him slammed open and the sound of metal-shod footsteps preceded a figure that dwarfed not only Wally but Mizer himself. Wally found herself staring up at what was easily six and a half feet of broad-shouldered muscle clad in an ornate hauberk of silversteel.

Her eyes were deliriously wide and painfully blue, and her mouth was carved into a broad grin that was eerily unmoving, like marble. The woman looked less like a mortal and more like a statue come to life. Her hair even fell in two arrow-straight sheets of flaxen blonde on either side of her face, framing an expression that landed firmly on 'unsettling'.

She was a knight, that much was obvious, but in the most anachronistic sort of way. No one walked around wearing full plate anymore! It was ridiculous. Most knights of the Union used more modern body armor made of interlocking sigils under, at its heaviest, what might have been considered half-plate—the majority wore little more metal than a breastplate, greaves, and vambraces, favoring speed and relying on their sigilic arts to protect them. This woman was dressed like a tank, and her outfit and manner were so bright and impossible to ignore that Wally found herself cringing back as Mizer squared up against the woman.

"Erik, I implore you," she began in a strident voice that had Wally's ears instantly pinned back under her hair. "We've yet to come to amicable terms! It's bad form to simply walk out of negotiations!"

"It's worse form when the only terms you'll accept are total capitulation!" Mizer said dryly as he rounded on her. "Now if you don't mind, I have a business to run!"

The woman's face didn't change but something about her presence grew more menacing as she held her hands out to either side in a show of tolerance. And Wally was *certain* it was just a show.

"Erik, this isn't a matter of business, it's a matter of good and evil! Of light and dark! Of justice, Erik," she reached out and laid a hand on his shoulder, *"justice!"*

Mizer groaned and crossed his arms. "Cass, this is my territory, that was my dispersal, and the remains are mine to do with as I please, and you," he knocked her hand from his shoulder before jabbing a finger at her breastplate, "have no claim on any of it. I'm not handing anything over to you just so the temple can monopolize the knowledge."

"The Temple of Ys works for the good of *all*," the woman replied stonily through her masquerade smile.

"And the profit of the few," Mizer retorted acidly. "We're done talking, Cass, and you're not welcome here, you know that."

Finally, the woman's expression changed. Just slightly. It was little more than the faintest narrowing of her eyes, but the difference was chilling.

"Understandable." Her voice was still as bright and borderline stentorian as before. "Do tell Paulina 'hello' for me, though." She stepped past Mizer and paused as Wally came fully into view. "I don't know you," she said flatly. "I thought I knew all of Erik's ramshackle sixth. My condolences if you're a new hire."

Wally pressed her lips to a thin line as she drew back, and Mizer put a hand up between them.

"I said, that's enough," Mizer repeated darkly.

The woman turned to regard Mizer with that unchanging smile, then nodded down to Wally. "Your heresies in associating with the dead and the damned taint you and Paulina alike, and you should be ashamed of dragging others into your depravity, assuming this girl," she gestured to Wally like she was a piece of furniture, "isn't one of them already."

"*Leave.*"

Wally hadn't imagined Mizer could take that tone with anyone. Still, if anyone deserved it, she couldn't help but think that this woman definitely ranked among the top.

Perhaps that was what pushed her to actually speak.

"Ma'am?" Wally stepped out from behind Mizer to the visible surprise of Mizer, the woman, and Wally herself. "With respect," she began, "if it's a choice between someone like you, and people who care about me for who I am, then I'll take the dead and the damned, thank you."

The woman that Mizer called 'Cass' gave her that eerily narrowed gaze for a brief moment before her expression was schooled beneath that weird, marble smile.

"I'll pray for your soul, then," she replied.

Then she was gone, and her massive, choking presence following her as she left the building. It wasn't until she was gone that Wally realized how cloying just being around the woman was.

"I . . . really don't like her," Wally said quietly, and Mizer snorted out a laugh.

"Neither do I," he replied, patting her shoulder.

That much was comforting. She had struck Wally as the type of person who was used to bullying people into doing what she wanted. The sort who would tower and shout over anyone who raised a voice against her. The type of person that Wally could honestly say she hated the most.

"What did she want?" she asked as they turned to start walking down the hall. "And who is she?"

"Cass wants access to the body of the elven woman we recovered from the Burroughs," Mizer said as he led her back to the basement door, fitted a key, and opened it. "She says the mass infestation isn't an isolated event and they're trying to nail down the why of it, and as for who she is . . ." He grew quieter as he pushed the door open "That was the Knight-Commander of the First Precinct, and High Paladin of Ys, Cassidia Truelight."

It took Wally a few moments to process that.

"Truelight?"

Mizer nodded while Wally followed him downstairs.

"Yeah," he confirmed. "That was Polly's baby sister."

Privately, Wally wondered if maybe he could have chosen a descriptor other than 'baby' or if he had done that on purpose.

"Uhm, she seems . . . not nice."

Mizer nodded as he lead her into his office

"Polly and her family, they . . . they don't exactly get along," Mizer said as he walked to his desk, slumped down behind it, and carded his fingers through his hair while Wally sat opposite him and wrung her hands.

In truth, Wally couldn't really say she understood that sort of relationship. Her family life hadn't been good to start with and it had ended in about the worst way possible. To the best of her knowledge she didn't have any extended family. She knew nothing of her mother's parentage, and her father . . . well, that wasn't really an option, even if any of them *were* still alive.

"It's a complicated mess, to be frank," Mizer said. "Honestly, I'm surprised she actually came down here. They must be desperate."

"Why did she want the body?"

"To study it, same as us," Mizer answered.

Wally sat back in the chair and rubbed at the back of her neck awkwardly. "So, I know she's not . . . nice," Wally began a bit lamely, "but *shouldn't* we be working with the other precincts?"

"It is, and if working together was what she wanted I might have considered it, but she—" Mizer gestured up towards the street-level— "wanted a full hand-off, and all proprietary intel."

"What?!" Wally sat up sharply.

Mizer wore a thin, arid smirk. "Yeah, the illustrious First Precinct couldn't possibly be seen working alongside the ramshackle sixth," he said dryly.

"That's not fair! We did the work!" Wally's blood was up; something that didn't happen very often. She could count on two hands the number of times she really got angry . . . assuming she only counted Vess as 'one'. That woman could get under her skin disturbingly easily considering they hadn't known each other all that long.

Mizer crossed his arms and nodded. "And Cass hates that.

She hates that we're the ones who got our hands on the first real piece of evidence."

"First piece?" Wally asked with a small frown. "But you just said there were other events. Wouldn't the first have something too by now?" Wally couldn't imagine that a dispersal precinct with enough skill and resources to carve out territory in the wealthiest part of Colvus wouldn't be able to preserve a single body.

"Maybe, maybe not," Mizer said. "Cass only admitted to knowing of three other instances, and while she didn't say it as such, it's possible that this is the only intact host body to be recovered from one of those sites."

"How?"

Mizer shrugged. "There are plenty of ways to die that don't leave much of a body," he replied. "Or any body, in some cases. We only managed to get the body in as good of condition as it is because Vess was there. Necrosis does a number on living flesh."

That was probably fair. If the other precincts took more than a few hours to fumigate a location, the resulting miasma would saturate the host's cells, resulting in total disintegration after the exorcism.

"The real kicker is that Cass probably doesn't even have her hackles up because we got there first. I'm pretty sure she just hates that Polly got to it."

"Really? " Wally grimaced. "She hates her sister that much?"

"I think so, yeah, but she also believes that we'll botch the research of the body." Mizer shrugged, then laughed, and this time Wally couldn't help but laugh a little along with him.

The idea that Vess would botch something like that was kind of silly.

"We can do it, though, right? The research?" Wally pressed.

"We can," Mizer replied. "Jemma thinks the old woman was cursed before dying, and that it was *that*, and not the spectral of the woman herself, that caused the infestation."

"Then what's the problem?" Wally asked.

"The problem is that Jemma just *suspects* a curse. She can't prove it definitively yet, and even if she could, that wouldn't tell us what the curse actually did."

"But we *can* tell, right?" Wally asked. "That's why you wouldn't give up the body. Because we can do it." She had to believe that. Wally had to believe that Mizer wouldn't just hold onto something like that out of spite. Even if it meant giving one precinct an edge, it would be better than nobody knowing why these mass infestations were happening.

It was, quite literally, better than nothing.

"We can," Mizer confirmed, and Wally had to resist breathing out a sigh of relief. "The only issue is that the person able to do it is currently . . ."

Now, Wally did sigh, and it was not a sound of relief.

"Sulking in a soup can?" she asked.

"That."

"And I guess you've tried to talk to her?"

Mizer nodded. "Mm, yeah, 'tried' being the operative word," he looked forlorn. "Polly can't enter Vess' chamber without someone proxying or some weapon's-grade sanctification, and every time *I* go in it feels like she's trying to throttle me."

Wally frowned. "Why would she be doing that?"

"She's not," Mizer replied quickly. "Or at least, not intentionally, she's just mad at me and the miasma she exudes recognizes that so it gets hostile on me immediately."

Vess really was a complete disaster.

"What about Jemma? Or uhm, Siobhan?"

"With the best will in the world, Jemma has no idea how to stand up to Vess. She practically worships the woman," Mizer said. "And Siobhan? Maybe . . . but if Siobhan gets involved she'll just pick a fight. Not maliciously, she just likes riling up Vess and that's the last thing we need."

That put Wally's hackles up, although for that mostly just meant she frowned a little harder than normal.

"You, on the other hand, can talk to her, although I hate to ask you to do it after what happened," Mizer finished.

"I don't regret it, and I'm happy to try," Wally replied.

And that was the honest truth. Wally regretted nothing about her decision to proxy for Vess except for the way it had ended. Even that wasn't anyone's fault. According to Polly, Vess had good reason to be angry about Mizer skipping steps, even if it hadn't been as dangerous as she'd made it out to be. Moreover, Mizer had given the impression that he'd known what would happen when he'd proxied Wally to Vess. He had known she would be furious, and he'd done it anyway. He'd done it because he'd wanted to keep her safe, and Wally agreed with him. Vess was a little *too* fine with putting herself in harm's way.

"Good," Mizer smiled, "and you remember where her room is, right?"

Wally nodded. "I'll go see if she's awake if that's okay?"

"It's fine, swing back by here before you leave though, we still need to do your hiring paperwork," Mizer said with a laugh as Wally got up and bowed herself out of his office.

Right, that *was* something. In all the excitement, Wally had nearly forgotten that she'd successfully gotten a job, and a good one at that. The pay was way above subsistence, although part of the reason for that was the automatically-included hazard pay. Dispersal was a dangerous job, after all, and her first experience had proved that beyond a doubt. But hey, maybe if she saved up, she could get Tipsy one of those fancy spark-powered leg prosthetics that were on the market now! They were spendy but it would be a nice goal to aim for.

With that thought on her mind, Wally made her way down the hall in silence. With everyone still recovering from the battle, she wasn't surprised the place was quiet. It was a small miracle that there hadn't been any serious injuries.

Well, none that stuck since, for obvious reasons, Polly didn't count.

Pausing in front of Vess' door, Wally took in the layered wards with a more critical eye.

The first time she'd seen it, she'd been too off-kilter to really appreciate the artistry of it, but it really was a sterling example of wardcraft. The whole room was a seamless combination of cultural symbology designed to throw back ill will, harm, and dark magic. It went far beyond anything Wally had studied back at university. It was more than just a theoretical study, it was a practical application that demonstrated a thorough understanding of the underpinning thought processes. The arrangement of the eyes and monads showed a clear knowledge of the ideologies and cultural beliefs that developed the symbols, and their placement in relation to one another corresponded beautifully with geometric magical theory. Wally had no doubt that the interior of Vess' chamber, assuming she had the opportunity to study it, would prove to be the same writ much larger. Whoever designed this door should have been a professor.

"Okay, enough dallying," Wally muttered.

Taking a grip on the door's handwheel, she tensed and turned it. It was heavy but well-used and well-oiled, so it gave with only a little protest. Cracking open the door, Wally stepped inside, and immediately staggered as silver fire flared and flashed around her body, and she clapped a hand over her mouth reflexively. The air wasn't poison, but her body was still *convinced* that she was standing in some kind of . . .

"Miasma."

Wally gasped out the word. This was Vess' miasma, but it was stronger than anything Wally could have imagined! She hadn't gotten the full force of it before because Vess had been calm, but that had clearly changed.

"V-Vess?" Wally called out weakly. "Vess, *please*, it's me! Can you . . . can you please just talk to me?"

There was no answer. The only reply Wally got was the thickening of the miasma around her. In theory, she knew she could breathe just fine, but her body was fighting her. Every time she tried to get a breath, her throat closed up like she was trying to inhale smoke! She was fighting her body's own autonomic functions just standing there! That must have been what Mizer was talking about, and it had probably been several times worse for him since he wasn't a reflector.

"Vess I s-swear!" Wally coughed weakly. "You—! UGH!" Wally stomped her foot. "You're such a child!"

No response. Mizer *had* said she wasn't doing it intentionally. She was 'sleeping'. That meant that this is what Vess was like when she 'went to bed mad' as they say. Wally needed a better plan than just choking to death, so she staggered out of the room, shoved the door shut, and took in a deep, grateful breath. There was no talking to Vess like that. She couldn't even get her attention, and Wally had no idea how long she would be in that state. More than just a plan, Wally needed to rouse Vess for another reason. While she'd been in there, she had been able to feel Vess' anger, sure, but more than that she'd felt Vess' misery. Vess was angry, but she wasn't really angry at anyone here.

She was angry at herself.

"Stupid," Wally muttered weakly as she massaged her throat and grimaced. "You're such an idiot."

How was she supposed to even get her to talk, she couldn't even breathe!

. . .

"Oh." Wally blinked owlishly, then smiled. "I just need someone who doesn't breathe."

The next day found Wally standing outside of a room she'd had no prior cause to visit. The door itself was made of sturdy wood that didn't match anything else in the building, and it had the oddest smell of woodsmoke about it.

Mizer and Polly had assured her that the room's occupant was perfectly friendly if a bit quiet, but that didn't make Wally any less nervous. Mizer had warned her again that Siobhan might not be the best candidate, but Wally was sure that, if she explained the situation, things would work out. Besides, the pair of them needed to meet properly regardless of whether or not Siobhan agreed to help with her plan. They were going to be co-workers, after all, and Wally couldn't just ignore the seven-foot-tall corpse in the room for her whole tenure.

So Wally rapped her knuckles against the door.

"Uhm, M-Miss Siobhan? It's Wally? Wally Willowbark, I—*eep!*"

The door opened with disturbing silence, and Wally had to struggle not to bolt as Siobhan towered over her. There really was no getting around just how dead the woman was. She was too big, too broad, and she had that same distortion of features common to most corporeal necrotics. As much as Wally didn't want to admit it, just looking at Siobhan made her guts twist.

Mortiphobia, they call it: an instinctive and intense revulsion in the presence of necrotic entities. Almost everyone would experience it at some point. Mortals feared death. That was basic biology. The living were wired to avoid death at all costs. It was why people often reacted so strongly to necrotics; because necrotics were both dead *and* a threat, and had been since time immemorial.

The real revulsion was physical, though. It was the pallor of the skin, and the musty, not-alive scent, but more than that . . . it was the face. When a corporeal rose, it mutated. The body changed and adapted, becoming stronger in response to the powerful miasma animating it. The result of that was a subtle reseating of the muscles all over the body giving them the inhuman movements they were capable of. It also resulted in a face that was *almost* normal but not quite, which was, scientifically speaking, more repulsive to most people than something that was outright monstrous.

Knowing that, Wally forced herself to breathe and focus on something other than Siobhan's face. The difference between Siobhan's face and her own, just structurally, was easy to see now that Wally was looking for it.

"Well, you didn't vanish this time," Siobhan's voice was an oddly pleasant rasp. "Good on you."

"Oh, r-right, sorry about that," Wally replied shakily. "Can uhm, can I come in?"

"Suit yourself."

Siobhan turned and walked back into her room, and what a strange room it was. Originally, Wally thought it might have been a large storage room of some kind, but the interior had been made up to look like the den of a cabin. There was a hand-carved table in the middle with four chairs, also handmade, and a large bed in the corner. A faux fireplace crackled at the far end of the room, and it was the only light inside other than a lone candle in the middle of the table. There were all the accouterments of a messy home strewn about; quilts and embroidery hung from the walls, there were some dishes and plates here and there, and even some dolls.

"Sit where you like," Siobhan said as she trudged back to her bed and sat down. She moved with an odd, stooped posture that made her seem like nothing so much as a great, emaciated bird.

Gingerly, Wally closed the door, then walked over to seat herself at the table while Siobhan settled in, laid the axe she was still carrying across her knees, and took up a whetstone to begin sharpening the head.

"I came to ask a favor," Wally said quietly. "And I know that's not really fair considering you don't know me, and that we got off to a uhm . . . a rocky start."

"I've had worse starts," Siobhan replied without looking up. "Speaking of, I was wondering how you did it," she glanced up at that. "The invisibility, I mean. Mizer's been dying to ask, too, but he's waiting til the gut's have stopped hitting the fan."

Wally laughed weakly, started to open her mouth, then paused. "If I tell you," she said, "will you help me?"

Siobhan chuckled at that "A trade? Sure, why th'fuck not?"

That was a lot less painful than it could have been. It helped that Mizer was right, Siobhan was surprisingly amiable if one bothered to actually talk to her. She *looked* terrifying, but that wasn't her fault.

"It's reflexive, so I can't control it," Wally started. "It has to do with my fight-or-flight instinct. My fear response . . . and I think it has something to do with my reflector talent, too, but I'm not sure. All I know is that when I'm scared enough, I turn invisible."

"Sounds like a hoot," Siobhan replied wryly. "Must'a been fun learning that the hard way."

"Y-Yeah," Wally nodded. "It's silly . . . after Bressig, when I was a teen, I had the worst anxiety, so any loud noise and—" Wally made a popping noise with her lips— "I'd just vanish."

Siobhan's inhuman face softened at the mention of Wally's hometown.

"I . . . I always thought I'd grow into it, you know? Learn to control it?" Wally shook her head. "But I never did, and no one could figure out how it was happening because it wasn't easy to replicate under controlled circumstances."

"How'd you stop—" Siobhan replicated the popping noise—"anytime you got spooked?"

"Uhm, anti-anxiety meds and a buttload of therapy, mostly," Wally said sheepishly.

"Huh . . . fair enough, I guess." Siobhan set the whetstone down and stood up. "Mind if I ask another question?"

"I uh . . . sure." Wally found she didn't actually mind Siobhan's company now that she wasn't halfway to a panic attack.

"Where in Bressig are you from?" She asked softly.

"Oh, uhm . . . right in the middle of town, basically. My house was off Geffner avenue about a half-mile from the park, why?"

Siobhan looked distant for a long moment, then shook her head.

"No reason, let's go talk t'Vess."

Wally frowned. "How did you know?"

Her response was a dry, raspy laugh as Siobhan opened the door and led Wally out of her room. "Seriously?" she asked, glancing over her shoulder and down at Wally with that not-quite-human grin. "Why else would you have come to talk to me?"

Well, that was fair, but still . . .

"It's . . . It's more than that," Wally replied. "I wanted to apologize for reacting like I did."

"You weren't the first and won't be the last," Siobhan said as she trudged down the hall.

Wally's ears pinned back. "That doesn't make it okay," she said. "So I'm sorry."

Siobhan paused in the middle of the hall, then looked back at Wally with an odd look on her face. At least, Wally thought it was odd. Once again, the seating of the muscles made it a little difficult to parse her expressions.

"You're a funny kid, y'know that?" Siobhan said.

"So I've been told," Wally replied wanly.

Siobhan left her at the door to Vess' chamber, and Wally

didn't bother trying to listen in. She would wait. Siobhan had promised to rouse Vess enough for Wally to get her to calm down and stop siccing her miasma on the rest of the team and ideally, she would manage that *without* riling the ornery sorceress up any more than she already was.

CHAPTER 14

WALLY WAS BLUSHING FROM her toes to the tips of her ears as she stared dumbfounded up at Siobhan while trying to process the words she'd said.

'—*y'wife's done sulking.*'

"Vonnie," Vess growled from the shadows of her chamber. "Get. *Out.*"

Apparently, Mizer hadn't been kidding when he said that Siobhan liked riling Vess up.

The towering dreadnought moved out of Wally's way, giving her an oddly genial nod before turning silently and starting back toward her room, leaving Wally in front of Vess' chamber door with rosy cheeks and a tied tongue.

'*Well,*' Wally thought miserably as she forced herself to take a step forward, '*Mizer did warn me.*'

As before, Vess' chamber was several degrees colder than the hall, but Wally didn't mind it so much. It was a dry, mostly pleasant chill, rather than the damp cold of Colvus, although Wally was well aware that she only enjoyed it because her reflector nature repelled the worst aspects of Vess' miasma.

Speaking of, it was much more tolerable now. Almost nonexistent, actually.

"Close the door, if you don't mind." Vess' voice came from

the shadows.

Wally paused, then nodded and did as she'd been asked. The door clanged shut, leaving them both in darkness. A moment later, the lights from Vess' sarcophagus flickered on, and the woman herself, or at least her projection, stood illuminated at the stasis unit's side.

The closer Wally got, the more she saw the effects of Vess' condition. When they'd spent the afternoon and evening together, she'd look entirely human, a far cry from the daemonic apparition she'd shown off before. Now, though . . . now, Vess was somewhere in-between. Her sun-kissed complexion was threaded with dark veins, and her eyes were deeply shadowed. They weren't quite the black-pinned embers of blue that her combat form had, but the suggestion was there. A reflection of her body's degeneration, maybe? Wally wanted to ask, but there would be time for that later.

"How are you doing?" Was what she asked instead. An easy ice-breaker.

Vess huffed out a laugh. "I'm fine," she replied. "I'm always fine."

"You didn't look fine back at the Burroughs," Wally said quietly.

A scowl etched itself onto Vess' face, and that suggestion of darkness deepened, showing a stronger hint of the daemon beneath the skin of her soul.

"Yeah, I guess not," Vess said after a long moment. "Sorry about that, by the way . . . you didn't deserve that."

Taking a risk, Wally moved a few steps closer, and when Vess didn't pull away, she reached out until her fingers were brushing the arm of Vess' greatcoat.

"I'm sorry too," Wally said.

Vess' frown turned to a look of confusion, and it had the pleasant effect of leaving her face markedly more human-looking.

"You're sorry?" Vess repeated. "For what?"

Another step closer, and Wally took a gentle grip on Vess' arm. Vess still didn't pull away. If anything, she leaned almost imperceptibly into the touch.

"For scaring you," Wally said.

Instantly, Vess bristled. Her skin began darkening from dusky olive to ruddy red, the blackened veins shot through with ice blue, and her shadowed eyes deepened to the color of pitch as—

"Stop that!"

Vess froze. Her transformation was arrested at Wally's snapped command, and honestly even Wally was surprised that it had worked. For a moment, the pair of them just stared at one another. It had been reflexive. It didn't take a genius to see that Vess got defensive at the drop of a hat, and that she had a tendency to follow up on that by going all-in and getting *angry*. Before Vess could get her mental footing back, Wally pushed forward, grabbing Vess' hand in both of hers.

"You . . . You keep doing that!" Wally continued. "You did it when we met and I surprised you! And you did it again at the Burroughs! And just now! *Just now!* You were about to do it again!"

"Do what?!"

"Run away!"

Vess' expression went slack and she tried to pull back, but Wally refused to let go. Admittedly, it wouldn't have taken much for Vess to reclaim her hand, but the moment Wally put pressure on her grip, Vess just . . . stopped. The black-pinned eyes faded back to unhealthy shadows, her veins and skin lost their unnatural hue, and Vess came back. At least, to Wally's eyes, Vess had come back. She wore her anger like a cloak around her, shrouding herself in violence, and Wally hated to see it. She hated seeing someone as gentle as Vess grow bitter and wicked so easily solely because it was easier to be that than to be afraid.

Softening her grip on Vess' hand, and she began to relax. Her fingers curled around Wally's and the tension bled from her shoulders in a visible slump. As she watched it happen, Wally had a curious thought; that there was no reason for Vess to physically do any of that in her astral form. Her body was a projection of her mind, and yet she still showed all the habits of a living body. Or at least, she showed a lot of them.

"Turn around," Wally said, acting on a hunch.

"Why?" Vess asked, even as she put her back to Wally obediently.

"I'm testing a theory."

Wally pulled at the corners of Vess' greatcoat, sliding it down to Vess' elbows and letting it hang there while Vess watched her with a small, wry smile from over her shoulder. Wally patted the shoulders of Vess' shirt down flat, then laid her hands on either side of Vess' neck and laid her thumbs over where the muscles of a normal persons' shoulders would be.

"Wally, that's not going to—*ohmygods*." Vess went slack as Wally dug her thumbs in deep and began massaging.

Vess hung her head forward and started making quiet, mumbled sounds of relief while Wally chuckled and continued to massage what should have been, for all intents and purposes, a set of imaginary muscles.

"I didn't actually think this would work," Wally said around quiet bubbles of laughter. "You're a mess back here, by the way."

Vess groaned. "*How* is this working? I've been using this spell for years! It *shouldn't* work like this!"

"Honestly, I'm not really surprised," Wally replied. "You're almost a spectral, you know? This spell puts you better than halfway there, I'd guess."

"So?"

"So spectrals are more than a shape. You're not just projecting your magic when you build this body, Vess, you're projecting your mental stress into it, too." And, as it turned out, Vess carried her stress in her shoulders.

"How could you tell?" Vess' voice had taken on an endearingly sleepy quality.

"Because you're always rolling your neck and shoulders like someone trying to work a kink out of their back," Wally replied.

"And?"

Wally shook her head. "And you shouldn't *have* to do that with an astral body. Which means you do it because you're stressed out and you're trying to release."

"Mm . . . I never noticed."

"Probably because you've been doing it for so long." Wally

continued to move her hands in relaxing patterns across Vess' back, and Vess let out another sigh.

"You're far too patient with me, you know," Vess said. "It's only been a few days and I'm already starting to get possessive."

Wally laughed quietly. "That's uhm, that's okay. I don't really mind so long as you're not biting other people's heads off about it."

A warm palm covered Wally's hand, arresting her movement as Vess took hold and slowly turned until she was facing Wally again. Her eyes, even shadowed as they were, were so, so bright.

"Be careful about giving me permission for something like that," Vess said softly as she brought her other hand up to cup Wally's cheek. "I might just take advantage of it."

Normally, Wally was the sort of person to avoid eye contact whenever possible. She much preferred to blend in than be noticed if she had a choice. The problem here was that, maybe for the first time, she *wanted* someone to notice her. She wanted *Vess* to notice her. So Wally didn't look away. Instead, she met Vess' gaze evenly, and pointedly leaned her cheek just slightly into Vess' palm.

Vess' lips curled back, baring teeth that were starting to go unnaturally sharp in an almost-bestial display. Still, Wally didn't draw back or flinch away. Instead, she just smiled because she could feel it, deep in the hollow of her chest, just like before. A complete and total lack of fear.

Most wouldn't understand what that meant to Wally. She wasn't even sure *Vess* would understand. It wasn't just that Wally wasn't afraid of Vess. It was that, when Vess was nearby, Wally wasn't afraid *at all*. That was notable because, other than those moments, Wally was always afraid. She was afraid of being seen. Afraid of failing. Afraid of being judged. She was afraid of going outside and afraid of becoming a shut-in by that same token. Wally was afraid of public transport, and she was afraid of crowds. She was also afraid of living the rest of her life alone. The first time she'd felt the fear fade, not diminish but actually fade, was the day she had met Vess Gibson.

Slowly, Vess relaxed, and that look of confusion was back on her face as she ran her thumb over the line of Wally's cheek.

"I don't understand you, Wally Willowbark." Vess brushed the hair from Wally's eyes. "You're not afraid of me, and without that . . . without fear, I'm not really sure how to interact with you."

"Do you want me to be afraid of you?" Wally asked.

"No," Vess shook her head violently. "Gods' hooks, no, it isn't that, I just—"

"You said you liked me," Wally cut in, "and uhm, I think it's pretty obvious that I . . . I like you too, so I need you to try and show a little more patience from now on, okay? And not just with me."

Wally reached up past the veil of auburn that hung across Vess' face and brushed the strands clear so she could see the woman's face more easily. Wally smiled as Vess let her tuck the stray strands behind her ears. Even after all these years, rounded human ears always looked a little funny to Wally.

"Why do you hide your ears?" Vess asked suddenly, and as she did she moved her hand a little to brush her hair away from Wally's delicately tapered ears.

Wally flushed.

"Because it's . . . normal, I guess? Jemma's the weird one for wearing her hair back like she does."

Vess cocked her head curiously. "Really? Since when?"

Not for the first time, Vess struck Wally as being incredibly anachronistic. The first time had been her reaction to Tipsy. ESA's weren't uncommon by any stretch. They'd been a common psychological healing technique for the past few decades, so even allowing for Vess not getting out much, it seemed strange. This, though, was even stranger.

"Elves only bare their ears around friends or family, really," Wally said slowly, watching Vess' expression carefully as she explained. "Our ears show off our emotions pretty, uhm . . . clearly. If an elf is disappointed or upset—" Wally forced her ears to pin back briefly in mimicry of dismay, much like how a human might make an exaggerated frown, before relaxing again— "we can't really hide it like a human or a dwarf, you know. It makes people uncomfortable."

Vess snorted. "Since when have elves cared about that?"

"Since . . . always?" Wally couldn't remember a time when that wasn't the case, but, thinking back to her History and Culture classes, she was fairly sure she knew the beginning. "Since the end of the Sunfall Rebellion, so a century and a half at least," she continued, and Vess frowned. "Between the Rebellion and the civil war, elves don't have a great reputation."

For a long moment Vess was silent, but her eyes lingered on Wally's revealed ear. The intensity of her eyes really was something else, they were a shade of blue that Wally couldn't look away from even if she wanted to. And she didn't. Still, right now there was something else there. Something beneath that sharp, frigid color that was as hard as stone.

"I guess . . . a hundred and fifty years is barely more than an elven generation, huh?" Vess said, finally.

Wally shrugged weakly. "Yeah, full-bloods don't uhm, breed quickly, but there are talks of conservation efforts, I think. I don't really follow Oreliaun politics . . . or politics in general."

"Probably wise." Vess dropped her hand and scoffed. ". . . civil war . . . what a joke."

"Hm?"

"Nothing," Vess shook her head, "so I assume Mizer sent you in here because he needs me for something, and you're the one person I won't pick a fight with and who won't—" she jerked her head towards the door where Siobhan left— "pick a fight with me either."

"Uhm, more or less," Wally admitted.

"Jazzy, well, let's get to it, then."

Vess leaned back against her sarcophagus and nodded to the door, drawing a questioning look from Wally. "They'll need you to proxy for me," Vess clarified. "Assuming you're up for it, since I can't work any magic outside my room without melting my insides."

"Oh." Wally swallowed thickly. "I'll uhm, let them know."

Vess nodded, but before she could fade back into her containment unit, Wally reached out and seized the lapel of her greatcoat.

"Vess, wait I—" Wally got a raised eyebrow from the woman in question.

She was going to ask Vess something, Wally had been certain of it, but as Vess turned, the electric light of the sarcophagus glinted off of something hanging from a slender chain now revealed in the low light by her open jacket.

A ring of stunningly beautiful quality hung from a chain of fine silver links. It was gorgeous, with minutely detailed, flaring wings forming the setting for a stone of deep crimson that perfectly matched Vess' hair when the light caught it just right, to make her tumbling locks burn like blood.

Then it was gone. Swept away by Vess' hand and dropped back down her shirt.

This was, Wally reminded herself, an astral form. This wasn't Vess' real body, it was a projected facsimile. The same was true of all of her clothing and accouterment. For someone as powerful as Vess, she dressed quite conservatively. Nothing about her outfit was particularly flashy, matching the dark shades favored by most Colvians.

Which was why that ring was such an incongruity.

It was so perfectly detailed, down the vanes of the feathers on the winged setting and the shade of the gem. And it was a projection. A memory.

"Tell Mizer I'll be preparing to be proxied, please," Vess said as she pulled her coat more tightly around herself.

Wally desperately wanted to ask about the ring. She didn't want to proxy, and she didn't want to pursue the investigation, even though that was her purpose. She wanted to ask about the ring.

She didn't.

"Okay," Wally said softly.

As she turned away to start towards the door of Vess' chambers, a memory came back to her, and Wally turned to look over her shoulder at the shadowed figure staring down at her own pale body inside its container.

"Vess?"

Vess looked up, and her eyes were weary.

"You said you betrayed someone dear to you, right?" Wally asked softly, although her voice sounded overly loud to her own ears in the enclosed space.

"I did," Vess replied hollowly.

Wally looked away and down at her shoes. Her heart was beating so hard in her chest that it was almost painful. She had no proof of it, but she felt in her bones that that ring was no heirloom, not given what Vess had revealed about her family. She had shown nothing but contempt for them, so the idea of her keeping something of *them* that was so precious to her that it featured with exacting detail in her astral form was laughable.

No, Wally was certain it had been given to her, and her insecurities and fears told her that the person who'd given Vess that ring was someone that Vess had loved deeply. Someone who, perhaps, had loved Vess just as much.

It wasn't new to Wally for her to dwell on the fact that, at the end of the day, she wasn't a very good person. She knew that she had an exceptional ability to ignore things she probably shouldn't, and had a tendency to be quite selfish when she actually wanted something. Enough so that she counted herself morally fortunate that she didn't want very many things.

The problem, of course, was that she wanted Vess.

She wanted her very, very much.

So the sight of that ring put a deep, angry ache in her chest, and a knot in her throat, and at the same time it made her hate herself for how ugly she was being. Whoever gave Vess that ring was probably gone—dead maybe, but definitely out of Vess' life—and that should be enough, but . . . but it wasn't because Vess was still wearing the ring.

One day. Was one day with Vess really all it took for her to show this side of herself? Gods' hooks she was ugly.

Once, twice, three times, Wally opened her mouth to say something else to Vess, even though she had no notion of what those words would be. She just felt compelled to say something. Another apology, maybe? For what? For thinking?

In the end, Wally said nothing, and left the room in silence.

• • •

Mizer stood over Wally as she laid supine on the gurney in the prep room watching over the process as Jemma dipped a thick-bristled brush into a jar of specially prepared paints. Wally was stripped down to her slacks and a long-sleeved linen tunic, simple but warm, and looking remarkably relaxed, all things considered.

Given her shyness, Mizer had expected her to be a lot more bothered by the process, at least the first time, but for the moment Wally looked like she was a million miles away. Her only real reaction was to jump slightly as Jemma painted the first warding symbol over her right palm. It was ice-cold because the substance the paints were made from had to remain refrigerated or else they would separate and start to spoil.

"You okay, Wally?" Mizer asked.

"Mhm."

"You've just been uh, pretty quiet since you got out of Vess' room," he continued conversationally.

"I'm fine."

Mizer winced. That was unusually terse. Even given that he didn't know Wally that well, she was usually livelier than this. "Can I uhm, ask what you're doing? If you don't mind, that is." Wally was looking up at Jemma, whose narrow features pinched into a faint scowl.

"Jemma . . ." Mizer warned. "Don't just scrawl on the girl, if she wants to know what you're doing she has a right to."

As talented and powerful as Jemma was—especially for her age—she really did have an unpleasant personality. She was contentious, ill-tempered, and bristly even on the best of days. Mizer hoped that Jemma would mellow out enough over the next few weeks for Wally to see the good person beneath all of that.

"I'm warding your lambda junctions," Jemma said tersely.

"With the Maw of Akur?" Wally sounded incredulous, but Jemma actually looked impressed, stopping briefly with her brush hovering over Wally's left palm.

"Yeah," Jemma said cautiously, her dark eyes narrowing. "You know it?"

Wally nodded. "The cults of Ghislaine and Fah'Akur are two

of the only daemon-cults whose worship is legal in the Union, and I went to a few lectures by practitioners."

"Hm . . . well, yeah, the mark I'm using is the Maw," Jemma confirmed, gesturing down to the stylized shape of an open mouth filled with fangs. "And, technically speaking, it's not a ward, but the Maw of Akur will devour some of Vess' miasma before it gets into your lambda system so you won't have to reflect as much, meaning it works the same way."

"Oh," Wally relaxed a little, "that's pretty clever, actually."

Mizer suppressed a grin and pretended not to notice how Jemma had started moving with a little more ease and confidence. The poor girl wasn't used to compliments. She got so few of them, after all. The dark faith of Akur might be legal but most people still equated it to illegal cult activity half the time, and many treated her as little better than a Sunfall cultist. Jemma suffered from that, as she'd suffered from a variety of prejudices in her life. It was probably relieving for someone to treat her like a normal person for once. Dolin had been . . . less than receptive when he'd found out about her worship.

"I've always been curious about how the Maw is supposed to work," Wally started as Jemma painted another mark at the hollow of her throat. "Is it just an energy funnel?"

Jemma shook her head.

"No, that's a common misconception," she replied, and Mizer thought there was significantly less bite to her tone than usual. "Akur blesses those who face foes and threats head-on, and the Maw is a part of that." She drew out the symbol with a flourish before moving up to Wally's forehead and brushing her hair out of the way. "If you face a curse down without flinching, the Maw will catch the curse and devour it, but if you turn away, it'll hit you."

"Like catching a lumma nut in your mouth," Wally said.

A snort of laughter escaped Jemma, and she barely kept her hand steady as she scribed the fourth Maw over Wally's symbolic third eye. "Yeah," she said through a bubble of laughter, "like catching a lumma nut."

Once she finished the fourth and final Maw, Jemma tucked

the jar of paint away, took up a bound cord of fragrant sticks, and grasped the top of them with her hand before muttering an invocation. The moment she opened her palm the tips of the bound sticks all lit aflame at once, and a thick, savory-scented smoke began pouring from them.

With slow, even motions, Jemma moved the bundle in ritual patterns, whispering in the fel tongue of Akur's faithful to draw the eyes of the Master of Daemons to her. She moved the smoke around herself first, completing a full circle around her own body, then moved to Wally and began the process over again. No matter how many times Mizer watched the process, it still gave him a little chill. Akur was a being that was diametrically opposed to the spirits of the world. It wasn't evil, per se, but it was 'other' and so the spirits had a deeply negative reaction to its power.

"I g-guess this—" Wally's words were interrupted by a short staccato of coughs— "is l-like the Maws?"

"Akur's Mist hedges out magic," Mizer confirmed. "Akur is a visceral entity and disdains underhanded tricks like curses. The Mist will double down on the Maw's mitigation of Vess' curse."

"All of this just so Vess can leave her sarcophagus?" Wally asked. "We're not fighting anything, though."

Jemma shook her head as she finished the cleansing spell and lowered her hand.

"It's not about that," Jemma said. "It doesn't matter if you're fighting or playing a round of Shatranj, you're taking a curse into your soul when you proxy for Vess and that's dangerous, so unless you want to end up on the floor for another two days, let me work."

Wally wilted back but nodded as Jemma reached into the pouch at her hip and brought out a necklace. It was large, heavy, and crude. The cord was crafted from knotted hairs taken from the mane of a warhorse, while the broken scraps of dull metal that were secured to it via those knots were taken from a blade shattered in combat. It was a coarse, heavy thing, and Jemma shook it three times over Wally in tune to a muttered invocation. A moment later, an odd sense of weight and solidity fell over the room before tangibly settling across Wally.

"Alright, all that's left is the IV and the proxy itself."

"Thank you, Jemma," Mizer said warmly, patting her on the shoulder. "Go prep yourself and meet us in the morgue, I'll take Wally to Vess' chamber."

"Will do, boss." Jemma bobbed her head once and left, and Mizer watched her leave for a moment before looking down at Wally.

"This is what Vess meant about skipping steps," he said wanly.

"I can see that," Wally replied.

"It's all necessary, though . . . imagine how bad you'd feel if you'd proxied for her for more than an hour or two?"

A shiver ran through Wally, and Mizer couldn't help but chuckle a little. Dolin had been miserable even after short proxies with the full panoply of wards layered over him, but then, he'd been a middling reflector. Wally was significantly more powerful.

"Don't worry, this will be much gentler than the first time," Mizer assured her. "This is the sort of thing that *should* have been your first time, in fact, and I'm sorry it wasn't."

"I'm not," Wally said as she looked up at him. "I'm glad I was useful to her."

All Mizer could do was nod as he moved to the head of the gurney and began wheeling her out into the hall. Something about the way Wally said that cut at him. She said 'useful' like she was an object. This wasn't the time for that conversation, though. Mizer wasn't sure there would *be* a time. He was her employer, not her therapist. He did hope she had a therapist though. Gods knew the poor girl seemed like she could use one. He could at least make sure she was aware of their health coverage. Dispersal precincts got fantastic health subsidies from the Union which included a generous mental health care package. It was a necessity given the horrors they could witness in their line of work.

That was another thought. Polly described the scene on the eighth floor of the projects as a hellish scrum of corpses and gore, but Wally came out of the proxy where she would have gotten a front-row seat to all of it without so much as a dry heave. At least, nothing that wasn't just the usual vertigo of displacement. It was almost like she was inured to that kind of horror, and on the heels of that thought, Mizer couldn't help but glance down at her forearms and what he knew the sleeves of her tunic hid.

They reached Vess' chamber and Mizer muttered a quick prayer of protection over himself, imploring the spirits to shield him from the miasma. It was strong enough to let him converse with Vess for a time, and lasted long enough to engage the proxy.

Even with the protection of the spirits around him, Vess' miasma gave him pause.

Taking a deep breath, Mizer wheeled Wally into the room, and up beside Vess' sarcophagus, reached beneath the gurney for the bag of saline from the Jiani's blessed pools, and secured it to a pole that he telescoped out from the corner of the gurney. Carefully, he rolled up her sleeve, doing his best not to touch her scars, and affixed the tourniquet before readying the IV itself.

"No one else will come in here, right?" Wally asked softly.

Mizer nodded.

"No, it's just you and—"

It only occurred to Mizer as he started to speak that he probably should have put the IV on Wally's arm *before* they'd come into Vess' room. He could have done it and then given her a blanket. That would have been easier and smarter, but he hadn't because he'd been moving out of habit the way he'd done a hundred-plus times with Dolin and hundreds more with Nella before him.

Wally had clearly come to the same conclusion and was even now staring up at him with wide, horrified eyes. No, not up at him. *Past* him.

"What . . ." Vess's voice came from over his shoulder and sounded nothing less than throttled. "Wally?" She moved into Mizer's peripheral vision and stood over the gurney, and her eyes were as wide and horror-struck as Wally's own as they fixed on Wally's arms.

Well, *shit*.

CHAPTER 15

WALLY WAS NUMB.

'This wasn't how this was supposed to happen.' Was her prevailing thought, followed quickly by: *'this wasn't supposed to happen at all!'*

That last thought was, honestly, a little too optimistic considering that working in close quarters for long periods of time practically made revealing that part of her life—and her body—inevitable.

Still, this wasn't how it was supposed to happen. In any other circumstance, the completely dumbstruck look on Vess' face might actually be a little funny. Normally she was so confident, strong-minded, and centered. This wasn't funny. Nothing about this was funny.

Wally jerked the sleeves down over her arms. "Th-That's not me! N-Not anymore. It's not me, okay?" She stared pleadingly up at Vess.

Mizer stepped back, looking mortified. This wasn't his fault. He hadn't thought about the fact that Vess might manifest, and neither had Wally. It wasn't right to be mad at him.

She was still a little mad at him.

"Vess?" Wally spoke the name softly at Vess who was still staring down at Wally's arms.

The sound of her name seemed to snap Vess out of her stupor, and she looked up sharply. Her body kept futzing out in staticky bursts as her concentration on her astral form repeatedly faltered. When she was stable, there was a tremble in her breathing, not unlike how she'd looked back on the street in front of the projects. She looked sick, but it went deeper than that. That cut deeply enough, though. Apparently, just looking at Wally's body made Vess sick, and that was enough.

Tears sprang unbidden to her eyes. This was stupid. It shouldn't hurt this badly, but it did. It *absolutely* hurt that badly and . . . no, no, no. She wasn't that person anymore. She was better now and she didn't *want* to do that anymore. It didn't help. Not really. Wally knew that down to her bones that a relapse would just make her feel so, so much worse.

'*But* Gods *I want to.*'

The knife-sharp sound of a finger-snap—*redact*—jarred Wally out of her fugue as something warm fell over her body, and Wally looked up to find a coal greatcoat lying on her, and the incongruity somehow broke through her panic in that curious manner of things, where the mind will latch on to some absurdly inconsequential detail like flotsam in a storm. In her case, the detail was that the coat shouldn't be there. It was an astral projection like the rest of Vess so the moment it left her grasp it should have dissolved into the aether.

"Later." Vess' raw voice drew Wally's attention.

Vess was still wearing her coat.

"If it's okay," Vess continued quietly. "We . . . We can talk about that later, or not if you don't want to."

"I'm sorry." The words came out wet and garbled, but they were at least intelligible enough to make out.

Cocking her head, Vess' expression had schooled back to a hard, confident expression. "Sorry?" she repeated. "For what?"

"That you saw," Wally said shakily. "I didn't . . . you sh-shouldn't have seen them, they're uhm . . . I'm just . . . s-sorry." Sorry that someone as beautiful as Vess had seen something so disgusting. Sorry that someone as strong as Vess had to see something so miserable, pathetic, and weak. Sorry. Wally was so sorry.

So, so, so sorr—

'*You know I can hear you, right?*'

Wally froze absolutely rigid at Vess' mindspeak voice. In truth, she actually had forgotten. Belatedly, she realized that, for all of Vess' playful mockery during their first meeting, she had been good about not mindspeaking at Wally after being admonished.

'*Not that I'm trying, but I'm a psyk-talent, remember? Telekine, telepathy, all that jazz? You're practically screaming in my ear.*'

If there were a way to make the world just crack open and swallow her, Wally would have been extremely grateful to know it. "I'm sorry." Wally repeated aloud in a breathless squeak like air escaping from the world's saddest balloon.

A warm palm rose up and pressed to Wally's cheek, pulling gently until Wally was looking straight up at Vess through a veil of tears. Part of her wanted to clench her eyes shut. She didn't want to see the contempt or the pity, not again, and especially not from Vess. She wanted to close her eyes so badly, but . . . but she couldn't make herself do it.

Vess deserved to at least look Wally in the eyes when she judged her.

To Wally's surprise, there was no contempt. There wasn't even pity. There was just a cold, hard look almost like . . . commiseration.

"Never be sorry for those," Vess's tone was like glacial ice. "No one gets out of a war without scars." Her voice cracked. "Most don't get out at all. Most fucking *lose*."

Vess moved her hand moved to grip Wally's chin, holding her there so she could see it when Vess' eyes began to burn like dead stars.

"So don't you dare apologize for winning a war, Wally Willowbark. Not to me." Vess' fingers were trembling from the effort of not clenching, and vaguely, Wally wondered if Vess' astral form could cry.

Despite not needing to breathe, Vess dragged in a breath all the same. It was a reflexive action. Like the way she shrugged and rolled her shoulders. Vess was trying to regain her composure, and if the way she was shaking was any indication, it wasn't working very well. When she did get enough of herself under control to speak again, Vess loosened her grip on Wally, cupped her cheeks with both hands, and wiped the tears from Wally's cheeks with her thumbs.

"Don't you *dare* apologize for surviving long enough to meet me."

A ragged hiccup escaped Wally's lips as she stared up at Vess. There was no contempt. There was no pity. Just hard blue eyes that somehow seemed to see her more clearly than ever before.

"No more tears, alright?" Vess brushed another droplet from Wally's cheeks. "We'll . . . talk." Her touch was so gentle, and the sheer relief that flooded into Wally in that moment of realization made her want to collapse. "Later, after we've both done our jobs, we'll talk, okay?"

"Mhm." Wally nodded, swallowing thickly as she did, then tugged gently at the collar of the greatcoat that was covering her. "H-How is this . . . ?"

"Hm? Oh, that." Vess let go of Wally's cheeks—something she was a little disappointed by—and smoothed out the coat that was acting as a blanket. "I keep my personal effects in a pocket dimension so they don't clutter up the precinct, so this," she tapped the coat, "is the real article."

"It's warm," she muttered. "And soft."

And it was. It was nicer than anything Wally owned, that was for sure. The outside was a smooth fabric that Wally couldn't name, but that felt even nicer than the facsimile of it that Vess projected, and it was lined with something like doehide. The whole thing was just sinfully soft and pleasant, and, from the feel of it, Wally guessed that it was probably more expensive than her whole apartment.

"Keep it," Vess said with a small smile, and Wally's jaw dropped. "What? Gods know I'm not using it, so someone might as well."

"R-Really?" Wally asked, her voice cracking at a high note.

"Yeah, really." Putting a hand to Wally's shoulder, she pushed her gently down until she was lying back on the gurney. "But we have a job to do now, right?" Vess gave Wally's shoulder a gentle grip, and Wally nodded as she started to relax.

"Vess?"

"Hm?"

"I know you're just trying to distract me and make me think of something other than . . . y-you know." Wally pressed her lips to a thin line. The horrified look on Vess' face stung at the back of her mind.

Vess snorted softly. "Guilty as charged." She was wearing that infuriatingly attractive cocked smirk of hers when she admitted it, too. "Is it working?"

Despite herself, Wally gave a weak chuckle and nodded. "Yeah, I think so," she replied, then shook her head. "You really are shameless."

"And *how*."

Oh, for the love of—Vess actually *waggled* her eyebrows.

Now she was just playing the fool for laughs, and damn her if she didn't get a little laugh out of Wally. How was it that Vess could slip right past one of Wally's biggest fears and sources of shame and come out actually making her laugh?!

No one should be allowed to be that good. It just wasn't fair.

"A louse," Wally repeated, shaking her head again and sending her short brown hair tumbling, "you're a louse, Vess Gibson."

And yet, she felt better. Better than she'd ever felt after a near-relapse. Usually, she'd be stuck in a self-destructive funk for days, barely able to muster the energy to feed Tipsy and water her plants. Those were always her gateways back to the living world. That wasn't to say she was aces. Wally still felt worn thin and exhausted; her limbs were leaden, her mouth was dry, and she was probably going to wake up tomorrow with one hell of a migraine, but still . . . this was better than usual.

"You still alright to proxy, Wally?" Vess asked, her voice dropping and becoming more serious. "I know I said we have a job to do, but you don't have to."

"I'm alright," Wally replied. "Really."

"You'd tell me if you weren't, right? Because once we proxy I'll know anyway," Vess said pointedly.

Wally nodded. "I'm a little . . . drained, but I promise, I'm okay, you really helped."

That last part put a smile on Vess' face, one that lit up the whole room if Wally was any judge. It was broad and toothy, and most importantly warm and genuine. It was a good look, and Wally decided she would very much like to see it more often.

"Okay, then, I'll go get Mizer," Vess nodded toward the door. "He's probably flagellating himself outside."

Sure enough, Mizer had slipped outside to give them some privacy at some point during Wally's miniature panic attack. Technically, that meant he had abandoned her with Vess, but it had turned out well enough. Mizer had probably known that Vess would be able to knock her out of her spiral, even if, Wally couldn't say how she'd done it. There was just something stabilizing about Vess. An obdurate, stony quality that promised unmoving support, and the moment Wally had come into contact with that support it was like all the momentum of her spiral just scattered.

As Vess left, Wally laid back and closed her eyes, turning her arm up as she did to wait for Mizer to return and attach the IV.

That could have gone a lot worse.

. . .

Right?

Vess was numb.

What were those?

What . . . What precisely was she looking at on Wally's arms?

Scars. Obviously, they were scars but they weren't scars that someone so gentle as Wally was supposed to have. She had seen scars. She had seen thousands of scars in a thousand different shapes and sizes. Vess *knew* scars. Vess had seen the scars in stone carved along the battlements of House Kassifor by Nera's warspells. She'd seen the identically patterned scars leftover from the stigmatic wounds that burst into being across a hundred bodies from Ro's horrific sympathica.

The worst scars, though, were the ones she herself had left behind.

So yes. Vess knew scars. She knew them intimately, and these were sickeningly familiar. In the blackest quarters of Vess' mind, she remembered the look of scars inflict by their owners' own fingernails as they tried to dig nightmares out of their own skulls. As they tried to carve imagined *things* from beneath their own skin. She remembered those scars most terribly and most easily, and *those* were the scars that Wally wore.

Down along the thick vein of Wally's forearm were raised ridges like the spine of a weatherworn mountain. Around that ridge were dancing patterns of blade nicks and dull-edged wounds.

They were old.

Thank the Gods they were old.

Wally jerked the sleeve of her tunic down over her arm in a panic. Vess could taste the panic in the air. She could feel it like the thrum of a bass chord in her mind, growing and growing like a crescendo until it felt like her teeth were vibrating in their sockets. This was pure animal terror, and it was coming from *Wally*.

"Th-That's not me! N-Not anymore." Her voice was so brittle. "It's not me, okay?!"

In the corner of her senses, she could feel the internal sickness, the poisonous guilt, digging at Mizer as he slunk away. This wasn't his fault, though. It was a struggle to keep her astral form coherent. There were so many thoughts in Vess' mind. Too many to keep in one place. They were interfering with her concentration on the bi-location. Despite only being a few feet from her physical body, it felt like she was miles and miles away. Like she was reaching across vast, illimitable vistas just to reach this handful of feet towards Wally.

"Vess?"

'. . . *looks sick . . . sick of me . . . n't right to be mad at him . . . still . . . at him*'

Vess snapped her head up and jerked as an icepick headache lanced into her left temple. Mindvoice. Mindspeak. This was—'*stupid . . . shouldn't hurt . . . badly*'—Wally's mind. Wally's thoughts. They were in Vess' head because her mind was so damn loud, and Vess couldn't hedge them out!

'*No, no, no . . . n't that person . . . nymore . . . better now . . .* '

No! Vess didn't want to be hearing this! She shouldn't be hearing these thoughts! She shut her eyes, tried to force the wall back up between them, but she couldn't. A part of her didn't want to. Too much of her didn't want to because she didn't want to put a wall between her and Wally. She wanted to be closer to Wally! Not further away! But Wally—*'better now . . . didn't want to . . . anymore'*—was shaking. She was terrified. Her pupils were blown wide with primal fear. Fight or flight, locked onto flight. She was trying to run. Trying to flee. Trying to spiral down and down and down, as far away as she could.

Far from Vess.

No. She had to stop that! Had to stop Wally from spiraling, if only she could hold her mind in place long enough to—*'relapse . . . make . . . feel so . . . much worse.'*—Yes! That's right, Wally. It would make it worse! Hold on to that! Don't spiral. Don't. Just hold on and—*'But* Gods *I want to.'*

NO!

It was like plunging into an icy bath, and at the same time like coming home after a long day. This old, familiar power. So cold. So ruthless. The power she tried so hard to push away and never touch again. But now . . . now she had to, right?

There was blackness all around. It was a darkness so deep that it devoured the light. All lights. All but two. One was flickering like a candle flame. It was so weak; so fragile and so delicate that it made Vess want to weep. It spilled from Wally's unshackled soul, and it was so soft that it barely cast shadows around her, but that was okay. Vess was there. She would make new lights.

In the ocean of darkness that was the depths of Wally's mind, Vess stared down at the amalgam of Wally's psyche and consciousness: id, ego, and superego, all bound into one luminous being, and Wally, in turn, stared up at her. Fortunately, Wally would forget this shape of hers. At the accelerated speed of thought, this was a fraction of a fraction of a second. Still, in that moment, Vess knew what Wally was seeing. She knew because she could see her reflection in Wally's mind-eyes. Vess saw hints of her 'true' body. Her luminous, astral body, unrestrained by the low, songless coils of flesh. She saw storms of shadow wrapping around bones made of diamond and dead-star eyes set beneath a crown of long, thin horns like white scars in space.

Oh, how she missed this body. This freedom. This *power*.

But no. *Wally*. She had to keep her mind together for Wally. She needed to save her because Wally was more important. Vess raised one clawed hand that was wreathed in black fire and caught the thread of Wally's consciousness between her middle finger and thumb. Wally was spiraling. She could feel the deep, bleak despair that was dragging that thread into a terrible place. The place where Wally got those scars.

She couldn't let Wally go back there, no matter what.

Any two-bit psyk-talent could play with memories—it was a crude thing that was barely worth being called a talent at all. Memories weren't just pictures and sounds, though. They weren't movies or broadcasts. They went deeper than that. True memories went to dark, painful places that left aches and wounds which lingered long after the moments themselves were forgotten. That was where Vess went, following that thread she had caught, and reeling herself in. She reached through the threshold of Wally's mind—not too deep. Too deep and she'd never get out—and found the pain.

The source was too old. Too dense. The shock might kill Wally if she tried to touch it, but this moment? This new pain had yet to be transcribed. It was still lingering in the soft quarters of her mind. There she found the visceral reactions. Fight or flight, locked into flight.

It wasn't fair to Wally. To go in like this, but if she didn't then Wally might be in real danger so . . . so Vess pressed her finger and thumb together, and at the same time slipped her claws painlessly meat of Wally's mind to find the instinct. The reaction. The visceral twisting of the guts that was smaller, quieter, and oft unnoticed. Like a vagrant child, so easily overlooked.

'REDACT'

The command came on the heels of a sharp snap of her fingers before reality came rushing back in.

• • •

The quiet settled around Vess as she released her astral form and fell back into her sarcophagus to await the proxy spell taking hold.

Mizer was attaching the IV to Wally who was doing . . . better, which was good. Wally was a little better. Still drained, still fragile, but better, and that was the most Vess could ask for. She'd managed to arrest Wally's spiral, at least for now, but it wasn't something she could—or *would*—do again.

Not without Wally's consent.

Going that deep had left Vess with a sickening knot of guilt and uncertainty as to whether or not she had truly done the right thing.

'*We'll talk.*'

That was what she had promised Wally. That they would talk.

Vess had the deep-seated feeling that she was going to be the one doing most of the talking though. No, call it what it was. Confession. Vess was going to tell Wally what she had done, beg her forgiveness, try to explain if Wally was willing to hear it, and what happened after that would be up to her.

She'd taken Wally's choice, but she could give her one back later. She owed Wally that and much, much more.

They would proxy do their job, and then . . .

Then they would talk, come what may.

CHAPTER 16

There was no pain as the proxy took hold of Wally's mind beyond the kind of aching stretch of a muscle that was a little bit sore.

The first time she had proxied for Vess, their minds had come together like the crash of a church bell. This time was much more graceful. There was a faint sensation of joining, and it felt like nothing so much as taking Vess' hand. Then they were together again, and when Vess opened her eyes, Wally saw too.

'*Oh, that was much more pleasant,*' Wally said, and the gentle sensation of Vess' laughter rippled through her mind.

'*That's how the first time* ought *to have been,*' she replied. '*It's much easier when the spell gets fully cast, and not half-assed.*'

'*Mizer did his best with a bad situation,*' Wally admonished as she settled comfortably into the back of Vess' mind.

There was a faint pull and a sense of motion, and suddenly there was more color and sound than before. They'd still been in Vess' sarcophagus—her soup can, Wally thought with a small laugh—and Vess had just projected them out.

'*I know, I know,*' Vess grumbled. '*Doesn't mean I have to be happy about it.*'

'*Well it helped you, so I get to be happy about it. So there.*'

A long-suffering sigh echoed through Wally's mind,

prompting another ripple of laughter. It was strange. Her mood was never this light after anything to do with her scars, but for some reason, it didn't seem to be hanging on like it usually did.

'Am I ever going to get the last word in with you?' Vess asked.

'No.'

Another sigh issued from Vess, and Wally's mood buoyed as she relaxed. It wasn't unlike floating in water. There was a sense of weightlessness, but it wasn't quite total. Moreover, there was a feeling all around Wally of genuine warmth. If she'd still had a body, Wally would have smiled. It felt like the evening she'd spent with Vess when they'd been relaxing on the couch together, and a moment later the coin dropped as she realized what it was.

The warmth was Vess herself. Her mind was nestled within Vess' where she could absorb the worst impact of the curse, and Vess in turn was wrapped around her, protecting her. Just like she promised she would.

The world moved around them again, and Wally steadied herself. She found that if she mentally relaxed and trusted Vess to carry her rather than try and keep track of each and every movement, there was a lot less vertigo.

"Alright, what am I looking at?" Vess' real voice echoed tinnily in Wally's ears like she was hearing it in stereo, where one of the speakers was slightly poor.

The room they'd landed in was dimly lit save for a single sharp sparklight hanging above the slab where a body lay in repose. Given where it had come from, it was surprisingly undamaged. She was old but had aged gracefully in the usual manner of her kind. The body was naked save for a white sheet draped over her body, and there were no signs of damage.

Jemma stood at the side of the table with her dark hair tied neatly back, wearing grey scrubs with warding eyes scribed on them, along with the Maw of Akur that decorated her body back in Vess' chamber on Jemma's skin.

"Full-blood Oreliaun elf, female, deceased." Jemma rattled off the words with clinical detachment. "Records give her name as 'Delona Barrowbridge', aged one hundred and eighty-seven years with no major health problems beyond just being old as dirt, and one listed next-of-kin, also deceased."

"The grandson?"

"Yeah." Jemma flipped through the papers, then said, "Vincent Barrowbridge."

Wally felt Vess grimace as she paused in front of the corpse. "Cause of death?" she asked.

"Technically? Heart failure. But it's hard to say for certain," Jemma said. "If I had to guess, though? A curse, and a subtle one, too. Maybe degenerative. Something that slowly weakened her soul's grip on her body until something gave out."

"A long-haul deal, then," Vess said as she circled the body, looking over it with a critical eye.

Wally watching through Vess' senses. The old woman was delicately built. Probably quite willowy in her youth, though age would have stolen that somewhat. She was beautiful, too, in the fashion of the very old and graceful.

'A curse would've left stigmatic marks, wouldn't it?' Wally asked, then clammed up, but Vess didn't argue.

She nodded instead, then looked up at Jemma. "What about stigmata?"

"Not that I could find, but it could be internal. I haven't done an autopsy," Jemma said.

"And there's no sign of how it triggered the infestation?" Vess asked in the tones of someone who knew the answer to their question but needed to ask it all the same.

Jemma shook her head.

"Shit." Vess glared down at the body. "I really don't want to go in there if I don't have to."

'Go in there?' Wally asked, alarmed.

A gentle susurration surrounded her, and Wally vaguely recognized it as the mental equivalent of someone taking her hand and giving it a reassuring squeeze.

'Yeah, I can skin-ride bodies if they're properly preserved.'

Wally did not like that notion one bit, and her feelings on the matter clearly bled over into Vess' mind because that sensation of a hand on hers repeated itself.

'Don't worry, I'd hedge your senses out so you wouldn't feel the body,

believe me, I don't like it either, corpses are kinda squidgy.'

'*S-Squidgy?*' Laughter bubbled out of Wally, and Vess sighed.

"Anyway," Vess spoke aloud again, "what are the odds I don't have to ride that corpse to figure out what she died of?"

"Not great, Gibs, sorry," Jemma replied, looking genuinely apologetic. "I did my best."

Vess sighed physically this time, and reached out, setting a hand on Jemma's shoulder and giving it a soft squeeze. "I know you did, this isn't—'*will you calm down?!*'—your fault."

Wally almost jumped at Vess' mental interjection and a moment later she realized she'd been almost growling. There was an angry burn inside of what passed for her chest, and a tightness around her mind like the beginnings of a headache. Where had that anger come from?

'*Gods' hooks, Wally, I didn't realize you were the jealous type.*'

'*I'm sorry!*' Wally squeaked through their mental link. '*I didn't mean to!*'

There was a snort, followed by raucous laughter, and it took Wally a moment to realize Vess was actually laughing for real, not just in the confines of the proxy. Jemma was staring incredulously at Vess.

"Sorry." Vess held up a hand to her lips in a vain attempt to capture the rest of her laughter. "Wally just . . . said something funny."

"Seems like poor timing," Jemma said in an icy tone.

"Oh hush," Vess brushed off Jemma's admonishment and leaned in over the body, "it's not like being dour's going to make her any less dead, now stand back, I'm gonna scrape her brain."

'*EXCUSE ME?!*' Wally blurted.

'*Don't worry about it.*'

'*I'M WORRYING ABOUT IT!*'

Before Wally could lodge another protest, Vess moved around the morgue slab, held out a hand on either side of the dead woman's head, curled her fingers into arthritic claws, and spat out a word that left a rancid taste in Wally's mouth even from inside the proxy.

The corpse jerked spasmodically and its eyes flew open as

brackish sparks of light began flowing from the tips of Vess' fingers. A gust of vile-smelling air left the corpse in a disturbing groan as its thrashing depressed its lungs, and the whole time Vess maintained an eerily unperturbed look on her face.

'V-Vess?'

'Sorry. Concentrating.'

She sounded strained, and Wally couldn't help but wonder if exerting her spellcraft through her astral form was painful. Using one's astral self as an origin point for spells was one of the crafts few uses, but the spells that someone could project through them were fairly limited; casting something too complicated or too powerful would short out the astral projection spell like a power surge through a badly insulated wire.

'*I wonder if . . .*' Following her instincts, Wally leaned in and was suddenly hit with the sensation of taking a slightly-too-hot metal weight onto her shoulders.

'*Wally wha—?!*'

Whatever Vess was about to say was cut off Wally was suddenly bombarded with images. Most of it was nonsense; snippets of old radio jingles, the smell of woodsmoke, the taste of a certain filet of fish imported from Arka Menais.

But there was something else.

Something familiar.

Some memory in the dead woman's mind resonated with Wally's mind and a brief and horribly familiar battery of sensations slugged her across her jaw; the taste of rot and gore, the smell of new death, and visions of a burning township. The feel of crumbling stone and wood beneath her fingers. And—*stay down*—a voice in her head that she didn't know.

Without warning, the sensory bombardment vanished, and she was pulled back from the drowning flow of memories.

'*Wally?!*'

'*Bressig!*' Wally gasped. '*She's a survivor of Bressig!*'

Vess' mental presence was stunned insensible for a moment, and Wally was suddenly pulled thin in all directions as she struggled to maintain the proxy on her own. Thankfully, Vess snapped out of it and took up her end of the spell a moment later.

"Hey, Gibs, what gives? You just went rigid." Jemma snapped in fingers in front of Vess' face. "You okay in there?"

"Y-Yeah," Vess replied, waving her off. "Wally just sort of barged into the memory feed while I was sifting through it."

"*What?!*" Jemma looked livid. "Is she trying to kill herself?!"

'*Kill—? What? I'm fine . . . a little winded, but I'm fine.*'

And she was. She had a little more of a headache than she'd had before, and it would probably be more like a minor migraine when she got back into her body but that wasn't the end of the world. She'd gotten worse headaches renewing her certifications because standing in lines amongst crowds of people messed with her anxiety.

"She's fine," Vess repeated Wally's words. "And better yet, Wally got us a lead."

"You're joking," Jemma said flatly.

Vess shook her head, then tapped a finger on the dead woman's forehead.

"Our vic survived the Bressig exclusion."

Jemma's eyes went wide, and Wally watched alongside Vess as some series of connections was made in the ornery young woman's mind.

"It was latent saturation." Jemma muttered, turning back to the body, almost in answer to Wally's mental question.

Vess nodded. "My guess is that someone managed to activate and release the miasma that was leftover in her body from the exclusion event, then harness it for a mass conjuring."

'*That's horrible . . .*' Wally felt sick.

Despite not knowing her personally, this woman had been a survivor of the same thing that haunted Wally's nightmares. Knowing that she had survived that only to die the way she did? Wait . . .

'*Harnessed?*' Wally repeated hollowly. '*As in, on purpose?*'

'*Yeah, this isn't something someone could do by accident,*' Vess replied softly. '*Meaning this isn't just a dispersal, it was a murder.*'

"Jemma, tell Mizer to contact the justicars let them know there's either a cursemonger or a necromancer on the loose," Vess said grimly. "I'll stay here and keep working. This was one hell of a spell, but if they were targeting the latent energy in her aura then there should be a trace of it leftover."

"You got it, Gibs," Jemma said before sprinting out the door.

'*Vess?*'

"Yeah?"

She spoke aloud as she worked, hovering her hand over the dead woman and coaxing out a visual representation of her aura as it had been at the moment of her death.

'*Do you . . . is this my fault?*'

Vess frowned as she continued to work, slowly building up a reasonable facsimile of the aura as she mentally chewed on Wally's question.

'*Sorry but,*' Vess shook her head, '*how could this possibly be your fault?*'

'*Well, it's kind of a coincidence, isn't it?*' Wally pressed in a panic. '*You bring on a Bressig survivor and then suddenly an entire tenement floor gets infested with corpses and spectrals?*'

A little huff of a laugh escaped Vess' lips as she finished generating the image of Delona Barrowbridge's aura. '*If this were the only instance, I might agree, but according to Mizer this isn't the first infestation.*'

'*Oh . . . right.*'

Memories of Cassidia's porcelain smile and Mizer's irritation over the woman's demands came back in a rush. But how many did this make? How many had Mizer said? Two? Three?

"Wally, I'm going to need you to get a *fucking* grip, or I'm going to lose this whole spell," Vess bit out.

She'd gotten angry again. Not just angry. Wally was absolutely *volcanic*. This wasn't a coincidence, it was a hunt. Someone was *hunting* the survivors of one of the worst tragedies in the past two decades and—

"*WALLY!*"

She clamped down on her anger, forcing it to the back of her mind and away from Vess.

'*Sorry! I'm sorry!*' Wally sobbed. '*I just . . . I c-can't think straight! I'm so, so mad!*'

"So am I," Vess said softly as she began stabilizing the

manifested aura, "but if either of us starts to get too unstable the proxy can fall apart, alright? And you know we can't let that happen."

'*I know,*' Wally replied, as she forced herself to calm down. '*I'm sorry.*'

"I'm not asking you to be sorry, Wally, I'm asking you to stay calm so we can save lives," Vess said sternly. "This is bigger than you or I."

Wally nodded from within the proxy, and went through her mental routine of distancing herself from her emotions. Her therapist had told her several times that one of her biggest problems was perspective. She got too deep into her own head, where everything became the worst possible version of itself. So, over the course of years, Wally had learned to pull *out* of her head and force herself to get perspective, and it helped.

A little.

In the proxy, it was easier. There was already some distance from the visceral reactions of her body, so it was a bit of a cheat. Honestly, though, it was kind of nice that it wasn't as difficult as usual.

"On another note, Wally, if you're going to try and share the burden of my spellcraft then you need to warn me before you do it, okay?" Vess said as she began circling the aura, leaning in now and again to nudge at it with her finger and cause ripples of light through the floating mass of colors.

'*The burden of what?*'

Vess breathed out a weak, laughing sigh.

"What you did when I was scraping Delona's brain for residual memory fragments," Vess clarified.

'*Oh . . . y-yeah, uhm, sorry about that.*'

"Honestly? I'm impressed," Vess said, and a warm set of butterflies took flight in Wally's stomach. "Dolin *never* got the hang of taking on my casting burden, so I was always a little limited with him, but you did it almost instinctively."

'*I don't even know what I did.*'

Vess waved her hand and the field of colors making up the shape of Delona's aura shimmered into a kind of film-negative of itself. "Casting and maintaining a spell requires mental and physical energy, right?" she began as she continued to mess with the projection.

'*Y-Yeah.*'

"Well, for me, all of that energy is mental because I'm projecting it, so my mind is pulling double duty anytime I cast, but my proxy can take some of the load off my shoulders by handling the basic background processes of the spell."

That made sense in theory. Arcane spellcasting was fundamentally made up of three different skills: mental maths for energy calculations, manual dexterity for somatic runeshaping with your fingers, and the focus to maintain concentration on the shape of the finished spell matrix once the spell itself was cast. The latter was, in Wally's opinion, fairly easy. It was a bit like making yourself look at one thing and nothing else for a long time, which for some people was agonizing, but for her wasn't all that difficult. Wally used to just zone out and think about Tipsy while she did it back in class.

'*Why couldn't Dolin do it?*' She asked, more curious than anything.

"Probably because he was too stubborn. It's one thing to be able to keep the shape of your own spell matrices in your head, but everyone casts a bit different so focusing on someone else's spellforms can be a lot harder to—*gotcha!*" Vess cut herself off and lanced out a hand to grab onto something in the floating aura projection. It was like a stray black hair or thread caught in the fluctuating dimensions of Delona's dying energy.

"What have we here?" Vess cooed as she plucked it out and examined it with a bare-toothed grin. "Aren't you just a nasty bit of magecraft . . ."

Wally watched in awe as Vess splayed her fingers and caught the thread in a matrix of light that leapt into being between the tips of her fingernails. Slowly, the matrix became more and more complex. It was like watching someone play the most complicated game of cat's cradle imaginable, and at the center of the net of light was that black thread. Slowly, painstakingly, Vess caught the thread in the snares of her spell and began pulling at it with the careful regard of an archaeologist brushing away dust from a priceless fragment of pottery.

Her eyes narrowed, and Wally could feel the strings of Vess' mind snap taut without warning.

'*Vess?*'

"*Horseshit,*" Vess spat over Wally's words. "This isn't possible . . ."

Vess brought her other hand up and added another layer light-threaded network to the spell to begin peeling the thread apart. Wally's stared agog as she watched Vess pull the spell sequences, equations, and coefficients directly out of the fragment to hang around her like a university chalkboard covered in arcane theoretica. Even with her degree, Wally struggled to piece together what she was looking at. The work that went into the spell that had killed Delona Barrowbridge was a thing of hideous mastery, complicated beyond anything that Wally had ever seen even in the halls of Colvus University.

But one thing did stand out to her. One thing she was absolutely positive of.

'*Vess, that's . . . a harvest ritual, right?*'

"Yeah," she breathed the word out through gritted teeth. "Yeah, it's a harvest ritual, and worse," she waved a hand a banished the whole mess from their collected sight, leaving the morgue in darkness once more. "It's a ritual based on *very* specific forms of Sunfall cult sorcery."

Even through the veil of the proxy, Wally felt her stomach plummet.

'*Which . . . uhm, which one?*'

The Sunfall Cults numbered five, each one devoted to a different member of the so-called Ephorate that prosecuted the Sunfall Rebellion which devastated the elven homeland of Oreliaus a century and a half ago. The end of the Rebellion and the civil war that marked its inglorious finale left behind a nation that was little more than a shadow of its ancient and storied glory, leaving it's people as an orphaned race ruled by a weak and ineffectual regency.

Of the five cults of Sunfall, the worst were the ones devoted to the two nominal leaders of the Ephorate. The first was the Maidenguard, the Cult devoted to the legendary Sunfall herself which was named for her personal retinue, while the other—

"This is Star magic," Vess spat, and Wally's blood ran cold.

Star magic? Wally echoed weakly. *As in Dark Star Mizrahi?*

The elven sorceress who was so synonymous with bad luck that her title had spawned the epithet Vess was so fond of using against herself.

Vess nodded dully.

"Yeah, it's . . . hers. This cursemongery belongs to the Cult of Dark Stars."

CHAPTER 17

"Tipsy, no! Bad kitty!"

Wally winced as a cup full of pens hit the ground with a deafening clatter, sending its contents spilling across the floor as it rolled away to the left, pursued by a cat.

"For only having three legs she's surprisingly dextrous," Polly remarked blithely as she watched Tipsy bat the cup around.

"I'm sorry, she's usually much better behaved, she's just excited," Wally explained as she juggled an armful of her belongings.

Mizer stepped out from behind her with a duffel bag full of clothes over one shoulder and a box filled with potted plants in the other.

"You know, most cats are terrified when they're brought to a new place," Mizer pointed out.

"Yes, but Tipsy has no fear of man nor gods, so—*damn it Tipsy, come back here!*" Wally pushed her things onto Polly's desk which had already been made a mess of by her errant cat and ran off in pursuit of the small animal.

It wasn't the ideal situation, but if someone was hunting Bressig survivors then that put Wally neatly in their crosshairs and Vess had staunchly refused to allow her to go back to stay in her apartment alone. Not that Wally had disagreed. She wasn't exactly keen on the notion of living alone while someone was roaming Colvus actively plotting her murder. Besides, it would give her and Vess a chance to talk like they'd both promised to.

"Oh!" Jemma turned the corner ahead of Wally and stumbled back as Tipsy plowed into her shins and flopped over. "What—? Who's this?!"

Wally's eyebrows went up at the sudden and *drastic* change in Jemma's tone as she dropped to a crouch with the biggest, broadest smile Wally had ever seen on anyone, much less the recalcitrant Jemma Corsivo, and began outright lavishing Tipsy with affection. Jemma tousled the fur between Tipsy's ears, rubbed her belly, and caught her paws now and again to poke at her little black toe-beans all the while cooing out baby-talk to the small feline, and Tipsy, naturally, was loving the attention, and had rolled onto her back to bat playfully at Jemma's fingers with mismatched paws.

"Baby girl! Who's a fuzzy baby? Who's a fuzzy little sweetheart?!" Jemma bopped Tipsy's nose gently before rubbing at her cheeks, which was one of Tipsy's most favorite kinds of pets.

"Her name is Tipsy."

Jemma froze, apparently realizing only at that moment that she was baring her shame for all to see, and slowly raised her head to stare, mortified, up at Wally, who just smiled weakly and waved.

"She's uhm, she's my ESA," Wally explained as she crouched down beside Jemma.

"I see," Jemma mumbled as she looked back down at Tipsy who was still batting at her fingers.

"Sorry, she's kind of a little slut for attention," Wally said as she stepped closer and knelt beside Jemma to start petting Tipsy's belly. "I keep losing track of her because she's a lot braver than me, and just goes wherever she wants."

"Mm, she's a feisty thing, huh?" Jemma said, more than asked, but Wally nodded all the same. "Can I ask how she lost her leg?"

"She didn't," Wally replied. "The vet said it was congenital, but I'm hoping I can save up some money to get her a prosthetic with this job," she looked up at Jemma with a small smile. "One of those new ones, you know?"

Jemma laughed and nodded.

"Yeah, that uh, that sounds good." She continued to pet Tipsy who was, true to form, rumbling loud and clear.

Wally hummed quietly as she stroked Tipsy's side while Jemma scratched her head and occupied her excitable little paws. Eventually, Jemma looked up with a strange light in her eyes.

"You make it really hard to hate you, you know that?"

Wally paused in her attentions to Tipsy, chewing on that sudden statement, then shook her head. "Not in my experience," she said after a moment. "Maybe you just don't want to hate people."

Jemma blew out an angry breath and dropped down to sit beside Tipsy and Wally, massaging her legs to get the blood flowing to them again after spending too long crouching. Wally did the same after a moment as her own legs started to cramp up.

"That's the thing, though . . . I do want to hate you," Jemma admitted.

That wasn't the most heartening thing that Wally had ever heard, but in a way it was refreshing. At least Jemma wasn't pretending. Wally didn't know how to deal with people who acted one way but felt another, it didn't compute for her. More than anything, she hated when people pretended to like or understand her, only to pull the rug out from under her later.

So maybe bare-faced dislike was for the best.

"I see," Wally murmured. "Can I ask why?"

Jemma leaned back against the hallway wall and stared up at the ceiling for a long moment, and as she did, Tipsy stood and hobbled over to loudly demand her attention again. Jemma laughed again quietly, and put a hand on Tipsy's head, rubbing between her ears obediently.

"Vess is . . . incredible, you know?"

Wally did know. A person would have to be blind, deaf, and suffering massive brain damage to not see that.

"I've known her for years, and she's always been this cool, aloof, master of magic who could wave her hand—" Jemma swept her hand in a sharp arc over her head— "and just spit out spells more complicated than I can even imagine."

"She's pretty amazing," Wally agreed.

"But she was always distant . . . always kind of sad and taciturn, and hard to talk to." Jemma shook her head like she was trying to clear cobwebs from her face. "She's a great listener, and gives good advice, but she's so walled up and just . . . cold."

Wally frowned. That didn't sound the Vess *she* knew. The Vess that Wally knew was confident, sure, but she'd never really been cold or taciturn to Wally. Quite the opposite, in the short time they'd known each other she'd been quite open. She'd been warm, patient, gentle, and protective. Sure, Vess could get defensive, and she certainly didn't seem to like being confronted about things, but . . .

"And then you come along and she's just . . . *different*." Jemma turned to Wally with a hard stare. "It's like a flipped switch! And I can't figure it out! What . . . What are you doing that I . . . !"

Jemma clenched her jaw and turned away. So that's what it was.

Wally was no great shakes when it came to dealing with other people but it didn't take a genius to see how Jemma felt about Vess. While they were in the morgue, Jemma had barely been able to take her eyes off of the woman, and it had really made Wally bristle, which was awfully selfish. Jemma had known Vess longer, but it wasn't about that. Vess said she liked Wally, and she'd said it in a way that Wally had never heard before.

She wasn't naive. She didn't believe in something as trite as love at first sight. But chemistry at first sight? That wasn't impossible. Something that had definitely *clicked* between them the moment they'd met, and, whatever it was, Wally wasn't willing to give it up without a fight.

"Are you afraid of Vess?" Wally asked softly.

Jemma didn't answer right away, but the sudden stiffness in her posture suggested the truth.

"Am I . . . ?" Jemma trailed off before picking up the thread of her thought again. "That's kinda complicated."

"No it's not," Wally said firmly. "It's a simple question: Are you afraid of Vess Gibson?"

Jemma clenched her teeth as she turned to glare at Wally. "Fine! Of course I'm afraid of her! Have you *seen her?*" She swept a hand violently towards Vess' room, and Tipsy made an awkward hop to bat at her moving arm. "She's *crazy!* She can tear corpses apart from the inside out, grab spectrals by the neck and throttle them, and wear dead bodies to learn their secrets! That's insane! That's some of the blackest magic I can even think of!"

She dug her fingers into her hair and leaned back against the wall as her breath started coming in ragged heaves.

"She can do the stuff of *literal nightmares*, Wally! And you're asking if I'm afraid of her?!" Jemma let out a brittle laugh. "Gods' hooks, aren't you?!"

Wally raised an eyebrow, then shook her head.

"No," she said softly. "I'm not."

Silence reigned in the hall for almost a full minute, disrupted only by Tipsy's rumbling as she continued to demand attention, and Wally and Jemma continued to absent-mindedly provide it as they stared each other down.

"Bullshit," Jemma said softly. "I call bullshit."

"It's true," Wally countered. "I'm not afraid of Vess, and I'm not faking it. I'm really not."

"Why?" Jemma demanded. "*How?!*"

Wally frowned again and leaned back against the wall as she absently scratched at the base of Tipsy's tail. "I don't know," she said finally. "All I know is that Vess would never, ever hurt me." She turned and smiled faintly at Jemma. "I believe that from the bottom of my heart."

The silence came back, and this time it seemed to stick hard around Jemma as she slouched and scowled down at the floor. Tipsy nudged at her now and again, though, receiving the demanded attention while Jemma stewed.

"I don't get it," she finally said.

Wally shrugged. "Neither do I, honestly." Admitting that felt almost sacrilegious, but it was true. She had no idea where her confidence in Vess really came from, only that it was there. "But I know it's true . . . I know that she'll protect me."

Jemma nodded, then sighed and stood up, and Wally followed

her, scooping up Tipsy in the process. "I guess maybe that's the difference, huh?" she muttered.

This wasn't an ideal situation, but Wally nodded all the same. Jemma's feelings for Vess were at least as obvious as her own and Wally wasn't going to pretend she wasn't attracted to Vess. She wasn't even going to pretend that her attraction wasn't *irrationally* intense, even if she couldn't pin down why she felt so drawn to the woman aside from the obvious.

Vess was, simply put, *smoking*. She was gorgeous, confident, powerful, and despite all of that, surprisingly grounded and thoughtful. She definitely had her flaws, that temper of hers being the most problematic, but no one was perfect, and Wally was confident she could work around that. Without fear, anger tended not to find much traction, which was one of the reasons Wally felt so strongly towards Jemma. Wally had seen firsthand how awful of a dynamic that could create, and Vess deserved better than that. Jemma did too, if Wally were being honest. Jemma's fear and Vess' temper seemed like a terrible combination, and Wally was certain that Vess knew that, even if the Akurian exorcist didn't.

The coin dropped in Wally's mind. That was why Jemma saw Vess as cold and aloof. Because that was what Vess *wanted her to see*. Vess wasn't oblivious to Jemma's advances, she just wasn't engaging with them, and that would make anyone seem cold.

"You know she cares, though, right?" Wally asked finally as she stepped closer, with Tipsy cradled belly up in a peace offering to Jemma.

Jemma chuckled and rubbed the proffered tum, much to Tipsy's pleasure, and nodded.

"Yeah, I know."

That was probably as close to peace as they would get, so Wally turned and began walking back to the main arming room where the majority of her things had been abandoned in her pursuit of Tipsy. She and Jemma emerged together to find most of the boxes gone, most likely moved into her new room by Mizer and Polly.

She'd been both surprised and pleased to find that there were a number of private rooms in the lower level of the precinct. According to Polly, it used to be common for employees to live at their precinct for long periods of time back when Colvus was more spread out and keeping the unit in one place for emergencies was a stricter necessity. With widespread public transit, the canal ferries, and the fact that most people lived in closer quarters, it was less of a priority. Since then, Mizer had repurposed most of the rooms for storage but had left enough of them open and tidy for employees to claim so they had a place to sleep off the odd long shift.

With that said, Mizer did actually live in the precinct full time, as did Jemma and Siobhan since, apparently, most landlords weren't too keen on renting anything out to daemon-worshippers and sanctioned, so the two of them had nowhere else to go.

That made Wally mad. Especially since Jemma was surprisingly nice when she wasn't being purposefully bristly, and Siobhan was only intimidating if you didn't talk to her.

"Can you, uhm, grab the last of those boxes? I can show you the room I took," Wally offered, and Jemma eyed the few belongings leftover on Polly's desk, then nodded.

"Sure." She gathered them up and fell in behind Wally.

Mizer and Polly were both in the room, moving things around to make space for Wally's limited collection of things. It came equipped with a bed, dresser, desk, and chair, but was otherwise rather spartan.

"Do you think we can put the plants upstairs where they can still get sun?" Wally asked.

"So long as you don't mind watering them," Mizer said, looking up from where he'd shoved the desk in place to make room for a small table that Polly was dragging in.

"I don't mind," Wally replied as she tossed Tipsy haphazardly onto the bed.

The three-legged cat landed with surprising deftness before curling up to supervise, as was her remit. Jemma dumped the last of Wally's belongings onto the table Polly had pushed to the middle of the room, then looked around, flushed, then shrugged and gave into temptation by sitting down on the bed beside Tipsy to continue petting the cat.

"Thank you all for your help," Wally said, bowing her head slightly, "I'm really lucky I met you all while this was going on."

"Believe me, we're just as happy to have met you," Polly said brightly to which Mizer and, to everyone's surprise, Jemma, nodded in agreement.

Mizer turned to Wally, who just shrugged. "We talked," was all she said before going over to join Jemma in lavishing more attention on Tipsy.

Her cat was going to get spoiled rotten while they were here.

A feeling like a nudge at the edge of Wally's mind distracted her as she made to kneel and start petting Tipsy. It was a decidedly strange feeling, almost like someone tapping on her shoulder except the phantom pressure wasn't localized anywhere specific.

Acting on a hunch, Wally stood and closed her eyes.

'*Vess? Was that you?*'

'*It was, sorry.*' Her mindspeak voice was weak and muffled by the wards of her room. '*I didn't want to just intrude like before.*'

'*No, I appreciate it. Did you need me?*'

A quiet sigh rippled across Wally's mind in reply, and after a moment her mental voice returned.

'*Yeah, after a fashion, can . . . can we talk?*'

Vess Gibson, insofar as standing up to challenges went, was no slouch.

From corpses to spectrals to proto-daemons like the wraith at Bressig, she had stood toe-to-toe against all of them and come out ahead. Shying away wasn't in her nature. That wasn't to say she was stupid. Vess knew the difference between confidence and arrogance. Her power was considerable, but not limitless, and there came a time and a place to fall back.

With that said, there were some battles that falling back simply wasn't an option. The Bressig exclusion was one of them. It was a fight not even Vess had been one hundred percent confident she could win, but she'd done it because the other option had been condemning the population of an entire town to a horrific death. She wouldn't have been able to live with herself if she hadn't at least tried.

The talk with Wally was another such battle.

A quiet rapping of knuckles against metal heralded Wally's entrance as she cranked the handwheel of the bulkhead and pushed it open.

'*Hey.*' Wally's thoughts rippled out along the link Vess had been maintaining since she'd contacted her in her room.

The moment Wally was inside and the door was shut, Vess detached her consciousness and projected it out to manifest in physical form in front of her sarcophagus.

"Hey," Vess said, and had to suppress a wince at how subdued she sounded.

If Wally noticed, she didn't show it, she just smiled faintly and walked over.

"Mind if I sit down?" Wally asked, nodding to the chair to the left of the sarcophagus that was tucked against the containment unit's control console.

"Go for it." Whatever made her more comfortable.

Wally pulled the chair out, seated herself, and immediately began wringing her hands. Her brow was furrowed and Vess was left waffling on how to open the conversation.

Fortunately, Wally was the one who broke the ice.

"So . . . my scars," she started quietly.

"Y-Yeah," Vess carded her fingers through her hair. "Sorry, by the way . . . for uh, staring. When I saw them, I just . . ."

"Mm, no, it's okay, anyone who sees them pretty much has the same reaction." She laid a hand over her forearms and shrugged. "They're pretty grotesque."

"They're—"

"Don't say they're not, please," Wally interrupted, and Vess clammed up. "Because they are. Scars are a lot of things, but they're . . . they're not pretty, okay? And I'm not proud of them."

Vess wilted back. For once, she felt completely at a loss for what to say. What *could* she say that wouldn't sound inane at best or patronizing at worst?

"I hate looking at them," Wally continued in a soft voice.

"Every time I do it's like I get flooded with feelings I don't know what to do with, and . . ." Wally shook her head. "I'm sorry you saw them like that."

Leaning against her sarcophagus beside Wally, Vess held a hand out in a silent offer, which Wally took, laying her palm over Vess'.

"I'm sorry I saw something that you weren't ready to show me," Vess said. "That's not how it should have happened . . . it shouldn't have happened at all unless you wanted it to."

"It wasn't your fault, though," Wally said. "So uhm, yeah . . . I guess I should explain, at least—" and she held up her other hand to forestall Vess' protest— "because I want to, not because I have to, okay?"

Vess pressed her lips to a thin line but nodded. There wasn't much she could say to that. It was Wally's choice.

"After Bressig, I was kept in seclusion for a year to make sure I wasn't going to like, spontaneously die and animate, or something," Wally started. "At ten, I . . . I was made a ward of the state, and I lived in a community home with twelve other kids from the exclusion, the 'Bressig Kids', but even among them I was a weirdo."

"Why?"

Wally shrugged. "Because I was a weird kid, honestly." She laughed quietly. "I was never outgoing, even before the event, and afterward I just . . . got worse, I guess. Public school was a nightmare, and," she tightened her grip on Vess' hand, "I spent most of it alone."

The thought of that broke Vess' heart. Whether or not she was the girl that Vess thought she was, she still felt responsible for Wally.

"Didn't you have a mandated therapist?" Vess asked.

"Yeah, but I wasn't a very good patient," Wally admitted.

Well, that was probably fair enough, even if it didn't do Wally any good.

"I don't really know how to describe it," Wally continued with a frown. "It was like, my head was filled with this deafening white noise, and at the same time it felt like I was completely empty, and it was like that day in and day out, and . . . and the uhm, the cuts, the pain . . ."

Wally swallowed thickly as she trailed off. Vess wanted to say something, anything, to help, but what could she say? Her silver tongue had no place in this conversation.

"There were days where I couldn't move because the world just felt too big and empty, and there were days where I couldn't breathe because everything was so claustrophobic, and I . . ." Wally's voice hitched with a wracking sob. She bit it back though, swallowed, and took a shaky breath. "F-For nine years, I just . . . sort of waded through life, and then I got out of high school, and into my first year of university, and that was where I just . . . I lost it."

"Lost it?"

"Mhm," Wally mumbled, "whatever was keeping me stable enough? Whatever . . . I don't know, equilibrium I'd managed to scrabble together that had left me more or less intact? It just crumbled." She squeezed Vess' hand again and then, to Vess' surprise, Wally drew their hands in to press Vess' knuckles to her cheek fondly. "One day I was chugging along like normal—not healthy, but alive—and the next I just . . . I woke up with my heart pounding and my blood racing, and all I could think was that I had to get out."

Vess squeezed Wally's hand, then let go to run her fingers through that short, wavy brown-and-green hair. Wally leaned into the touch with a faint smile, despite the shadows under her eyes and the tracks of tears on her cheeks.

"I just had to get out," she repeated hollowly. "So, eventually, that's what I tried to do."

Just the thought of that made Vess shiver. She'd seen the scars. Those weren't the kind you survived. They certainly weren't the kind inflicted by someone who *expected* to survive.

Wally had really meant it when she tried to 'get out', which of course, begged the question—

"How . . . ?" Vess bit her lip. This wasn't an easy question to ask, but she wanted to know. She didn't need to, though. Not if Wally didn't want to go into it.

"I don't know how I survived, honestly," Wally said. "Just that I woke up in the hospital something like a week later," she laid a hand over her forearm again and shrugged. "Someone called on the Jiani quickly enough, but I don't know who . . . I was alone in my apartment, I didn't have any family or friends, and they didn't leave a name. To this day, I don't know who saved me."

Odd. Most definitely odd. A neighbor maybe? Regardless, that wasn't really important. Vess was grateful to whoever that person was, obviously, but it wasn't relevant. What *was* relevant were the rest of her thoughts.

"I see." Vess continued absently to stroke her fingers through Wally's hair, as she formulated her next words more carefully. "Can I ask something else? Something personal about that?"

"At this point, I think we're about as personal as it gets," Wally said in a weary attempt at humor. It drew a wan smile from Vess all the same.

"Fair," she admitted. "So, in the spirit of that, you know that I mentioned you were projecting your thoughts uh . . . pretty loudly?"

Wally grimaced, but nodded. "I didn't know, I'm sorry."

"Nothing to apologize for, like you said, you didn't know," Vess said, waving it off. "But I have to ask, one of your thoughts that came through . . . it was . . . that is . . ." Gods, but this was hard to say. "You still . . . I mean . . ." Vess trailed off as her words floundered in her mind.

The truth was, she didn't *want* to say it. Saying it gave it weight. Saying it made it real. Just the thought of Wally hurting like that was a physical pain inside of her, and saying it felt almost as bad.

A warm hand captured hers again, gripped tightly, and Vess looked up to find Wally giving her a smile that had gone from wan to simply sad.

"You . . . want to?" Vess asked dully.

Wally nodded. "It helps—helped—me feel anchored, I guess," she replied. "Helped me feel real. Or just calm. It's almost like a . . . a factory reset for my senses, and the worst part is that it's so, so easy. Even though I *know* it's not healthy it's just . . . easy."

Her voice shook on the last word, and Vess lowered herself down to kneel by Wally's side so she could take Wally's hand in both of hers. She didn't interrupt. She didn't speak. She just held on and waited as Wally regained her composure.

"I want to," she continued quietly. "When I'm anxious or scared or sometimes even just when I'm not doing anything at all I'll just . . . want to. That's what happened before," she returned Vess' grip gently, "but it passed, and went a lot easier than it usually does, so that was nice."

Vess gritted her teeth, but nodded. "I see," she bit her lip. There was no 'pain' precisely, in her astral form, but chewing on her lip was a habit. One Vess had retained for years, among others.

The ring hanging from the chain around her neck felt especially heavy at that moment.

"You're much stronger of a person than I am, Wally Willowbark," Vess said in a hushed voice. "And a better one, too."

Wally turned back to her with a frown and began to say something, but before she could get a word out, Vess let go of her hand, moved back, planted her fist, knuckles down, hard against the cold steel floor, and hung her head.

"Vess?"

"I need to tell you something," Vess said softly, and Wally drew back at the tight strain in the older woman's voice. "But before I do, I want you to know I'm not . . . I'm not making excuses, and I'm not . . . asking anything of you," she let out a shaky breath and forced the words out in a rush before she could choke on them. "I'm telling you that I'm sorry because I did something to you that I shouldn't have done because I . . . I panicked."

Silence congealed around the two of them, and Vess licked her lips as she waited for Wally to say something. The last thing Vess wanted to do was talk over her. She deserved a moment, at least.

A moment to decide if she *wanted* to hear Vess out or not.

"Vess, I need you to look at me."

That wasn't what Vess wanted to do. Telling her—confessing to her—would be hard enough without looking her in the eye while she did it. But then, that was just Vess being true to her absolutely *cowardly* nature.

In the end, she really was the worst.

But she was trying to be better.

Vess looked up, and Wally's eyes were steady and hard.

"Vess," Wally said softly. "What did you do?"

CHAPTER 18

IT'S CALLED 'REDACTION', AND it's ... probably something I should swear off ever using at all considering the moral implications, but it's incredibly useful and—" Vess gave a weak wave of her hand paired with a faint grimace of a smile, "—I'm naturally an amoral *jackass.*"

An ice cube hit the well of Wally's gut at the word 'redaction'. It didn't take a genius to put together what that might mean for a telepath.

"*Vess.*"

"Right, sorry, I use humor to deflect, uhm . . ." Vess shivered and licked her lips.

"Vess did you . . . did you mess with my memories?" Wally asked, praying that the answer would be no but not expecting it to be.

"Not exactly," Vess said quietly.

Wally clenched her jaw but didn't say anything. She wasn't sure she trusted herself to say anything at that point. At the same time, Wally *also* wasn't sure letting Vess continue to dig herself extra vertical footage for her grave was any better.

"Define 'exactly'."

In the end, at least she would know what was done. After that, she would decide what would happen.

Nodding, Vess rubbed awkwardly at her arm then said: "It's not really the memories that are ever the issue, you know? It's how we feel about them."

"What do you mean?" Wally asked softly.

"You're angry with me because you found out I went into your head and did something, but answer me this," Vess looked up and into Wally's eyes. "If you *knew* all of that, factually, but the only thing in your mind was the cause and effect, that is, I went in, I stopped you from spiraling down, then I left, and that's it, and there was no sense of violation or offense or . . . or anything like that . . . would you care?"

Would she care? Wally leaned back, trying to collate everything Vess had just said. Would she care if she didn't feel any one way or the other about what had happened? She wanted to scream that 'of course she would care!' because *of course* going into someone's head is *wrong*. But that was the point, wasn't it? Right and wrong were just words. They weren't real unless everyone agreed they were real, and something was only wrong if enough people cared. If people didn't care then the difference was academic.

"So . . . you made me not care?" Wally said hollowly.

"Sort of," Vess replied. "I . . . redacted a portion of your short-term memory and long-term transcription, leaving the factual memory of what happened while blocking the binding of a few key neurotransmitters and eliminating the neural ties that trigger your fight-or-flight reflex." Vess bowed her head again. "It kept you from going into a full panic attack, so . . . if you think back to what happened in the room right now, how do you feel about it?"

Wally thought back to the moment when Vess had seen her scars. It had been an objectively awful situation all around, but honestly, looking back, it wasn't *that* bad. She'd been surprised, Mizer realized he'd messed up, Vess had been horrified but of *course* she would be. Those scars were pretty horrible. Anyone would have been.

Really, though, she . . . she didn't care.

Wally's mouth went a little dry, and she smacked her lips

as she tried to dredge up some attempt to *care* about what happened, but really what bothered her the most wasn't that it happened. What bothered her was that she didn't care.

"You get it, right?" Vess asked, still not looking up. "You get what I did to you now?"

Wally nodded.

"Then you know why I'm apologizing, and why I . . . I had to tell you."

"No, actually, that's what I *don't* get," Wally said suddenly, looking up at her. "I don't get why you had to tell me."

"Because I went into your head!" Vess snapped her head up to glare at Wally.

"And?!" Wally bit back, leaning forward, and Vess flinched back. "Would I have *noticed* if you hadn't said something?"

Vess worked her jaw soundlessly for a moment, then stepped back and shook her head.

"That doesn't matter! What matters is that I—"

"It matters!" Wally cried. "It matters because the only reason you'd be telling me is that *you knew it was wrong!*"

She probably couldn't have hurt Vess any more deeply if she'd cracked open her sarcophagus and stabbed her. Vess looked absolutely gored. Her body flickered and shuddered with astral static as her concentration cracked and wavered. What was Wally supposed to do with that, though? Vess saw her scars and her first reaction was to . . . what? Erase the moment? No, not erase. Numb it. Numb the impact. Numb the pain, not heal it, because they were scars, not wounds. They couldn't be healed. They weren't even the kind that would fade.

Those scars were too deep.

If only those damn scars weren't there. If only *she* hadn't been the one who put them there.

"I knew," Vess admitted in a ghostly whisper. "I just ignored it because I didn't know what else to do." She buried her face against Wally's shoulder and shuddered. "I wanted you to stop hurting, and I panicked, that's all, I just panicked . . . I won't ask you to forgive me."

Wally furrowed her brow. "Why not?" she asked softly.

She could practically *feel* Vess frown at that. The older woman blew out an angry breath and shook her head. "Because I don't deserve it!"

Wally pulled away and glared at Vess. Vess, whose blue eyes were sunken and shadowed, and whose face was pallid and washed out—a far cry from the warm tawny shade she'd had not so long ago. "Then do you want me to just hate you for it?" she asked.

"No!"

"Then why won't you just *ask?!*" Wally sobbed.

Because she wasn't worth asking. That was what her mind said. That was what the traitor in her brain told her. That Vess wouldn't ask so she would have a reason to leave. She didn't ask because being around Wally was far more trouble than it was worth. Vess wouldn't ask—

'*Please . . .*'

Wally froze as Vess' mindspeak voice echoed in the lonely chambers of her consciousness. It was faint, a weak plea that was barely more than a whisper, but it was there.

"Vess?"

'*Please forgive me . . .*' She lowered her head silently and started to shake.

'*I'm sorry I'm so terrible at this,*' Vess sent, her mental tone still fluctuating and drawn. '*I'm sorry I can't make my tongue make the words. Every time I do, something inside me seizes up. But I don't want you to hate me, and I . . . I do want you to forgive me. Please know that my mind and heart would have you stay, even if my tongue betrays me.*' Vess was clenching her fists, and this time she spoke in her real voice. "I want to keep you."

Wally took a shaky breath of her own, then reached out and took Vess' trembling fingers in her own. "Then promise me—" the words came uneasily, but at least they came— "that you will *never* go into my head like that again."

"I swear it," Vess hissed. "On the dawn and all the stars, I swear it."

Strange. This wasn't the first time that Wally had thought that the way Vess occasionally talked could be . . . strange.

Anachronistic was the best way she could put it. The tail end of her mindspeak sounded like echoes from another era, and she didn't say 'I promise' as a regular person might have. She said 'I swear it'. And when she went to admit her wrongdoing, she knelt and bowed her head.

Vess, at that moment, reminded Wally of nothing so much as a knight.

Maybe one day, Vess would tell her more. Maybe it would happen on a day that Wally felt courageous enough to ask, but that wasn't likely to come any time soon. It didn't need to, though. She didn't need to know *that* badly. There were more important things to do for now.

"Then I forgive you," Wally said softly. "Because I don't want to leave, either." she sniffled quietly. "And because you probably could have 'redacted' all my bad feelings about this conversation if you weren't being honest."

"Is it terrible that I thought about it?" Vess asked weakly.

"A little."

"Sorry."

Wally shook her head. "Don't apologize for that," she said. "Just do better next time."

"And what if I'm not able to be better?" Vess' tone had grown solemn. "What if this is all the 'better' that I'm capable of?"

That was a grim question. Wally wanted, in her heart, to believe that everyone was capable of good things, but during her time in recovery it had been drilled into her to accept that everyone *isn't* the same. Wounds of the mind don't heal easily, for some they don't heal at all, and ultimately in order to heal you have to want to.

And some people don't.

Maybe that was true of being 'good' or being 'better', too. Maybe some people just didn't have that in them.

"I guess that's why you have me, then," Wally said and pulled away to give Vess as encouraging of a smile as she could. "To tell you when you're not being better."

Vess chuckled, and the huskiness of it warmed Wally from her heart outward. "All of my instincts and reflexes are to do terrible things, Wally, so you'll forgive me for saying that sounds like a raw deal for you." But Vess didn't let go of her hand. She didn't push Wally away. Instead, she was tugged closer to lay her head in the crook of Vess' shoulder, and relax her body against the taller woman.

"I guess that means I'll uhm, I'll have to stay around you forever, huh?" Wally said, only half-joking.

"I reiterate the 'raw deal' part," Vess repeated with another, weaker laugh.

Wally shook her head.

"I don't know," she said quietly. "It doesn't sound so bad to me."

At least there would always be someone who needed her.

Certain things were agreed upon by cultures across the world as being objects and symbols of power. The effigy. The eye. Both were identical across the span of time and space.

Objects and symbols.

Places, too, shared in that certain agreement.

Homes had power; not just dwellings, but *homes*. Ask anyone bearing ill will and they'll tell you the difference. Places that were in-between had a power all their own, too. The alleyway, the middle ground, the space between spaces, and the crossroads. The place where the could-be's met would-be's, and during that intermingling, there happened, at times, an exchange.

The darkly dressed young man stood at one such place on the outskirts of Colvus, rolling a piece of fine jewelry nervously between his forefinger and thumb. The place where the roads came together was north and west of Colvus, just over ten miles outside the city limits. It was also a place that was in between in another sense if one considered it in the context of being 'between' two locations, even if one of the locations had been rendered uninhabitable fifteen years ago.

The young man eyed the ring he was holding cautiously.

He really didn't like it. Not that it wasn't pretty. It was beautiful. He'd examined it over and over and knew if he were to hock it to the right person he'd never have to work another day in his life.

Of course, that was ignoring who the ring belonged to.

Swallowing thickly, he pocketed the ring and wrapped his arms around himself. Despite the fact that he was dressed warmly, this place gave him chills. It wasn't the nighttime air or the cold Colvian spring, or the lack of tree cover from the bracing winds. It wasn't even that the night was so very clear.

If he had to put a finger on it, he'd say it was the stars above that shone mercilessly down on him like watching eyes. Eyes that knew what he was doing and what he was planning.

He checked his watch.

Six more minutes.

A brief and unreasonable roil of panic settled into his stomach as he considered his position. It was a terrifying one, objectively speaking.

Considering who it was he was treating with, anyone would be afraid. He still had—he checked his watch again—five minutes. He could run. He could cut his losses, and wash his hands of it. The first time was bad enough. The second and third were worse. This last one would have been the worst of all if the precinct hadn't intervened. He revised his earlier assessment, deciding instead that the roil in his stomach was entirely reasonable. That twist in his gut didn't necessarily mean he was doing the wrong thing, just that his survival instinct wasn't dead, the way *she* had always said it was.

The young man grit his teeth. Anger replaced fear, and he dug in his heels.

Two minutes.

He was staying. The young man tapped his foot and licked his lips as he tried to work some moisture back into his suddenly dry mouth.

One minute.

He reached back into his pocket and pulled out the ring, looked around at the empty roads, and then stepped into the center of the crossroad.

"Three," he muttered, "two . . . one—"

"Hello, boy."

Another shiver ran down the young man's back.

Her voice was smooth like poisoned cream and honey, and the warm weight of a hand settled on his shoulder as she moved around him. He could smell her. A heady and cloying perfume hung around her, woody and floral and thick as molasses.

Dropping to his feet, the man bowed his head, his brown hair falling heavily over his eyes so that only her finely crafted boots remained in his vision, and held his hand, palm up, offering her the ring. "Hail the Sunfall. Hail to thee, the Dark Star at the end of days." He spoke the word carefully, forcing his voice not to crack with the terror that was gnawing at his chest. "The fourth ritual succeeded, but Vincent, he . . . I had to pry the ring from him, I barely made it out before they reached the core."

The woman clicked her tongue, then chuckled. "Dark Star," she said, her tone twisting mockingly, "such a graceless title. As for the boy, I'm not surprised. He was weak. He panicked and called the dispersers, and nearly ruined it all." She plucked the ring from the young man's open hand. "A pity, it's still not full."

"Th-The power requirements you're asking for are—!" the man stammered, but his words cut off as her open hand settled onto his crown, patting him like he were a dog.

To her, he supposed he might as well be. After all, she was near enough to a god. If only a smaller one.

"I'm well aware that I'm asking a great deal of a single individual, but you are the only one capable of fulfilling this role," she said gravely, and despite himself, the young man grinned. It was a vicious baring of teeth, the kind that one wears at the heart of a great vindication.

"More is needed," she continued. "More miasma, more death, and more torment are needed to reach her, and you, child . . ." Her hand settled on his cheek, and he shivered. She was so cold. "You are the lynchpin of it all."

Her hand left his cheek and he was thankful right up until she took his still outstretched hand, pressing the unnatural chill of her flesh against his once more.

She forced his hand open and pressed the ring into his palm.

"Once more, boy, and this time it must be you," she said

warmly.

Forcing himself to swallow back his fear once more, he nodded and closed his hand. "M-Me?" he began as he returned the ring to his pocket. "After what happened to Vince?"

"Young Barrowbridge was weak," she murmured, her voice slithering across his mind like numbing oil. "His talents were weak, unlike yours . . . you're a reflector, and you are *strong.*"

Strong. Yes, he was strong. He could do it! But . . .

"But the precincts are watching now!" He resisted the urge to raise his head and look at her. That would end poorly. "Last time, the ritual had barely begun before the sixth ended it! I only just got the ring out!"

She clicked her tongue again and paced around the young man in a manner that was far, far too much like a predator circling a potential meal for him to feel comfortable.

"The sixth," she said, "has a trump card that the others don't, and you know it."

The young man bared his teeth again.

"*Gibson.*"

"Is that what she's calling herself now?" The woman asked, and her voice had a curious lilt to it. "Gibson," she rolled the word around on her tongue, then laughed. "Funny . . . what a normal name for such a disaster of a woman."

"I thought you said you knew her," the man asked, narrowing his eyes.

"I did, an age ago, but she wore a different name back then, as I did."

His throat constricted almost violently at those last two words.

"Back . . . Back then?" He said shakily. "How—" he swallowed thickly as he tried to force his thoughts into coherent words past his fear. "How *old* is she?"

The godling woman made a soft, thoughtful hum.

"The five of us were a matched set, equals . . . call us all soulmates," the woman said, a faint smile coloring her voice. "And we almost ruled the world together, so you do the math."

"Matched set . . . ?" He breathed. "She's one of the *Ephorate?!*"

Gods, no wonder she killed her first proxy! Who knew what

that thing's soul even looked like now! And he'd shared his soul with her! With *it*. Vess Gibson. No . . . that wasn't her name. She was one of *them*. The Legion, maybe? The Titan? The Void? He felt sick. Utterly sick.

"She was," the woman said softly. "But it's irrelevant. The ritual must be seen through to the end."

"W-Wait! If I'm serving you, Lady Star, then doesn't that mean I'm serving her, too?!" He asked in a panic.

"No," she said quietly. "No, that woman walks a different path, and our will is not hers, not yet . . . but one day, perhaps." She tapped his head playfully. "Don't fret, though. If that day comes, you will already be too deep in *my* good graces for her to touch you."

That notion was a cold, dark comfort, and he tried to swallow back the knot in his throat, but there was too much fear. Too much panic. This was a mistake. He was *re*-reassessing his prior reaction. But of course, it's wasn't like he could back out anymore.

"What . . . What should I do?" His voice shook as she stared down at her boots. "She so powerful . . . even with my talent she could kill me as soon as look at me!"

"You're right, she could," the woman replied warmly. "Which is why you won't be going in alone." She knelt and he nailed his gaze straight downward, desperate to keep from seeing her again as she took his chin in a hard grip and started dragging his face up. "You've already shared your body and soul with one of the Ephorate, Dolin McIntyre—" he tried to resist, but she was *so* strong— "what's one more?"

The empty crossroads echoed with a high, cracking scream.

CHAPTER 19

IN THE DEPTHS OF the proxy, Wally was straining.

'*Focus!*'

'*I know!*' Wally shot back. '*But it's hard when you—*' her vision swung violently as Vess flickered backward out of the range of Siobhan's axe— '*do that!*'

The enormous dreadnought was in top form, advancing like a surge tide of brutal, arching swings that devoured the space in front of her. Vess, by comparison, moved like a dancer. Her body flowed between physical and astral states with liquid grace to the point that Wally couldn't tell how solid they ever really were, and it was *really* starting to twist her stomach.

Vess moved in jolting, staggering, rhythmless steps, slipping between the metronome blows of Siobhan's swings. The way they were moving, Wally had no idea where she even was in relation to the rest of the room anymore. Every half-step saw Vess flickering left, right, or back seemingly at random.

Flickering. It was such a tiny word for such a *freakishly* complicated action.

Flickering meant that Vess would project, then cast her bi-location spell to physically get where she wanted, only to *uncast part of it* to reduce herself back to an astral state, then *recast the part she just uncast* in order to become physical again, all at practically the speed of thought! Just thinking of doing that many things at once was enough to make Wally's head hurt. That was to say nothing of keeping track of those things, and her own location, *and* her enemies' locations, all in the middle of a pitched battle!

'*Wally, you're slipping again.*'

'*I know!*'

The proxy wavered. Wally clamped down on her frustration, forced herself to focus. The thread solidified again and she felt more than heard Vess breathe a quiet sigh of relief as the strain of maintaining it herself faded as Siobhan executed another series of brutal, threshing swings that Vess deftly flickered between, folding her physical self away for the split-second of the axe's passage before solidifying again and spinning around Siobhan's side, forcing the Siobhan to stagger as she tried to twist and follow Vess' motion.

As a dreadnought, maneuverability was her weakness. That was one of the many things that Vess had drilled into Wally over the past three weeks they'd spent training. Dreadnoughts were big walls of muscle and they were definitely faster than they looked. They could clear distance in a straight line faster than anything that big had any right to and their reflexes had ended the careers of more than one dispersal agent that confused their ponderous size for sluggishness.

With that said, the one thing dreadnoughts didn't do was corner well.

"Shit!" Siobhan swore as a sound like splintering wood cracked through the training hall as her leg folded beneath her, and Wally grimaced at the sight of bone poking through the bloodless flesh of Siobhan's right ankle and calf where her own weight had torn through muscle and skin.

"You win," Siobhan said with a dry laugh as she grabbed the offending extremity and wrenched it back into place with a sickening snap. "You're getting better, Willowbark."

Vess smiled for both of them as a warm feeling followed the praise.

"She is," Vess agreed, and that warmth doubled over. "I haven't been able to move like this in *years*."

'Really?'

'Really.' Vess replied through the link. *'Look, I liked Dolin well enough, but he wasn't what anyone would call . . . skilled.'*

'That's kind of mean,' Wally said, although secretly she was a little giddy. It was bad of her, she knew that, but still, it was nice to know she was better at something than someone else. That wasn't something she got to experience very often.

'I'm not saying he was stupid or anything, but holding the proxy link is more an art than a science.'

Wally pulsed a sense of confusion over the link; a wordless combination of clarification requests and a sense of misunderstanding. *'But it's not that hard,'* she said atop her sending.

A soft chuckle escaped Vess' lips and she spoke aloud. "Hey, Vonnie, Wally just said that holding the proxy *'isn't that hard'*."

Siobhan's laughter was a harsh, guttural bark that came out around the grin full of unnaturally sharp and jagged teeth.

'What?' Wally grumbled. *'What's wrong? Why are you laughing?!'*

Vess shook her head. "I'm laughing," she said, speaking aloud mostly for the sake of Siobhan, "because you think holding the proxy isn't hard! I never really articulated it before, but one of the reasons I was so mad at Mizer was because, with Dolin? It took him *weeks* before he could proxy me for more than an hour at a time! It took *months* before we could tandem fight."

'Tandem fight?'

"Yeah, tandem fight," Vess repeated playfully. "Y'know? The thing you and I have been practicing for the past *week?*" She shook her head, sending her auburn locks tumbling around her face. "The first time Dolin proxied for me he ended up with the worst flu of his life for near a fortnight."

'Why was it so hard on him? He was a C-grade reflector, right? That's not that weak.'

"It's not about your grade," Vess replied, waving a hand dismissively. "Or at least, that's not all it's about. There has to be a balance between the proxy and the main. Not a give an take, but mutual support. Here, Vonnie, can you help me out?" She stepped back and gestured for Siobhan to stand up.

Siobhan tested her foot against the floor, leaning her weight on it cautiously. Her regeneration was incredible. That was one of the hallmarks of a Dreadnought, and one of the things that differentiated them most heavily from wights, ghouls, and stalkers; dreadnoughts could heal themselves. They could draw in miasma, to recover from even the most devastating of mortal wounds—even ones that destroyed their entire bodies. That was why Dreadnoughts were one of the few corpses that required an exorcism in addition to putting them down physically.

The thing was, it was usually a slow process.

Wally's university studies tracked the rate of cellular regeneration for deep muscle and bone trauma on the span of hours. Siobhan had just recovered the damage enough to be fully functional in under a minute. Then again, that was why dreadnoughts usually got prioritized for dispersal. The longer they lived, the more miasma their cells and tissues absorbed, and the harder they were to put down, and Siobhan was over a decade old. Wally had never even *heard* of a Dreadnought that old.

"Here," Vess held out a hand and gripped Siobhan's forearm, and Siobhan did the same to Vess. "Now, lean back and balance on your heels, Vonnie."

It was an odd request but she did it and leaned backward. It was an awkward motion, especially for someone as tall and heavy as she was, and Wally had half-expected her to just fall over. Except that the moment Siobhan leaned back, Vess did too, pulling back and letting her body weight act as a counterbalance to Siobhan's. It was a little ungainly given the disparity between their height and weight, but, with a little effort, they made it work.

"What're you trying to prove, Gibs?" Siobhan asked dryly.

"This," Vess said. "Pull me."

Siobhan frowned, then shrugged, and pulled.

Instantly the pair of them fell over.

"Ow! Shit! Why?" Siobhan sat up, rubbing the back of her head.

"To prove a point to Wally," Vess said as she flickered to her feet. "You can't *control* a proxy. Give and Take? Push and Pull? That doesn't work when you're proxied, and Dolin never really got that."

"That makes a lot of crap make a lot more sense," Siobhan muttered as she got to her feet and raised the hand gripping her axe to scratch at the back of her head with the smile of the weapon.

"Yeah," Vess muttered quietly. "It wasn't what I'd call . . . comfortable. Not like it is with Wally."

'What do you mean?' Wally asked, almost afraid to ask, but at the same time feeling compelled to.

Vess sighed. "Dolin was always trying to . . . control," she said. "Or more like he could never just *trust me*. He could never give his half. He always needed me to give more, whereas you and I—" Vess tapped her temple— "share the load split evenly most of the time, and neither of us tries to push or pull the other."

'Isn't . . . that what you're supposed to do?'

'I like to think so,' Vess replied silently as she rolled her neck and plopped down next to Siobhan. "Here, lemme see that ankle," Vess reached out and Siobhan moved to give Vess better access to the wounded leg.

Vess hummed thoughtfully as she moved her fingers down Siobhan's cold flesh, and Wally was vaguely aware of threads of magic spooling out from her and into the dreadnought.

'Did Dolin ever get you hurt?' Wally asked as Vess worked on Siobhan's leg.

'Mmm, not really, I can't really be *hurt when I'm projecting,'* she replied. *'Honestly, I was fine. The only one he was hurting was himself.'*

The thought Wally had next was one that she kept studiously walled off from Vess. A better person might not have thought it at all, but Wally was, at least in that instance, kind of okay with not being the better person, and contented herself with a single word in the back of her mind.

Good.

What she actually said was, *'What was he doing wrong?'*

Vess ran her finger up Siobhan's leg, tracing the outline of the bone where it was wrapped in unnaturally powerful muscle. Wally could feel her doing . . . something, but it was so faint and so fine-tuned that she couldn't really comprehend it.

'All Dolin knew how to do was pull, so he thought that's how everything worked,' Vess explained, and even her mental voice was quiet. *'When we proxied, he would seize hold of my mind and pull, and I'd immediately have to start pulling back, turning the thread into a constantly taut cord that would, inevitably, snap.'*

That sounded wrong on a number of levels. First and foremost, the way Mizer had explained it to her, the proxy was supposed to be a balance of equals, not a constant fight for dominance.

"There," Vess said as she stopped channeling whatever it was she was doing and patted Siobhan's leg. "You should be able to corner a little better now."

"Thanks, chief," Siobhan replied gruffly as she stood up tested her weight on the leg Vess had been working on. She gave a stiff nod after a moment, then gestured with her axe. "Wanna go again?"

"Yeah, I think we need a practical demonstration," Vess said before swapping back to mindspeak and asking, *'You good for it, Wally?'*

'Mhm, I'm fine, what do you mean practical demonstration, though?'

"Hey Vonnie, keep the swings slow, I wanna make a point," Vess said by of an answer.

Siobhan nodded and hefted her axe. "On your call, chief."

'Vess?'

'Do you trust me, Wally?'

'You know I do.'

'Then close your eyes and shut off your senses.'

For a moment, Wally wavered. Shut off her senses? The notion of it terrified her, in part, because it felt too easy. To let everything go, to let nothingness take her? Letting herself sink into that hazy drift of nothingness felt far too close to the sharp edges that she'd tried for so long not to acknowledge, and Vess had to know that. She knew, at least in part, how tempting that dark place was, which meant that she wasn't asking Wally to trust her with her senses and her safety.

Vess was asking Wally if she trusted her enough to pull her

back.

'*Okay.*'

And the world went black.

No, not black. That wasn't quite right. It was just . . . nothing. Her mind interpreted it as blackness out of habit, but really it was just nothing. Nothing but the firm, powerful thread of the proxy humming distinctly around her, but there was no vertigo. No motion. Just . . . just warmth.

In her mind, Wally had imagined the link to be akin to holding onto Vess' hand as she dangled herself over a well of power that was just as likely to consume her as not, but now, with all of her senses condensed solely down to her awareness of the thread that connected them, she realized it was so much more than that.

This wasn't nothingness. Not really. It was just Vess.

Nothing but Vess.

Wally could feel Vess' arms tight around her waist, cradling her from behind, holding her up and steady. At the same time, Wally could feel Vess leaning her weight forward, trusting Wally not to collapse and bring them both tumbling down. She could feel Vess' cheek on hers as the taller woman pressed against Wally's shoulder. She could feel the rise and fall and the heart-thunder in Vess' chest.

—*aster, Siobhan, go faste*—

Words trickled through the link, words that Wally imagined Vess was probably speaking aloud. She ignored them. This was so much better than trying to keep track of the world while Vess was moving. It was probably the most comfortable she'd been in ages.

—*on now! I said faster!*

The world outside of the link was moving so quickly, but here there was only peace and quiet and warmth. If she could just stay here forever, that would be—

'*Wally!*'

Light exploded around Wally followed by a crash of sense and sound, and she let out a low, pained groan as everything began orienting once more.

The training room was a mess. Siobhan was moving

sluggishly—could dreadnoughts even *get* tired?—and was leaning heavily on her axe where she'd planted it, head-down, on the impact mats of the floor

'What?' Wally asked, trying not to let on how grumpy being pulled out of the link had left her.

'You were going into torpor, Wally!' Vess said. *'I didn't think you'd go that deep.'*

'What do you mean? You asked me to shut my senses off.'

"Hey, uh, I'm gonna go recharge, okay?" Siobhan grunted as she jerked her thumb towards the training room door. "But uh, Gibs? I've *never* seen you move that fast. Not even with Nella."

"Yeah," Vess replied quietly. "No, I . . . I know. Go uh, take the rest of the day and tomorrow, Vonnie, I'll have Polly pick up any dispersal calls. Wally could use the rest, too."

"Sure thing." Siobhan gave a weary nod, then turned and trudged out the door.

'Vess?'

She didn't answer immediately, she just watched Siobhan leave, then shook her head and turned to start picking up. Wally winced at the disaster around them. Weapons racks had been knocked over. Mats had been torn fully off the ground from where they'd been seated against the concrete.

It looked like someone had waged a war.

'Vess, please . . . please don't give me the silent treatment, I don't . . . you know I can't handle that.'

Vess sighed softly and sent a pulse of gentle reassurance over their link that did wonders to soothe Wally's nerves. *'I'm sorry, I'm just trying to formulate my thoughts,'* she replied.

'I just did what you told me to do.'

'Right, yeah, I know that, I'm just . . . I don't know why, but I keep underestimating you, okay?' Vess said, and the link shuddered as Vess' emotions rose in pitch. Out of habit, Wally extended a mental hand and laid it on the thread, quieting the sudden surge, and Vess let out a breath.

They'd been training almost non-stop over the past three weeks. The first time had been the day after she and Vess had had their talk. It had been a test of sorts. A reassurance that they both still trusted each other enough to proxy. It went off without a hitch which was a relief to Wally, especially. During the training, Wally had realized something, which was that *all* emotions were shared over the link. Not just chaotic ones. Whenever Vess started to get worked up, she could reach out and steady her, and Vess had learned to do the same. It was comforting. Moreso than Wally had ever imagined anything might be. So much so that after the first few training sessions she dreaded leaving the proxy despite the fact that it always left her feeling a little like she'd had a fever that had only recently broken.

The proxy was better. There, she knew she wasn't alone.

'Can you tell me what I did wrong?' Wally asked after a long moment.

Reticence pulsed along the thread of the link.

'And don't tell me I didn't do anything wrong, Vess. You don't get like this unless you're worried about me and I don't want to worry you.'

A soft grunt of effort escaped Vess as she shouldered one of the toppled weapon racks holding blunt practice blades that Wally had seen Polly utilize to deadly effect back into place.

'You know the proxy is more than just a shared experience, right?' Vess asked, and Wally pulsed a wave of understanding. *'Your soul is making a little bit of space for mine, and vice versa. The thing is that, because I'm the one piloting us, you can just kind of disengage.'*

'Right, that's what I did.'

Vess made a low noise which suggested that that wasn't quite accurate, and the bevy of emotions that spilled across their shared thread supported that.

'Or uhm, did I not?' Wally asked nervously.

'No, you . . . you did,' Vess replied. *'You just went too deep. Your soul drifted so close to mine that we almost merged.'*

That put a knot of panic somewhere deep in Wally's metaphysical gut.

'M-Merged? That can happen?'

'Uh, well, the short answer is 'no, but actually, yes', which I realize isn't super helpful,' Vess replied sheepishly. *'The 'no' part is that it can't actually happen by accident, so the worst-case scenario should be that you go into a kind of coma, but one I can rouse you from given enough time.'*

'So what's the 'yes' part?' Wally asked.

That low noise squeezed out Vess again, a kind '*ehhhhhh*' sound like air struggling to escape from a very small hole. '*It can't happen on accident, but it . . . can happen on purpose,*' Vess said finally.

'*Can I uhm, can I ask you to explain?*'

Vess huffed out a quiet laugh and nodded as she walked over to the corner of the room and sat down, leaned her head back, and sighed.

'*I probably should have explained a while ago, so yeah.*'

Wally pulsed warmth across the link. It was the feeling of having your hand taken by someone you trusted combined with having your head hit your pillow at the end of a long day. It was comfort.

'*You don't have to,*' Wally said. '*I trust you.*'

Vess returned the pulse and nodded.

'*I know that, but you deserve to know.*'

Vess ran her fingers through her hair. It was starting to take on that lank, greasy look that Siobhan had. A side-effect of the miasma pooling in her body which reminded Wally to ask Mizer to run a purification bath on Vess later. All the training was causing some buildup.

'*The process is complicated, mechanically speaking, but . . . you're familiar with the function of the lambda system, right?*'

'*I sure hope so since a grad degree in necromancy kind of relies on understanding the flow of magical energy through the body,*' Wally replied wryly.

'*Fair, so when I'm talking about merging, I mean it literally. I mean that you've sunk into the proxy so deep that you've hollowed out your soul, in a sense.*' Vess' tone took on a lecturing quality that reminded Wally of some of her favorite teachers back in university. The ones that could really engage with their students and make complicated subjects seem approachable. '*The lambda system governs the circulation of thaumic energy, and each persons' is unique. When we proxy, we sync up our metaphysical pulse, so to speak. That's a gross oversimplification, but that's the gist.*'

'*Now syncing up our pulses is one thing, we match beats, we operate on the same wavelength, you following?*'

Wally pulsed a tentative agreement.

'Okay, so anytime you have a beat, you have an interval. That's—' Vess clapped her hand, once, then twice, then held— *'a space between the beats—'* then clapped again. *'What you did was effectively slow your pulse to the point that there was so much space between your beats that I could have created a syncopation, a counterbeat, then slipped in and taken control.'*

'CONTROL?!'

Vess winced, and Wally pulsed a soothing apology as she tried to steady her emotions. This time, it was Vess who was there for her. She returned the soothing emotions with her own, calming hand. There was reassurance and a soft, gentle touch riding the core of the thread between them, and Wally let that feeling permeate her.

'Yes, control, but I would never, ever do that to you without your permission and, honestly?' Vess leaned her head back and sighed quietly. *'It's not something I ever want to do again.'*

'Why?' Wally asked, genuinely curious.

'Because the process I just described?' Vess replied grimly. *'It's called 'wearing' and it's the hard-drinking, cracked-out-on-pixie-dust cousin to skin-riding.'* Vess' fingers dug furrows into the mat she was sitting on as she took a steadying breath. *'It's dangerous. It exposes my proxy to the full brunt of my curse and my own power, which is . . . not pretty. It's also how my first proxy died.'*

'Oh.'

Wally wasn't sure what she was supposed to say to that. Ever since the first time she'd proxied for Vess, the name Nella had hung over her like a shadow. She'd known that Nella was a former proxy, that she had passed, and that Vess blamed herself for it. Knowing that she died like *that*, though, was . . . different.

'I'm not going to pretend she died easily, Wally. Nella died screaming because of my curse. Because it overwhelmed her nature.' Vess' mental voice was threadbare and stony at the same time, and Wally tried to send out a pulse of comfort, but, for the first time, it fell short. *'Don't ever let anyone tell you there's any such thing as a good death. They're all bad. They're all ugly. Death isn't glorious. It's not beautiful. It's a shit-stain coil of tar and effluvia dragging you into the sewage while it tries its*

damnedest to shove its way into every hole in your face, all so it can drown you in stink and muck.'

Vess' fingers curled into a hard fist and her jaw clicked as she grit her teeth. The proxy was a maelstrom. A torment of emotion that Wally was barely riding out. She could feel Vess trying to pull herself back. She could feel her trying and failing. No amount of pulses across the steadily fraying link were helping. Nothing was calming her down.

It was too much.

'*That's why I respect you so much, Wally,*' Vess whispered. '*Because you never let death have its way, even when it was in your head. That's why I lo—*'

The maelstrom froze on that final sentence, and Wally's heart almost stopped.

'*V-Ve—?*'

The thread snapped, and Wally dragged in a violent breath back in the icy warding chamber down the hall.

CHAPTER 20

"Y*OU'RE A LOUSE, VESS GIBSON!*"
Polly winced as the warding chamber door was slammed deafeningly shut. Vess must have really screwed the pooch. Wally was normally so soft-spoken, but the exception to that invariably involved her angrily shouting at Vess.

In her defense, Vess usually deserved it.

Wally came storming out of the hall, her hands curled into dainty fists and her face scrunched up with rage that was, tragically, kind of adorable, but before Polly could ask what was wrong, Wally stomped past her desk and spat: "Vess is in her *soup can* in case anyone needs her!" with about a gallon of venom.

Mizer poked his head out of his office wearing a frown, looked down the direction Wally had come from, then turned to look down where she'd gone, then looked squarely at Polly.

"Oh no," Polly said before he could say a word. "I am *not* putting myself in the middle of those two again."

"You're better at this than I am," Mizer replied.

"And they're grown-ass women! They can handle it!"

He nodded, but didn't back down. "I don't disagree, but you and I both know that when Vess ends up in the doghouse, it's usually—"

"—her fault, yes, I'm aware," Polly finished. "Which is why

those two need to learn to find a middle ground between newlyweds and an old bickering married couple on their own!"

"And why should they have to find it on their own?" Mizer asked pointedly.

"Because—!" Polly bit down on her next words.

It really wasn't fair to say something like 'because we had to'. Obviously, that was unfair. The point of being older was to teach the younger generation to do *better*. Not to force them to make the same mistakes out of spite. Well, not unless you were Polly's family, that is. In that case, spite-fueled mistakes and shared misery were practically the only forms of family bonding they recognized.

Polly sighed.

"Fine." She pushed away the paperwork she'd been fiddling with and stood up, running her fingers through her hair as she did. "I'll talk to Wally. You wanna talk to Vess?"

"Deal," Mizer said with a faint smile. "Although I think you're getting the better end of this."

"Oh definitely, Wally stormed off to her room which means I get to pet Tipsy while I talk to her, and you get to freeze your ass off talking to a pissed-off sorceress in a 'soup can'."

That earned her a frown from her boss which she soundly ignored as she turned to follow Wally's stormy path down the hall to the private rooms.

In truth, she'd already been thinking about talking to Wally, although not about this specifically. Over the past two weeks, Wally and Vess had bonded on an almost instinctual level. The constant proxying had accelerated the development of their relationship to, at least in Polly's opinion, an unhealthy degree. They weren't talking like normal people because they'd skipped that step entirely. Instead, they were sharing the essence of their minds and souls, and while that had deepened the relationship itself, it hadn't made them any better at just *talking shit out*.

Polly blew out a breath as she stood in front of Wally's closed door. She had to be careful about this. Even when they were fighting, Wally was still *insanely* protective of Vess. They had already reached the point where neither would hear a word against the other unless it came from their own mouths.

Gritting her teeth, Polly forced herself to relax, counting down from ten as she uncurled her hands from the firsts they'd balled into.

"Damn it, Mizer, you colossal dumbass," Polly muttered.

He'd been reckless. Too reckless. He, like Vess, *kept underestimating Wally*. She wasn't just a reflector, she was easily the best reflector that Polly had ever heard of! Much less seen! She made a mental note to look into exactly *when* Wally had been evaluated because if she was actually still a B-Grade, then Polly would eat her own machete. Wally recovered from a half-prepped proxy in under two days. That would have been a lot to ask of Nella back in her *prime*, Gods rest her. Now, Wally was proxying almost every day! She could recover from hours-long training sessions with little more than a decent meal and a good night's rest!

Absurd.

It was absolutely absurd.

Wally was a high A-grade, without a doubt. *Maybe* even a Special-grade reflector, which Polly had never even heard of existing. The S-grading scale was theoretical as it applied to reflectors since there were so few of them.

Polly knocked twice, quietly, on Wally's door, and was rewarded with the sound of Tipsy meowing, and a muffled 'come in'.

The room's owner was curled up on her bed. She was still wearing her usual long-sleeved tunic and slacks that she proxied in. Over that, however, she had wrapped herself in the enormous coal greatcoat that Vess always wore in her projected form. Polly still didn't know quite what to make of that. Vess had been wearing that coat the day they had met and had worn it every day since. She'd never let anyone touch her personal belongings before, and yet now . . .

Tipsy poked her head out from the greatcoat, looked up at Polly, and let out a plaintive meow, pleading for help from the new entrant into the room.

"Hey," Polly said softly. "You okay?"

"No."

The lump beneath the coat shifted and pulled it more closely around herself.

"You and Vess fighting again?"

A quiet sob sounded from within the coat.

Polly sighed again, crossed the room, and dragged the chair from the desk over to sit down beside the bed.

"W-Why won't she just talk to me?" Wally mumbled from under the coat. "Why does she keep shutting me out?"

"Because she's scared," Polly said as she laid a gentle hand atop the coat.

"She's not going to hurt me." Wally lifted her head, disturbing the pile of the coat and allowing Tipsy to flee to freedom which happened to be no further than Polly's lap where she curled up for more pets.

"Traitor," Wally muttered, eyeing Tipsy neutrally.

"*Mrow.*"

"You know I feed you, right?"

"*Mrrrow.*"

Polly chuckled and scratched Tipsy behind the ears. "She's not afraid of hurting you, Vess only says that because she's too proud to admit that she's afraid of *being* hurt, Wally."

"I'd *never* hurt her."

Both of Polly's flaxen eyebrows rose up to her hairline at the cold iron in Wally's voice. Her gaze, normally so soft and unassuming, had taken on a quality that Polly had only ever seen a handful of times. Gods. She almost looked like an angry Vess for a moment there.

"I know," Polly said softly. "But it's not you, it's Vess, okay? She was . . . was hurt very badly before, I'm sure she mentioned something to that effect."

Wally lowered her head and looked thoughtful for a moment. When she looked back up, it was with concern in her eyes, rather than that iron-hard threat.

"She said she betrayed someone dear to her."

Polly snorted. "Of course that's how she would phrase it. Damn martyr complex."

"Was that . . . not what happened?" Wally asked. She

furrowed her brow, and again, Polly couldn't help but appreciate the look.

Even without her personality and talent, Wally really was just too cute. She could see why Vess was so smitten.

"Ugh, yes and no, but it's not my story to tell," Polly replied after a moment. "Vess is a private woman and is entitled to that privacy, especially about her personal life. The short answer, though, is that yes, that is what happened, but no, that is *not* the whole story and is a horrifying oversimplification of events."

Polly hoped desperately that, of all people, Wally would understand the difficulty that Vess faced in talking about her past even if she couldn't possibly understand the magnitude of it. The only ones who knew were herself, Mizer, and Vess—the three who walked out of Geddenheim so many years ago. Polly wasn't sure she could put into words what that hellscape was really like, and she'd only endured it for a day.

"She doesn't need to tell me," Wally said quietly. "I don't need her to dig up old wounds, I just . . . I just need her to stop running away from me the moment she starts to get close."

For all the iron in her spine, Wally really was too soft. Polly continued to scratch Tipsy along the cheek and under the chin as she organized her thoughts.

"The problem," Polly began, "is that if you want her to stop running then she *does* have to dig up those old wounds." She leaned her head back against the chair and sighed. "Vess needs to talk about it or else she'll just keep shutting down."

Wally sat up looking despondent as she moved Vess' coat around herself until it was settled properly on her shoulders. She pulled it close and buried her nose against the coat's collar as she let out a quiet little sigh.

"I don't want to hurt her," Wally mumbled against the fabric.

"Well, right now, you're both hurting *each other*, and that's not exactly aces for any of us," Polly said flatly, and Wally sunk more deeply into the coat in response.

Silence reigned between them for a long moment as Wally visibly mulled things over. It was telling that even while the two of them were fighting Wally still sought comfort from Vess. She wasn't sure how healthy that was, but she still believed that the two of them were ultimately good for each other; Vess had become more lively, more talkative, and more approachable over the past two weeks than Polly could remember her *ever* being, and while Wally would probably never be a social butterfly, the young woman she'd met the day she'd been hired had been withdrawn in the extreme. That changed around Vess. She would speak her mind, even if it was only to yell at the woman.

"Tell you what," Polly said as she picked up Tipsy and passed the little animal back to Wally who took her gratefully. "Ask Vess about the ring she wears around her neck. If she's willing to talk about it even a little bit, that will give her the chance. If she's not, then that's her choice."

Wally nodded. "I think I can do that." She leaned in and nuzzled her nose against the top of Tipsy's soft head. "Can you uhm, do me a favor, though?" she muttered against the silken fur.

"Sure."

"Can you run a purification bath for Vess? She keeps forgetting to ask and her miasma is building up. I know she's in pain because of it but she keeps ignoring it." Wally hugged Tipsy one more time, then lowered her off the bed and let her go.

Polly watched as Tipsy did her little hobbling run over to her food and water bowl, and as she did that she marveled a little at Wally's gentle nature. She still was worried about Vess despite being in a fight.

"Yeah, no problem," Polly said quietly.

Mizer pressed his palm to the cold glass of Vess' sarcophagus and wiped away the frost and condensation. He could feel Vess' tainted consciousness buried deep within the astral spaces of the warding chamber. This was the closest to slumber that Vess got but it was both unfair and dangerous to call it that. Slumber, after all, wasn't something you could inflict on yourself.

"Damn you, Gibs," Mizer muttered.

There was nothing else. Just. Damn her.

There wasn't anything Mizer could do to alleviate her pain. There was nothing he could do to take away the nightmare her existence had become. How was he supposed to even try? He couldn't undo what had been done. He couldn't undo what *she* had done.

"If you're going to do it, do it. If you're going to chicken out then chicken out," Mizer said gruffly. "But don't you dare string that poor girl along. She's already been through enough."

He knocked his knuckles against the glass, but there was no response. No mental prodding. No tickle in the back of his mind. Vess was giving him the silent treatment. She'd really buried herself this time.

Gods' hooks, she really could get herself worked up when she put her back into it.

Mizer paced around the room for twenty minutes, calling out to her, vocally, then mentally, and even twice resorted to sending out pulses of raw spiritual energy. That last one was a waste of time, as he'd suspected it would be. The miasma in the room was so thick that anything he put out immediately necrotized. Vess wasn't even in that bad of a mood. She couldn't be. If she was angry her aura would be trying to throttle him.

"You really scared yourself, huh?" Mizer said finally as he settled into the chair and tapped out a few commands into the system. Might as well run a diagnostic on her sarcophagus while he waited.

With the program running, Mizer stood and stretched. His muscles were starting to ache from the cold. He was no stranger to the chill but this wasn't any kind of natural cold. There was something more deeply biting about a chill produced by a being like Vess, or any spectral of significant power. Spending too much time around them wasn't healthy.

Not that Wally seemed to notice.

There was something off about that girl and he hated to even lay hands on that thought. She was such a sweetheart, and all fights aside he believed in his heart of hearts that she was good for Vess, but something was . . . wrong. Proxying wasn't a skill you could *learn*. Nella's compatibility with Vess had been a fluke. Pure luck. Dolin was what Mizer had expected. Not because Dolin was weak, either, but because proxying was so . . . intrusive.

Wally took to it the way fish took to swimming and in Mizer's darker hours he had to admit that it terrified him.

"You made the damn spell so you know this better than anyone, Gibs," Mizer said quietly. "Wally is a one-in-a-million proxy for you specifically because there's so much *space* inside of her for you," he pounded his hand on the glass and grimaced, "so why aren't you taking better care of her?"

'It's not like that.'

Of course bringing Wally into it would dredge her up.

"Isn't it?" Mizer snapped, his temper truly rising. "You're going to tear her apart if you aren't careful, Gibs!"

'I . . . I'm sorry, I know, I just . . . I lost the connection and I couldn't—'

"—so tell her that!" Mizer shouted. "Don't ignore her! Talk to her! Admit to her that you lost it! Just *tell* her you had a panic attack! You know she would understand! She thinks you cut the thread and kicked her out!"

There was no response. Mizer rolled his eyes and carded his fingers through his hair.

"You know," he began more quietly. "It's not as though Wally isn't *aware* that you fuck up. Admitting it won't make her think less of you."

'I'll . . . I'll talk to her, I promise,' Vess sent weakly. *'I'm sorry.'*

"I don't want your damn apologies, Vess, I want you to be careful with that girl because if I'd known when she walked in what I know now, I would *never* have hired her." Mizer loomed over the sarcophagus, and he swore he could feel Vess sink deeper into herself. "You are not *allowed* to keep fucking up with Wally, alright? If you do—" Mizer jabbed a finger against the glass right over Vess' face— "I will fire her."

In an instant, the temperature dropped another five degrees and Mizer found himself being hauled up into the air. Telekinetic force closed around his limbs, locking them in place, and what felt like a collar of tempered steel constricted around his neck. Beneath him, the nightmarish figure of Vess Gibson's battle form, all ruddy-skinned, blue-veined, and clad in shadow, manifested.

And she was glaring death at him.

'You'll take her over my cold, dead body.'

"If that's . . . what . . . it takes," Mizer choked out as he struggled in vain against the mystic bonds holding him still.

Darkness closed around his vision as colors began to grey out. Mizer tried to conjure, tried to call out to the elements, but they were deaf to him here. The only element that ruled in this room was death itself, and right now it wore a face that was contorted in possessive fury. Then, without warning, the pressure released, and Mizer dropped straight down to the ground, hitting the cold metal hard as he coughed and tried to drag air into his abused lungs at the same time.

"Gods, M-Mizer, I—" Vess muttered as she pressed her palm to her forehead. "I'm sorry! I didn't . . . I was just so *angry*."

"Yeah, believe me, I got that," He massaged his throat cautiously as he stood up. There was no bruising. Not yet anyway. Maybe there wouldn't be. She may very well have just been constricting his airway directly. "I wasn't bluffing, though, Gibs, you have got to shape the fuck up because I'm not leaving that girl in your care if you're going to treat her this way."

Vess hung her head miserably.

"You *know* why she can proxy so easily, right?" he said, and she gave a small bob of her head.

Slowly, Vess lowered herself to the floor, sat down, and curled up against her own sarcophagus before burying her head against her knees

"I'm *trying*, alright?" Vess mumbled. "I'm trying to get closer. I'm trying to make her happy. I'm trying to . . . to give her a reason to stay."

"She already has a reason and she found it before she met you," Mizer said. "You don't have to be her absolute everything! Gods' hooks, even if you could, that's not healthy!"

Vess curled in even more on herself and shuddered, and Mizer found himself, once again, joining her on the floor. He wasn't sure why she always ended up like that when she was miserable. He suspected it was a holdover from when she was still properly alive. It really did steal a lot of her gravitas, seeing her curled into a shaky ball of shadows, ugly-sobbing on the floor.

"What if . . ." Vess swallowed thickly and looked up at Mizer. "What if that's all I know how to do?"

Mizer thumped the back of his head against the sarcophagus.

"She's not your ex, Vess. She's nothing like that woman," he said softly as he stared up at the ceiling while Vess lowered her head and curled even more miserably in on herself, and a soft sigh escaped Mizer's lips. "*You're* nothing like her either."

"I beg to differ."

Without warning, Mizer curled his broad hand into a fist and slugged Vess hard in the shoulder, sending her sprawling haphazardly onto her back with a squawk of alarm. Vess blinked owlishly up at the ceiling as Mizer stood, stalked over to her, and looked down.

"Then beg," Mizer said grimly. "If that's what it takes for you to differ from that narcissistic psychopath, then *beg*. Or is Wally not worth your pride?" He softened his expression and held out a hand to her.

Vess hesitated for a moment, then reached out and took it, taking care to avoid cutting him with her claws.

"I'm dead serious, Vess, I'm not going to let you lead her on and I'm not going to let you hurt her, even if I have to be the one who steps between you two." Mizer said the words more as a statement than a threat, and Vess hesitated again, sighed, then nodded.

"It . . . it really shouldn't be this hard for me to just talk to her like a Gods damned adult," Vess mumbled.

"It would sure make my life a lot easier," Mizer muttered.

Vess gave a wan laugh and nodded, then held up her fist to Mizer. The elementalist smirked back at her as he knocked his knuckles against hers.

"Amen to that."

Myriam had been staring down into her mug for the past ten minutes, barely able to keep her eyes open but too stressed to actually want to sleep.

Not that sleeping would matter. Being one of the unlucky sods tasked with scraping the canals clean every Gods damned day meant she only had one day off a week, half of which was expected to be spent at the Temple of Jiani'Kai for worship, and two days off every two and a half weeks. No sane person would want the job which was why heretics did the dirty work.

So she'd desecrated a shrine on a teenage dare. She'd been stupid! It wasn't fair! She'd paid her dues a hundred times over and still the Jiani held her leash. Hell, she'd been orphaned fifteen years ago along with a slew of other kids out of Bressig. She figured she was owed a little grace for that alone! But no. Immortal sins and all that. Well, she'd show them sins. If they wanted to brand her a heretic to the water god for the rest of her life, so be it. She'd show them heresy.

Myriam lifted her mug and swallowed back the rest of the bitter drink inside of it, grimacing at the taste all the while. "So this stuff . . . it'll work?" she looked up at the man who was sitting across from her.

He was young. A pretty boy, after a fashion. Not burnt out from hard life and hard work like her. His face was a bit wind-worn and he had the darker complexion of a born Colvian, and his hair hung around his face in a manner that might've been ragged if he were less handsome, but he managed to come off as endearing rather than messy.

"It'll do, Myr," Dolin said with a smile. "Takes a few hours, though. It's gotta soak in."

Her heart was racing. Was it the drink or the excitement? He'd been waiting for her at her apartment door. Dolin McIntyre. She recognized him from the few cult gatherings he'd attended. He was newer, only joined a few months back, but he'd had a furtiveness about him—a fear—back then.

That fear was gone.

"It's inevitable now, so relax, kick back, and put your feet up," he continued as he reached into his jacket and fished out a foil-wrapped packet of hand-rolled cheroots. "Here, it's good for the nerves."

"Right, I'll have one gladly," Myriam chuckled as she took it and held it under her nose. The leaf was sweet and fragrant. "This is the good stuff, huh?"

Dolin nodded. "Sure as shit."

Myriam tucked the cheroot between her lips and started looking around for a matchbox. She'd never really stopped smoking, she'd just stopped being able to easily afford even her cheapest vices. The Elemental Union wasn't as draconian about criminals as, say, Arka Menais, or New Ghereve, but they sure were a bunch of killjoys.

"Damn it all, where'd I—"

"Here."

Myriam looked up at Dolin who was reaching across the table with an upturned palm full of gray fire.

"Fire?" Myriam looked up at Dolin. "Since when're you a pyro, Dol?"

"I don't need to be," he replied, waving off Myriam's remark. "What, did you think those promises of power the cult made were empty?" Dolin asked with a wry laugh. "Why'd you join, then?"

Myriam frowned, then leaned in to light her cheroot, breathing in the pungent smoke, then sighing it out with relief. "I . . . I dunno, I guess in the back'a my mind, I wondered if it was all for show, y'know?" she said quietly as she leaned back in her chair and took another drag.

Dolin closed his hand and snuffed out the flame as he leaned back as well. "It's all real, Myr . . . I've seen it. She showed me things you can't even imagine."

"She?"

Myriam pulled the cheroot from her lips and stared across at Dolin. There was something in his eyes she wasn't sure she liked.

"I met her, Myr," Dolin said with that curious mixture of calm and excitement that only the truly insane possess. "The Dark Star . . . she showed me what to do and how to do it."

Grey fire lit between his fingers and around his palm.

"She taught me to make fire with my soul."

Myriam stared into the flames he was holding. It wasn't like any fire she had ever seen. It burned though, sure as all hells. Slowly, she turned her gaze to the empty mug that was still sitting between them, and swallowed back a sudden knot in her throat.

"What uh," she looked up at Dolin, "what's gonna happen when I die?"

"You'll burn, too," he said with a raw, strained excitement, "and you'll be so bright, that for a moment, you'll be a star like her."

A moment. Myriam couldn't help but wonder how long that moment would last. It was too late for regrets, though. The poison was already killing her. It would take her in a few hours, like Dolin said. She took another drag and tried to relax. All her life she'd never had any power. No inborn magical talent to speak of and no money to go to a university to learn real arcana. Sure as all hells she wasn't pious enough to join any priesthood. But thanks to the Cult of the Dark Star, for a brief, shining moment, she'd be powerful.

The tip of the cheroot glowed as she took another deep drag, and then grinned around it.

"Sounds like a clean deal to me," Myriam said. "After all, who does Misery love?"

Dolin grinned toothily at the cult phrase. They were strange words. Secret words. Words by which the cultists of the Dark Star could know one another. The funny thing was, no one knew the exact answer. Myriam always thought it was like one of those philosophical riddles the Jiani'Kai were so fond of—the ones whose answer was whatever made the most sense to the person who was answering.

"Aye," Dolin replied after a moment. "Who indeed?"

His answer was odd, even by cult standards. Who indeed? He said it as if he knew. Who knows? Maybe he did. Still, to Myriam, the words had only ever had one answer:

Misery loved her, because no one else would.

CHAPTER 21

A TIMID KNOCK SOUNDED at Wally's door, and she looked up and over the black lump of fur on her chest with a frown.

"Can I come in?"

It had been a full day since their argument. Long enough for Wally to stew and eventually simmer down from her spike of anger. Hopefully, someone had also taken that time to run Vess a purification bath. Wally wouldn't know. Other than getting up to tend to her bodily needs like food and bathroom visits, she'd been far too busy lying on her back, sprawled gracelessly on her bed while Tipsy purred contentedly on her chest. Wally's small, differently-legged cat leveraged her meager weight to pin Wally to the bed by the power of loud rumbles and general apathy. At the rate Wally was going she would be up for a promotion to *Commander* Apathy. Or maybe it was Lieutenant General Apathy. Wally couldn't remember.

"Wally?"

"Yeah, go ahead," Wally said as she wrapped her arms around Tipsy.

The door creaked open and Vess Gibson stepped inside, and apparently Wally's heart didn't *care* that she was supposed to still be mad at Vess because seeing her the way she'd been back at Cuppa's and in her apartment made it do a little flip. Gone was her pallid complexion, replaced by that warm shade that Wally knew would tan rather than burn. Vess' hair fell in searing waves of auburn, flashing crimson on the occasions when the lights of her room struck the strands just right.

And those eyes. Who gave her the *right* to have eyes that blue? Damn that purification bath. Wally should have thought that through. It was a lot harder to stay mad at her when she was so pretty.

Vess tugged her greatcoat around herself nervously. It was the twin to the one Wally was currently lying on top of, and which Vess had clearly noticed by the fact that she was trying not to wear too hopeful of a smile. Well, so much for staying mad.

"I'm stuck."

Wally scratched Tipsy between her ears, and the rumbling grew in volume for a moment as the cat began kneading at Wally's chest.

"Ow . . . ow . . . Tipsy, you gremlin."

"*Mrrow.*"

Vess snorted, then laughed as she walked over to the bedside, pulled the chair that Polly had been using a little closer, and sat down.

"I uhm . . . I'm sorry about before," Vess said quietly as she fiddled with one of the buttons of her coat nervously. "I didn't cut the cord, I promise . . . I just . . ." Vess hung her head and grimaced. "I panicked."

Wally leaned up to nuzzle Tipsy for a moment before relaxing back against her bed and turning her head to stare up at Vess. "You couldn't have just told me that?"

That earned a quiet groan from Vess as she pressed the heel of her palm to her face. "I . . . should have, I know, I just . . . locked up and . . . and I . . ."

On instinct, Wally reached out and laid her hand over Vess', and Vess returned the gentle grip, twining her fingers with Wally's in a way that felt far too natural for it to be fair.

"You ran away," Wally said.

"I ran away," Vess agreed.

"I really wish you'd stop doing that," Wally said quietly. "At least . . . at least to me."

Vess snorted again and nodded. "Yeah," she muttered. "Me too."

That was fair enough. It wasn't as though Wally wasn't familiar with the kinds of panic-response neuroses that led people to do things which, in the moment, seemed rational and perfectly well-reasoned only for it to become glaringly obvious at how stupid they were later on. Maybe all this time it had been Wally who'd been being unfair to Vess. She was always so dynamic, so confident, and so self-assured most of the time that it was easy to forget that there was something deeply broken inside of her. No, Vess struck Wally as being the type of person who was just very, very good at walling up the bad things in her mind. Wally had been good at that for a while too. The scars on her arms itched as she remembered all too well where that had gotten her. Vess was stronger than she was, Wally was sure of that much. Still, maybe she could have been a bit more . . . gentle.

Suddenly and without warning, Tipsy sat up, her eyes dilated until they were completely black, and she bolted away in a dead sprint, running a circuit around the room, screaming at the top of her tiny lungs before hauling ass out the door, yowling all the way while Vess stared after her in shock, then turned back to Wally who just shrugged as she sat up.

"It's scream'o'clock."

"W-What?"

"Scream'o'clock," Wally repeated as she nodded towards the door. "Tipsy is letting everyone know."

"Is . . . Is scream'o'clock always at—" she glanced on the little digital clock on Wally's desk— "five at night?"

Wally shook her head. "No, only Tipsy knows when scream'o'clock is, but don't worry," she nodded towards the door where the Tipsy klaxon could be heard echoing down the halls, "she'll let you know."

"Huh." Vess furrowed her brow, then looked back at Wally. "So she did this back in your old apartment?"

"Yeah."

"The tiny apartment with all the plants?"

"Uh-huh."

"Did she ever knock over—"

"Every. Fucking. Time."

Wally pressed her lips to a thin line as she recalled all the times she'd come home from classes to find that scream'o'clock had arrived in the middle of Applied Arcana or Lambda Biology, and left half of her potted plants spilling their sod across the tile. And Tipsy, of course, would be sitting on the couch, calmly cleaning between her toes.

"Huh," Vess repeated, then laughed softly. "That's funny."

"And frustrating," Wally admitted. "But I love her so much that I don't care."

Vess made a quiet pensive sound, then said, "I . . . I always wanted a cat." Her voice took on a distant, almost grainy quality as her astral form shivered. "I never got the chance, though. Growing up, I couldn't even take care of myself, then the orphanage wouldn't allow animals, then the dorms wouldn't, and then . . ." Her free hand drifted up and she laid it over the center of her chest, right where the ring on her necklace would have fallen.

"Vess?"

Wally squeezed Vess' hand and her form abruptly sharpened back into focus as she snapped out of wherever her mind had wandered. She looked over at Wally, her eyes wide and faintly terrified for a moment before the emotion vanished under that mask of calm that Wally was learning to despise.

"Will you come with me somewhere?" Vess asked. "It's about an hour's drive outside of town."

Raising an eyebrow, Wally sat up the rest of the way and rolled her neck. In the distance, the Tipsy alarm was still going. She was tempted to ask why, but that, she felt, was probably the wrong response. She wasn't sure why. She just knew. So instead she said, "Okay."

Vess stood, keeping hold of Wally's hand, and tugged.

"Follow me."

Wally picked up the coat from her bed and followed as Vess led her out of the room and down the hall, and Wally's cheeks bloomed rosy red as Vess kept holding on to her hand the whole way through. Vess pointedly ignored the raised eyebrows and faint grin she got from Polly as the two of them walked past her desk. There's was strength in Vess' hand; warm living strength. That was why it was, at times, hard for Wally to remember that Vess had a buried pain so much like her own. Unlike her, Vess held her head high. She kept her chin up, her shoulders squared, and her eyes clear and steadily fixed forward.

There might have been an awful needle of fear buried deep within her but, when she was like this, Wally found it difficult to say precisely where that needle was. So yes. Vess had fear, but she was strong enough to overcome it, sometimes it just took her a little bit. Wally envied that.

"Here." Vess turned the crank on her warding chamber door and pushed it open. "I want to show you something."

Wally nodded as she followed, her mind still occupied by the fact that Vess hadn't let go of her hand.

"My sarcophagus goes with us on some dispersions, which you know," Vess said casually as she walked Wally to the containment unit that housed her physical form. "The loading process is easier than you'd expect, though."

She turned and shot Wally a smirk. No one should be allowed to have a smile that charming. It was far too dangerous.

"C'mere." Vess gave Wally's hand a gentle tug and brought her closer. "Look here." She knelt and ran her hand over five broad cylinders loaded into the base of the machine. "These are holy reliquaries," she said solemnly. "They each carry something inside of them that's imbued with pure spark, magic untainted by the hand of mortals."

"The power of the Gods," Wally said softly.

She reached with her free hand to touch one of the cylinders. It was just cold metal. Odd. She had expected it to feel different.

"Mhm, and they serve to neutralize my power anytime I'm projecting outside of the chamber," she said. "Without them, I'm hemorrhaging miasma into the air." Vess scowled as I looked back up at her. "Every beat of my heart curses the world around me, that's why I need a reflector to purify the magic I'm using as I use it."

"That sounds awful," Wally said softly as she stood. "But I don't understand . . . if you have the reliquaries—" she gestured to the cylinders— "then why not just use them all the time?"

"Because they only work for a short while, and without a reflector, I'd corrupt the spark within them in about thirty hours, give or take." Wally's eyes widened. She'd drastically underestimated the Vess' curse. "There's a reason I call myself a bad star," Vess said somberly.

"How?" Wally breathed.

"The one who cursed me made it special," Vess replied, her voice falling low as she looked down at herself, at the shadow of her own vital form that was practically laid in state in front of her. "Not only did the curse contain the sum total of *her* power, it was also designed to not allow me to die until it necrotized every last drop of magic within me." She laid her hand over her chest again and tension corded along her jaw. "Then, and only then, would it let me die, and, well . . ." she gave Vess a wan look, "I don't have to tell you what happens when someone steeped in that much miasma dies, right?"

She didn't. Gods. With how powerful Vess was, combined with the power of the curse itself? The resulting exclusion zone would be downright apocalyptic.

"Come here," Vess said after a moment and towed Wally over to the computer screen. "Sit down, my handler should know how to run my release programs."

Wally obeyed, and over the next several minutes Vess walked Wally through what turned out to be a relatively simple set of commands designed to release a series of maglocks that secured her containment sarcophagus.

"How do we get it to the hearse?" Wally asked as the last of the locks hissed loose.

"Easy." Vess grinned and nodded up. "We're right underneath it."

Wally stared, then looked down at the floor. She'd never really examined it closely before because why would she? It was a floor. Unlike the rest of the room, it wasn't covered in eyes. There was no reason to. The earth herself was a powerful enough ward. A living entity of power that repelled ill will. On closer inspection, though, there were subtle seams in the metal surrounding the sarcophagus, and the coin dropped.

"It's a freight lift," Wally said, looking back up at Vess who was grinning proudly. "Your sarcophagus is installed on a freight lift, isn't it?"

"Mhm," Vess nodded and pointed back at the screen. "Go into the system files and you should find the lift commands, it's pretty simple. Just 'up', 'down', 'on', 'off', and 'test'."

Wally nodded and keyed her way through the system, turned the lift on, then went to tap the 'Up' command.

"Hold on." Vess grabbed hold of Wally's hand again and shook her head. "You can't bring me up without engaging my restraints, the reliquaries, I mean."

"Oh." Wally froze, then swallowed hard.

"It's okay," Vess said softly, "it's right here."

She tapped a section of the screen, and Wally keyed through the system commands.

"Restraint level five," Vess said. "You have to engage all of them in sequence," she tapped the icon marking restraint level one, "up to the fifth seal, then run the program on the side there," she pointed to the sidebar. "It takes about a minute."

Wally followed Vess' instructions meticulously. It wasn't really the sort of thing she was allowed to mess up. She engaged each reliquary by the numbers, and they came to life with monotone groans before settling into a dull background hum. Lights flickered a healthy green along the rims of each cylinder, which Wally took to be a good thing, and once they were all going she moved to the sidebar program and examine the executable.

"The Ro Incantation?" Wally looked up at Vess. "I . . . I don't think I know that God. What pantheon do they belong to?"

"None, because Ro isn't a God," Vess replied, and there was a sudden edge to her voice. "Ro was a sorceress who specialized in taking objects imbued with spark and causing them to harmonize to multiply their effects."

A sorceress who could enhance pure spark? Wally stared in

disbelief. That was supposed to impossible. That was the whole point of spark! It was unsullied magic! Well, technically Vess just said that Ro harmonized it with other relics. So, once again, *technically*, it was still unsullied. That was brilliant! Using spark to enhance spark was *brilliant!*

"How have I never heard of this?" Wally asked, staring up at her in shock. "This is groundbreaking! How are there not whole schools dedicated to this?!"

"It's . . . complicated," Vess replied hollowly.

Then she leaned in past Wally and ran the program, and immediately, the room filled with a soft, bell-chime harmony, and Vess furrowed her brow.

"Right, sorry," she said, through gritted teeth. "S-Should've warned you . . . this part . . . is . . . g-going to get . . . kind of . . . *rough*—*!*"

"VESS?!" Wally's ears pinned back and she stood sharply as Vess staggered, clutched her head, and dropped to her knees.

The harmony was so pure and bright that it brought tears to Wally's eyes. It lifted her soul. Elevated her. It was like standing in the center of the Cathedral of Ys during the Convocation of Light surrounded by the clarion voices of a thousand choristers as the dawn streamed through the mighty, vaulted windows. It was impossible not to feel heightened, but it looked like it was *killing* Vess! Her body flickered and phased, burns scorched across her skin, only to be regenerated a moment later, and her veins blackened, rotted, and then cleansed.

"I'm . . . *fine*," Vess bit out. "It's okay!"

A moment later, the note struck a soaring crescendo and Vess spasmed violently at its highest note. Then the song cut off as abruptly as it had begun, and Vess sagged.

"V-Vess?" Wally knelt, and Vess waved her away.

"I'm fine, I'm sorry, I wasn't thinking," she said, shaking her head before getting unsteadily to her feet. "The Invocation tunes the relics to one another," she explained through deep breaths. "Then, it attunes all five of them to *me*, which, with all the miasma inside of me," she thumped a fist against her chest and gave Wally that infuriatingly cocky grin of hers, "isn't a comfortable process."

Wally sagged and let out a quiet groan.

"*Please,* don't do that to me."

"Sorry, I'm sorry, okay?" Vess said as she stood up, holding up an apologetic hand. "I really am." The expression on her face was truly contrite, and Wally forced herself to relax.

Nodding, Wally stood and took both of Vess' hands in hers.

"You're sure you're alright?" she asked softly.

"Yeah, I'm sure," Vess replied with a small smile. "The reason I forgot is that I've done that literally *hundreds* of times, so it only occurred to me how it would look from the outside as I was doing it."

Nothing about that sentence sat particularly well with Wally. The fact that every time she had to go outside, she had to endure that pain was definitely not on the list of Wally's favorite things. The fact that she just . . . did it. That definitely wasn't right.

"Isn't there another way?" Wally asked. "Or at least a less painful way?"

Vess shook her head. "Not that I know of, now, come on," she gestured back at the control panel. "Bring us up and, also, I guess I should've asked," Vess chuckled weakly as she rubbed the back of her head. "You can drive, right?"

The hearse wasn't what Wally would call a particularly graceful piece of machinery, but it was old, reliable, and had an engine that ran off of second-generation sigil plates rather than the newer thaumic circuits that were an absolute pain to get repaired.

The first-gen sigils were all hand-made custom jobs so it took specialized skills to fix them, but any artificer who had half a clue what they were doing could get a second-gen plate functional again. Circuits might have been a lot more efficient in terms of energy consumption and construction, but they were also a real nuisance to repair when things inevitably went wrong. Not that Vess had any clue about that because, as it turned out, the one thing that Vess Gibson could not do was drive any kind of vehicle.

"I guess it *would* be hard for you to get licensed, huh?" Wally said with a laugh as Vess telekinetically maneuvered her own sarcophagus along the rails from the freight lift to the rear of the hearse.

"Well, yeah, there's that," Vess said with a small shrug. "But uh . . . even given a license, I still can't drive."

"Why not?"

Vess made an odd noise in the back of her throat, then laughed weakly as she slotted the sarcophagus into place and the autolocks engaged, sealing it to the body of the hearse.

"Because I lose focus on my form when I do," she admitted quietly.

"What?!" Wally poked her head out of the driver's side door where she'd been adjusting the seat and stared at Vess. "You can focus on more things than I can keep in my head at once!" she said. "How is it that *driving* makes you lose focus?"

The hearse shook as Vess threw the rear door shut and moved around to the passenger side, pointedly looking anywhere but at Wally.

"Vess . . ." Wally settled back into the driver's seat and stared over at Vess as she got into the hearse.

"Because driving gives me anxiety, okay?!" Vess threw up her hands before folding her arms over her chest, jerking her head to the side, and slamming the passenger door shut with a burst of kine energy.

Oh. That was . . . shockingly normal, actually.

"I have to rely on other people not being complete morons on the road and I do *not* trust like that!" She continued huffily.

Wally put a hand on Vess' shoulder, and the older woman relaxed a little.

"So . . . yeah," Vess bit her lip, then shrugged. "It's kind of hard to drive when the wheel occasionally phases through your hands, that's all."

"I guess it would be," Wally agreed.

She didn't push anymore after that. Something Wally had learned about Vess was that she was painfully aware of her own faults, there wasn't any need to needle her about it.

"Which way are we heading?" Wally asked as she thumbed

the keystone on the dashboard to start the engine, then tapped the rune hanging from the rearview mirror to start opening the garage door.

"West," Vess said. "Just head west."

That was easy enough. The interior of Colvus was a grid system, but the various ins and outs were made up of a trio of freeways that carved through the heart of the city. The Internal-Forty—or just 'the forty'—was eight lanes and ran east-west and there was an exit every mile or so *somewhere* in downtown Colvus. That meant that the main issue wasn't finding a way out, it was getting the old beater up to speed.

As it turned out, the speed wasn't particularly fantastic but didn't Wally mind it so much. Not with Vess leaning back in the combination gurney and passenger seat with the window open and her arm hanging out, and her auburn hair rippling in the wind as she watched the city pass her by. Wally found herself growing more and more fond of the comfortable quiet, as soft tunes played from the weavedeck. Wally thought it was a little sad that weaveplay was dying out. There were so many personal devices that could store music nowadays, but there was an ineffable sort of romance about music that came on over the weave. They were projected by old-school sonothurges, most of whom were the last of their discipline since strict sonothurgy had been supplanted by more intersectional disciplines. They also relied on outdated old harmonikords—durable crystalline disks etched with sonic patterns—to project their music, and only a few vintage crafters even made them anymore.

One day they would be gone, but for now, it was still around, and Wally loved it.

There was something so grounding about music that came on over a long drive. It felt like being joined by a voice from a solid past, rather than just a whisper coming from a nebulous future, although maybe that was just her being nostalgic again.

"Oh, I like this one!"

Vess leaned in to turn up the volume, and a smile found its way across Wally's face as the strumming, light-hearted chords of a mandolin came over the weave. Its voice was joined a moment later by a deeper-bellied guitar, and the airy tones of a fiddle backed by a tapping percussive four-and-four beat.

Heartland Road was a classic piece somewhere between folk and rock that was some three decades old and could comfortably find play across any station on the weave. Personally, Wally liked it because it was the right sort of melancholy. A pining song for the homesick. It was one of those songs that, if it came on in the right place where everyone was at the right level of inebriation, it would be sung along to with varying levels of skill without fail. Unsurprisingly, Vess needed no such liquid courage and Wally's jaw dropped, her ears perked straight up beneath her hair, and she very nearly ran them off the road when Vess picked up the opening lines of the song.

Vess' sang in a toasty contralto that filled the space around her in a calmer, more sedate way than her usual dynamism. If Vess hadn't been a top-notch sorceress, she probably could have cut it as a professional singer. Not necessarily a stadium-filling sensation, but the lounge-singer kind whose tradition all but died out a half-century ago, but could still be found here and there in the right sorts of nightly establishments.

Wally thought, in a silly sort of way, that Vess might have been happier doing that if she'd had the choice.

The rest of the drive was quiet, filled intermittently with old, nostalgic songs, and a very few times with Vess' warm contralto, until the freeway bled out into the long-bodied open highway. When they did pull off the main road at Vess' behest, it was onto an older route that had fallen into disuse after the Union internal had passed through. They followed it some ten miles down through an old town where it served as the main drag before Vess had them meandering even deeper down country roads until they came to a stop where the road simply ended at the verge of an old-growth forest.

"Here?" Wally asked, looking to Vess, who just nodded as she stepped out of the hearse and out into the evening air.

"Yeah," she said. looking up at the sky which was lately darkening, and whose first stars were just beginning to make themselves known. "Right here."

CHAPTER 22

The forest breathed in a soft susurration as Wally walked beside Vess along the narrow, wooded path. The tree cover was sparse, leaving the sky open to the star- and moonlight, and for the first time in a long time, Wally's eyes began to adjust. Elven eyes were precise things, capable of seeing clearly even on a moonless night. It was one reason why the Homeguard of Oreliaus were so famed. It was said they could strike a target at range even in the pitch black of night.

The eyes of a half-elf like Wally weren't quite as good, but they were better than a human's by a shout, and after a moment Wally's vision had sharpened enough to take in the detail of the undergrowth, the foliage, and the gleaming stars overhead.

It really was beautiful.

"Where are we going?" Wally asked.

"A grove."

Vess' answer surprised Wally. Groves were rare nowadays. Elementalism was a bit of a dying art, except as it pertained to the temples, and the art of druidic magic was even rarer except in isolated Pykan enclaves and some of the more conservative Dwarven holds.

"I didn't know there *was* an active grove out here," Wally said as she fell in behind Vess. The path was narrowing considerably in the choked underbrush.

"There isn't," Vess said quietly. "Not anymore, anyway." She sounded sad, and Wally couldn't help but feel the loss, too. The wilds were retreating as civilization advanced.

"I guess the grovekeepers must have left after Colvus expanded, huh?" Wally said, trying to keep the conversation going. "But that must've been . . . Gods, half a century ago at least?"

"At least," Vess agreed.

An ache settled in Wally's chest as she followed Vess. This was a side of her that Wally wished she knew more about. She wished she knew the Vess that sounded so sad when she talked about things long gone. It sounded less like nostalgia and more like . . . genuine loss.

She wanted to ask.

No, she *needed* to ask.

Wally believed that Vess was telling the truth when she'd told her that she wanted to have something real. She believed that more firmly than she had believed anything in a very long time. So she needed to know. Wally needed to know about this woman named Vezha Gibson who could work magic like other people breathed and who knew things that no one else knew.

"Hey, Vess, can I ask you something?" Wally started, and Vess paused in her tracks briefly.

"In a moment, we're almost there."

Vess pushed through the narrowing foliage for another few minutes until the thicket of branches and undergrowth suddenly gave way to a broad, open glade, and Wally gasped as she stumbled forward into the starlight-drenched clearing where a single mighty tree soared up from the center, reaching out like an immense hand towards the heavens. Wally walked towards it in a daze. It was ancient. She could feel that. It might even be a methuselah. She was no druid and no follower of the old, wooded ways, but she *was* Pykan—a wood elf—on her mother's side. The deep places of the forest called to something in her blood in the same way it called to all of her people. Her chest was aching again, but this time it was different. It wasn't sympathetic. It came from a place that she hadn't even known was there. It was a place that remembered the feel of grass between her toes and a taste of a good, clean breath of fresh air that flowed between wild trees and over babbling brooks.

The Pykan in her *ached* for this place. It pined for a grove long abandoned and, without warning, a trickle of wetness slipped down her cheek.

"You feel it, right?" Vess asked as she joined Wally at her side to stare up at the tree. "The magic in the air? The first magic, I mean. The real stuff."

"Yeah," Wally breathed the word hollowly. "I do."

"There were more of these places once, a long time ago," Vess said, raising a hand to lay it over her chest. "In almost every forest, Pykan Grovekeepers tended the woods and the surrounding land, keeping the world green, and now they're gone, and so much more of the world is metal."

Wally looked over at Vess, at the tired expression she was wearing as she stared up at the lonesome tree, and wondered. "How . . . old are you? Really?" she asked.

"Old enough to remember when the song of this grove could still be heard strong some forty miles from here, though." Vess answered. Those eyes of hers really were like ice sometimes.

A century. No, more than that, probably, given that the grove's influence must've declined drastically before it was abandoned. But how? Longevity magic was a bad joke unless you were a biomantic like Polly, and that sort couldn't be shared. It was really just a battery of hyperspecific healing spells meant to combat the symptoms of aging and couldn't do much more than add on a couple of extra decades if the person was already healthy. Age still caught up, regardless with its grey hairs and liver spots. Weakness, sickness, and all of the other associated brittleness of getting older all still happened.

Stasis tech like what was keeping Vess alive only came into being in the past couple of decades, so it couldn't be that. She was human. She should have been dead a *very* long time ago.

"This isn't my world anymore but I'll do whatever I can to protect it, even just a little bit, even if it's just putting down petty ghosts . . . I owe it that much." Then Vess turned and smiled, and it was a radiant thing, and it was honest, and Wally couldn't help but smile a little bit back. "Besides," she said with a faint laugh beneath her voice. "You're in it, so that's all the reason I really need."

A flush crept across Wally's cheeks, but she didn't look away. "You're a louse, Vess Gibson."

"And *how*."

She flashed that toothy grin of hers, and Wally laughed for real. She couldn't help it. She laughed for several minutes and through it all Vess just watched, her smile broad and warm, and her eyes glittering with humor and mischief. Maybe the most charming thing about Vess was how sometimes she would look at Wally like she was the most beautiful thing in the world. It put an indescribable expression on Vess' face, but it was one that was so enthralling, even if Wally didn't understand how it got there.

When she finally mastered herself, she was sitting on the ground and gulping down breaths of cool air. Vess flicked her greatcoat off, and it vanished into the astral as she sat down beside Wally and took her hand.

"Will you tell me how?" Wally asked suddenly. "How you can be that old, I mean?"

Vess' expression fell, and after a moment she shook her head.

"Not . . . Not yet," she replied. "I don't want to tell that story at all, honestly."

"Why?"

"Because, sometimes, you look at me like I'm a hero, and even if it's selfish, I don't want that to stop."

"Who says it will stop?" Wally asked.

Vess frowned and shook her head. "Who says it won't?" She looked up at Wally. "Who I was is gone, is that okay?"

Well, Wally would have to be the world's *biggest* hypocrite to tell her no. Who she'd been was gone too and she was happy to leave it that way. She didn't have the right to ask Vess to dig that deep, not if she really didn't want to.

"It's okay," she said finally. "Can I . . . ask something else?"

"Shoot."

"Your ring?"

She fell silent as her hand closed around what lay beneath her pale button-down. After a moment of consideration, she nodded and laid back, relaxing on the grass, and patted the spot next to her. Wally smiled and joined her, sprawling on the soft grass and loam of the clearing to stare up at the stars through the ancient branches.

"It's mine, and it's not," Vess began. "It was given to me by someone who was once incredibly near to my heart."

That familiar knot of jealousy formed in Wally's chest, but she'd been expecting that. In her mind, at least, the only reason to hold on to something like that was that it had been given as a gift, either by family—and Vess had shown nothing but contempt for her family—or else, a lover.

"Girlfriend?" Wally ventured cautiously.

"No," Vess replied, to Wally's surprise. Surprise turned to cold shock at Vess' next words. "My wife. It was my wedding ring."

A thick, heavy silence settled over the two of them as Wally tried to digest that information. She had been ready for a girlfriend, someone who had meant a great deal to Vess, she had been ready for a lot of things. She hadn't, as it turned out, been ready to find out that Vess was—or had been—*married*. Wally found that she hated that. She hated that Vess had been married, but she hated even more how *much* she hated hearing it. It felt so petty and unworthy. Just because Vess had been married didn't necessarily mean anything to Wally.

Or at least, it shouldn't have.

But it did, and Wally hated that it did.

"You uhm . . ." Wally had to lick her lips to get a little moisture back in them before she could get her voice out. "H-How . . ."

"I was young, and too stupid to know better," Vess replied without looking at her. "We married when I was twenty and she was thirty-eight, but she was also an elf so," Vess gave a dismissive wave of her hand, "by their standards we were about the same age."

"What happened?" Wally asked, not really certain she wanted to know but possessed of sneaking suspicion that she *should*.

Vess let out a bitter huffing laugh and shook her head.

"She wasn't who I thought she was," Vess said. "Or, no, it was more that I let myself believe that she was better than she was." Her hand began shaking, and Wally shifted over onto her side. "I let her use me. I let her just tell me things I knew weren't right, things that weren't true, but that I uh, that I wanted to believe. I let her convince me to do things that I . . . that I'm ashamed of."

The way Vess' voice was trembling broke Wally's heart into a thousand pieces. Her form swung wildly between inconstant—shimmering and phasing through static—and being far too real. The pallid color of her skin and the way she was sweating, the way her pupils were blown wide, and how she swallowed almost convulsively, all spoke of a bone-deep pain that had existed unchecked for far too long. Her right hand was clenched into a white-knuckled fist around the fabric and the ring beneath that. Wally couldn't take it. She couldn't just watch. She reached out, sidling closer, and laid her hand cautiously over Vess' rigid fist.

Vess froze, almost like she'd momentarily forgotten that Wally was there, then turned her head slowly to meet Wally's gaze.

And her eyes were still so beautiful.

The idea that someone had hurt Vess this badly absolutely *killed* Wally. Vess let go of the ring and grabbed Wally's hand, squeezing almost painfully.

"I'm bad luck, Wally," she squeezed a little tighter, "a bad star, and I don't . . . if I ever hurt *you* I . . ."

"How long?" Wally asked gently.

"What?"

"How long?" she repeated. "Were you with her, I mean . . . how long?"

Vess paused, then swallowed. Then . . .

"Ten years—"

Wally's jaw dropped.

"—and married for seven. It wasn't all bad, though." Vess's voice shook as she said the words. "She was good . . . most of the time, so it's hard, you know?"

Vess tried to let go, and Wally knew if she did then it would only be to grab that damn ring again, so she didn't let her. After a moment, Vess seemed to realize Wally's intention, and relaxed, letting their fingers twine.

"It's hard to put the two together," Vess breathed. "And it's just as hard to keep them apart . . . it's easier to pretend they were two different people altogether, even though I know that isn't true."

Vess laid her other hand over her eyes and took several deep, shaky breaths.

"Sorry," her voice cracked, "I uhm, I'm sorry, I . . . I should stop."

"That's okay, I'm sorry too, I shouldn't have pushed," Wally said as she moved a little closer.

She pulled Vess' arm to her and dared a little to lay her head on Vess' shoulder, if for no other reason than so Vess would know she hadn't chased her away. That she wasn't alone. Not anymore. To Wally's surprise, Vess didn't pull away. Instead, she turned and wrapped her arms entirely around Wally. She held on hard, burying her face against Wally's shoulder. The sudden warmth, the closeness, stole Wally's breath, but only for a moment.

Past that moment, Wally returned the embrace and held on tight. This wasn't a side of Vess that she was willing to share with anyone. The fact that this was happening here, in a place so far removed from the rest of the world, was, maybe, the only place it was allowed to happen. This time, Wally was happy to let the rest of the world pass on its own beyond the domain of the grove. Here, there was old magic and green grass, and tall, ancient trees, and here Vess felt more real than she ever had before. This wasn't the dynamic bombast that moved magic that shook the foundations of mind and memory. This was Vess Gibson, a woman who had been hurt and was still hurting, and who wanted the hurt to stop for a little while.

"Are you okay?" Wally whispered.

"With you, yes," Vess replied wetly, then trailed off before finally amending herself to: "and no . . ."

Wally tried not to jump to conclusions. This wasn't a rejection. Not yet. "Why?"

"I told you, I'm a bad star, and I don't want to curse you, too, but I don't want to give you up, because your soul fits against mine just right," Vess said with a bitter edge of self-reproach.

Tears pricked at the edges of Wally's eyes as she squeezed Vess a little tighter, then pulled away gently to look her in the eyes. "I don't think you're a bad star," she said. "But even if you are, I'll just reflect it all away, won't I?" She closed her eyes and touched her forehead to Vess'. "You can't curse me, Vess Gibson."

"How do you know?" Vess muttered

Wally opened her eyes. Their noses were brushing, their lips too close to retreat anymore. Vess wasn't pulling away for once, and this time neither was Wally.

"Because without hate, you can't curse, and you . . ." Wally's lips practically brushed against Vess' as she spoke, ". . . you're the only person I really believe won't ever hate me."

They closed the distance at the same time in a slow but urgent meeting of lips. There was fear there; the sort of fear that's buried deep in an old wound and in the memory of old scars, but it wasn't enough. The fear wasn't strong enough, not this time. This time, Wally pushed past it and pressed hungrily against Vess.

Something soothed over in Wally's chest as she felt Vess push back with just as much passion. This was a first. In the past, Wally had watched. She'd looked. She'd pined. She'd had her little crushes here and there and always, always buried them. They were never worth it. Never worth the pain. Never worth exposing herself to the hurt. She was never brave enough because she was always too scared. Too afraid. She wasn't afraid of Vess, though. She knew that Vess would always be there. She knew that Vess would protect her. With Vess, she knew she was safe.

Wally's fingers scraped down Vess' side and up her abdomen and found the gentle slope and hills of muscle. Her body was limber and powerful with compact, brawler's muscle. She had the body of an in-fighter and for a moment Wally felt a little self-conscious. Unlike Vess, Wally had nothing like that. She wasn't so much slender as she was underfed, and she certainly had no real muscle to speak of. Gods' hooks, just going up the stairs at the precinct winded her! That inhibition lasted all of a moment before Vess' hands returned the affection, tracing over every soft and meager curve of Wally's, and a moment later Wally found herself on her back as Vess moved over her. She was panting, her cheeks were flushed and her hair fell in an auburn veil that separated the pair of them from the rest of the world, and her eyes burned painfully blue.

'*Stars.*' That was the absurd thought that darted through Wally's mind. '*Her eyes are stars.*'

Bad stars. Cursed stars.

But Wally was a reflector.

Before Vess could move, Wally had her arms around Vess' shoulders and was dragging her down to drown against her lips again.

More. She wanted *more*.

Vess gave it to her. Her lips parted, and Wally let her deepen the kiss as much as she wanted. The question wasn't whether it would be too much for Wally, it was whether or not it would ever be enough, and Wally suspected the answer to that was a solid '*no*'.

They kissed desperately. Vess' weight was a welcome anchor against the intensity of the feelings that were storming Wally's heart. Every time Vess tried to lever herself up, to relieve some of the pressure on her, Wally pulled her back down. She shook her head in silent denial.

"Please stay." Wally was breathless as she drew back from Vess. "Please."

"Aren't I too—"

"No, I . . . j-just . . . stay?" Wally hated how pathetic she sounded, but Vess didn't comment on it, she just brushed her fingers across Wally's brow and nodded.

"Okay," she said softly.

Vess laid her palm over Wally's cheek and drew her back up into another kiss. This time, the desperation was faded, and underneath it Wally found a warm, deep-seated contentment. Vess settled against her, indulging her, and Wally reveled in it. Her awareness of the world around them faded. There was just her and Vess, and a pulse between them

For a moment, she swore she felt the thread of the proxy, lying just out of reach. Wasn't this how it was supposed to be, though? A meeting of souls? Of equals?

Wally writhed softly beneath Vess, pawing at her now and again, dragging her fingers against Vess' neck and down her chest. She wanted more. Gods, she wanted more, but . . . not here. It wasn't right and she wanted it to be just right.

"Wally?" Vess pulled back again and stared down at her. "We . . . can go home, if you want."

She heard the silent offer there, and it occurred to Wally that, given Vess' restrictions with her curse, this would be the only time within the next three to four weeks that they could be together like this, but . . .

"No, not yet," Wally said. "I don't want this to end yet."

"It doesn't have to end," Vess said with a frown.

"The moment, I mean, this place . . . everything. I just want to stay here with you."

Forever. That was what Wally really wanted. For once, she wanted to *be* somewhere. It was just one place with just one person, but for so long Wally had lived her life disconnected from the world. No place held any greater draw than any other. It was all just the big, bad world. But not here. Here it was quiet and there were stars and Vess, and everything was warm and, for once, safe. She was *safe*.

"C-Can I ask you something else?" Wally's voice cracked on the last word, ending in a heart-wrenching sob that sparked worry across Vess' face.

"Anything," Vess said. "Ask me anything."

Wally swallowed thickly and licked her lips. She felt her nose clogging and tears pooling at her eyes. She knew she looked awful, but she had to get the words out. She *needed* to.

"Is it ok-kay that I w-want you to love me?" Wally sobbed. "B-Because I do . . . I r-really do."

Vess stared, wide-eyed, then took in a shuddering breath before nodding. "Only if it's okay that I say it," she replied.

"Because I fall fast, and I fall hard, and I've fallen so hard for you, Wally Willowbark."

Words failed her so, instead, Wally just nodded frantically against Vess' chest as Vess gathered her up in her arms, sat up, and pulled Wally into her lap before brushing the hair from Wally's eyes and meeting her gaze evenly.

"I love you, Wally," Vess whispered, "and no one will ever take you from me."

Wally leaned in until their lips were touching. "I think I love you too, and I'm scared of just how easy it is."

"Are you scared of me?" Vess asked softly.

By way of answer, Wally leaned in and pressed her lips firmly to Vess' catching her off-guard and drawing out a satisfying squeak, before pulling back.

"Never," Wally replied with a shy smile. "I don't think I know how to be."

Wally all but draped herself against Vess, nestled into the crook of her neck, and let out a quiet, satisfied sigh.

"I'm not scared of you, Vess Gibson," Wally muttered. "You're just . . ."

"A louse?"

Wally snorted and laughed, then nodded.

"Sometimes, yeah," she replied through a swell of giggles.

Vess threaded her fingers through Wally's hair, letting the strands play between them as she stroked down and then back up, and Wally let out a soft, happy sound.

"I'm very possessive, you know," Vess said.

"I know."

"And I have a temper."

"I remember." Wally pressed a little closer until she was flush with Vess' neck, and brushed her lips along the tawny skin she found there. "And I'm still not scared of you."

Vess let out that small, huffing laugh of hers, and nodded.

"Okay then," she said. "I guess . . . we're doing this."

Even if she'd wanted to, Wally wouldn't have been able to keep herself from smiling against Vess' neck as she hugged her tight.

CHAPTER 23

The false hearth in Siobhan's room flickered its light lazily around the small expanse as its owner sat cross-legged before it. The light was dull, but it still hurt her eyes. Light of any kind hurt Siobhan's eyes, but that was her life—or maybe existence was a better word. That was the lot of a creature like her; to be repelled by light.

There was a reason her kind were generally nocturnal. Unlike spectrals, dreadnoughts could stand in the light of the sun without burning, they simply preferred not to. Siobhan had long since grown used to the way her eyes functioned. They were larger and darker and tracked both light and motion more easily, but to do that they had to be quite sensitive. Despite that, Siobhan endured the prickling pain of staring into the dull firelight. It stirred something in her. Memories, she thought. Memories of older places, older times . . . times when her heart still pumped blood and her lungs still drew in cold air.

Siobhan's broad hand tightened its grip on her axe, and the unearthly wood groaned like a disturbed corpse. It was a hateful tool and a dear one. She couldn't remember why she hated it, though. Nor could she remember why she clung to it. Every dreadnought was born from the womb of death with a weapon in hand—a tool of violence drawn from their souls to enact whatever repeating vengeance or rage brought them back from beyond in the first place.

A weapon that they could never lay down.

In the years since her second birth, Siobhan's right hand had never once uncurled from the haft of her axe. It went with like a misshapen limb.

Most days were like a dream to her. Not a good dream. Simply . . . a dream. An odd and hazy thing that sharpened only in rare circumstances. Her mind came back to her most easily when she had a purpose. When she was deployed to put down her erstwhile cousins-in-death. There were other times though, like when she would speak to Vess and her mind would come back to her and she could remember things.

And Wally.

That was another time, oddly enough. Maybe it was Wally's nature as a reflector. Her presence was supposed to repel miasma and curses, so perhaps it did the same for the cloud around Siobhan's mind. Or maybe it was just because she was Pykan. Something about her reminded Siobhan of trees. Of sunlight glinting through colored glass. Of chants and dancing around open flames under the moons.

Maybe it wasn't Wally at all, but someone that Wally reminded Siobhan of.

Someone that—

"Siobhan?" The Dreadnought looked up and over her shoulder at Jemma who stood on the threshold of her door. "H-Hey, sorry, for barging in but I tried knocking and there was no . . ." Jemma trailed off and narrowed her eyes at Siobhan. "Are you okay?"

Siobhan blinked tears from her eyes. When had those gotten there? She couldn't remember.

"Fine," Siobhan replied gruffly and forced her stiff legs straight as she stood. "Are we called?"

Jemma scowled, and Siobhan could feel the bellicose young woman mulling over whether or not to press the issue. Ultimately, though, whatever her purpose was here seemed to win out, and she nodded.

"Chief Mae of the Fifth requested backup for another housing block, like the Burroughs, called the Stymphalian Heights. Her Wardsmith, Baelion, says its on the edge of exclusion."

Siobhan nodded and rolled her neck, eliciting a faint chorus of pops and cracks.

"We're all going?" Siobhan asked.

"Yeah." Jemma pressed her lips to a faint moue. "Vess and Wally are . . . out, but Polly phoned them and they'll be meeting us there."

Out? That made Siobhan smile a little, although she wasn't sure why. She liked Wally well enough, although in fairness the girl was difficult to dislike. Even Jemma had to work at it. She was almost painfully inoffensive, in Siobhan's opinion, and could probably stand to put her foot down more. Except with Vess. There, Wally seemed to have no issue whatsoever, and that tickled Siobhan immensely. Vess needed someone to stand up to her and Siobhan couldn't be bothered. She didn't have enough of her own mind in one piece to deal with someone else's.

Siobhan followed Jemma out into the halls. She didn't have any gear to carry with her. Nothing but her axe. Beyond that, her body was her weapon. Cut a corpse in the right place, and it would fall apart, the same was usually true of a spectral. Some needed a little more oomph or some more specific witchery, but that's where Jemma came in. Between the two of them and Polly, they had the staying power even the larger precincts lacked, and that wasn't even counting Vess. With a good reflector backing her, Vess could fumigate an entire building by herself, and Wally wasn't a good reflector, she was a great one, with a soul that tasted of hand-polished silver.

Keeping her hulking frame in Jemma's shadow, she followed her through the precinct and up to the garage where Mizer and Polly were loading Katee with Jemma's ritual equipment, along with extra weapons for Polly, the tools needed to do an on-the-road purification for Wally so she could go into the proxy fresh, and a spare power unit for Vess' 'soup can'.

If nothing else, hiring Wally was worth getting *that* nickname for Vess' tank.

"Siobhan! You ready to get stuck in?" Polly was giving her a broad, toothy grin.

"Always."

"Well, load up, we've got a loud one."

"The fifth chief called us?" Siobhan asked as she ducked into the rear, seated herself, and gave two solid knocks on the partition separating the rear and fore-cab, and Polly slid open the dividing grille and peeked through from the passenger seat.

"Yeah, ol' Isshin herself," Polly said more soberly. "It takes a lot for that warhorse to ask for help, but if it's as bad as the last one then she's going to need us."

Siobhan nodded. The housing project they'd recovered the old elven woman's corpse from had been a difficult one. That it hadn't gone into exclusion was a small miracle, and had probably only been held at bay by their quick removal of necrotics as they manifested. That's what they were good at though. Siobhan and Polly, between them, could afford to fight fast and reckless because of their healing factors. In fact, the worse off a place was, the faster Siobhan healed.

The fifth had no such advantages. They were more specialized. Their team could isolate and contain threats that the sixth could only brute-force down, so they saved on collateral, but in situations like this that bit them in the ass.

"How long ago did the call come?" Siobhan asked, looking up at Polly.

"Ten minutes ago," she replied. "And we're about twenty-five minutes out from the fifth's jurisdiction in evening traffic, even with sirens on."

"Vess and Wally?"

"Forty minutes out by now." Mizer's voice cut in as he loaded a crate and shoved it under the bench and between Siobhan's feet. "Fortunately, they're coming from the west, so they should get in around the time we're done setting up."

"Tch . . . shame to bother them while they're out," Polly grumbled as she settled into her seat.

Siobhan chuckled but didn't comment. No need to rile up Jemma who was clambering in beside her. "Akur calls out, and

I'm trying to answer him, so if you three are done chatting can we get the lead out?"

Mizer clapped a hand on her shoulder and nodded, and she endured it with all the grace of a patronized daughter, which was to say, with a snap of her teeth and a muttered oath.

Leaning back, Siobhan closed her eyes as Mizer shut the door, moved around, climbed into the driver's seat, and kicked the old Hideback to life. The garage door groaned open and Katee rolled out, and a moment later they were on the road. Once more into battle. Once more her body would be the bulwark between this awkward little family of hers and their painful deaths.

It was a worthy role. Death was not a place where she could follow easily, if at all.

Siobhan tested her leg against the metal floor, the one that had snapped under the pressure of her hairpin turn when she'd been sparring with Vess. The one Vess had knitted and reinforced. It felt stronger, more durable. It felt more even with her other leg.

It had to be enough. Hopefully, this time, she would be fast enough.

This time? Siobhan frowned. *This time?* She took in a deep breath and smelled woodsmoke and pitch. She smelled fire and . . . blood. Then it was gone.

"Vonnie?" Jemma was looking at her from across the narrow cab with concern.

"It's nothing," Siobhan waved her off, "just . . . thought I smelled something."

Polly pressed her head back against the seat cushion of the passenger seat as Mizer pulled them onto the westbound forty and gunned it with the sirens going at full volume. Her machetes were laid out on her lap in their leather sheaths, ready for use.

Just like her.

A weapon ready to be drawn.

"This is going to be different, Mizer," Polly said suddenly, turning her head as she did to face her old friend.

He didn't look at her. He didn't need to. Mizer just nodded

faintly.

"You can feel it, right?" Polly pressed. "This time? It feels like—"

"I know damn well what it feels like, Pols." Mizer bit the words out, then grimaced and blew out a breath. "Sorry . . . yeah, I know."

Polly shrugged and offered him a small smile. No harm done. Mizer wasn't angry. He was worried. He and Vess had that in common, sometimes. On rare occasions only, though, since Mizer was so seldom afraid and even more seldom angry. It wasn't difficult to rile up Vess, on the other hand.

Not if you knew the trick.

"It won't be like Bressig," Polly said as she turned away and stared down the road as Katee's inexorable gait devoured the asphalt in front of them, dragging them towards the housing project they'd been called to. "We're better now, and there's more of us."

"More to lose."

"We didn't have Siobhan back then," Polly pointed out. "She's a Dreadnought, she's just going to get more dangerous and harder to put down the worse things get."

"And if she loses her grip on her mind?" Mizer made the point with the grim fatalism of someone planning for the worst.

Polly frowned. If that happened then the best they could hope for was that she'd go berserk and bring down whatever was in there on her way out. Dreadnoughts tended not to discriminate between the living and the dead in their rages.

"We didn't have Wally, either," Polly said softly.

Mizer grimaced. "Vess didn't *need* Wally, or any reflector, back then."

So Vess said. Back then—fifteen years ago—and for the years prior to that after the events of Geddenheim, Vess claimed she was fine. That she was counteracting her curse herself. The purifications, the sarcophagus, all of it, she said, slowed its progress enough for her natural magic to fight back.

"I'm not as sure about that as I used to be," Polly admitted as she looked back up at Mizer, who finally flicked his gaze in her direction briefly before looking back at the road.

"You think she lied?"

"No . . ." Polly replied in as politic a manner as she could. "Vess doesn't really lie but—" she massaged the bridge of her nose as she fought off an oncoming headache— "I do think that she may have . . . given us an optimistic estimation."

The frown on Mizer's face deepened.

"You think she should have been proxying even back then?" Mizer asked.

"Don't you?"

His expression gave the answer that his voice didn't.

Maybe if she'd had a proper proxy, she wouldn't have deteriorated. Then again, they only developed the system after Vess had blown out her lambda system during the Bressig Exclusion.

But they could have tried harder beforehand.

"Do you think there will be an exclusion event in the city?" Polly asked.

It took Mizer almost five minutes of silent driving to finally answer, and when he did it was only with a tight, wordless nod.

Ten minutes.

Fifth Precinct Chief Isshin Mae crossed her arms in front of her face and willed her Qi into the reactive tattoos that were etched across her forearms. Patterns of vibrant green became folded layers of armored scale that caught the downward thrust of a kitchen knife. The tip should have shattered with the kind of force it had behind it, but it didn't. The weapon of a Dreadnought doesn't break that easily.

"*Bastard!*" Isshin spat as she flexed and knocked the blade away, then slid her right foot forward and rode the momentum with a sharp intake of breath as she lanced her fist out.

Pallid skin that should have been weak and brittle in death took the blow from her like a ceramic plate, but it wasn't enough. Necrotic flesh ruptured, bones snapped, and the Dreadnought buckled around her strike before the impact caught up with his body and sent him rocketing backward.

Mae dragged in a shaky breath as she glanced down at the

scales on her arm that are even now folding back into the intricate tattoos they were born from. A new scar marred one of the scales.

This was the first time Isshin Mae had ever seen a kitchen knife scratch *dragonscale*.

"Mae-shii! We have to get out of here!" Baelion stumbled into the room she'd been fighting in, snapping his fingers through runic patterns and threading a seal of protection over the threshold as he did. He looked awful; neither of them were spring chickens, but his normally well-kept blonde hair was hanging lank over a pallid face.

"Where are Yusuf and Idol?" Mae snapped.

"Holding the elevator shaft!" He snapped back.

Mae clenched her jaw as the Dreadnought got back to its feet. It had once been a man in his early-to-mid forties; human, or human-passing, and thick-set with hanging jowls and watery eyes. There was something deeply unpleasant about him, even ignoring his undead nature. A murderer maybe. One evil enough and cursed enough to bypass becoming a Stalker altogether.

And he was strong.

"Civilians?" Mae asked as she moved forward to meet the Dreadnought with fists raised.

"There are no more civilians, Mae," Baelion said tightly. He didn't use her honorific that time.

"Shit!" Mae carded her fingers through her short, ragged hair, bared her teeth at the Dreadnought, and bellowed.

Qi flourished across her neck and back and over her shoulders carry chitin and brutish muscle in a liquid wave over and beneath her skin, along with hide as tough as steel plate. Isshin Mae struck in a staccato rhythm, hammering the points of her knuckles into the Dreadnought's reinforced body. She bellowed her rage at him, at the thing he had been and the thing he had become. It was over in a second, and the Dreadnought staggered back, blinking in confusion as it flicked its hand up to brandish its knife; the arm rotted away with a sound like a wet sheaf of paper ripping in half. The Dreadnought frowned, then coughed, and a gobbet of flesh came up, followed by a stream of black bile as it collapsed to its knees. Its own miasma was tearing it apart.

That had been stupid. Summoning the Manticore's power had taxed her limited reserves, but *Gods* it had felt good to just shut off the Dreadnought's ability to channel its own necrotized magic. Without it, its body was remembering that it was dead and oughtn't be moving, and with that much necrosis suffusing its tissues it was decaying in fast motion.

She shouldn't have used that much power, though.

"Mae!"

"I KNOW!" Mae spat as she turned to face him, then bit her lip, and let out a shaky breath. "I . . . I know . . . yes, let's go."

Ten minutes.

They'd barely been inside for ten minutes and already it was a shitshow.

As the pair of them stepped outside of the room, the floor shuddered. The air shook, too. The walls cracked and the whole world around them seemed to *flex*. It was like taking a step down off a set of stairs expecting the landing and finding another pair of steps beneath your foot. It was a shaky, vertiginous sensation of falling only briefly before gravity reoriented itself.

"Oh no," Baelion muttered, and he looked up to find his expression of horror neatly mirrored on his precinct chief's face.

"That . . ." Mae swallowed thickly as her other two employees came careening around the corner with haunted looks on their faces.

Idolatry Friese looked terrified and furious at the same time. Her prosthetic arm hung limp and mangled at her side and at some point her dreadlocks had come loose from their tie. Blood from dozens of shallow cuts was staining her uniform. Yusuf came huffing and swearing up behind her with his toolbox rattling at his belt and a few replacement pieces for Idol's prosthetic arm still in his hands.

"Chief! That drop? Was that what I think it was?"

Isshin Mae nodded. "That was translation vertigo," she confirmed quietly. "The laws of physics and magic just got rewritten, and this building just got excluded from reality."

From somewhere far down the hall, a deep, single note

thrummed, and Yusuf looked up.

"I know that sound," he said softly as he moved back between Idol and Mae.

The note repeated itself, closer this time, and deeper, and there was a harsh growl to the edge of it.

"Yusuf?" Idol hissed. "What is it?"

"A . . . it's a bass," he said shakily. "A powered one."

Mae frowned and stepped forward, raising her fists. A bass? As in a bass guitar? Who would be—the bass note thrummed again, and the world around Isshin Mae exploded.

CHAPTER 24

By the time Wally pulled the hearse up alongside the street and put it into park, the justicars had already sectioned off a five-block radius around the nineteenth street housing project, the ostentatiously named Stymphalian Heights, which death had already swallowed the lion's share of.

'Vess? Is that what I think it is?' Wally glanced over her shoulder towards the sarcophagus housing her now-girlfriend's half-sleeping body.

'Unfortunately, yes.'

From the first floor up to the fifth, the Heights looked relatively normal; concrete on concrete, grey on grey, it was a standard example of the mass-produced habitation blocks raised by the Earthworkers of Penikken. From the sixth floor up, however, things became markedly different, and demonstrably worse. Floors six, seven, eight, and nine had vicious furrows carved into them like scars left from impossible claws and a sickly purplish light spilled from the rents in the structure. The tenth floor was little better than floating rubble, with gravity distortions twisting the air around the upper levels as chunks of concrete drifted away only to find their way back moments later where reality met exclusion.

Shadows could be seen, too; unwholesome shapes moved

past open windows and the wider portions of shattered walls. Wally's heart was hammering in her chest. This wasn't what she'd signed up for. Of course, intellectually, she knew it had been a possibility that she would be called upon to help deal with an exclusion zone, but the point of operating *inside* the city was that these things just didn't happen! Or at least they weren't supposed to!

"Wally!"

Mizer appeared at the driver's side window, nearly sending Wally into arrhythmia as she startled in her seat. The chief of the sixth precinct rapped his knuckles against the window, and once Wally had gotten her breathing back under control she opened the door.

"Is she ready?" were the first words out of his mouth.

Wally nodded. "Yeah, the power supply has a while left on it," she reported shakily. "S-Sir, is that really a full exclusion?"

"A small one," he confirmed grimly, "but not for long if we don't nip it in the bud, so we're going to have to prep you for proxy ASAP, sorry about the rush job."

"No, it's okay." Wally unbuckled herself from the driver's side and awkwardly shuffled one seat over onto the passenger-side gurney-seat. "I ran myself a purification bath this morning."

Mizer raised an eyebrow as Jemma joined him at his side, and she froze as she looked over Wally, her eyes lingering on the familiar coat she was wearing.

"Weren't you and Vess still fighting this morning?" Jemma asked while she knelt with her pot of odd-smelling paints and began quickly drawing out the Maw of Akur on Wally's palms.

They had been, but . . . "It was just an argument," Wally said after a moment, then glanced fondly at Vess' sarcophagus before looking back at Mizer and Jemma.

'*Right?*'

A wave of warmth spilled over Wally from Vess reaching out telepathically.

'*Right,*' Vess replied.

"Disgusting," Jemma muttered, "but lucky, I guess." She put the final touches on Wally's left hand before reaching up to her face, brushing the fringe of her hair aside to begin painting the final maw over her 'third eye'. "This is gonna be a rough one, Willowbark, make no mistake," Jemma continued. "There's a good chance one of us bites it in there, and by one of us I mean me since I'm the only one not undead, immortal, or projecting."

'You'll be fine, Jem,' Vess spoke gently across the minds of the three of them. *'You know I won't let anything happen to you.'*

Mizer and Jemma both winced slightly, and Wally raised an eyebrow.

"Are you two alright?"

Jemma massaged her temple and nodded. "Yeah, you don't . . . You don't feel that? When Vess talks to you?"

"Feel what?" Wally looked between them, and even Mizer looked surprised.

"Pain," Mizer said, tapping his own forehead. "Just a little, like a pinched nerve, from the mental connection."

Wally shook her head. "There's some pressure, or . . . there was, at first, I guess. I don't even feel it anymore."

Both Mizer and Jemma shared a look that Wally wasn't sure she liked, and even Vess seemed suspiciously quiet.

"Well, we can't really unpack that *now*," Mizer said, waving a hand. "Let's get you hooked up and situated, and we'll deal with whatever that is later on."

'Vess?' Wally sent, mentally prodding the sorceress, who gave a sort of cerebral shrug in reply.

'Honestly, I was wondering about it, too, but for once I genuinely couldn't say why you're different in that regard.'

Well, that wasn't the ideal answer but Mizer had a point, now wasn't the time, so she relaxed back against the gurney, curling up as much inside of the comfortable black coat as possible, while her precinct chief set about hooking up the IV. He'd shooed Jemma away to make her own ritual preparations to give them privacy which Wally was thankful for. She'd already had to explain her scars sooner than she'd have liked to, and she *liked* Vess, whereas Jemma and Wally had a . . . working relationship, at best.

'We're going to be alright, Wally.' Vess' mental voice rippled over

her, drawing out a small smile.

'I know, I've just never been this close to an exclusion since Bressig, and I barely even remember that.'

'You won't be going in, don't worry,' Vess said.

'Technically, I will be, I'll just be with you.'

'You're allowed to just let me comfort you, you know.'

Wally chuckled, drawing a raised eyebrow from Mizer as he taped down the IV, and she just shook her head and mouthed 'nothing'.

'I don't think I am, actually,' was her actual reply.

'You're insufferable.'

'And you're a louse.'

Vess Gibson laughed. It was an incredibly strange sensation, hearing a telepath laugh. It wasn't a sound, it was a sensation. It was like being surrounded on all sides by bubbles that tickled just a little bit, and Wally couldn't help but giggle along with her. Whatever she said, Vess *did* make her feel better. Being around Vess made her feel better, and just the fact that she was trying really did help.

'Hey, Vess?'

'Mhm?'

'You'll protect me, right?'

There was a stretch of silence like a wide lake covered in ripples suddenly going still all at once. It lasted all of a heartbeat before the silence was replaced by a rush of warmth.

'I . . . yeah, of course I will, Wally.'

There was an edge to the words, one that Wally couldn't readily identify. It was like the phantom sensation of their proxy-thread going taut, except more nebulous. Underneath it all, Wally felt a thrum of reticence from Vess. Like she knew something and wasn't saying. That was probably wise, though. It wasn't the time.

"Ready to proxy?" Mizer asked as he knelt beside her, and Wally looked up at him with a calm smile and nodded.

"Always."

Vess opened her eyes at the edge of the gleaming circle of

silver-blue dust that ran a broad circumference enclosing the Stymphalian Heights. She felt stronger than she had in the forest now that she was proxied with Wally. If she had to measure the difference between this, and proxying with Dolin, she would say there was no comparison. Even Nella, Gods rest her, didn't compare. Being with Wally—that is, she mentally amended, being proxied with her—felt like nothing Vess could readily put a finger on. It was comfortable in a way she'd never known. She was faster, sharper, and more agile than ever. Her magic sparked at her fingertips more easily than it had in decades.

She almost felt alive again.

"I recognize these markings," Vess said as she flicked an appraising gaze across the runes marking out the circle. "This is Baelion Magni's work, isn't it?"

"I'd wager so," Polly replied as she knelt down and looked it over.

Vess nodded. "He's a good man and a better wardsmith. I'd bet money to love this circle is the only thing keeping the exclusion zone from spreading faster than it has. How long til the city's greater ward goes up behind us?"

"Mizer's making the call for a five-block lockdown right now, and once it's closed we're locked in with whatever is in there—" Polly nodded grimly towards the Heights— "and with exactly bupkis for backup."

Jemma stepped up to the ward's edge and toed the line. "It's gonna be a bitch for you and Siobhan to get through that, Gibs, you gonna be alright?"

The hulking Dreadnought had already clambered out of the back and was moving up behind Vess. She could feel Siobhan like a pulsating nexus of miasma behind her, tightly contained and as ready as a loaded cannon.

"A year ago I'd have agreed with you," Vess said with a smirk, then turned her thoughts inward. *'Hey, babe, mind lending me a shoulder so I can cast something halfway decent for once?'*

'B-Babe?!' Wally blush carried over the proxy, and Vess barked a laugh out loud, earning a few odd looks. *'Could you at least warn me next time?'* Wally said sullenly, but it was tinged with a playful

smile. *'And yeah, go ahead'*

It said something that Wally didn't even question her. There was just a warm press of understanding, then suddenly Wally felt so much closer. Her mind was practically bleeding into Vess', drifting thoughts—mostly complimentary ones about Vess or stray memories of their stolen moments in the woods—found their way into Vess' mind. As much as she would have loved to dwell on a few of those, she hedged them out, all while carefully maintaining the distinction between her mind and Wally's.

'Okay, let's try this—Gods' hooks~!*'*

Wally's concentration wavered, then solidified again.

'Vess?! Is everything okay?!'

'Y-Yeah, I just . . . Gods, is this what it used to be like?'

It was like finally being able to breathe and move freely again after years—literal years—of being trapped in a box and buried underground. It was seeing starlight after being blind! Or tasting fine wine after drinking nothing but tepid water!

The magic just *flowed*.

Somewhere in the back of Vess' mind, she remembered how it had been before the sarcophagus and before Geddenheim, but two decades of sleep and deprivation had numbed those memories badly. Now, with Wally taking so much of the mental processing load, she could finally move magic the way she'd used to. The way that had earned her the accolade of a one-in-a-million prodigy.

Baelion Magni was a wardsmith par excellence. His warding circle was nearly perfect. It would have to be in order to stand up to a full-blown exclusion event. Even a small one. Still . . . almost perfect wasn't perfect.

Vess slipped her fingers into the arcane calculus of the ward that encircled the Heights and began running the numbers. There were mishaps here and there; transposed variables, clunky equations, and other bits and bobs that were interfering with the ward's consistency, or making it less energy efficient than it could be.

Initially, Vess had just been intending to use Wally's help to pry open a temporary passage for herself and Siobhan, but now that seemed almost helplessly quaint! Why stop there?

Baring her teeth in a manic grin, Vess began correcting the ward. She used her own internal reserves to alter and perfect the flow of Magni's spark that he'd imbued the circle with to keep it running while manipulating the actual, physical runes with nudges of her telekinesis. Slowly but surely, she perfected the circle until it was a work of art, and in the meantime she added personal exceptions for herself and Siobhan, allowing them to cross it at their leisure.

'Uh, V-Vess? I don't mean to complain but can you uhm, wrap it up?'

Vess' eyes widened. *'Shit! Sorry!'*

Vess closed the circuit and completed the loop before backing out of the spell matrix and re-establishing the proxy's usual distance. The moment the burden lifted from Wally, even her physical body let out a sigh of relief. Her astral presence was thready and weak, and Vess reached out across the proxy to impart an apology laced with a surge of her own willpower.

'Gods, Wally, I'm so sorry, I . . .' Vess drew back as shame welled up in her. *'It's just been so long, I . . . I'd forgotten what it was like! I got caught up and—'*

Vess was silenced by a sound like a clarion chorus mixed with the tactile sensation of warm silk pajamas on her skin and the floral scent of a garden in bloom.

'It's okay, I promise I'm alright.'

'O-Okay, I'll be more careful next time.' Vess opened her eyes and stepped back from the ward.

All of that had happened in under a minute. Magic at the speed of thought. Gods, how long had it been since she'd been able to just *cast* like that? How long since she'd gotten five knuckles deep into fifth base on someone else's spell and just *fixed it* like it was her job?

"Alright, we're good," Vess said, gesturing to the ward. "Let's get to work, ladies."

Before Jemma, Polly, or Siobhan could say anything, Vess took a quick step across the warding line. Jemma let out a sharp, half-formed noise of concern that trailed off with a weak noise of disbelief.

"What . . . how?" Jemma looked up at Vess who grinned toothily.

"Wally's a hell of a proxy, that's how," she replied.

'Vess!'

'What? It's true,' Vess replied to Wally's weak protestation as she turned to look up at the excluded floors. *'If it weren't for you I'd barely be able to get Siobhan and I across without breaching the ward! With you, it's child's play!'*

Polly moved past her with Jemma and Siobhan in tow as she drew her machetes, then shot a look over her shoulder at Vess.

"You coming, Gibs?"

Vess made a quiet huff and nodded.

"Yeah, I'm coming," she said quietly.

Something about the zone they were walking into felt off. It wasn't big but it was potent. Stronger than it ought to be for something confined to a handful of floors. Vess followed her team in, flickering to close the distance as they moved into the main lobby. Siobhan entered first, axe up and shoulders squared with Polly moving in her blind spot. Jemma took up the middle while Vess performed back-to-back mental scans of their surroundings.

"First floor's clear," Vess said as they stepped in. "Second and third floor, too . . . it's getting fuzzier the closer we get to the exclusion, though."

"If there's anyone still on the fourth floor or higher, they're not human anymore, I guarantee it," Jemma said grimly.

As much as she hated to admit it, Vess agreed. The place was already infested. If the exclusion swallowed four whole floors it was almost a guarantee that the corpses and spectrals in the building would be moving boldly downwards, and destroying them would be ultimately pointless since all of their gathered necrotic miasma would just flow back into the exclusion rather than dispersing as it should.

"Do you hear that?" Siobhan said softly as she approached one of the far walls and lowered her axe.

Putting out her free hand, she pressed her open palm to the wall and closed her eyes, and her foot began to tap to an odd rhythm.

Polly moved to Siobhan's side and put her hand out next to the Dreadnoughts. "What are you—? Oh . . . that's . . ."

Despite lacking a physical body, Vess' stomach flipped and she lunged out to grab onto Jemma's shoulder as she moved to join Polly and Siobhan.

"Don't," Vess hissed. "There's something wrong!"

Jemma scowled, then looked back to Polly and Siobhan. They weren't moving. They were barely breathing. Something *was* wrong. Vess held out an arm between Jemma and the other two and stepped closer. There was a sickly sound in the air; a grinding, twisting, thumping beat that put the oily smell of incense in Vess' nose.

'I don't like that sound, Vess,' Wally muttered, and Vess felt her withdraw deep into the proxy. *'Make it stop . . . please make it stop!'*

Vess let her war-form bleed out around her. Her dark coat burst into a living, snapping mantle of shadows. Her skin boiled to a ruddy red and her veins ran blue with vicious ice. Hideous claws split out from her fingers that she jabbed into Siobhan's dense skin, and Vess used the connection to send a pulse of necrotic energy into her, briefly disrupting her mind-body connection, and Siobhan stumbled away from the wall, her eyes wide and haunted as she stared at it.

"You alright, Vonnie?" Vess asked without turning.

"F-Fine," Siobhan gasped. "Sort of."

A full-body shake had settled into Siobhan's bones as she put the head of her axe to the floor and leaned her weight against it. She looked, for all the world, like a woman trying desperately to catch her breath despite the fact that she hadn't breathed in decades.

Stepping up beside Polly, Vess put a hand on her shoulder and tried to drag her away from the wall. The moment she pulled, Polly tensed, dug in her heels, and pushed back, and a faint trickle of milky, pinkish blood leaked from her nose.

"Shit," Vess let go and instantly Polly relaxed.

"What's wrong?" Jemma's eyes were wide, but she was, thankfully, doing as Vess had told her and staying back.

Rather than answer, Vess let her mind slip across the surface of Polly's, just enough to find the edges of her surface thoughts. There weren't any. There was just the thunder of bass and a dull, atonal chanting underpinning it all. It was drowning everything out as it pried apart the wrinkles in the meat of her brain, slithering in and—

'Hey, Wally?'

'Uhm, y-yeah?'

'You're gonna want to shut yourself down for this next part.'

She didn't answer, but Vess felt Wally take her advice to heart and retreat deep into the proxy. Once Vess was certain that all of Wally's physical senses were disconnected, she reached out, and put a hand on either side of Polly's head.

"Jemma, close your eyes!"

There was no time to wait and see if Jemma obeyed. Polly didn't have that kind of time. That noise. Those words. That *chant*. Vess couldn't allow those words to seed themselves in Polly's subconscious. *That* would be a fate worse than death.

"Sorry Pols," Vess muttered, then tensed, flexed, and *pushed*.

Polly Truelight's skull cracked and splintered like rotten firewood, and she crumpled bonelessly to the floor. Vess grimaced as she shook blood and other more wretched fluids from her hands as Polly twitched spasmodically on the ground beneath her.

Somewhere behind Vess, Jemma was throwing up.

Damn it. She'd told her to close her eyes. Then again, maybe it was the smell.

Slowly, Polly's skull knit itself back together. Normally, brain damage was something that not even a regenerator wanted to try to shrug off, but Polly was tougher than most. In truth, she was an absolute freak of nature. Vess had *never* seen a biomantic heal like her, but she was still probably going to wake up tomorrow with the mother of all migraines. It took her almost three whole minutes, which was saying something for Polly, who could regrow an entire shorn limb in a handful of seconds if she was actually trying. By the time she was sitting up and cradling her head like it was made of glass and filled with bees, Jemma had gotten control of her stomach and Siobhan was looking steadier on her feet.

"What happened?" Polly mumbled as she smacked her lips. "And why do I taste spinal fluid?"

"You and Siobhan got caught in an enchantment," Vess replied as she reached through the proxy to nudge Wally and let her know it was safe to come back out.

Polly frowned. "How? The last thing I remember . . ."

"The beat." Siobhan looked up at the wall and grimaced. "That sound . . . I can still hear it."

"Try not to," Vess said in a strained voice. "It's emanating from the exclusion all the way down here, and if you let it inside your mind it will start making . . . changes."

'Vess, are we going to be okay?' Wally asked softly.

'We'll be fine, I know this spell, it's only dangerous if you don't know how to drown it out.'

Of course, the larger problem was that she knew the spell.

No one else alive should know it. Not anymore.

"Stay close to me," Vess said as she motioned for them to advance. "I'm going to project a . . ." she trailed off, then looked back at her team. "It's called a murmur, and it's basically telepathic white noise. It should shield you from the effects of the enchantment. It's short-range, though, so it loses effectiveness after about five meters."

"Five meters isn't much to work with," Jemma said grimly.

"Would you rather have an unspeakable sentience pry open your brain and carve graffiti into the meat?" Vess asked dryly, and Jemma blanched.

"Yeah, I didn't think so."

Their formation shifted, keeping Siobhan at the fore while Polly took up the rear while Jemma stayed glued to Vess' as they advanced to the elevator shaft. That beat was all around them, but with the murmur hedging it out, none of them fell victim to that unpleasant trance state. Good thing it hadn't been Jemma who touched the wall otherwise Vess would have had to go in after her manually. It was doable, but she didn't want to vouch for Jemma's condition once she got out.

Siobhan jabbed the call button for the elevator, but there was not response.

"Can you crack these open?" Vess asked, nodding at the closed elevator doors, and Siobhan's smile stretched to that wide, unhealthy rictus as she hefted her axe, gave it a few test swings, and slid her food back, braced, and swung in a hard downward arc. The smile of the axe bit deep into the metal seam dividing the doors, and Siobhan put her necrotic muscle to work prying it open.

The elevator itself was stuck about three-quarters of the way down from the second floor.

"Naturally," Vess muttered. *'Wally? Shoulder for me. I just need to drag that thing down.'*

'Of course.'

Gods it was far too easy to get addicted to the feeling of being so close to her. Not just to her body but to her mind. Her spirit. Wally was so *good*. It wasn't just the feeling of comfort from having her take the burden of casting. It was so much more than that. It was the feeling of not being alone. Of being trusted and . . . and loved. That last one especially, at least she thought so. That was a new one. What she'd had before? That wasn't love. What she had with Wally? It might be.

Putting *that* thought out of her mind, Vess let Wally take on the simple chore of handling the background of her telekinesis. It wasn't that she couldn't do this on her own, but it would preserve her energy for what was coming, and Vess had the unpleasant feeling that she was going to need it.

"First floor—bad music, dead people, and tired lesbians," Vess remarked as she mentally gripped the elevator and dragged it down.

It ground noisily along its rails until it reached the first floor. The internal doors were still closed, fortunately, they had a key that was shaped suspiciously like an enormous dead woman with an axe.

"Vonnie?"

"On it." Siobhan stepped in and swung hard, digging the blade into the doors before pushing hard to—

"*SCREEEEEEEEEEE~!*"

"MOTHERFUCKER!"

Vess flickered back as the door exploded open and an oily black stalker tore its way out of the elevator cab, its long, bony, blade-tipped limbs thrashing wildly. Siobhan cursed as her left arm went flying, and Jemma nearly lost part of her nose before Polly dragged her back. The stalker's sinuous body snapped like an eel in midair as it lunged at Polly and Jemma, the two most obvious sources of actual *life* in the room, with a tinny shriek. Siobhan buried her axe it deep into the stalker's meaty back as it dove past her, and the dreadnought levered the thrashing corpse down, keeping it pinned as Polly snapped her machetes out of their sheaths and darted forward like starlight dancing across still water.

The Stalker's head went flying along with two of its limbs as Polly executed a flensing pattern of hacking strikes, and she dove to the side as Jemma followed with her right arm stretched out fully.

"*Akur take you!*" Jemma snarled as she plunged her hand and arm down to her elbow into the thing's hideous body.

Jemma glowed with a grim, ominous light as the stalker crumpled, bit by bit, collapsing in on itself with a sickening snapping noise before disintegrating into ash.

"Gods *damn* I hate those things!" Vess cursed as she stood from where she'd landed in a crouch.

"Let's keep that to a minimum," Jemma gasped out. "I can't consume many of them if they're all that . . . meaty."

"Agreed," Vess said, "and good thinking, by the way," she nodded to the soot that was all that was left of the stalker. "That was some impressive work, Jem, I mean it."

Despite her dark complexion, Jemma's cheeks colored, and she smiled. It was an impressive bit of spellcraft, wielding the hunger of a daemon-god like that. Feeding that thing to the Master of Daemons would at least mean its power wouldn't return to the exclusion.

In the back of Vess' mind, Wally was still shivering and trying to pull herself back together. She'd fled to the furthest extent of the proxy when the stalker had made its attack and, to be fair,

Vess didn't blame her. She hadn't expected an entire-ass stalker to have wedged itself inside the elevator cab either, and she already knew Wally was no great fan of jump-scares.

"Oh, gross," Polly recoiled from the cab and wrinkled her nose. "Guess the last few evacuees didn't uh . . . quite make it."

Vess clicked her tongue and scowled. "We'll make it up to them as best we can," she said quietly as she moved past Polly, Jemma, and Siobhan, and stepped into the cab amidst the ruin of broken bones and shredded flesh the stalker had left behind.

"Yeah," Polly muttered as she stepped gingerly inside. "For now, we have a job to do."

Siobhan followed with Jemma behind her, the latter of which paused at the sight before her, closed her eyes, then stepped inside.

"May Akur find your souls," she whispered as she passed a hand in benediction over the mess, "and may your miseries be lighter in your next life."

Not likely, Vess thought, but for once she kept those opinions to herself. Maybe Wally *was* rubbing off on her.

CHAPTER 25

WALLY WILLOWBARK FLOATED BODILESS in the depths of the proxy as the strain of Vess' casting began to settle across her mind. Gods, she was so powerful; moreso than Wally had imagined, and her imagination hadn't been modest about it. It was just that, the way Vess used magic? It was breathtaking.

'*You ready?*'

'*Ready.*'

She was more than ready. Despite how much it taxed her, being this close to Vess while she moved magic was worth it. It was like being allowed to stand beside a master illuminator and watch them filigree parchment with gold and silver leaf.

'*Okay, here we go.*'

The pressure doubled, then tripled on Wally's mind as Vess wrapped the whole of the elevator cab in a sheath of telekinetic energy, and began to lift. The cab shuddered as it ascended the floors, but even with this kind of brute-force method of magic, Wally marveled at Vess' expertise. She wasn't just seizing the elevator in an invisible fist and lifting, she was manipulating all of the fine mechanisms of the lift itself. The gyros and the cogs, the wire and winch, everything was moving according to her will and she was doing it all manually, which was staggering. Most telekines could only manipulate two or three distinct objects at a time unless they were familiar with them. A talented one might be able to manage a half-dozen. That limit was due to the fact that they had to create a precise and differing amount of kinetic pressure on all sides of the object to achieve lift without breaking anything. So in order to lift, say, a vase, a mug, and a plate, they would have to produce that pressure on all sides of each individual object, each of which would require different amounts of force applied to different curvatures of surface area.

In other words, when given the option, Wally had opted out of the telekine course back at uni because it turned out to require an absolute *fuckton* of calculus and Wally hated math. It did, however, give Wally the perspective to appreciate that Vess, in that moment, was manipulating over twenty distinct objects, including fine machinery and cables. It wasn't dissimilar to one person playing every section of a full orchestra by themselves at the same time! It wasn't just a matter of power, it was a matter of precision and attention. Vess was attending to a thousand tiny details every moment that she raised the lift, and the best Wally could do was handle the background load—the most basic thaumic power equations and calculations—and provide an extra well of spark for her to tap into while she watched Vess performed a feat of magic that would be considered the next best thing to a miracle if the person watching understood enough to appreciate what they were seeing.

"We just passed the fifth floor," Vess hissed through gritted teeth. "When I open the door—"

"Get ready to axe some questions?" Siobhan offered.

Jemma and Polly both snorted and Vess rolled her eyes, while Wally, on the other hand . . .

'Will you stop laughing? It wasn't that funny!'

'Th-That was hilarious! C'mon! Axe! Like ask but—'

'Yes, I get it, ugh, Gods, of course I'd fall for someone with a garbage sense of humor.'

Wally's presence rippled with indignation.

'Excuse you, but puns are the highest linguistic form of humor! Making a good pun requires the greatest level of language fluency.'

'I would agree with you save for one crucial hole in your argument,'

Vess replied.

'And what's that?' Wally asked, her suspicion wafting across the proxy like a cloud of cloying jasmine.

'There are no good puns.'

'For the sake of our relationship I'm going to pretend I didn't hear that.'

Vess huffed. 'You wound me. Are we building our love on lies now?'

Wally couldn't contain her mirth any longer, and it rippled over the proxy in a flood. The light of it danced over Vess, illuminating her smile in gold and silver as her laughter joined Wally's. It was a beautiful sound, hearth-warm and husky, and it made Wally smile all the wider.

The rock and rattle of the cab reaching the sixth floor and locking into place dropped them back into silence, and Wally's smile faded.

"Get ready to fight, ladies," Vess grunted as she withdrew her telekinetic sheath from the cab and steadied herself.

'Can I ask why we didn't just go in through the window?' Wally ventured softly. 'Wouldn't it have been easier?'

Vess shook her head.

'Exclusions aren't permeable bubbles, Wally, they're fortresses,' She replied grimly. 'They can only be entered and exited at certain points, usually thresholds. The exclusion zone's border is always thinnest in places where people have moved in and out because the world remembers it as a place of passage.'

'That's . . . Way-Magic, isn't it? Passing and threshold arts?'

'Is that what they call it now? Hm. We used to call it fairy-law.'

Fairy-law? Wally tucked that away in the back of her mind for later. Fairy-law was a *very* old term for the magic governing passage between places of power.

"Moving out," Siobhan said as she slipped between Vess and the door, wedged the blade of her axe into the sixth floor doors, and wrenched them apart.

There was no shrieking corpse waiting for them on the other side this time, just an eerie silence disrupted occasionally by an ugly, atonal beat that stirred the stagnant air. Siobhan took a deep breath, though it wasn't air she was truly inhaling. Miasma flooded her limbs, energizing her muscles and suffusing her bones, and Siobhan's grin widened as her slowly regenerating left arm congealed back together.

"Still with me, Vonnie?" Vess asked cautiously as she followed the large woman out.

"Still with you, Gibs," Siobhan replied. "Just getting a taste for the atmosphere."

Jemma and Polly emerged on their heels, their hands held over their noses and mouths.

"Gods, I could have lived my whole life never stepping into another one of these things," Polly muttered.

"Don't invoke the Gods so casually, Polly," Jemma replied in an uncharacteristically somber tone. "We are closer to their homes than ours right now."

"Think your patron could make a house call, then?" Polly asked blithely as she turned to keep her gaze leveled opposite of Siobhan.

"Don't tempt him."

"She's right and you know it," Siobhan said quietly. "The spirits are close here. Daemons are closer. This place is far from the borders of the Hedge and the other bright, living places of the Otherside," she raised her axe and scraped it along the wall, making a deep furrow, "we should be cautious until we know where this marble of reality rests in the Dream Eternal."

'The Dream Eternal?' Wally echoed.

'It's an old name for the collective cosmology of the planes, the upper realms of the Gods, the lower realms of the daemons, and all the middle realms, too like the Hedge of the Fair Ones.'

It wasn't a name that Wally was familiar with, but in fairness there were as many names for the realms as a whole as there were cultures and peoples.

'Why call it a dream?' She asked as Siobhan led them down a dark, concrete hall stained with noisome fluids. Part of asking was to distract herself. The last thing Wally wanted to think about was being back in an exclusion zone, even if she wasn't physically there.

'Because that's what we are,' Vess replied softly. *'Because the world is sleeping and it's dreaming of trees and mountains and oceans and strange*

little creatures who build strange little structures, then put on strange little hats and call themselves kings.'

A dull bass thrum made the air around them shake, and Siobhan scowled. "Anyone else feel like it's far too quiet for an infested exclusion zone?"

"I was trying not to think about it, thanks," Polly replied dryly.

Siobhan carved another mark in the wall, and said, "This is going to go badly."

Jemma made a quiet growl in the back of her throat, and shook her head. "Then it goes badly, we still have a damn job to do."

"Enough." Vess held up a hand and scowled. "We're not doing anyone any favors by bickering, but yeah . . . we should be wading through necrotics right now, this doesn't make any sense."

'Vess . . . listen.'

'I told you to ignore the sound, Wally.'

'No, listen! It's changin—!'

The explosion came down the hall riding the paradox of a slow-patterned bassline, *Da-da-dum*, like an arrhythmic heart, and the walls cracked, the floor shattered, and the world spun on its axis. The hallway flew apart, exposing them to a screaming alien vista that stretched to eternity. In the distance, Wally saw something like a sun, but whose color was drenched in film negative hues that made her stomach curl. Chaotic strings and drums and flutes filled the air along with strange voices in a language that made Wally want to vomit. Jemma was on the floor clutching her head and screaming, and Polly was draped over her, trying to shield her like a mother covering her child. Siobhan was staring, her eyes blown wide and her jaw slack.

Only Vess stayed cogent.

'SHUT YOUR EYES!'

Wally closed off her perceptions. She blacked out her vision, plugged her ears, drew back from their shared skin and blanked out everything, but despite that she could still feel that image worming its way through her mind.

Ba-ba-bum.

That bassline struck through Wally's self-imposed numbness and collapsed the world. Despite herself, Wally opened her eyes. She forced herself to keep track of everything. Vess grabbed onto Polly and Jemma and dragged them with her towards Siobhan as the deafening impacts of concrete slammed down over and over. The walls and the floor. Everything was coming down in a different order.

Da-dum.

The last block slid into place with an echoing thud, and suddenly it was quiet. If Wally still had a heart it would be hammering. Vess was hunkered down over Polly who was curled protectively over a terrified Jemma, while Siobhan stood over the lot of them, axe up and muscles tensed.

"It's okay, Jem, it's okay," Polly was murmuring, "you're okay, we've got you." She sat down and pulled the young half-elf into her arms and cradled her as she looked up at Vess with wide eyes. "Gibs . . . what was that?"

Vess worked her jaw silently for a moment, and Wally could feel the turmoil roiling through her. She followed the thread of the proxy, soothing the torment where she found it until she reached Vess herself, and pulsed through a reminder that she wasn't alone.

'I'm still here.'

Nodding, Vess licked her lips and reached out to pat Siobhan on the arm to let her know to stand down. "That was the Dreamtime . . . somewhere far beyond the Gate of Horn." Vess curled her clawed fingers into a fist, and Wally had to draw back her tactile sense as she dug into her own skin. "But that's irrelevant now, we need to get out of here."

"Out . . . what?" Polly stared up at Vess. "You're joking, right? We have a job to do, Gibs," she jerked a hand out and around them, "we're not just abandoning this!"

A freezing cold settled around Wally, it felt like rime forming over Vess' soul. It was an alien feeling. Wally had no idea how to define this sensation that was bleeding across the proxy to her.

"We *are* abandoning this, Pols," Vess said in a flat, iron tone.

"We are going to tuck our tails, bow our heads, and run from this, because with all due respect and all the love in my heart, fuck this," she pointed to the ground, "fuck that," she jabbed a finger down the hall, "and *fuck you*."

'Terror.'

'What?!' Vess snapped, turning her attention inward.

Wally realized what it was the moment Vess' voice started to crack. This wasn't fear, like the panic attack that had struck her in the training room and severed their link. This was terror. Bone-deep terror. The kind that chills the soul and turns the bowels to water. The kind that leaves your mouth dry, your throat convulsing, and your legs simultaneously itching to flee and locked in place.

Vess was terrified.

'You're scared,' Wally said quietly. *'You're . . . actually scared.'*

'Of course I'm scared! Are you kidding me?! Did you not see that?!' There was no real 'volume' in the proxy, but Wally winced at the sharpness of Vess' voice.

'No! I didn't!' Wally countered. *'I have no idea what I saw! And I don't think they did either! You can't just tell us to abandon everything without a—a damn good reason!'*

Wally could feel Vess grinding her teeth. Polly was staring furiously up at her, trying her best to calm Jemma was also staring up at Vess, in shock rather than anger. Siobhan seemed to be waiting, phlegmatic and ready for action, however it went.

'Talk to them, Vess,' Wally pleaded. *'Talk to me.'*

Despite the numbing cold of Vess' terror, Wally reached across the thread of the proxy, thawing the ice with as much affection as she could. Vess shuddered, bit her lip, and nodded.

'I . . . I'm sorry,' she whispered across the thread. *'You're right. Sorry.'*

'I know.' Wally closed the distance between them, briefly moving as if to shoulder one of her spells. There was no spellcraft to take up, but the closeness helped.

At least, Wally hoped it did.

On the outside, Vess opened her eyes, and looked down at Polly.

"I'm sorry," Vess began quietly. "But we *do* need to leave. This isn't a normal exclusion zone we're standing in, it's a domain, and whatever corpse or spectral owns this place," she gestured out around them, "is strong enough to manipulate its physical structure."

A bovine stare was Polly's initial response until she snapped out of it, shook her head vehemently, and said, "That's not possible."

"I don't give a damn if it's possible," Vess snapped. "That's what this place is, whether it's possible or not!"

"This place was just excluded!" Polly shouted. "A domain takes *years* to form . . . naturally . . ." she trailed off and her face went bloodless.

"Did the coin just drop?" Vess asked bitterly.

"The cult ritual?" Polly asked hollowly.

Vess nodded. "Yeah, this is . . . it's a real nightmare of a working. Someone did this on purpose, but at least now we know where all the necrotics went."

'*What do you mean?*' Wally had been following, mostly, up until that point. '*Where did they go?*'

Vess huffed and her mouth stretched to a humorless grin that was less smile and more sharp shark-teeth.

'*It takes a lot of miasma for a necrotic to yoke control of a whole demiplane to its will, even—*' she nodded around them— '*a comparatively small one like this. It takes decades of existence and feeding to build up that kind of power, unless, of course, someone happened to make a spell that could funnel the miasma of hundreds of manifested necrotics into one place and shove it down the gullet of a specially prepared vessel.*'

A . . . vessel?

"It's unstable, though." Vess reached out and scraped her claws against the concrete. "This whole place . . . it's coming apart at the seams. The one at the middle of all of this isn't strong enough to hold it for long and when they pop that five-block cordon won't be anything like enough room."

"Then we have to stay!" Polly snapped.

"And do what?" Vess flicked her gaze down to Polly derisively. "Die on them?"

Polly's jaw hung open, and even Jemma was looking hurt at the disdain in Vess' voice.

'Vess, are you saying we just abandon hope?' Wally asked quietly.

"Abandon hope?" Vess replied aloud as she tapped her temple. "Wally . . . there was never any hope here to begin with, and I'm not losing the closest thing I have to a family to this shitstain."

"That's not what you said when you went into Bressig!" Polly spat.

Vess froze. The proxy thread froze. Everything on the inside of Vess' mind simply froze. Deep within the proxy, Wally sat poleaxed as she tried to process what she'd just heard.

"You *bitch*," Vess snarled.

Polly Truelight's throat bobbed as she swallowed thickly and drew back from the furious apparition in front of her. Vess advanced on her with murder in her heart as she flexed her claws, cracking her knuckles with the motion alone.

'V-Vess?'

'Not now.'

'YES NOW!'

For the first time, Wally didn't just follow the thread, she didn't just lay a hand on it. This time, Wally grabbed hold of the thread that bound them and *heaved*. Silver light and fire flared in the dark and Vess' astral body went slack and crumpled to the floor like a doll as her consciousness was hauled out of it. The magic and the shape remained, but the animation was gone. There was a sharp pain as the twin consciousnesses of Vess Gibson and Wally Willowbark collided with one another. They tumbled in the shadows of their shared mental space and Vess let out a sharp cry as Wally kept hold of her.

'Wally stop! You have to stop!'

'You lied to me!' Wally snarled, the deep ache in her heart spilling out across them in ruddy red light. *'You were at Bressig?!'*

'I never said I wasn't! You . . . You never asked!'

'OH THAT IS SUCH HORSESHIT!' Wally shoved Vess away furiously. *'You were there and you didn't think to maybe mention that?!'* Not a lie, maybe. It was true that Wally had never asked, but she

shouldn't have had to! Vess knew where Wally had come from! *'Why didn't you say anything!'*

'BECAUSE I DIDN'T WANT YOU TO OWE ME ANYTHING!'

The ache numbed and the light dissipated to a dull aqua shade surrounding them as the pair of them floated in the dark. Wally stared across at Vess, knowing and *feeling* that she was telling the truth, but . . . but it still hurt.

'I didn't want it between us, okay?' Vess sobbed. *'I didn't want you to know because it doesn't matter!'*

'It doesn't matter to you, *Vess!'* Wally's tone was wet with angry tears as she gave Vess a hard mental shove. *'It matters to me! I can barely remember what happened! It's the thing that's defined me my whole life and I can't even remember it!'* Her chest heaved and the aqua light leaking from the wound in her heart deepened to a heavy navy blue. *'I lost everything to Bressig! I lost my home, my family! I lost my* life, *Vess!'*

Vess worked her jaw for several moments, then swallowed hard and drew in on herself. Her form was washed in deep, deep blue, and it clashed with her fiery hair, and yet somehow those eyes of hers still pierced the darkness.

'You're so fucking selfish, Vess,' Wally continued bitterly. *'Did you even think that maybe I would want to know? Or that maybe I'd want to talk about it? Did you even think about me at all?!'*

For a long, long moment, Vess hung there in the darkness in front of Wally, utterly defeated. She looked like someone had run her through and left her pinned to the wall like an insect on a corkboard.

The shade of blue softened to a clinging shade of turquoise that was thick with emotion as Wally bit out: *'You're a* louse, *Vess Gibson.'*

Vess just nodded.

'I'm sorry, y-you're right, I didn't think,' she replied after a short stretch of silence. *'I was afraid you'd . . . no, I . . . fuck,'* Vess shook her head angrily, *'I was just scared you might not want me, or something . . . I don't know.'*

Wally trembled in the depths of her mind. Rage and fury bubbled out of her and around her, and she shook with it. The world around her shook with it. The cloying color redshifted, drenching them both in shades of gore as Wally glared at Vess.

'*You . . . You don't get to just make that decision for me!*' Wally hissed. '*I don't care if you want to keep your past in the past, Vess, but Bressig killed me* twice—'

'*—beg pardon?—*'

'*—and you don't have the right to hide my past along with yours if you had a part in it!*' Wally ran over her interjection with the unyielding momentum of a falling cinder block.

They stared at one another through a grim film of red rage. Silver flames licked across Wally's soul like moonlight off of water. It lit her eyes, too, turning what was once a soft brown to searing starlight that was almost blinding.

'*You owed it to me to at least tell me!*' Wally finished furiously.

Despite her power. Despite her age. Despite everything she could do, Vess looked for all the world like a whipped dog. She drew back, curling in on herself with wide, brittle fear in her eyes, and suddenly Wally felt a surge of regret. Hadn't Vess just told her? Had she just confided that the last person she'd given her heart to had abused it without a care? None of that made Vess' decision right. Her fear didn't justify anything, but still . . .

'*I'm sorry,*' Vess sobbed as she lowered her head and curled into a floating ball of misery in front of Wally. '*Y-You're right, I just . . . I wasn't thinking.*'

'*You're not allowed to do that ever again, okay?*' Wally said softly. '*You're not allowed to just ignore me like that.*' Vess looked up with a spark of fragile hope in her eyes. '*We're not leaving here, understand? We're not leaving the Fifth to die, and we're not letting the exclusion break. If you stopped Bressig, then you can stop this, right?*'

Her face fell, and she glanced away.

'*That's . . . I'm not as strong as I was before,*' she replied. '*It was before I had a proxy, and before I really needed one. I dropped three out of my five restraints and overburnt myself to seal Bressig but it blew out my lambda system. I can't do it again.*'

'*Restraint level . . . two, right?*' Wally said, and Vess nodded.

She chewed on that for a moment, then sighed.

'*Do you trust me, Vess Gibson?*' Wally asked.

Vess looked up with a frown.

'I . . . yeah, I do.'

'Good, because even if you don't deserve it right now, I trust you, too.' Wally drifted closer as her anger faded, and the red shadows softened to a gentle green like sunlight filtering through leaves. 'I trust that you'll protect me, okay?'

Vess shook her head. 'Wally, no, we aren't—! You've never even proxied at level four!'

'Will four be enough?' Wally asked sharply.

The look on Vess' face was all the answer she needed. If it took her at level two to bring down Bressig, then two was probably the best bet.

'Maybe . . . three?' Vess put in weakly.

'Are you sure?'

Vess sighed and shook her head.

'Then do it.'

Wally grabbed Vess by the hand, their proxied forms melding for a moment as Wally bled her honest trust into Vess. It was fragile, but it was still there.

'I don't want to be the one who hurts you,' Vess said quietly.

'You already hurt me,' Wally replied, and Vess flinched, but Wally didn't let go. 'But you weren't trying to, you're just kind of . . . dumb,' she continued with a weak smile.

'Trust me,' Wally finished. 'I can take it.'

Heaving a quiet sigh, Vess nodded, and together they rose up through the nullspace of the proxy, and Vess' consciousness bled back into her physical form, bringing Wally with it.

'By the way . . . where uhm, where did we go?' Wally asked pensively.

'Your mind,' Vess replied as her body twitched back to life and stood up, earning shouts of alarm from Polly and Jemma. 'Sort of like how you're with me right now, you dragged me to you. That was how Dolin got control enough to turn off my restraints manually.'

'Oh . . . I didn't know I could do that.'

'This is two-way, remember?' Vess said as she rolled her neck and shoulders. 'It's supposed to be a partnership of equals, that's how the proxy works . . . now, are you sure? Even Dolin never touched level two.'

'I'm better than him,' Wally said firmly, and for once she really believed it.

She believed that she was actually good at something. It was, honestly, kind of a novel and terrifying experience for her.

"Vess?" Polly started, and Vess held a hand up.

"We're staying," Vess said simply. "And you're all going to get behind me, because I'm about to run hot."

Polly's eyes widened and she grabbed Jemma and staggered back. "How hot?"

'Do I need to do that again? To turn it off?' Wally asked.

'No, so long as we're in agreement I can do it from here, so . . .' Vess cleared her throat and said aloud. "Wally Willowbark, do I have your full and knowing consent to lift restraints five, four, and three, til battle is done and the foe is made silent?"

Wally vacillated for a moment as a weight of power fell over her. It was a ritual of some kind, obviously. There was no time to ask for a greater explanation, though.

'You have my consent, Vess Gibson.'

"So mote it be." Vess lifted her hands to either side of her head and splayed her fingers. "Conditions have been met to initialize the restraint release program." The blue of Vess' eyes flared and her miasma redoubled on itself, and suddenly Wally felt like she was choking. "Invert the Ro Invocation, reverse process from canto twenty-five to canto ten, releasing limiter restraints five through three in three . . . two . . . one."

CHAPTER 26

Far below on the streets of Colvus, Erik Mizer was crouched on one knee with his fingers laced praying fervently to the spirits. Something had gone wrong, of that much he was certain. His team had yet to check in since entering the exclusion which was definitely bad, but whatever it was clearly wasn't bad enough to break the proxy. If Vess' projected form had taken enough damage to suffer disjunction it would have thrown both her mind and Wally's back into their bodies, and Mizer trusted that, so long as Vess still stood strong, his team would be safe.

The question then of course became: what if?

What if whatever was going on up there *was* strong enough to disjoin the proxy? What if Vess wasn't able to keep them safe?

"Hear me, spirits of all, I implore thee, walk with they who share my home and hospitality and safeguard them through their trials," Mizer murmured.

The steady rumble of a powerful, high-grade engine broke through his meditations, and Mizer grit his teeth as a sudden flash of anger coursed through him.

"No," he hissed. "Not now!"

Mizer flicked his gaze to the side to where a four-door Model-V Phoenix had pulled up along the empty stretch of road to park. It was painfully bright ivory chased in gold, with deep, broad wheel-wells, a high-roofed cab, and an enormous engine grill stained silver and emblazoned with the sunburst insignia of Ys the Illuminator.

A tall, narrowly built half-elven man with a look of graceful age about him stepped out of the driver's seat and moved back to open the rear door.

"Ma'am," the driver said as he stepped back with a low bow.

The click of metal on asphalt sounded as armored boots struck the street, and the Model-V gave a slight heave as if a great weight had suddenly been lifted off of it as the boots' owner emerged and stood straight.

Even in the dark of the night, what little light there was from the city and the street lamps seemed to reflect a hundredfold off of her shining plate armor. The breastplate and faulds were decorated in images of angels and dragons rampant cast in polished silver, and her broad pauldrons and gorget shone with her symbols of office. At her throat was the monad, the most ancient numeral for 'One'. On her right pauldron, she bore the insignia of Ys, a wingless dragon coiled around a sunburst on a field of gold and on her left was the heraldric symbol of the House Truelight: a downthrust blade over two crossed spears resting against a sunburst field to show the House's long devotion to Ys, and framed by words written in old Oreliaun elven.

'Cast In The Light Of Our God, We Are True.'

"Erik Mizer!" Her voice was the tenor clarion of a trained chorister. "Rejoice, for your salvation has arrived!" She spread her gauntleted hands wide and Mizer's expression twisted.

Her long hair flapped in the evening breeze like a banner of liquid gold, and her sharp, sky-blue eyes were open wide on a fair face over a smile that showed teeth so white that Mizer could probably have checked his reflection in them.

"What do you want, Cass?" Mizer snapped. "This is Fifth Precinct jurisdiction! We are here as reinforcements, but you are *not* welcome."

Still smiling, Cassidia gestured for her driver to leave, and he obeyed with the alacrity of someone used to taking orders. As the vehicle rumbled away, she lowered her arms and laid a hand over her heart, her unchanging grin still soldered in place.

"Erik, you *wound me*," she replied as she towered over him. "To think you would imagine that I, a Paladin of Ys, would come here against the laws of the Accord? Do your heresies know no bounds?!"

Gods, Mizer always forgot how tall she was. Polly was tiny but, for some reason, the three Truelight sisters had an inverse height-to-age relationship. Cassidia might have been the youngest but she stood six foot and six and was monstrously broad, and that was without her enchanted Silversteel plate.

Standing up, Mizer squared his shoulders against the woman.

"This is still an ongoing dispersal, Cass, so get your bright and shiny arse out of the cordon or so help me I—"

"This is *not*—" Cassidia bellowed over Mizer, stunning him backward— "dispersal business! I am here as an agent of Holy Ys! Be glad that my respect for you is such that I came to take control of this exclusion myself!"

"Bull*shit* you will," Mizer snapped. "The temple only has the right to interfere if the exclusion has *breached!*"

"INCORRECT!"

Mizer staggered back at her stentorian bellow as she shoved a gleaming finger under his nose.

"Agents of Ys may take control of any necrotic event whose miasma has reached critical mass!" She all but declaimed. "Can you not feel it, dear Erik?" She slung an arm over his shoulder and towed him around until they were both looking up at the housing project. "Can you not *feel* the wound in the world and foulness that rules it?! That is no mere exclusion!"

Normally, Mizer would have shoved Cass' arm off of his shoulders in a heartbeat, but her words had dropped his heart cleanly into his stomach and his limbs had gone weak.

No mere exclusion . . .

"Ah~, you feel it now, don't you? Even with your pagan soul, you can feel the corruption!" Cassidia gripped his shoulder in what might have been an act of comfort coming from anyone else.

It was difficult to tell, but while Cass may have been a variety of unpleasant things, she was a Paladin, not a liar.

"A . . . domain?" Mizer shook his head and gave a brittle laugh. "No, that's not possible, that would be the smallest domain in recorded history!"

"And yet," Cassidia gestured outward towards it, "there it—"

Her voice went silent with the finality of a cut throat as Cassidia Truelight's body dropped slack. The whole of her weight sagged as she fell to a knee with the clangor of a cracking church bell, and tremors rolled through her powerful body, setting her armor clattering against itself as she stared up at the housing project. Mizer felt it too, deep in his soul; a sudden and terrible premonition of disaster. It was the sensation of being chained to the ground and watching a blade falling point-down at his neck. Helplessness froze his limbs, spasmed his guts, and sent arcs of electric terror up his spine.

"*What is that?*" Cassidia breathed the words out as she raised both hands, palms up and outstretched to the heavens. "Heresy . . . vile and unspeakable heresy . . . vicious and tainted! Unholy! GODS! DEAR GODS! *WHAT IS THAT?!*"

Mizer bit his lip, shivered, and risked a glance over at the hearse. Thanks to the ongoing proxy spell, his senses were tuned to the spirits of water and air—air being the more operative one as it strengthened his hearing among other things. With that, he could hear Vess' sarcophagus cycling. He could hear the click and whir of her life support system, and the hum of the generator's spark cells.

He also heard the sound of three of Vess' five limiter restraint reliquaries go silent.

"Don't you dare fucking die on me, Magni!"

Isshin clutched her oldest friend to her chest as she knelt in the dust and filth of a studio apartment near the east corner of the Heights. Magni's long, pale hair, fair in his youth and made lighter with age, fell across her tattooed arms as he rested his head against her shoulder.

"I'll do—" a wracking cough choked his words for a moment before he mastered himself— "m-my best, Izzy."

Izzy. He hadn't called her that since they were both much, much younger, and he'd been specifically *trying* to get under her skin. She'd only just abandoned her monastery back then and still had a stick up her arse about a lot of things. She felt very lucky that Magni had had such a good sense of humor about her antics all those years ago. Mae lowered her head and pressed her face to his crown. Her lap was soaked in Baelion Magni's blood. Only his own magic sealing the wound had managed to keep him from losing more than just that.

"*Mae~Shii~*"

The familiar voice echoed dreamily through the halls, and Mae shivered. Something had gone wrong. Terribly wrong. From the moment the translation had trapped them, Mae had known that it wasn't a normal exclusion event. It was far too stable. It had taken her moments too long to realize why that was, though.

There were a lot of names for it; Lair. Reality Marble. Demiplane.

The most common one in the dispersal business, however, was 'Domain'.

"*Mae~~Shii~~*"

Mae clenched her jaw and focused, stilling her breathing and slowing her heart rate, then turned her remaining Qi in on itself to mask her and Magni's presence. If she was lucky, the one hunting them would pass by without noticing.

"I'm sorry," Mae muttered quietly to her second in command. "This has all gone so wrong."

"S'not your fault," Baelion rasped.

She wished she could see him and, at the same time, she was glad she couldn't. This way, she could still hold him in her mind's eye as she had before her eyes had been taken—with his fair, dry-humored smile and bright gray eyes. Now, his spine was broken, his legs were useless, and his guts were opened up. He was barely alive, and then only by dint of his powerful preservation magic.

Planes and layers of force and will were keeping his insides *inside* while what little healing magic he knew tried desperately to knit his ruined body. It wouldn't fix him, he wasn't a strong enough healer for that, but Isshin Mae prayed it would keep him alive long enough for extraction.

If they could just get him to the Temple of Jiani'Kai, then maybe . . .

"M-Mae?" Magni's voice was weaker, fainter than before.

"Sshh, save your strength."

"Th-The ward—!" Mae felt him move, felt him reaching out, and realized too late what he meant.

The same ward that was hedging out the deleterious mental effects of the domain would also be impossible to hide, regardless of how well she masked them.

A dull pair of thuds sounded against the cheap wooden door. It was a metal sound: lightweight, solid, and built for combat and ease of movement, and to interfere with its owner as little as possible since a dreadnought took her flesh and blood limb two years back.

"*Mae~Shii~*"

Idolatry Friese's voice had a junkie quality to it, it was the voice of someone whose sane mind was far, far away.

"Idol! *Please!*" Mae begged as the knocking grew louder and more insistent. "IDOL!"

Sanity was drowned by high, ecstatic laughter as the pounding on the door grew more frenetic. Cracks appeared on the surface as rapid staccato thumps and bangs rattled the door in its frame.

"Magni, will the ward keep her out?" Mae asked quietly.

"N-No," he replied. "You've—"

"—don't you dare finish that sentence, Magni, or I swear to all the gods I will kill you myself!" Mae snapped as she hugged him closer.

The door shattered and hung in pieces as Idolatry Friese stepped into the cramped little one-room apartment. Her soul burned fiercely with curse-tainted sickness, so much so that she was illuminated in Mae's vision like a soiled lantern. Dark, frizzy hair hung blood matted around her face and over eyes that swam with madness. Streaks of blood and mucus trailed from her tear ducts and her nose, and she licked cracked lips as she laughed shrilly.

Her arms, flesh and metal, hung numbly at her side as she staggered forward. "Listen! Listen, Mae-Shii!" Idol pleaded through bubbles of laughter. "The dreams! You can't imagine the dreams!"

"Enough!"

Baelion Magni snapped out a hand, his fingers twisting into a runic shape, and an arrow-thin spear of force lanced out of his palm. It was a killing shot, armor-piercing, the kind of thing wielded against necrosis-fueled dreadnoughts, not people.

The shot took Idol just above the left eye and drilled a coin-shaped hole in her skull, through and through.

"MAGNI!"

To Mae's senses, it was like a bolt of migraine-sharp sunlight had blown through Idol, who staggered drunkenly backward. She stood with her limbs hanging bonelessly around her like a pupped kept up by a single string. It was like her body wasn't quite sure she was dead yet.

"I'm s-sorry," Baelion coughed as he went slack. That kine-spear had taken the last of his strength.

Mae closed her eyes, wishing for the first time that she'd never learned to open her third eye to counteract her blindness. It was something that, once done, could not be undone.

An eye that could not close.

"*Mae~Shii~*"

"No . . ." Magni looked up weakly, and Isshin pulled him closer as she swallowed thickly.

Idol's body moved with stilted jerks as she straightened and grinned down at Mae and Magni, at her Chief, and her friend. There was nothing of Idolatry Friese's mind behind those glassy eyes, Isshin realized.

Nothing at all.

She was already dead.

Lowering Magni to the ground, onto the central axis of the ward-rune he'd laid into the floor before his wounds stole his strength, Mae stood, cracked her knuckles, and fixed her one-time subordinate with a pained glare.

"Goodnight, Idol," she murmured. "I'm so, so sorry."

Idol's smile was a horrible thing to look at, especially through the third eye.

The atmosphere of the excluded domain had a toxic quality to it. Something about it poisoned the mind and shredded the personality within. Magni hadn't had the opportunity to determine exactly what caused the mental infection, only that it was related to the nature of the domain itself, before both Idol and Yusuf had been lost to it.

Yusuf . . . Gods, poor Yusuf.

He'd been stronger than Idol, in a way. He'd felt his mind about to shatter and he'd known, somehow, that it would be a thousand times worse than just dying. If they got out of this, Mae knew that she would be hearing the deafening report of Yusuf Orne eating a shot from his own sidearm til the day she returned to the cycle. She would beg his forgiveness in the next life, later if the Gods and Spirits were kind, and soon enough if not.

Pushing her Qi into her skin in a protective sheath, warding her body and her soul alike, Isshin darted out of the veil of Magni's ward with her fists up.

Idol cackled and stumbled forward like an inebriate. All of her hand-to-hand combat grace was gone, not that it mattered terribly much. The shock runes etched into her arm crackled to life as she swung a wild haymaker at Mae who bobbed beneath the blow and doled out a pair of punishing jabs to the Idol's torso in payment for the clumsy attack.

Ribs shattered gruesomely under Mae's iron-hard fists, but Idol continued unperturbed, laughing through mouthfuls of blood as she swung her arms in childishly wide arcs.

One swept close to Mae, missing her nose by fingerbreadth, and—

"W-What?!" Mae spat as she staggered back, her vision doubling as her head jerked to the side.

She executed a quick backflip, lashing out with her legs in a Dragon's Tail at Idol to create space for herself before landing.

Mae lifted a hand to her right cheek as she touched down,

and winced. Bruised, and badly, and she tasted blood in her mouth. It was like she'd just got slugged in the face, except Idol had *missed*.

It wasn't magic, her Qi would have reacted. No, that had to have been a physical force.

"The wake," Mae muttered in disbelief as she watched Idol cackle mindlessly to herself before taking another pair of shaky steps forward.

Her arms were hanging limply at her side.

No, not limply. Bonelessly.

Mae's stomach twisted and clenched, and her gorge rose up into her throat as she realized the truth.

Her arm was broken.

Those attacks she'd been making hadn't been haymakers. The thing that had once been Idolatry Friese was just using her own broken arms like flails with enough force that even missing caused bruises. Shattered ribs, broken arms, and a hole in her Gods-damned *skull!* And she was still coming!

"Shit," Mae hissed as she took a step back. "I . . ." she looked back at Magni who was unconscious in the ward. If only he had fire magic or acid, something to destroy her body! "Damn it!"

Mae looked back up at Idol and spat on the ground between them.

"*Mae~Shii~*" Idol chanted as she took another step forward.

'*I think that's enough dreams for you.*'

"AAH!"

Mae dropped to her knees clutching her head. Pain like a frozen icepick pierced her temple and buryied itself in her forebrain! And that voice! It was cold. Cold, like emptiness. Like the deepest, darkest places of the ocean. Or space.

Idol froze, then turned her head to the wall dividing the apartment from the hallway slowly.

The wall came apart like a jigsaw puzzle. Wallpaper peeled away, drywall disintegrated, and the concrete beneath separated into neatly divided blocks that self-dismantled.

"*Who are*—"

They were the last words out of Idol's mouth, and she didn't even get to finish them before her head vanished in a wine-dark flash of light that left behind a painful, brackish afterimage. Idol's headless body staggered back as blood spurted uselessly from the now-open vein and artery, then it staggered impossibly forward towards the hole in the wall.

'Hm, the Dreaming Priest's eye is wide open in you, isn't it?'

Mae cried out and dropped to the ground. That voice put a bone-deep ache in her body and filled her mouth with the taste of frozen iron. More than ever, she wished she could close her third eye. Anything not to see that stumbling corpse-thing that was once her friend blindly charging forward.

Another snap of that unwholesome light filled the air, wider and darker than before, and Idol's body was simply gone.

'Your eye is closed here, Old One, go back to sleep.'

Light broke through the shadows and from that light a shape resolved. Mae tried to focus on it. She tried to see through the light. It took her a moment to realize that that was precisely her problem. The light wasn't blinding her to the figure.

The light *was* the figure.

It was power.

Pure power.

Isshin Mae's mouth went dry and her heart hammered as she stared with blind eyes into the light that was approaching her. Her third eye, so useful against spectral entities like poltergeists, was useless here. Seeing it wasn't the problem. Perceiving it, was.

"Mae!"

Mae's head swiveled as a small, warm body collided with hers, and it took a long moment before her nearly-blinded third eye could pick out the riot of greens and golds that made up Paulina Truelight.

"Vess! Reel it in a little! You're hurting her!"

A new voice broke through, one that sounded almost like the one that had been piercing her mind. It was softer, though. Warmer.

"Sorry, it's . . . hard when I'm like this. When I'm so close to the Dream," the voice replied. "Wally, I need your help holding back . . ."

It was like watching a supernova in reverse. Bit by bit, the light was swallowed by the shadow at its center. The spear-bright pain in her third eye became a dull ache, then faded to blissful numbness as the figure became fully realized, and all Isshin Mae could think at that moment was that she wished more than anything else that the lights had stayed on.

"*Daemon* . . ."

The word left her lips like an oath as Mae began to shake. She never actually fought one, nor had she ever seen one. True daemons were, thankfully, vanishingly rare in the Real. She had seen the depictions and heard the sermons and admonitions the same as anyone, but she had never seen one.

Not until that moment.

It stood with regal bearing, wearing a coat that flapped around its limber frame like an obsidian battle flag. Its face was arterial crimson, etched with curvilinear symbols of pure white light that traced the lines of high cheekbones and around the ocular frames of its burning blue eyes. Its hair was a wildfire mane that rolled and twisted around its head, face, neck, and . . . a crown?

Mae stared at its head.

No, not a crown. Twelve points rose out from beneath her mane of fire, their tips jagged and broken, and at first it looked to Mae like a circlet or crown beneath the hair, but no. Horns. They were horns.

Mae pushed herself away from the daemon, scrabbling across the dirty floor towards the warding circle and towards Magni. She might cover him if she were fast. Maybe the daemon would take pity on them. On him. Maybe spare him for her. She wanted to close her eye. To be mercifully blind to the crowned daemon.

"Mae! Mae stop!" Polly was grappling her! Trying to hold her down, trying to feed her to the daemon! Was she enthralled?! Was she *mad?!*

"Sshh, sleep~" the daemon whispered

It was in front of her. It hadn't moved, it was simply *there*.

There was no snap of displaced air from teleportation, no planar vertigo from a dimensional shift. Just a flicker of color, and then it was kneeling in front of her. It spoke soothingly as it reached out. Its hands were wickedly clawed, and Polly gasped as it pressed the tip of one of those awful needles to Mae's brow to slide it into her third eye silently and bloodlessly.

"Dream your dreams," it murmured, "of quiet things, of roots and mountain clouds—" Mae's body was suddenly heavy, and she couldn't recall why she'd been so frantic— "and walk again those old oak roads beneath the autumn rain. In those dreams of quiet things," it—no *her*—voice was so soothing, "sleep, and dream again."

For the first time since her third eye opened, Isshin Mae knew darkness, and her mind plunged gently and deeply into the caverns of slumber.

CHAPTER 27

The mental unspace of the proxy was a tempest of silver fire.

Prior to the release of Vess' limiter restraints, maintaining the proxy on Wally's end had largely been a passive experience. All she really had to do was keep her emotional levels synchronized with Vess' own and soothe Vess when she got worked up.

Truthfully, despite having more experience with the proxy, Vess was kind of bad at keeping it stable. Her emotions were all over the place most of the time.

With the restraints gone, however, the game had changed completely. What had once been a cool, dark sanctuary broken only by the warmth of Vess' emotional presence was consumed by a torment of magical and psychic energy. Wally had to strain to keep the connection stable at every moment. Her astral body was at once too hot and too cold, like the worst sort of fever minus the delirium that usually accompanied it. If she had to equate a physicality to the sensation, it would be like having every single one of her muscles and tendons pulled taut.

Over the quarter-hour that the restraints had been lifted, Wally had slowly begun to understand her role. She wasn't a calming thread anymore. She was a stabilizing pillar holding up a fortress that was caught in an earthquake.

'*Wally, I need your help holding back . . .*'

Vess' voice echoed across the link, and Wally sent back a wordless transmission of assent. Slowly, she forced her right index finger to curl inward.

'*O-Okay, just let me—*'

What had once been a single thread connecting them was now ten, each one bound to one of Wally's fingers, each one pulling her inexorably in a different direction as the silver firestorm raged around her.

It was all an illusion, of course. A paradigm of thought that allowed her to take the formless and create form, and thereby create function. It was among the most basic principles of magic: to shape the shapeless, the mage must have a clear image in their mind of what that shape must be and then have the will to impose that shape upon the world. When the restraints had first been lifted and Wally was suddenly forced to try and juggle all of the different aspects of the proxy that were suddenly at her fingertips without losing track of them, the most absurd thing had popped into her mind.

If you need to remember, tie a string around your finger.

The thread attached to Wally's index finger was like spider silk; fine to the point of invisibility and stronger than steel, and it creaked with strain as she drew it inward. The rage of the tempest began to taper, and the constant strain gradually lifted from Wally's astral muscles, leaving her feeling thin and shaky until she managed to stabilize herself and catch her metaphorical breath.

Twitching each of her fingers in turn, she checked the stability of the various fragments of the proxy she'd carefully divvied up.

Power regulation was good, psyche balance was mostly stable which was honestly about as 'in the green' as Vess ever got. Her emotional stability was swinging like a pendulum but that was normal.

Gods she really did have to go and fall for a total mess, didn't she?

The astral conduit and link were both steady, and synchronization was clean and green, like always, but those rarely ever wavered since they represented aspects of her and Vess' actual proxy link. Vess' power draw was a little high but it was dropping slowly as Vess relaxed. Her curse was spiking though . . .

Wally curled her left ring finger and silver flames immediately leapt to life around her as she forced the flow of Vess' curse to realign back into her before the fires died slowly back down as her reflector nature adapted and began countering the magic.

'Wally?'

'Gimme a sec, this isn't easy.'

'Sorry.'

A small laugh escaped Wally as she checked the last two threads, the arcane maintenance and mental outflow, both of which were almost slack since she wasn't currently casting anything intensive other than the telepathic murmur.

'It's fine, we're okay, just give me a little warning before you go apeshit on a wall next time, please and thank you?'

'I'll do that.'

Wally sighed. *'You could have just blown through it, you know. You didn't have to seize control of the local dimensional matrix like that.'*

An insouciant little tremor rippled down the thread of Vess emotional range that attached to Wally's right ring finger. Gods, she could be such an insufferable ass sometimes. Still, Wally couldn't deny that it had been fascinating to watch. With three of the five limiter restraints lifted, their minds had become almost one. They were in no danger of losing coherency with one another, but it allowed Wally an unparalleled ability to observe precisely *how* Vess cast her spells.

Despite not being terribly good at arcane calculus, Wally knew mathematical elegance when she saw it. Vess' spells displayed a creative flair and graceful, almost stylish, application of various formulae to generate masterpieces of magecraft. Every working she wove was as much art as science, so getting to see Vess weave her magic into the fabric of space-time and begin casually contesting control of the exclusion domain was absolutely *fascinating*. Moreover, she found she actually understood some of the concepts. Being so in tune with Vess' psyche meant she had the equivalent of a tutor speed-teaching her not only terminology and theory but how to comprehend both.

It really was beautiful.

She was beautiful.

'Sync up your senses, we're moving to the next step,' Vess sent, and Wally returned another assent

Twitching both her right pinky and thumb, Wally opened the astral link that connected them wide and increased the conduit flow, joining her senses back up to Vess'.

The process wasn't smooth.

With the limiters gone, the flow and flux of power Wally was dealing with was a constant, shifting pressure over every inch of her body, and it had only been fifteen minutes. No wonder Vess' old reflector ended up hospitalized. As it was, the extra sensory input bordered on pain, and she had to bite back a sharp hiss as she forced herself to focus on one sense at a time to get used to it.

"You back with us, Wally?" Vess asked aloud.

'I'm here, just . . . acclimating.'

"Take your time," she replied.

A relaxing wave of warmth from Vess sank into Wally, and she sighed softly.

Vess looked back up and Wally's vision followed suit. The two remaining members of Fifth precinct were in bad shape— both unconscious and incapable of defending themselves. That wasn't as big of a problem as it might have been since there were no roaming necrotics, but there was no telling what sustained exposure to the excluded domain would do. The elven man looked to be on death's door, too. He'd die the old fashioned way if he didn't get help in the next hour or two.

"Alright, here's the plan," Vess turned to Polly, Siobhan, and Jemma who straightened under her gaze.

It was odd, but at the same time Wally understood. There was something about Vess. She possessed the sort of aura of command that Wally imagined belonged to generals in war fictions. The ones with steely eyes and unswerving voices, and who charged the teeth of the enemy line with their men. Vess spoke and everyone just . . . listened.

"You three are going to evacuate these two—" she held up

a hand sharply to forestall the complaints from Jemma and Polly— "this isn't an argument!" Vess snapped, then gestured to the prone figures. "Siobhan needs to carry Baelion carefully, move him wrong and he loses his guts, literally, so Polly," she turned to the pint-sized blonde berserker, "you get Chief Mae, and Jemma needs to triage Magni while you move."

"So you're staying in here alone?!" Jemma snapped.

Wally felt Vess' smirk as much as everyone else saw it as Vess tapped the side of her head.

"I'm not alone, Jem," she said casually. "I've got Wally up here, and we're not leaving until we've sealed this domain."

"How do you plan on keeping us sane if we're splitting up?" Polly asked, thankfully not arguing the point.

Over the few weeks Wally had spent getting to know everyone better, she'd gotten the impression of Polly being eminently practical. She didn't *like* leaving Vess behind, but she clearly saw the logic. Their options were to leave Vess behind, leave two veteran dispersers to certain death, or abandon the dispersal entirely, and those last two weren't even options.

"The murmur is just psychic white noise on autocycle," Vess said with a shrug. "I'll hang the effect on Siobhan before you leave. It won't be permanent but this domain is tiny," she made a squishing motion with her finger and thumb, "so once you're down in the lobby you'll be out of the area of influence anyway and it won't matter."

"And you?" Jemma asked. "It doesn't affect you?"

The proxy grew cold for a moment. Wally still wasn't sure what it meant when that happened. All she knew was that Vess suddenly felt painfully far away. Then it warmed again, and Vess shook her head.

"No, it doesn't."

That distant tone wasn't encouraging, but Wally knew she was right. Even before she'd put up the murmur, she'd heard whispers on the edges of the proxy, but something was hedging them out. Something the others clearly didn't have.

"Now, enough talk, move out, I'm not having the old guy croak while we bubble around." She jerked a thumb over her shoulder.

Jemma gave her an odd look, but didn't argue. Siobhan moved past Vess with the same phlegmatic acceptance she did everything with, and Polly did the same, stooping down to pick up the crumpled form of Chief Mae. Since they had a moment, Wally decided to indulge her curiosity.

'Did you just say 'bubble around'?'

Vess stiffened, then frowned.

'Uh, yeah, I . . . I guess that one went out of style too, huh?'

'About a century ago.'

'Damn. I liked bubble around.'

Wally giggled lightly within the proxy, sending a small flush of delight up the thread towards Vess. 'Well, who knows? Maybe you can bring it back.'

'Hilarious.'

'Hey, I'm sorry, I didn't mean to tease . . .' Wally reached out across the link and let herself slip closer to Vess' astral presence.

Being this close was dangerous during combat. Without the restraints, Wally had to maintain a more careful distance or else she risked suffering psychic blowback from Vess' spellcrafting, but when things were quiet she could give Vess a little more comfort.

'Are you okay?'

Vess leaned into the embrace and nodded.

"I am, yeah, sorry, I'm just kind of . . .' she trailed off, and Wally sent another small, soothing wave over her.

'Miserable?' Wally supplied.

The proxy went cold.

No, not cold. It went almost *dead*. Terror flashed through Wally; terror, pain, and whispers that were so loud they were like thunder in her ears. It was quiet and yet all-consuming. Silent and deafening at the same time, and it was all coming from Vess!

Desperate, Wally reached out and—

"—come to bed."

"I can't, there are too many reports from the front to go over before dawn."

A soft and comforting weight fell over shoulders that were bowed with responsibility, and Vess let out a sigh that turned into a long-suffering laugh as warm breath tickled her ear and a rich, savory perfume wafted past her nose.

"Don't be so miserable." Her tone was playful, but at the same time there was a barb buried underneath it.

There always was.

"I'm always miserable, remember?" But Vess leaned up from the desk she was sitting at to encourage the embrace all the same.

"Mhm, I remember." Lips brush her ear. Lips whose shape she knows intimately. "Hey . . ."

She groaned and closed her eyes.

"Don't say it, Phee! You know I—"

"Who does Misery love~?"

"Ugh."

"Come o~n."

Vess sighed and turned her head to catch the women's lips in a warm and casually intimate kiss before pulling back and smiling.

"Misery loves—

Wally gasped as she was shoved out of the painfully intense memory. Her skin was crawling and she almost wished that she could throw up. Gods' hooks, she might just do it once she got back into her body anyway if it meant getting the feeling of that . . . of those *lips* off of hers!

'S-Sorry, I'm so sorry!' Vess gasped as she pushed Wally away, widening the buffering void between them in the proxy. 'That— That shouldn't have happened.'

'What . . . Vess?!' Wally reached out and Vess flinched back, and the proxy link jerked taut and turned tenuously brittle. 'Vess! Stop! Stop pulling away! You're going to snap the link!'

I-I'm sorry! I'm trying!' Vess' mental voice cracked and Wally reached out again, trying to bridge the gap.

'Vess, come back! Please!' Wally begged. 'Please! It's okay! I promise, you're okay! We're okay! Everything is okay!'

Slowly, the brittle link began to steady and strengthen again and Vess' astral form resolved out of the darkness. She looked now as she looked outside. Like a cross between an angel and daemon. If she'd been wearing some kind of distant beatific expression on her face, the image would have been complete. As it was, her eyes were wide, and her face pallid with fear. Her chest was heaving despite lacking lungs, and she looked at least as nauseated as Wally felt.

'Later, okay?' Wally said softly. 'We can talk about . . . about whatever that was, later.'

Vess nodded gratefully, relaxing as Wally sent a calming ripple over her. They would talk later. They had to. Vess never seemed keen on dredging up her past but that . . . that memory at least, had to be addressed or else it would fester, and they both knew it.

But later.

The pair of them re-engaged their senses and opened their eyes to the outside world again.

Vess' orders had been carried out with some degree of success. Jemma had managed to fashion a kind of hammock-style sling for Siobhan to carry the man Vess had called Baelion in. It was already soaking slowly with blood, but it was holding. Polly, by comparison, had Chief Mae slung over her shoulder in a fireman's carry.

"Ready to move?" Vess asked, her voice was strained but steady, and if anyone noticed the change they were circumspect enough not to mention.

"Ready," Polly echoed with a sharp nod.

Vess laid a hand on Siobhan, and Wally aligned herself with the controlled thrum of power that was released. The murmur shifted subtly around them. The others probably didn't notice, but Wally did. She saw Siobhan, briefly, the way that Vess must: as a complex, humming network of lines, rich with miasma. Like everything else Vess did with magic, the way she moved the murmur was singularly elegant. A normal sorceress would have simply dismissed the spell and recast it, but Vess was anything but a normal sorceress.

Rather than waste the power needed to cast the spell again, Vess untethered the formations of the spell that anchored it to her and, at the same time, charged it with an influx of power to keep it temporarily stable and running without a direct link to its caster during the transition. Then, as easily as tying off a piece of twine, Vess threaded the loose ends of the spell matrix into Siobhan's own corrupted lambda system.

Eventually, Siobhan's body would recognize the alien spell and destroy it, but until then it would run without error.

'Beautiful.'

'You'll make me blush if you say things like that.'

Wally startled, then let out a nervous laugh.

'I . . . sorry, I didn't mean to say that out loud.'

'Well, technically you didn't. We're just . . . you know.'

'I know, so what next?'

Vess answered her out loud. "Alright, follow me."

She led their party out of the room and into the hall, found a nice, wide expanse of wall, and reached out.

"Polly, Jem, Vonnie? Wally and I are going to contest control of the domain now. There will be a short window to escape but it won't stay stable for long, so you need to take it *immediately*, okay?" Vess said, turning her head to regard the others, who goggled for a moment, then nodded.

'Ready, Wally?'

'Always.'

A smile flitted across Vess' lips as she laced her fingers, cracked her knuckles, and then splayed her claws and drove them into the concrete with a grinding *crack*.

Wally gasped as the casting load doubled over on her, and all ten threads suddenly went taut and began thrumming like the strings of a powered guitar in the middle of a riff. A storm of silver fire exploded around her as Vess channeled more magic than Wally had ever felt her use at once, and the world bloomed into existence around her. She wasn't seeing it. Not through anything so crude as eyes, anyway. She felt the exclusion around her like it was a part of her. Every inch of wall, every tile, and every scrap of mortar and concrete. It was all soaked in miasma, and it was all *hers*.

Almost.

There was something else in there with her, and it recoiled

as Vess effectively bull-rushed it out of the way with a surge of main magical force. It was the equivalent of jumping someone in a dark alley and laying them out with a withering fusillade of right and left hooks. Wally had been expecting Vess to do something graceful like she had with the murmur. To steal the domain out from under its controller's nose.

She hadn't done that all.

She'd broken into their home and *robbed them*.

"GO!"

Vess snarled as the wall in front of them suddenly and violently opened and the space beyond reshaped into an internal stairwell that spiraled downward, leaving Vess fingers seemingly buried an inch-deep into thin air.

They bolted past Vess with Polly in the lead followed by Jemma and Siobhan in the rear.

"You'd both better come out of this!" Polly shouted over her shoulder.

Within the proxy, Wally was in a unique position to see what Vess had just done. When she'd seized control of the domain, she hadn't just stolen it, she'd *broken* it. Vess had turned her power into a magical comet of destructive impulse and blown through the fabric of the domain, leaving scorched holes in its metaphysical substance. So really, she didn't just rob the domain's owner. She also set their house on fire on the way out.

'*Uhm, Vess?*'

'*H-Hold that thought, babe.*'

Vess blew out a strained breath as she tracked the progress of their friends until they were beyond the boundary of the domain. The moment they were past it, Vess wrenched her fingers out of the air with a sound like splintering glass and staggered backward as she shook her hands out.

'*Alright, what's up?*'

'*You just blew the domain's foundations apart.*'

'*Ayup.*'

'*What about us?*' The issue was kind of null at that point but Wally felt the need to ask all the same.

'*We find the bastard in the middle of this place really fast and disperse* them.'

'And uhm . . . just hypothetically speaking, what happens if we don't?'

Vess let out a weak laugh as she put her fist to the side of her jaw and cracked her neck. 'Uh, best case scenario? This floor disintegrates, turning the upper half of the building into a ruin.'

'And . . . what's the not-best-case?'

'The domain implodes and takes most of the building with it.'

'. . .'

'But—!' Vess continued brightly— 'the domain will be gone either way!'

The threads of the proxy connecting the two of them practically shook with the weight of the sigh Wally heaved out. Well, it was probably better than the domain breaching and flooding several city blocks with miasma, but still . . . 'What happens to us?'

'Eh, we'll be fi~ne,' Vess replied with a wave of her hand as she started moving down the hall towards the thickest source of miasma.

'You're sure?'

'Probably.'

'Probably?!'

Vess carded her fingers through her hair. 'Well, yeah,' she said with a weak laugh. 'I mean, neither of us are really here.'

'Except . . .' Wally prompted dryly.

'Except I uh, might end up a little bit . . . comatose.'

The threads heaved with another sigh.

'I'll get better!'

'Are you sure?!'

'Uh . . .'

'Vess don't you dare say—'

'—probably.'

"*VESZHA GIBSON!*"

Vess blew out another strained breath as she massaged the bridge of her nose with her fingers. 'I know! I know! Alright? But it was the only way to ensure the domain wouldn't breach! You'll be fine! I promise! You're a reflector, you'll just bounce back to your body!'

'And what about you?!'

'I . . . I'll . . . be fine.'

'Probably!' Wally spat back. *'You can't just—!'*

'I can and I will, Wally!' Vess snapped over her, and the proxy threads shivered painfully, pulling Wally's body in ten different directions for a brief moment before Vess mastered herself again.

'I'm sorry, I didn't mean to yell,' Vess mumbled, and Wally had to force herself not to draw back. The proxy might not take the strain. *'But I meant what I said,'* she continued. *'This is my job, Wally, and it's yours too. We're dispersers, if we fail then people die.'*

'I just . . . I can't lose you, okay?' Wally replied softly, pushing as much of her feelings across the proxy as she could as she did so.

A sudden hitch in Vess breathing told her that her feelings had come across, and Vess nodded before speaking through a throat tight with emotion.

"I know," she said aloud. "But we'll be fine because—" she brushed her flowing fiery hair from her eyes— "I haven't had nearly enough time with you yet either, Wally Willowbark."

Wally forced herself to focus and said, *'so we win this.'*

'We'll win. With you, I can't lose.'

'Charmer.'

'I try.'

Wally loved and hated that smug little smile of Vess'. It really wasn't fair, how charismatic she was.

'You're a—'

'I know, I know.'

A small laugh echoed out from Wally through the proxy. Outside of the proxy, Vess' mouth softened to a warm smile despite the cloying miasma that surrounded them as they approached the densest thicket of darkness.

"Alright, let's do this."

Thin, bloodless fingers picked out another deep-bellied chord from the bass guitar cradled in its owner's lap. The instrument was a beautiful thing, a classic, long-necked four-string with a cherry red finish and deep black fretboard.

She had always wanted growing up; an Ulverike 1092 Special. They'd only been made by one manufacturer in the small northern empire, but were prized by bass players for their rich voice. They also cost a small fortune each due to their limited run. All the greats had owned one during the golden age of weaveplay, and it had always been her dream to own one of her very own, too.

Ba-dum~

The note rang out clean and bone-deep, and Myriam smiled. It was a dream come true: her very own 1092. She ran her palm over the curve of the body up toward the subtle horns that framed the neck, and then back down to find the strings again where she picked out another chord and all around her the world shifted lazily to the tune of her music.

"So? How's it feel?" Dolin asked as he leaned back in the chair.

At some point, they had moved to the living room. Myriam couldn't recall when that had happened. Had something else happened between the kitchen and the living room? She couldn't recall that either.

It didn't matter.

"It's perfect," Myriam muttered. "It's all I ever imagined."

"That's her specialty."

Everything was worth it. The long hours. The cult. The crimes. The long shitty hours at her day job. It was all worth it. All she'd ever wanted was to be good enough to hold one of these babies in her own two hands, and now she was doing just that.

The apartment shook and Myriam looked up with a frown. Dolin looked up too, but he was smiling as he eyed the door. Then he turned to Myriam and his grin widened.

"Times almost up, Myr, you remember your role?"

Some of the dream began to slip away, and Myriam remembered. She remembered the cup full of poison. She remembered the ritual. The plan.

Myriam nodded soberly.

"I remember," she said quietly.

"She's nearly here," he said.

Myriam pressed her lips together. Her mouth was practically a gash in her face. Her chest was empty of motion. She looked up and through the doorway that led to the kitchen where her body lay slumped in a pool of her own sick across the table. That's right. She remembered now.

Looking back to Dolin, Myriam brushed her hair from her eyes, then laid her hand across the strings.

"Do I have time for a last song?" She asked.

Dolin's grin was ear-to-ear, and it looked alien on his face, like someone was stretching him out beneath his skin.

"Darling," he replied in a voice that echoed strangely, like there was someone else repeating his words a split-second off-beat. "I absolutely *demand* it."

Then he turned, made a flicking motion with his fingers, and a wound in the air opened. Dolin, or whoever was underneath that face, stepped through the rift, and vanished, and Myriam went back to her 1092 Special. It didn't really matter what the plan was anymore. The domain was falling apart, just as planned. The Ascendant was coming, just as planned.

"And I guess that makes me the opening act," Myriam muttered, then smiled a little more broadly.

This was gonna be one *hell* of a concert.

CHAPTER 28

Unearthly metal scraped harshly against concrete as Vess dragged the tips of her claws against the wall of the excluded sixth floor while she walked. It wasn't a pleasant sound by any stretch of the imagination, but it soothed her. She couldn't really put a finger (ha) on why, but it did. It was an objectively obnoxious noise. It shouldn't have any positive qualities.

Maybe it was just the familiarity.

That and she needed to be physically linked into the domain to track where that near-constant *'dum-da-dum'* noise was coming from anyway. The geometry of the place wasn't lining up which was par for the course for exclusion zones; they didn't necessarily have to vibe with passing niceties like 'causality' and 'three-dimensional continuity' so the best she could do was move deeper into the miasma. It was the only reliable measure she knew of to find the center of a domain.

'How long before the collapse?'

Wally's voice was surprisingly steady considering what Vess had dragged her into. She would be fine, though. Vess truly believed that. If she'd thought there was even a chance that getting caught in the event horizon of a collapse would clap back on Wally, she wouldn't have done it. She wasn't quite as sanguine about herself as she had led Wally to believe, but she was confident enough to take the risk.

'Half an hour, maybe a bit less,' Vess replied. *'It's hard to say . . . a lot of it depends on the curser now.'*

'Shouldn't we be moving a little more quickly, then?'

Vess shook her head. *'The geometry of the exclusion zone is unstable. If we move too quickly we could step in a pocket of disjoined space and end up on the other side of the zone.'*

'Oh.' Wally's impatience rippled across the proxy thread to Vess. *'So we might just wander around for a half-hour and then explode?'*

A laugh shook through Vess and she nodded wanly.

'Implode,' she corrected. *'But yes, possibly.'*

It was more possible that Vess wanted to admit, to be honest. The area was large enough that it made searching for the center little more precise than a game of Hotter-Colder. If she stepped down a hall that lead them into thinner miasma then she would know she was moving in the wrong direction, but then she would have to backtrack. It was a narrow window of time whose only comfort was the fact that the only one who would be getting her fingers caught in it when it shut would be her and the curser.

Wally would be safe.

'Wait.'

Vess came to a stop as Wally's mental impulse traveled across their joined minds.

'What is it?' Vess sent back.

'I . . . I don't know, but . . .' Wally's presence wavered across the link and Vess sent ripples of calm across the thread to soothe her. *'Can't you feel it? Something is here. It's right . . .'*

". . . beneath my fingers," Vess muttered as she cracked her knuckles, and curled her claws.

They bit deep into stiff, cheap wood.

Turning her head, Vess stared at the door that had, a moment ago, been solid stone, the same as every other length of wall. Somehow she had very nearly walked right past it and would have if Wally hadn't said something.

'How did you know?'

'I don't know.' The thread wavered with Wally's uncertainty. *'I just . . . I felt something. Like an echo, maybe? Or like remembering

something that happened a long, long time ago.'

'You're not a seer talent, are you? I think I would've noticed.'

That notion scared Vess more than she was willing to admit. The last thing she needed was Wally seeing more of her memories involuntarily. There were secrets that ought to *remain* secret.

'No, they tested me for that,' Wally replied. *'I swear, I don't know how I knew but I just felt the door like . . . like I just knew where it was supposed to be.'*

That didn't bode well, but there wasn't any time to question it.

'If you did, then that means they were expecting us,' Vess began.

'But nobody knows that you exist!'

'I said us.' The thread drew taut as it caught in the gears of vess' mind. *'I wasn't the one who felt the door, Wally. So if you knew it was here somehow, then this—'*

'—is a trap.' Wally completed the thought even as Vess formed it. *'Vess, we're walking into a trap.'*

'I know.'

Vess lowered her hand from the door and looked it over.

It was, in all ways, an average apartment door. It had a small, tarnished copper plate that bore the numbers six-one-two-nine at eye level, and the brown paint was peeling from wood that looked to have been repainted many times, and there were signs along its surface of repairs both recent and old. There was nothing remarkable at all about the door, and yet Vess could feel the echo of a chill run down her spine as her distant body reacted to a gut instinct that something was very, very wrong.

"This is it," Vess said aloud. "This is the center of the domain."

'Vess, wait, please. If this is a trap then they know about you and me! We can't just walk into it!'

A small, huffing laugh left Vess as she shook her head.

"The trap was sprung the moment I collapsed the domain, Wally, maybe even the moment we stepped inside the building." Vess' tone was hollow and haunted. "Everything we've been chasing, these exclusions, they're Sunfall Cult sorcery and ritual, and somehow they already *knew*."

They knew about *her*. About both of them.

How?

'Back in the morgue, you said it was the Dark Stars who did this, right? That it was their magic?'

'Yeah.'

'Why would they go to this much trouble to trap you? To trap us?'

Vess lowered her hand to the doorknob and gripped it. Unsurprisingly, it wasn't locked and the knob turned with a muted click.

'It's a long story,' she replied as she pushed the door open, 'but I guarantee they're going to regret catching me.'

Jemma's vision was still swimming by the time they stumbled out of the elevator cab and into the lobby of the Heights, and she could still feel the poisonous grip of the domain above them dripping its toxic stream of miasma down over their heads.

"You still with me, Jem?" Polly caught her eye from ahead and Jemma gave her a shaky nod.

"Still with you," she replied.

"Good, because I highly doubt the cult is just going to let Vess and Wally have it all their own way," Siobhan added as she lumbered forward as carefully as possible which was surprisingly careful given her bulk.

Jemma shook her head. "There was nothing and no one left up there," she said. "Not even necrotics. Believe me, I could tell. There's no entering an exclusion from anything but a threshold and no getting in through the threshold—" she jerked her thumb back towards the elevator— "without getting through us."

As confident as she was about those statements, Jemma couldn't deny that there was something about the whole matter that felt wrong. It was a persistent question that had been digging at her since Vess had revealed the nature of the infestations as a ritual—why? What was the *point?* Thanks to her upbringing, Jemma was intimately familiar with the nature of curses and this one made no sense at all. A curse wasn't just a bomb you dropped on a building! It was purpose made *manifest*.

To curse something or someone, you needed hate, and lots

of it. Hate was personal. It was—

"Personal . . ."

"What?" Polly glanced over her shoulder at Jemma as they emerged from the Heights and into the cool evening air of Colvus.

"Nothing, just . . . I'm trying to figure out who the target of this curse actually *is*," Jemma replied.

"What do you mean?" Polly asked. "I figure all the necrotics and the dead people would answer that question."

Jemma shook her head as she took the steps two at a time to keep up with Siobhan's titanic gait. "No, those infestations were side-effects of the curse's wind-up," she explained. "They were by-products of all the miasma pouring out of the target! The curse tapped into the necrotic saturation of the Bressig survivors and just . . . magnified it, but what I can't figure out is *why?* Why release all of that power? And where did it go?!"

It didn't make any sense.

"Fuck me sideways." Polly spat on the ground and fumed as they got onto the street, and it didn't take Jemma long to see the source of her ire.

A familiar figure was kneeling on the asphalt near the hearse with her mailed fingers laced and her head bowed in prayer. Jemma had only had a handful of interactions with the woman, but it was hard to forget someone like Cassidia Truelight. It wasn't just her size, it was the manner of her. The intensity.

"Is that . . . ?" Jemma grimaced and looked back at Siobhan who was still plodding forward, although her expression had grown stony.

There was nothing for it. No one else could safely take Baelion Magni from her. Siobhan would just have to endure dealing with the Knight Commander of Ys. Given how everything had gone rapidly to shit, Jemma couldn't say she was surprised to see the woman here.

"I'll deal with her," Polly said sharply as she adjusted Mae's unconscious body over her shoulder, then stormed towards her younger sister.

"Right." Jemma nodded for Siobhan to fall in behind her.

They didn't more than a few more steps forward, though, before Cassidia raised her head. Those fiercely blue eyes shook Jemma like always. Meeting her gaze was like staring into the sun, unshielded; her naked faith left bare for all to see.

"Paulina," Cassidia stood and settled her hand on the pommel of her sheathed blade. "It heartens me to see you safe."

"Are you still talking like that you giant fucking nerd?" Polly said gruffly as she stopped in front of Cassidia.

Cassidia bristled, her eyes flashing with anger before the emotion vanished beneath the marble veneer of her expression. "Some of us," she began through a clenched jaw, "have a care for traditions that our family has upheld for over a century, *Paulina*."

Looking at the pair of them, their positions would seem reversed. Polly looked for all the world like the insouciant youngest sibling while Cassidia looked every inch the loyal and dutiful eldest.

In another ten years, they would pass for mother and daughter.

And eventually, grandmother and grandchild.

Jemma had never asked—it had never felt like her place—but always suspected that that was one of the greater reasons for Polly's estrangement. Being around them, year after year, watching them age while she stayed the same, was a constant reminder of the day she would have to bury them all, and none of them seemed to give a damn.

"If you're going to take up so much damn space at least make yourself useful and save the old man's life, will you?" Polly pointed over at the bloody sling hanging from Siobhan's shoulders. "Magni's barely clinging on as it is!"

Cassidia stared down at her sister for a stretch of heartbeats, and Jemma heard the faint grating of metal-on-metal as the woman's gauntleted hand clenched around the grip of her blade.

"As you say," Cassidia replied finally, and turned on her heel to march towards Jemma and Siobhan.

"Cass." Jemma gave a perfunctory greeting and nod of her head as Cassidia strode past her, paused, then looked back over her shoulder and down.

"Corsivo." Cassidia spoke her last name like an epithet. "I trust you're keeping to the terms of your pardon?"

Jemma scowled. "Fuck you, platehead."

Ignoring Jemma's jab, Cassidia approached Siobhan the way someone might walk up to a particularly fetid piece of roadkill.

"And you, abomination," Cassidia began curtly. "Will you permit me to lay you to rest yet?"

"I'm good, thanks," Siobhan replied flatly. "You mind doing something useful about the guy hemorrhaging against my chest?"

Cassidia sighed, then stretched out a mailed hand and laid it on Magni's shoulder.

"The light of Ys be upon you, for your work upon this land is not yet done." Cassidia thrust her fist into the air and a column of light fell like a hammer upon her, enveloping all three of them in golden radiance.

"Vonnie!" Jemma started forward, only to stagger back at the intensity of the light. Beneath it, she could hear Siobhan's agonized roar.

As quickly as it had been summoned, the light was gone, and Jemma rushed to Siobhan's side. The dreadnought looked a bit crispy but still—insofar as Jemma was concerned—alive. As soon as Jemma was sure that Siobhan hadn't been scorched beyond repair, she turned to Magni.

Despite herself, Jemma couldn't help but be impressed. The mortal wound that had been inches from killing the old man was just . . . gone, and in its place was clean unblemished flesh.

Breathing a sigh of relief, she turned to Cassidia who was lowering her hand slowly, her eyes glazed in rapture from the after-effects of communing with her god. In that moment, Jemma's breath caught in her chest. Before this, she'd never seen Cassidia truly invoke her power—she had never had a cause to. Her silver armor glowed forge-fresh, and her long hair, normally flaxen, burned like scorched gold.

And brighter than either of those things were her fiercely gleaming eyes.

She caught herself staring a moment too late, shook her

head, and asked, "Will he make it?"

"Ys has willed that he should live," Cassidia muttered as her eyes regained their normal, painfully sharp focus.

Jemma looked over the old man again, then turned back to Cassidia. "Thanks."

"The gratitude of heretics is wasted breath," Cassidia replied blandly as she put her back to both of them and began walking towards Polly and Mizer.

Jemma snorted. "Yeah? Well, fuck you, too!"

"Enough, Jem," Polly said as she returned, putting a hand on Jemma's shoulder and pushing her back. "Cass isn't worth it."

"Yeah . . ." Jemma blew out an angry breath and nodded. "Yeah, I know, she just pisses me off."

Siobhan shuddered as she shook off the avalanche of holy power she had just weathered, and Jemma laid a hand on her scorched bicep, silently willing a surge of miasma into her, siphoned out from Akur's realm.

"Thanks," Siobhan grumbled as she straightened out.

"No problem."

Mizer and Cassidia were back to arguing as the trio approached the hearse with the two unconscious dispersers from fifth precinct. Surprisingly, Cassidia was actually winning.

"You're precinct will be compensated for your time and for the successful rescue," Cassidia was saying, "but your place in this dispersal is over, Erik. A domain is Ysari business."

"You can't just seal it, Cass!" Mizer snapped.

"I can and I will." Cassidia's hand drifted back to the pommel of her blade. "The longer it remains, the more dangerous it becomes."

"Wait, Cass, no!" Polly settled Isshin Mae next to Magni by the hearse before sprinting up to her sister. "No, you can't seal the thresholds! Not yet! We're not all out of there!"

Cassidia raised a single sculpted eyebrow, then looked back at Mizer. "Your staff is all present and accounted fo—" She cut herself off, then looked back, and Jemma felt her eyes pass over each of them in turn, counting them off.

"There was a new hire," Cassidia said slowly as she turned

back to Mizer, her blue eyes blazing. "Mizer, did you bring a *greenhorn* into an *excluded domain?!*"

Mizer curled his fists and squared up to her. "She's projecting, and she's a reflector, a powerful one! Not even the domain could affect her! But I will not let you lock her up in that place!"

"You try," Jemma hissed as she took a step forward, "and we'll stop you, *paladin.*"

Cassidia's hand slid down the length of her weapon's haft until her fingers curled around the locket of her scabbard. "Will you now?" She muttered.

It was the softest that Jemma had ever heard Cassidia speak. "CASS, NO!"

Polly's scream was swallowed by an explosion of light as Cassidia wedged her thumb against the guard of her weapon and pushed the blade out less than an inch. Gold seared through the night like the break of dawn as Cassidia Truelight's voice thundered out a single word that beat itself into Jemma's mind like forgemaster's hammer coming down on a burning ingot.

"*Kneel.*"

The worst of it hit Polly, who was close enough to touch her sister. Her head jerked back with a sickening snap a moment before an unseen force seemed to hook into her ribcage and drag her to her knees so hard that Jemma heard bone crack. Mizer wasn't much better off. He staggered and dropped to a knee, his body coruscating with the power of the Elementals he was bonded to as they tried and failed to help him resist Cassidia's command. Worst of all was Siobhan, who howled like a wounded hound as she was driven to the asphalt by the divine word that was nailed into her necrotic body.

Light poured from the fraction of Cassidia's blade she had bared. It was so bright it made the rest of the world seem unfathomably darker—as if she were standing at the heart of a solar eclipse.

"Is that it?" Jemma spat blood. Her legs quaked as Cassidia turned to face her with a look that neatly bordered respect and surprise.

"You're still standing," she remarked.

"I can't tell you to go fuck yourself from the floor."

Unfortunately, standing was about all Jemma was able to manage. The weight of the command was still ringing in her mind, worming its way into her nerves and muscles, and it was taking everything she had just to keep her feet under her. Palming out her chisel from her sleeve with one hand and pulling her hammer from her belt with the other, Jemma focused on the feel of her tools under her fingers. The cold metal and smooth handle braced her and sharpened her focus, lightening the burden of the compulsion enough for her to straighten her bowed back.

"The exclusion is under my bailiwick, so if you stand between me and my holy purpose, I will have no choice but to cut you down." Cassidia pushed her blade another inch free of its scabbard, and the light spilled brighter across the streets, casting Jemma in harsh relief.

"And I'm sure you'll shed all kinds of tears for a dead heretic," Jemma snarled.

Her vision was doubling over on itself and her mouth was filled with the taste of copper. Her back felt like it was about to fold over on itself, but still, Jemma stood. She had to. There was no other choice.

'Akur look upon me,' Jemma thought as she raised her chin another inch to glare up at Cassidia. *'I will not bow. I will not break.'* Cassidia stopped in front of Jemma, those painfully bright eyes boring down into her. *'Never again.'*

"You could have sought absolution, Corsivo," Cassidia said in a surprisingly soft voice. "You could have sought redemption from the shadow of your sires and used that iron will of yours for grace." She shook her head dolefully. "Kneel and ask, and all will be forgiven . . . Ys is merciful."

"I'm not asking the person who's about to murder my coworker for shit!" Jemma pushed herself a little straighter.

"Her sacrifice will be remembered."

"*Fuck you!*"

Brackish, daemonic power snapped like viperous jaws around Jemma's body as she pushed every ounce of will and hate she had into her limbs. Just once. Just this *one time*. That was all she wanted!

Just *once!*

Clang

Cassidia raised an eyebrow and looked down at the chisel in Jemma's hands. The tip had stopped on her plate, scraping ineffectually against the enchanted silversteel. Slowly, Jemma pulled her arm back, spat another curse, and slammed the chisel down against, scoring a shallow mark on the metal.

"H-Her name . . ." Jemma could barely get the words out, her throat was constricting around them. Useless.

Even now, she was still *useless.*

Swallowing thickly, she forced the words out anyway.

"Her name," Jemma growled, "is Wally Willowbark."

Vess would make it out. She was so powerful. Too powerful, really. Jemma was sure that, given enough time, Vess could make it out, but Wally? No. Not even a reflector of her caliber could withstand being proxied for the amount of time it would take to slip the bars of a divine seal. Especially not in the heart of a collapsing exclusion, and certainly not with three seals released.

Armored fingers closed around her wrist, and Cassidia pushed the chisel from her armor. She was so strong that it wasn't fair. It was just like with Vess. Like there was just this . . . this category of existence that Jemma could barely even touch.

"Wally Willowbark." Cassidia repeated the name solemnly. "I will remember it, I assure you."

"You don't deserve to," Jemma hissed as Cassidia pushed her back.

Cassidia lowered her head briefly and the marble facade of her face shifted subtly. It was strange to see, and not unlike watching a statue come to life just long enough to scratch its nose before returning to unmoving stone. In that moment, Jemma saw a flicker of something different underneath the religious zeal.

She saw sorrow.

"Perhaps you're right," Cassidia said, "but I will fulfill my purpose all the same, and right now—" she jerked Jemma to the side, sending her sprawling to the asphalt— "you are in my way."

The moment Jemma struck the ground she was stuck fast to it, the overwhelming pressure of Cassidia's command pressing her down into the street. Her limbs seemed to weigh half a ton each, and it was all she could do just to raise her head from the asphalt.

"Murderer!" Jemma shouted. "You're nothing! You hear me?! Just another common, fucking murderer!"

Cassidia paused a few steps away, then, in a single, fluid motion, drew her blade fully from its sheathe, and the night was washed gold as Cassidia Truelight brandished her weapon.

Once, when she'd been *very* drunk, Polly had told Jemma the story; that her family's name was earned from the blade her bloodline carried. The blade that she, as the eldest, had been expected to carry before she told her parents exactly where they could stick their ancient piece of enchanted steel. The Truelight was more than a weapon, though. It was touched by the pure spark of Ys and could only be carried by a Paladin whose oath had never faltered. It was a weapon of myth persisting through the mists of time to the modern era, granted to her great-grandfather by a golden spirit, and remained one of the ultimate weapons against the dead and the damned.

Turning her blade tip down, Cassidia drove it into the street and its power rolled across the whole city block with an intensity that made Jemma's skin crawl. Words spilled from the Knight Commander's lips in a language that Jemma didn't speak but recognized instantly. It was the silverbell and chiming tongue of the heavenly realms. The tones and syllables were so pure that they brought tears to her eyes.

She was so close. She was *right there*, and all Jemma could do was watch as Cassidia locked the exclusion away, smothering it under the power of Ys to burn itself out until not even ashes remained.

"That's enough of that."

The invocation split apart and fractured, the words of power turning in on themselves until they became babble and nonsense. The command's weight lifted from Jemma's body and she could breathe again! Staggering to her feet, she found Cassidia working her jaw uselessly to recover the spell as the Truelight's divine radiance actually *dimmed*.

"B-Blasphemy!" Cassidia spat as she shook off whatever had taken control of her words from her. "What blasphemy . . . ?"

Shadows spilled from the entrance of the Heights and moved down the street like a living thing.

"Sorry, but I'm not quite done with that mess back there." A figure emerged from the heart of the shadows, which clung to him like tar. "So I'm going to have to ask you hold off on that whole 'divine purpose' business for the time being, can you do that for me, darling?"

"Dolin?" Mizer stepped up next to Jemma with an arm under Polly, his face was tight with something between anger and horror. "Dolin, what the hells did you get into?!"

"Another abomination?" Cassidia pulled Truelight from the ground and brought it up between her and the advancing reflector.

Silver fire licked around Dolin's body beneath the shadows as he smiled wanly. The months had not been kind to him. His roguish looks were pale and sunken, and his veins were a cold, icy blue. If it weren't for the fact that he was standing and talking, Jemma would have though he was dying. There was something deeply wrong with him. Jemma could feel it and she was certain that Mizer could too. He wasn't tied to the darkness the way she was, but his Elementals had to be telling him that the thing in front of him was unnatural.

"I got power, Mizer," Dolin replied. "I always told you Vess was holding me back! She was fighting me every step and never letting me do as much as I could!" He bared his teeth in a wolfish grin.

"But now look!" He threw his arms wide. "I found someone stronger and better than she ever was! And I can do everything she could and more now that she's not dragging me down!"

"I always knew you were a shitspit, Dolin, but this is beyond the *pale!*" Jemma snarled.

Before he could reply, Cassidia moved, and Jemma's stomach lurched at the sight.

Fast.

She was too fast.

Nothing that tall, that broad, and wearing that much damn armor should move that *gods damned fast.* Truelight flashed in her hands like an orphan star as Cassidia closed the distance between herself and Dolin in an instant. Dead he had to be dead. Anyone would—

Darkness exploded from around and beneath Dolin in a surge tide of grasping, spectral claws that collided with Cassidia in a deafening clangor. Noisome flesh hissed and bubbled as she swept Truelight through the flood, slicing through wrists, digits, and arms, but in moments she was overwhelmed, seized, heaved off of her feet, and thrown back to crash into the hood of sixth precinct's redoubtable Hideback.

Laughter bubbled out of Dolin's throat as the shadows retracted around him, and Jemma shuddered at the sound. There was something else underneath his laughter—another voice, echoing just between the beats of his words.

"That was fun." He opened his arms wide and smiled. "So who's next?"

CHAPTER 29

A VOICE SOFTLY HUMMING the opening bars of Heartland Road stirred Vess from her slumber, and she groaned quietly as her mind begrudgingly started to kick free of her dreams. And she *had* been dreaming, although of what, she couldn't say.

Probably nothing important.

"Five more minutes . . . or years," Vess grumbled as she turned over in bed and pulled the thick comforter over her head.

The humming faded and was replaced with a quiet laugh. The sound put a smile on Vess' face despite her best efforts to claw back the blessed oblivion of sleep. That smile widened just faintly as the sound of footsteps trailed in from the other room, and the door to the bedroom creaked open.

"Vess."

"No."

"Gods' hooks, Vess, you've got class in an hour and a half, now *get*—" the comforter was yanked cruelly off of her and Vess hissed as she curled up against the cold— "*up* and have some breakfast."

"Can't I skip?" Vess groused as she sat up shivering before trying and failing to pull the sheets around her bare skin.

More laughter. Vess was back to smiling as Wally sat down on the bed beside her, reached out, and prodded her cheek playfully.

Her two-tone hair fell around her face in carelessly attractive waves, and those expressive half-elven ears of hers were perked up happily through the delicate strands. For a moment, Vess just stared happily up at Wally, content to be right where she was.

"Given that you're the one giving the lecture, I'm going to say probably not," Wally replied, flicking Vess' nose.

Vess sneezed, then blew out a breath and flopped back over in bed with a deathgrip on the sheets. "But it's *co~ld.*"

"You are such a baby!" Wally slapped at Vess' shoulder. "Now get up! I've got coffee and breakfast waiting."

Rolling over, Vess brushed a tangle of hair from her eyes and smirked up at Wally. "Kiss me first."

"Brush your teeth first, you absolute gremlin," Wally said firmly, putting a finger on Vess' lips which Vess licked.

"Gremlin," Wally repeated.

"You love me anyway."

"Mm . . . I love you *because* you're a gremlin," she corrected as she leaned nuzzled her nose against Vess' before pecking a kiss on her lips. "Among a lot of other reasons, one of which is that you're an amazing professor who is regularly showered and on time to her lectures."

"That's a very specific reason."

But a convincing one, so Vess sat up, braving the cold while Wally returned to the kitchen. She had her own job to get to and Vess couldn't very well make both of them late. Besides, a hot shower sounded divine.

Stepping into the bathroom and cranking the hot water up, Vess let it run and fill the room with steam while she did her best to comb out the snarls that had settled into her hair overnight. Long hair was a hassle, but Wally liked it. She thought it was pretty. That was reason enough to want to keep it.

Vess hissed as she stepped under the flow before sagging in relief as she got accustomed to the temperature. Winter in Colvus was always brutal. The worst of Ulverike's winter winds blew straight down from the northern empire, across the plains, and down the Colver, bringing snowstorms aplenty with them. They would sweep in over the city and around the aerial spire berths of the merchant fleets, and coat the city in a heavy fall of pure white.

"And it'll be too damn cold," Vess muttered as she stepped out of the shower with a shiver before grabbing the towel and drying herself off.

Picking up her brush, she squeezed out some toothpaste and started in on getting rid of her morning breath. Wally would definitely make good on that no-kissing threat if she didn't, if only to teach Vess a lesson.

"Huh . . ."

Vess paused and stared at the fogged-up mirror. Written in the cloudy condensation, over and over, were six letters.

WAKEUP

Vess flinched as an icepick headache doubled her over the sink, and for a moment she felt foggy and disjointed. Her vision doubled briefly as the pressure between her eyes became unbearable. She took slow, even breaths through her nose, focusing past the pain, and when the sensation faded it left Vess winded and bracing herself while her swimming vision settled.

"Oof, wow, that was a bad one," Vess muttered, shaking her head as she massaged her temples and straightened out.

She swept a hand over the mirror, clearing away the fog. If that was the worst headache she got today then she'd count herself blessed. Running the comb through her hair to wring out the water, she got to work drying herself off before turning around to grab her clothes and—

"Shit." Vess chuckled weakly as she massaged the bridge of nose, then turned and thumped her head against the bathroom door. "Hey, babe!"

The door cracked open, revealing a smug Wally holding up her usual pair of clean dark slacks, undershirt, white button-down and tie, and a pair of unnecessarily lacy underthings.

"What would I do without you?" Vess said as she took the clothes she'd forgotten.

"Arrive half an hour late your own lectures with wet hair and no underwear?" Wally suggested.

Vess laughed softly as she caught Wally's hand on its way

out, pulled it close, and laid a kiss over the simple gold ring that glittered on her finger whose twin gleamed brightly on Vess' own hand.

"I love you."

"Love you, too," Wally replied with a grin. "Now get dressed."

"As you command." Vess cut a low bow, earning another laugh from Wally who put a hand to the top of her head and pushed her back into the bathroom.

"That's a lot less dramatic when you're naked!" She said as she shut the door on Vess.

Vess shook her long mane of red hair out and began the laborious process of drying it. "Are you complaining about me being naked?"

"Shameless," came the muffled response.

By the time Vess was decent—at least by Wally's standards—she had less than an hour left to get to class.

"Coffee, the gods own elixir," Vess muttered as she swept up her mug and took a long draught of the brew.

"Eat something, please," Wally said pointedly as she fiddled her purse at the kitchen counter. "I don't want you passing out halfway through your evening lectures."

"That's—"

"—again."

Vess pinned her mouth closed, then huffed as she scooped up a piece of toast covered in scrambled eggs. "That only happened once," she said before taking a bite.

"It doesn't happen to normal people *at all*," Wally pointed out, giving Vess a flat look over her purse.

Vess blew a raspberry, earning a chuckle and a roll of the eyes from her wife. The eggs were good if a bit cold, but that was Vess' fault for not waking up earlier. In her defense, their bed was *really* soft.

Taking another bite, Vess chewed thoughtfully as she tried to recapture her dream. There was something tantalizing about chasing it, but, like most dreams, it vanished into fog the moment she got her fingers around it. It was probably nothing, but curiosity had always been her greatest vice. It was, as Wally had pointed out more than once over their marriage, what made her such a good teacher.

Ding.

A message alert chimed from Vess' phone, and she frowned.

"Hey, babe, where did I leave—?"

"—left-hand coat pocket, like usual," Wally replied without looking up.

Vess chuckled quietly as she walked over to where her coat was hanging from the peg by the door and fished around the pocket with one hand while she took another bite of egg and toast from the other. Sure enough, her fingers closed around the slate of plastic.

"Huh." Vess hummed as she pulled it out and tapped through the lock screen. "No wonder I slept through my alarms."

"One wonders why you bother to set them," Wally chided gently.

"It's the thought that counts."

"I don't think that's true," Wally replied.

Shrugging, Vess tapped open her messenger app. The message was from an unknown number—but it was nonsense. Just six letters.

W A K E U P

Another icepick hit Vess right between the eyes. Her phone and her breakfast hit the floor as she staggered and put a hand to her temples and she hissed a sharp oath through her teeth.

"Vess?!"

Wally was at her side in an instant, steadying her as Vess blew out a breath. It was gone faster than the first one, leaving behind a numbing tingle in her brain.

"I'm fine," Vess mumbled as she got her feet under her again. "It was a quick one, I'm fine," she mustered a small smile for her wife and stroked a finger over her cheek. "I promise, I'm fine."

"Maybe you *should* skip your classes today," Wally said quietly, her ears pinning back in worry. "What if you get a really bad one?"

"I'm *fine.*" Vess got an arm around Wally's shoulders and pulled her close, pressing a kiss to the top of her head.

"Vess." Wally caught her face between warm palms and held her gaze evenly. "You just . . . you don't take care of yourself and it worries me, okay?" She lowered her arms to Vess's shoulders and hugged her tight. "I don't know what I would do if anything ever happened to you."

Settling her chin on Wally's soft, messy crown of hair, Vess slipped her arms around her wife's middle and rocked her gently back and forth.

"They're just headaches, babe, they're not that big of a deal," Vess said dryly.

Catching her wife's chin, Vess brushed her lips across Wally's before kneeling to pick up her phone and to sweep up the bits of egg and toast that had scattered in front of their apartment door. Together made quick work of the mess which Wally dropped into the trash while Vess tidied up the table. As she did, Vess glanced over at her phone again. No messages except for the ones about her missed alarms. Dismissing them, she snatched up her coat, pulled it on, tugged it straight, and turned to flash an insouciant smile at Wally.

"How do I look?" Vess asked as she dropped her phone back in her pocket.

"Brilliant and dashing, like always," Wally said as she reached out to straighten Vess' tie. "And don't forget your lecture notes." She nodded down to the briefcase by the door.

"That's—"

"—again."

Vess pressed her lips to a thin line.

"Will I ever get the last word with you?" She asked.

"N~ope." Wally popped her lips on the last syllable as she went up on her toes to kiss Vess again, more warmly this time.

Vess laughed quietly as she took up her briefcase, blew a kiss to her wife, then stepped into the clear, open space by the table to begin weaving a spell. Her fingers flicked through familiar motions while her tongue passed across phrases that unraveled the spatial sequences around her, linking her coordinates to the university's teleportation circles.

"Hey," Wally called out as Vess finished tying off the last

threads of the spell, letting it wrap her in a stable envelope of power.

"Hm?"

Her wife's smile was stunning, as always, and her eyes—brown, they were *brown*—sparkled with mischief as she blew the kiss back.

"Who does Misery love?" Wally called.

Vess chuckled. "Misery loves y—"

The envelope closed and Vess was whisked away to the university.

The world was awash in silver fire.

She was burning. Everything was burning. Threads were pulling her fingers painfully taut. Ten? No, twenty . . . a hundred . . . a thousand.

A thousand slipknot loops dug into her astral flesh as silver burned through her veins. She could feel her joints pulling loose and her fingers stretching. Every inch of her was being drawn and readied for quartering. The pain was beyond words.

There was no room in her mind for anything but the threads.

She had to make room for the threads.

Ten threads. Twenty threads. A thousand threads. However many were needed to pull her back from the brink.

One more thread, then.

A thousand and one.

Vess drummed her fingers across the face of the pulpit as she waited for her classroom to quiet down. She had almost eighty students crammed into a tiered lecture hall which wasn't strange for her. Her classes always filled up almost instantly come the start of each semester. It was always an even split, too, between people who were genuinely interested in the nature and history of curses, and people who just thought Advanced Maledictions sounded like a really cool course.

In their defense, they were right. It both sounded like, and was, a really cool course.

Her notes were neatly ordered in front of her, although per usual they were little more than an outline. Vess liked having room to improvise when she was teaching. Her students seemed to listen better when the lecture felt more organic.

Besides, she had it all memorized anyway.

"As I'm sure you all remember from last class—" the dying classroom chatter fell silent as she started speaking— "we're studying historical curses, of which there are about a billion." A ripple of laughter washed across the class. "We just went over plague curses, which were most common in the continental midlands, and why was that . . . Polly?"

The rough-looking girl near the back stiffened and sat up straight as Vess pointed straight at her. Paulina Truelight was one of the 'this course sounds cool' crowd, but she was also a lot smarter than the badly dyed black streaks in her hair suggested.

"Uhhh . . ." Polly stood up, doing an admirable job of throwing off her flop sweats as she did so. "Because . . . the midlands were—are—a breadbasket?" she began, but Vess could see her confidence start to rear its head. "Curses manifest through cultural fears, and, in farmlands, the fear of a plague spreading is powerful. Cursemongers take advantage of that zeitgeist to strengthen their workings."

"Very good," Vess said, and Polly practically glowed at the praise as she sat back down, and Vess turned her regard back to the class as a whole.

"So the midlands, regardless of kingdom or clan, most commonly saw curses in the form of disease and plague-spread. By contrast, the islanders of Arka Menais, if you all remember from last week, were more likely to experience storm-curses."

There was a general hum of agreement. Vess liked starting her classes this way. Taking a few minutes each day to refresh her student's minds before bombarding them with new information usually helped with retention, in her experience.

"But what about the north?" Vess asked, looking over the class whose last vestiges of distraction had melted away. "Here in the Union, our most northerly neighbor is, of course, The Rike Ulver, or Ulverike, more commonly . . . who can tell me the origins of that name, by the way?"

One hand shot up instantly, and Vess had to suppress a

chuckle. Jemma Corsivo had the worst and most obvious case of 'hot for teacher' that Vess had seen in a long time. Her ears were practically sticking straight up.

"Go ahead, Jemma."

"Rike is the old tribal word for a union of clans," Jemma began, her voice only cracking a little as her cheeks colored. "The clans would unite against common threats with a single leader at its head. The current Rike was forged by the matriarch of Clan Ulver, who united the clans against Oreliaun expansion in the early eighteenth century, which is why it was called 'The Rike Ulver', but unlike all the previous Rike's, the battle against the elves lasted for so long that by the time it was over, generations had passed, and the clans were all basically one when the armistice was signed."

Vess chuckled and nodded. "That's . . . yeah, that's true, but you digressed a little, there, Miss Corsivo," she said, and Jemma's cheeks went rosy. "The words?"

"Oh!" Jemma swallowed visibly and nodded. "R-Right, so, uhm, Rike came to be recognized as their word for 'Kingdom' but 'Ulver' just meant Wolf or Wolves . . . the uh . . . plural is the same as the singular."

"The Kingdom of Wolves," Vess said, pulling the class back on track from Jemma's impromptu history lesson. "That's right, and that tells us a lot about their culture, actually . . . especially in regards to what they fear."

"Fear?" Dolin sat up from where he'd been lounging near the middle of the class.

Vess grimaced. She wasn't supposed to have most and least favorites among her students, but the reality was that every professor did, and Dolin was far from her favorite. He wasn't lazy, but he was . . . entitled. He often acted like he deserved a better grade for his assignments regardless of the work he actually put into them, as if just turning in his essays should be enough to warrant a high pass.

"Yes, Mister McIntyre, fear," Vess repeated, fixing her eyes on him, and he shied back. Good. "Heraldry, armor, names . . . they're all masks of things we fear. We dress up as that which we fear because, in doing so, we take away the power those fears have over us," Vess said. "A wolf does not fear other wolves."

"Gods of aversion," he said quietly, and Vess raised an eyebrow.

He wasn't wrong. It wasn't often Dolin had anything particularly insightful to add to her classes so she was always pleasantly surprised when he did. Then again, he wasn't stupid. Just a bit obnoxious.

"That's right," Vess replied. "So now we come to our lesson . . . the curse of Rike Ulver is not plague nor storms, but *hunger*, and the ultimate symbol of ravenous hunger, in the culture and art of the Rike, is the wolf."

Turning, Vess flourished a hand, casting out streamers of light around her, and at the same time dimming the lights of the lecture hall. "There are thousands of legends pertaining to wolves in the Rike," she began, as the strands of light began coalescing into simple, artistic scenery, "but one of the most common variations is that of the Piper of Wolves."

The cascades of light she had conjured settled into the image of a snow-dappled village, with little figures moving about their daily lives.

"It always takes place during winter, and always during a lean season," Vess recited, her eyes occasionally passing over her notes to ensure she wasn't missing any of the primary details of the legend. "In the story, there is a huntress who dwells on the verge of a forest near the village, and each month she comes to the village with her best catches . . ."

Vess always preferred to tell the stories with her magic; with the lines and traceries of light that drew images in the air like a miniature movie. It certainly kept her students' attention better than just prattling at them, but, in truth, Vess did it more for herself. It was a way to keep herself in practice. Her students had no idea how much manual and mental dexterity it took to keep her impromptu pantomime moving smoothly. Each figure, each house, and each mote of snow was accounted for in Vess' mind, and the end product was beautiful.

In the floating images, the figure of the huntress went about her day, hunting lone djerda—a large, thick-furred ungulate native to the forests of the Rike that grew hard, knotted carapace over its flanks and shoulders. She downed it with skill and dressed the game before hoisting it over her shoulders.

"Night was falling, and the huntress made haste to the village," Vess continued, sending her little figure of light darting through the starlit snow. "She would sleep at the village inn and sell her catch at the morning market, but as she made her way down the frozen road, she heard the most curious sound."

Vess twitched her fingers behind her back, out of view of her class, and added sounds—an arrhythmic, atonal piping. Her students startled up, and Vess carefully kept the smile that threatened the edges off her lips schooled back.

"Pipes could be heard in the distance, and the huntress moved more rapidly, for they unnerved her. They were a devilish sound, you see." Vess turned her head just slightly. Enough to eye her students with an enigmatic smile. "Soon she was sprinting, then running. Fear had taken hold of her, and she considered abandoning her catch. No djerdi meat was worth being taken by a daemon, after all."

She had their attention, rapt and captured.

"But she kept hold of her prize and eventually reached the edge of the village," Vess blossomed a village made of spun light into existence in the middle of the darkened classroom, "and found, to her horror, that it was overrun by wolves!" Predatory shapes made of shadows darted from behind trees and buildings, snarling and gnashing their teeth. "The huntress cried out and threw her catch to the ground as the wolves raced towards her! She turned and fled deep into the snowplains, as wolves howled and the pipes bayed behind her. She ran fast and far into the night, and eventually collapsed!"

Vess snapped her fingers and the whole scene disintegrated, plunging the room into pitch black. Startled gasps were quickly stifled from her student, and Vess grinned as she slowly lit the stage again, this time in the shape of a small room.

"The huntress woke in a camp among other hunters, and she told them her tale." The classroom was deathly still, and she allowed her voice to fall low and carry. "They made haste back to the village, and found it to be empty not just of villagers, but of bodies! And most curiously of all . . . not a single wolf track could be found.

"The hunting party was baffled, and the huntress most of all, but she could still hear the pipes playing in the hills, and said to the others: *'Do you not hear them? The daemon pipes?'* and the other hunters looked at her strangely." Vess allowed the pipes to fall in volume, but remain in the corners of the room, barely heard.

"They did not hear the pipes," Vess continued, "and would not venture into the hills, for many wolves lived there, and the huntress grew angry! She resolved to go alone to search for the piper and the villagers." Vess twitched her fingers and showed the huntress gathering her tools. "She took her best bow, two quivers of finely fletched arrows, and her finest iron skinning knife, and went into the hills against the protests of the others."

The class was listening intently. Even Dolin was caught in her story, leaning forward on his elbows with his eyes wide as they stared up at the display she was weaving. Polly and her friends looked dazzled, and Jemma was grinning like a fool.

"She found many wolves in the hills, and killed them," Vess continued softly, "and lacking winter food, she took flesh from those wolves, and ate it. For days she traveled, deeper and deeper, always following the pipes, until finally, one night, she reached a great clearing where she found a strange, unnatural sight."

Vess wove a new scene; a wide and open copse, and populated it with wolves moving in strange jerks and leaps.

"It was like they were dancing, the wolves capered and howled, all to the atonal voice of the pipes, and finally the huntress beheld the piper." Vess conjured a shape that resolved with every word she spoke. "He had the head of a wolf and the body of a man, his skin was mottled gray like dirty snow, and the huntress called out, *'Begone daemon! And bring back the villagers you stole!'*"

Now, she really had their attention.

"The daemon lowered its pipes, but the piping continued in the huntress' ears, and the daemon said to her, *'I will go where I please, and I have stolen no villagers, little huntress, for they are before you!*' and he laughed as he spoke, for the huntress saw that he was right!" Vess flourished her hands, and the jerking, gamboling wolves turned upon the huntress' lithe figure. "The huntress cried out in denial, but even as she did she looked to the wolves, and saw that their eyes were not the eyes of beasts, but of men, and the daemon laughed louder as she fell to her knees while the dancing wolves that were not wolves circled her and swallowed her whole."

Vess swept her arms out and banished the image, and at the same time flicked the lecture hall lights back on.

"That huntress totally ate people, didn't she?" Polly said flatly as she blinked in the suddenly bright lights.

"Totally," Vess replied just as flatly. "But," she added, as she took her place back on the pulpit, "that was the point of the tale, wasn't it? The curse? The darkest fears of Rike Ulver are seated in starvation, a very real threat in the snowy north, and the most taboo thing to do following starvation is to resort to cannibalism."

"So curses in Rike Ulver . . ." Jemma began, raising her hand a bit redundantly.

"Curses of hunger and withering and delirium are the most common," Vess replied.

"Does that mean what happened to the villagers and the huntress was an illusion?"

Vess frowned and turned to scan the classroom. She hadn't recognized that voice. It had come from the rear of the class, the very back row, hadn't it? There was no one there.

"I . . . well, that's not really the point," Vess said. Pressure was starting to build painfully behind her eyes, and she massaged her temples as she tried to focus. "The uhm . . . the tale of the huntress is about fear in general, and uhm . . ."

For some reason, Vess couldn't get her eyes to focus.

"But what happened to the huntress? Was she eaten by the wolves? Did she become a wolf?"

"It doesn't matter!" Vess spat, and jerked her head up to scan to back of the classroom again. Was someone fucking with her?

No. Someone *was* there. How had she missed them? They

were right there but . . . but for some reason she couldn't make out their face because they were shrouded in silver fire.

"It . . . the huntress isn't the relevant part of the story," Vess said. Why was she suddenly winded? She felt like she'd just run a sub-ten-minute mile.

"Then what is?"

Vess blinked sweat from her eyes. She was too hot and freezing at the same time. Was she coming down with something? That would just figure.

"It's uhm . . ." Vess turned her notes over and tried to find her place, but every page said the same thing over and over again.

WAKEUPWAKEUPWAKEUPWAKEUPWA KEUPWAKEUPWAKEUPWAKEUPWAKEUP WAKEUPWAKEUPWAKEUPWAKEUPWAKE UPWAKEUPWAKEUPWAKEUPWAKEUPWA KEUPWAKEUP.

"Did the huntress ever *WAKEUP?*" The voice asked.

"The huntress doesn't matter!" Vess roared as an icepick lanced between her eyes.

Vess knocked her notes to the ground with a sweep of her arm as she glared up at the face, burning student in the back of the classroom.

"The story isn't about the huntress! It's about the curse! It's . . . It's about . . . about the uh . . ." Her head was pounding, her breath was coming in short, violent heaves.

Something was wrong. Where were the rest of the students? Where was *she?*

Vess looked around. Salt stung at her eyes from sweat that was pouring from her brow and down her back. Her hair was matted to her head and her button-down was clinging to her. What was going on? Something was . . .

"It's about . . . the curse." Vess swallowed thickly

In the back of her mind, the deep bass note thrummed hollowly.

"I . . . I need to go." Vess licked her lips as she grabbed her coat and pulled it on. "Class is dismissed."

She conjured motes of light around the tips of her fingers

as she focused on the spatial coordinates of home. She needed to get home. She needed to get back to Wally. Everything would make sense if she could just get back to Wally.

Vess threw out her hands and commanded the ways of space to open, and she was swallowed by a vortex of light.

CHAPTER 30

"—do not send backup! I repeat, *do not send backup!*"

Mizer winced at the feedback from the interlink. The justicar sergeant on the other line was, understandably, confused. Blowing out a breath, Mizer hunkered down a little lower on the opposite side of the hearse from the war that was being fought across the street and brought the transceiver back up.

"This is Chief Six to Justicar Station, we've got a domain-class exclusion down here with a Sunfall-cult ridden on the ground! Do not make that bastard's job easier by bringing him more meat!"

Mizer sighed and lowered his head, pressing it to the cold hard plastic of the interlink transceiver as they sent back a cautious affirmative. The mess they were in would be a lot less dire with the Justicars at their backs, but they were fighting in front of a ticking necrotic time bomb. If it went off, then every dead Justicar was not only a gap in the city's necessary safety net but an enemy that the remaining Justicars would have to fight.

Not only that but for all Mizer knew Dolin was just waiting for the city wardsmiths to open a gap in the seal. Teleportation wouldn't have been something he'd have thought to worry about with his old employee, but there had clearly been some changes.

Speaking of changes . . .

Sitting up, Mizer looked over his shoulder at Wally who was lying back on the gurney. Silver, heatless flames licked around her body. She was sweating like a hog, twitching and spasming with every other breath, and periodically calling out for Vess.

He didn't dare wake her. Not while she was still proxied and especially not while Vess was delimited. Something had obviously gone even more wrong upstairs than Polly had reported, though, because they should have been out by now.

Reaching across the driver's seat, Mizer muttered a quiet invocation and laid a hand on her arm to will a spirit of hearthfire and comfort to flow into her. It would soothe her and maybe offer her some support, but at this point, he was just guessing. By the same token that he couldn't wake her, he also couldn't offer any but the most generic support. Not without knowing what was happening. All he could do was trust that Vess and Wally would get out of that mess alive.

"We really doing this on our own, Mizer?" Siobhan asked as she hunkered down protectively beside him.

"We can't afford to breach the seal. We can't give that thing—" he nodded towards Dolin— "any more bodies to animate. And frankly, if *we* can't deal with him, then a bunch of justies aren't going to be much use."

It was a raw deal either way, because the flipside of that decision meant Mizer was asking his own team to face Dolin down without even the false hope of a little extra firepower.

Without warning, the hearse rocked violently as something impacted the hood. The windshield crazed with fractures and Mizer cursed, dropped, and rolled away before kipping up to his feet and lashing his arms out to either side. The asphalt streets rumbled beneath his feet as spirits of earth answered his call, and miniature cyclones wrapped themselves around his wrists and forearms.

"It's just me," moaned the slightly crispy lump on top of the hearse.

"Gods' hooks, Polly, you took ten years off me."

Mizer's second in command rolled off of the hearse and hit the ground with a meaty thump as her regeneration began twisting and snapping her shattered limbs back into place.

"Want some of mine? I've got a few *hundred* I'd rather not use," Polly groaned.

It had been a long time since he had seen Polly looking this rough. Her biomantic gifts could keep up with a lot of damage, but magic wasn't limitless. Eventually, even her durable lambda system would fail as it tried to regenerate through the wounds she was taking.

"How we looking out there?" Mizer asked as he tossed the transceiver back in the cab.

"Not great." Polly sat up, brushing gore-matted hair from her eyes. "I don't know how he's doing it, but Dolin's throughput is *unreal*."

"It's not him, he's being ridden," Siobhan said, looking over the cab of the car briefly, then said, "and whatever is riding him is strong enough that I don't trust myself to close with it."

Mizer nodded in agreement as he popped his head over the crumpled hood of the hearse as well. If Dolin *was* possessed by some patron of the Dark Star cult then fielding a corpse against them was the worst possible plan. Cursemongers had a nasty habit of being able to yoke the dead to their will, and, as strong as Siobhan was, Mizer had an ugly inkling that Dolin's rider was stronger.

Thankfully, Dolin and his tag-along were still at the entrance to the Heights playing guard dog for whatever reason. Cassidia was moving back and forth, her blade still shedding its false dawn over the street, and periodically darting in to test Dolin's defenses while Jemma stayed back, eyeing Dolin cautiously and waiting for Cass to give her an opening.

Shadows boiled around Dolin's feet, and every so often Mizer caught glimpses of motion inside that darkness. It was like seeing a great ocean predator move just beneath the waves in more than one way. He could feel a twist in his guts and a primordial, hindbrain fear of prey looking at an apex predator from afar.

"This *is* the work of the Dark Star cult, right?" Mizer lowered himself back down and looked over at Polly

She shrugged as she tested the grip of newly regrown fingers before looking back up. "That's what Vess said, but . . . something doesn't track."

"Yeah," Mizer glanced over his shoulder again at Dolin, "I can't parse out what kind of curse he's using. It's like he's carrying an infestation around with him in his shadow and I . . . that's beyond anything I've ever even heard of!"

"Sunfall cults get into some weird shit, Miz', maybe it's a variation on a calling curse?" Polly ventured.

Siobhan shook her head at that. "If it was a calling curse then I'd be able to hear it too, Pols," she rasped. "It ain't that."

"And where would they be coming from even if it was?" Mizer added. "Calling curses attract necrotics, and sure, maybe he could get a few dozen stray repeaters, and even amp them up, but nothing like whatever the hell those—" he gestured over his shoulder— "things are."

Sighing, Mizer massaged his temples as he tried to follow the logic. "And how is he keeping them caged up like that?" He asked, speaking more to himself than Polly. "It's like he's just conjur—"

The words died on his tongue, and Mizer licked his lips as he follow through on the idea. It *was* possible. In fact, given all the factors at play, it might actually be likely. If he was right, then he might know how to fight back . . . but he had to know for sure. If he went in half-cocked and was wrong then they would *all* die.

"You got something?" Polly asked, leaning in with narrowed eyes. "Talk to me, Mizer."

"Maybe," Mizer replied hollowly. "I have to confirm it though," he glanced back over the hood of the hearse and nodded towards Dolin. "I need you, Cass, and Jemma to keep him distracted while I call in a few markers from the powers that be, think you can do that?"

Polly chewed her lip as she followed Mizer's gaze, then asked, "How long?"

"Fifteen minutes, give or take, but you've gotta be loud, or else that thing riding him will *definitely* notice what I'm doing," Mizer said.

Especially if his suspicions were correct.

"C'mon, Miz', you know me, loud is all I know how to do, but what about Vonnie?"

"She'll stay here," Mizer said, looking to Siobhan who gave simple nod of acknowledgment before he turned back to Polly. "If that thing does . . . does get through you all, then hopefully it won't have enough grunt left to slave a dreadnought as old as Vonnie."

"Here that, Von? Mizer called you old." Polly's tone was soft, but had an edge to it that Mizer knew all too well. It was the sound of a soldier about to get dropped into a hot zone.

Cracking her neck, Polly smirked and rolled her shoulders. "Alright, then . . . time to get lou—oh!"

Mizer caught her by the wrist as she made to move, and she turned back with a frown forming on her face. The expression faded like mist in the sun as Mizer pulled her back and wrapped his arms around her. His enormous frame completely eclipsed hers, and she stood poleaxed in his embrace for a moment before cautiously returning the hug.

"You uh . . . you okay there, old man?" Polly asked quietly, her voice muffled against his broad chest.

Mizer let out a breath and shook his head.

"Be careful with that thing out there, Pols," Mizer muttered. "Because whatever that thing is, I don't think it's Dolin, not really . . . not anymore. And if my guess is right, and his rider goes all out? Even you won't be able to regenerate *that* fast."

Polly stepped back and flicked a look back at the roil of shadows that was Dolin. "What's stopping him from doing it now?"

"My guess?" Mizer began. "Miasma is hard to maintain. The stronger it is, the faster it burns, so as long as Dolin's rider is letting Dolin do the lion's share of the work, it can sit pretty for as long as it wants, but . . ."

". . . but I need to make it focus on me," Polly finished. "Not just Dolin, I need both of them—the rider and ridden—to focus on me, so the rider might actually attack."

Mizer nodded grimly as, in the distance, Cassidia dove in again, executing a technically perfect veil of blade-strokes in another attempt to cleave her way through the shadows to the center mass where Dolin sat laughing. She ripped through dozens of clawed hands and wailing faces, only for dozens more to billow out like an ash cloud and push her back.

"Okay," Polly said quietly. "Guess it's time to pull the manticore's tail, then."

Shadows spat and hissed around Jemma as she strafed around the torment of miasma that was spiraling around Dolin. His body was wrapped in layers of unholy power, and between those twisting, near-living shadows, she caught glimpses of silver fire flaring off of him.

"I don't suppose I could expect any help from a heretic," Cassidia spat as her latest foray into the tangle of claws pushed her back near Jemma.

"I might if you had a plan other than just headbutting the damn thing until it gave way," she replied. "But I guess that's the only tactic they teach you in the temple, so more fool me for expecting too much."

She could practically hear Cassidia's teeth clench. Normally that would satisfy her to some extent, but there wasn't much humor to be had for the time being.

Clicking her tongue, Cassidia raised Truelight en garde and looked back at Jemma. "I'm open to ideas."

"First time for everything," Jemma replied under her breath.

Cassidia bristled but didn't rise to the bait. In truth, Jemma didn't have a plan either. This was so far above and beyond her pay grade that it wasn't even funny. Jemma liked a challenge, but this was ridiculous!

"Isn't that fancy sword of yours supposed to be the *'ultimate weapon against evil'* or something?" Jemma asked as she moved up alongside Cassidia.

"Truelight is *a* weapon against evil," Cassidia replied tightly. "It is a blessing from Ys, but . . ." her voice trailed off, and Jemma eyed the paladin cautiously.

The few times she had laid eyes on Cassidia Truelight, she'd felt nothing but contempt. Her silversteel hauberk was always polished to a mirror shine just like her perfectly sculpted face was always plastered with that marble smile. She was an avatar of everything and everyone who had ever made Jemma's life miserable.

Now, though . . .

Her armor was dented and smeared with viscous black stains. That same ichor matted patches of her blonde hair to her scalp, painting her face with dull stripes of black. There were no more marble smiles, either, just lips pressed a hard line as she brandished her weapon against a foe that was proving to be more than either of them could handle.

Jemma moved to Cassidia's side and brought up her hammer and chisel.

"Stay behind me," Cassidia said. "Stand at my side and you'll only be torn apart."

"I'll stand where I want, *paladin*, now tell me you've got some kind of plan because my friends are in that tower and I'm not letting that thing wearing my old co-worker's skin keep them there!"

"That wasn't a request, *cultist*, that was an order!"

"Oh good, I love disobeying orders."

"If you're done flirting with my sister—" Polly stepped between them, flourishing her machetes around her— "then Mizer's got a plan and we're going to need you both to pull it off."

Jemma's ears pinned back. "I *can* find a way to kill you, Pols, you know that right?"

"What plan?" Cassidia asked, studiously ignoring her sister's barb.

Polly nodded at Dolin who was still stalking back and forth in front of the Height's entrance. He looked like he was talking to someone, his lips moving in rapid whispers. The muscles around his eyes and mouth twitched chaotically, as if there were two sets of expressions warring for dominance on his face.

"We're keeping the details close to the vest just in case," Polly replied. "All we need to do—" she raised her machete and pointed straight down at Dolin— "is hit that asshole as hard as we can for as long as we can until Mizer gives us the signal."

"What's the signal?"

Polly shrugged. "I assume we'll know it when we see it."

Rolling her eyes, Cassidia sighed and asked, "Are you at least sure that it will work?"

"Not even a little, but unless you've got a better idea hidden somewhere in your cast-iron panties, then this is what we're doing."

Cassidia grimaced but didn't argue the point. Instead, she reached out and laid an armored hand on her sister's shoulder. "The light protects, so too shall Ys protect you. Faith is a shield against the contempt of the shadows, may faith in Ys be that shield." With the whispered prayer, a veil of golden light settled onto Polly, who shivered as it settled into her skin.

"This time, and this time only, Cass," Polly muttered.

Rather than reply, Cassidia turned to Jemma and extended a hand, "Ys protects even those who stand willingly in the shadows, Jemma Corsivo, if they would but step into the light for a moment."

"Hard pass." Jemma stepped back and away from the proffered blessing. "My strength will see me through this or my weakness will kill me, Akur judges that fitness more fairly than your divine arbiter."

Cassidia withdrew her hand and scoffed. "Suit yourself, heretic, just don't die while you're at *my* back in this mess," she said curtly.

"That assumes you can keep up with me in all that tin," Jemma shot back.

Polly pushed both Jemma and Cassidia away from each other, meeting each of their gazes with a silent, respective glare. "You two can hate-fuck through your issues on the drive back, ladies, but for now I need you to nut up, knuckle down, and help me kick that colossal dumbass—" she nodded flatly toward Dolin— "in the bag so hard that his unborn children double over."

Dolin's head was a pounding, twisting mess of scattered thoughts and fevered memories.

Ever since the crossroads, every single day had been like a lucid dream. There was a strange disconnection to every action, as a kind of easy power flowed through his veins like a narcotic. It had been so simple to do everything he'd needed to do after the Dark Star had joined with him. So much easier than it had been when he'd been sharing his soul with the venomous bitch Gibson.

Up until this point, he'd been able to just glide through the world riding the most powerful high he'd ever felt. The concept that there could be this much power concentrated in a single person—in *him*—was mind-boggling, but he wasn't complaining. The Dark Star had promised him power and she had paid that power out in spades. All she'd wanted from him was the convenience of his physical body, and a few errands checked off her to-do list. That one of those things was sticking the bitch herself in a trap specifically designed to make her more miserable than ever was just icing on the cake but now something was wrong. He kept telling his legs to move forward, but they refused, while the power that had come as easily as breathing a moment ago refused to flow, and he was left pacing impotently in front of the damn building where they'd trapped Vess and along with whoever her new proxy was.

Of course, by now that proxy was either a burnt-out vegetable or just dead. Dolin had barely been able to handle Vess' strength. Some newbie with a month and a half of training under their belt didn't stand a chance.

So why, then?

Why couldn't he just *attack?!*

'Because it's not time, yet, darling.'

The muscles in Dolin's face twitched and seized for a moment as her words wrapped around his skull like a vice, exerting a brief inexorable pressure before letting go.

"We could take them! We could take all of them! Not one of them is as strong as we are! Not even that Ysari paladin bitch!"

'My, my, you really like that word, don't you?'

"What?"

'That word. Bitch. You say it in your head quite a lot.'

"I . . . well they're—"

'Tell me, Dolin . . . does calling women bitches make you feel strong?

Does it soothe the thin skin that covers that petty excuse for an ego?'

"Wh-what?"

'You know all of Sunfall's Ephorate were women, right? All . . . bitches . . . by your parlance?'

His muscles weren't working. His legs had stopped moving and his arms were pinned to his side. Dolin could barely get a breath through his slowly constricting throat as laughter bubbled through the meat of his brain, scattering his thoughts before it like a charge through a shattered phalanx.

"Th-That's n-not what I—" Dolin's tongue jammed up around his words as his jaw clicked painfully shut.

'I've endured your petulant self-aggrandizement for long enough. I mean, I know we needed a reflector talent for this bit but you? You were the best her so-called Cult could turn up? A petty little boy with a grudge? They really scraped right through the bottom of the barrel and into the sod to find you, didn't they?'

Fear coursed through Dolin like lightning. It was the kind of pants-wetting animal terror that he had only felt once—when he had proxied for Vess after delimiting her. That had been the more excruciating and terrifying span of minutes in his short life.

Until now.

He felt her fingers move beneath his skin, slowly caressing the muscles of his face and leaving them slack and numb.

'We're not attacking because killing them is a waste of time and power. We—and by we I mean you—are here solely to ensure that the Ascendant achieves her true purpose, and in order to do that we must simply watch and wait, and not waste our energy on trivial details like your pointless and frankly annoying little grudge against my lovely sister, are we clear?'

The pressure let up and Dolin staggered, and for a brief moment, he was aware that something was terribly, terribly wrong. Everything was cold and still. His fingers were stiff and unresponsive, and his eyes wouldn't blink properly, and he . . . he was choking! He couldn't breathe! He—!

'Oops! Poor boy, that was a close one, I pulled a little too far back that time, I'll own that that was my mistake.'

"What happened?" Dolin gasped as he drank in long, cold draughts of air. "I . . . It felt like I was . . . like my body was . . ."

'Everything is perfectly fine~' the soothing, narcotic wash of power flooded through him, chasing away his fear and leaving strength in its wake. *'See? Don't you feel better?'*

"Better . . . yeah." Dolin grinned as he nodded dully.

He felt much better. Much *stronger*. As strong as he knew he was. Deep down, he'd known that power was in him and that all he needed was time and someone who wasn't going to choke and rob him of his potential!

'That's right, you're doing wonderfully dear, now . . . oh, look at that, they're gearing up to take a swing at us. Your wish is being granted through a combination of sheer luck and zero effort on your part, just the way you like it.'

"What?"

'Oh, nothing. Go get'em kiddo, you got this.'

He *did* have this! He would have all of them! Polly, Jemma, Vonnie, and that Ysari paladin bi—Dolin spasmed as pain ricocheted through his nervous system before settling into a deep throb behind his temples.

'Language, if you please, dear.'

Swallowing back his gorge, Dolin nodded. Right. He had this, they . . . they would all pay. He was stronger than any of them. Stronger, even, than Vess-fucking-Gibson.

Right?

'Of course you are.'

Right.

CHAPTER 31

THE PEARL FLASH OF teleportation accompanied the faint snap of displacement as Vess reappeared in her home. Her head was pounding and her vision was spinning. Nausea roiled in her belly as she stumbled up to the kitchen counter and leaned against it, pressing her head to the cool, varnished surface as she took in ragged breaths.

Something was wrong. Right? Right or wrong? What was it?

Vess shrugged off her coat as she stood straight and carded her fingers through sweat-matted hair. Everything was a jumble in her head. Memories, dreams . . . and the nagging feeling that she was confusing one for the other. But which ones?

WAKE UP

An icepick struck her between the eyes, and Vess flinched and gasped as she rocked back, barely catching herself on the kitchen table before she fell.

"Vess? Is that you?" Wally came out from the hall that led down to their room.

Her brow was furrowed softly as she moved to Vess' side and put a hand to her cheek. "Oh, honey, you're burning up!"

Wally swept up a towel and moved to the sink to run cool water over it while Vess collapsed into one of the chairs at the table. Wally was here. She was here and everything was fine and okay and . . . yeah, everything was fine.

"Look at me, baby," Wally said softly as she caught Vess' chin and gently guided her face up.

Eyes the color of old-growth treebark in the summer sun stared back at her. They were such beautiful eyes. A beautiful—*mismatched blue and green*—brown color that . . . Vess blinked as the world flickered around her. It was brief. It happened so fast she barely registered it.

"Wally?" Vess mumbled as Wally brushed the cold, damp towel across her cheeks and brow.

"I'm here," she replied, "don't worry, I'll take care of you."

"Take care of . . ."

She felt almost drunk as Wally leaned down and got an arm under her before pulling her up and moving her slowly through the kitchen towards their bedroom. Vess forced herself to move, but every step was a labor. Her limbs weren't obeying her, her tongue felt fat and clumsy in her mouth, and her vision kept flickering and swimming.

Wait, why was Wally here? Why was she home? She had work, didn't she? At her job at . . . the . . . where did she work? Vess couldn't recall. It was like a gear was grinding in her mind and she couldn't get it to unstick and let the rest of her thoughts go on.

"Something's wrong," Vess mumbled. "Wally, stop . . . no, s-something's wrong!" She tried to push Wally away, but couldn't, she was so weak.

"You're sick, Vess," Wally said firmly. "You've got a fever! I knew you shouldn't have gone in today! You need to rest!"

Vess shook her head but didn't have the strength or energy to do more than struggled fitfully before Wally had her down the hall and sitting on the bed. Sweat was dripping down her face, burning her eyes and clogging her nose. Her mouth was so dry . . . she couldn't breathe and could barely see straight.

"What's going on?" Vess rubbed at her eyes and face. "I . . . I don't . . ."

"Sshh," Wally hushed her as she settled her hands on Vess' shoulders and guided her down to the bed. "Just sleep, okay?

You need sleep. You're sick, and you need to sleep."

"Need to . . . sleep . . ." Vess' head hit the pillow and instantly every ounce of exhaustion that had been bleeding through her muscles turned to lead. "Y-Yeah, I . . . no!" Vess shook her head. "Something . . . Wally, something is wrong!"

"Nothing is wrong." Wally knelt beside her and brushed a few damp strands from Vess' forehead. "You're going to be fine, I promise."

"But—!"

"I'll take care of you, Misery. I'll always take care of you."

Misery? Vess tried to push Wally away. That word; it sounded wrong coming from Wally's lips. There was something very wrong with the way she said that word. That name. Her name. A strong hand on her shoulder kept her down. Or maybe it was just the exhaustion. Vess couldn't tell anymore. Everything was so heavy. The world was a throbbing mess of fever sweats and . . .

And misery.

"Sleep," Wally whispered, "and dream, of quiet things . . ."

". . . of roots and mountain clouds," Vess mumbled.

"That's right," a gentle hand crossed her brow, sweeping away a layer of sweat. "And in those dreams of quiet things . . ."

". . . sleep and . . . and dream . . . again." Vess' eyes fluttered shut, and soft, rich laughter rolled across her ears.

"Who does Misery love?"

"Misery . . . loves . . . y—"

WAKE UP

—a voice softly humming the opening bars of Heartland Road stirred Vess from her slumber, and she groaned quietly as her mind begrudgingly started to kick free of her dreams. And she *had* been dreaming, although of what, she couldn't say.

Probably nothing important.

Right?

Vess pushed herself up from the bed, and the cool air of Colvus chilled her bare, sleep-warmed skin. She rubbed at her arms and looked around. Something was wrong, she had to—*W*

A K E U P—find Wally.

An icepick struck between her eyes, and Vess snarled a curse as she kicked the blankets away from her legs. She stood up and shivered. It took her a moment to find her clothes; a pair of pajama pants that had escaped the wash, some woolen socks that were definitely Wally's, along with a tee-shirt and a flannel button-down. It was barely enough to keep the cold air off, but it was better than being naked.

"Wally?"

Vess stepped out into the hall outside their room. It was empty and quiet. Eerily so. She couldn't even hear the sounds of the cars outside. Everything was so still that she could hear her own heart beating loud in her ears and the sound of a voice humming Heartland Road somewhere in the apartment.

"Wally?!" Vess cried out a little louder. Her voice didn't even echo. It was like the sound died the moment it left her lips.

The living room was empty. The kitchen too. Panic was starting to rear its head in Vess' heart. Where was Wally? Where was *anyone?* There was no sound except her own heartbeat and footsteps and the incessant humming.

No . . . no there was something else. Something beneath the humming. A beat. A thrum.

Ba-bum.

Vess whipped around at the sound of something small and delicate rattling behind her.

It glinted in the low light of the kitchen. The light flickered and danced strangely off of it, and the sight of it put an altogether different chill down Vess' spine than the one the cold air had given her. She was sure that thing hadn't been there when she'd come in. Licking her lips, Vess reached out and picked it up, turning it over in her palm as she tried to resolve what it was. It was bright. So bright that her eyes wouldn't focus on it.

No, not wouldn't . . . *couldn't.*

Scowling, Vess grit her teeth and forced herself to—*W A K E U P*—focus on the object. She focused through the light and the cold and the ringing in her ears and the agony of the icepick headache digging into the space between her eyes until she could finally—*W A K E U P*—see it!

A ring.

"You ever have a situation where you think that maybe you succeeded a little *too well?*"

Vess froze, then turned slowly to find Wally sitting on a stool at the kitchen counter, her head propped lazily up on one hand while the other gripped a tumbler full of some rich, dark liquor. What struck Vess most, though, was the voice. It had been Wally's voice but . . . the tone had been wrong.

Completely and utterly wrong.

"I mean," Wally continued, "the whole point was that she be strong enough, right? That was *literally* the point, but, and I don't say this often . . . but I think I might have overshot it."

The ring burned in Vess' hand as she tightened her grip on it while Wally sighed and knocked back the entire glass like it was spring water.

"Mm . . . still can't taste it," she muttered. "What a shame."

She stood and flicked the glass away to shatter against the wall, and Vess flinched as she backed up away from Wally who was advancing on her slowly. The ring in her hand was biting into her skin.

"You just won't stay asleep. No matter how many times I put you down she just wakes you back up . . . every single damned time. No matter how deep I bury you, no matter how hard I hold you down, she just keeps pulling you back up."

Dropping into the seat across from Vess, Wally flicked her fingers and produced a hand-rolled cigarette wrapped in cheap, brown paper. She snapped her finger, and a flame appeared above her thumb, and Wally took a few puffs to light the tip before blowing out a cloud of thick, pungent smoke.

Suddenly, Vess' gorge was in her throat. Her stomach revolted, her skin was crawling, and irrational panic was hammering at the inside of her skull.

It was dragonroot. Root was once a common vice in old Oreliaus—it was a mild stimulant meaning almost every mage's apprentice in the kingdom had indulged at some point. It could be found growing just about anywhere and was practically a weed. It was rare, now. After the rebellion, so much of Oreliaus had been rendered inarable. Whole swathes of the country were were magically scarred to the point that no living thing would grow there for generations . . . and anything that did probably wasn't healthy to be near, much less eat. The smell was unforgettable, though; heady and earthy, like incense.

"What's wrong?" Wally asked as she lowered the dragonroot from her lips. "You're looking extra miserable today, *Misery.*"

"Who are you?" The humming still hadn't stopped, neither had that persistent, irritating beat beneath it, and something tickled at the back of Vess' memory.

This was wrong.

"Don't you know your own wife?" Wally asked, flashing a grin and holding out her hand to show off the ring gleaming on her finger.

"You're not her," Vess said flatly, her temper flaring. "You're not my Wally."

"Ooh, *'your'* Wally? How brazen!"

"Shut up!" Vess slammed her fist into the table, then winced.

Blood trickled out from a tiny wound in her palm, and she forced her fingers open to allow the bloodstained ring she'd been clutching to roll out onto the table.

The spatter of blood was almost unnoticeable, crafted as the ring was from Oreliaun red gold. The two small holes that had bitten into Vess' hand were made by the setting which had been shaped to resemble the flared wings of a bird of prey, and borne within the grasp of the wings was a perfectly faceted crimson gemstone.

Ice sluiced down Vess' spine as she let out a quiet breath, then, all of a sudden, she started to laugh. It began in the hollow of her chest before moving down into a full, belly laugh that had her shaking in her chair as she grasped the kitchen table for support. Through it all, Wally watched, bemused, as she smoked her way through her dragonroot.

"It's . . . It's not real," Vess said quietly. "None of this—" she gestured vaguely around her— "is real."

"Why do you say that?" Wally asked.

Vess shook her head and rubbed at the bridge of her nose. The pressure wasn't going away, and she still couldn't put a finger on where she had been before this or what she'd been doing, but it didn't matter.

"Because you're gone," Vess whispered. "You're gone, and you'll always be gone . . . not even dead, just . . . gone."

She wanted to vomit. The smell of dragonroot was still thick in her nostrils. It was as overwhelming then as it always had been. It occurred to Vess, in that moment, that there was something she had never said before the end. Something she'd always thought, but never voiced because it seemed petty.

"I hate that smell."

"Hm?" Wally raised an eyebrow as she took another drag, then blew the stream of pewter-colored smoke out of the corner of her mouth? "This? You love this smell."

"No, I don't!" Vess hissed. "I hate it! I always hated it! I just told you I liked the smell because . . . because you always smelled like it! Because you were *always* smoking those fucking things!"

The dragonroot had burned down to the base, and the ember caused the shadows to dance darkly over Wally's face, making the shape of it look strange and wrong.

"Classic." Wally laughed leaned back in the chair, crossed her arms—Gods, Wally looked so much like *her* when she did that— and shook her head. "You're mad so you're picking a fight. Guess it was either that you'd storm off and lock yourself in the bedroom again, huh? You never change, do you, Misery?"

"FUCK YOU!"

The table shook violently as Vess slammed both fists into it, sending the ring rolling haphazardly around until it came to stop between them, and Wally eyed Vess calmly, the dragonroot smoldering between her lips, and after a moment, she sighed, then took the root between her fingers, and put it out on the table.

"And you still resort to tantrums, too, I see." She twisted the root back and forth on the table, grinding the ashen end into the surface. "Still yell and hit things whenever you don't get your way . . . you're lucky I love you so much, Misery. No one else would put up with that abusive shit."

Not real.

She's not real.

That look on Wally's face. It was the exact same look that *she* always wore; contempt and disappointment, like Vess had failed to live up to some invisible, unspoken test. She was shaking. She rubbed at her face, anything to push the memories away and to keep that monster out of her head!

"It's okay, though," Wally—no, that's not Wally, *that's not Wally!*—reached across the table and held out her hand. "We always got through our arguments. Everything always turned out fine in the end."

"Go away," Vess swallowed thickly and shook her head. "I . . . Y-You're not real. None of this is real. You're some spectral who's fucking with my head and I . . . and you're *not real!*"

"Take my hand, Misery," Not-Wally said. Her eyes had changed. No more soft brown; now they were odd and mismatched; left eye green, right eye blue. Those eyes . . . *her* eyes. "I still love you . . . even after what you did, even after you betrayed me, I still love you."

"Stop it!" Vess pushed herself away from the table, upending her chair as she stumbled back until she was pressed against the wall. "You can't hurt me!" she snarled. "Not anymore! You're not real and you can't hurt me anymore!"

Not-Wally's expression flattened and she stood up, then carded her fingers through her hair. She ran her fingers straight back along the center of her scalp and around the back of her head until she reached the back of her neck, where rubbed at the muscles that always bunched up there.

She always carried her stress in her neck.

"I would never hurt you, Misery," Not-Wally said quietly as she moved around the table towards Vess, then smiled wanly. "Too bad you can't say the same to me, huh?"

Closing her eyes, Vess tried to hedge everything out. She tried to find the divide between the curse that was trapping her in this . . . this horror show, and the real world, she needed to—*W A K E U P.*

The apartment shook, and Vess snapped her eyes open wide.

That voice. She knew that voice!

"Whatever you are," Vess snarled as she straightened out to loom over Not-Wally. "You are *not* her, and you are certainly not Wally Willowbark."

"Did you really think you got one over on me?" Not-Wally asked casually. "Did you really think I was *gone?*"

"You *are!*"

Vess snapped a hand out and the apartment rattled. The timbers of the floor exploded beneath Not-Wally's feet, only for her to suddenly be several steps back. With a graceful flick of her wrist, she turned the shards of dense wood away, sending them firing in all directions around her while Vess surged forward, wheeling her arms as she tried to seize control of the magic around her. This was a spell matrix. The whole damn thing was a giant spell! It was a curse and a curse was just a spell and every spell had *rules*.

With a snap of her fingers, she reversed gravity, and Not-Wally barked out a laugh as the ceiling suddenly dragged her towards it, and executed an acrobatic flip to land on her feet.

"Take off that face!" Vess snarled as she mentally grasped the table as it was falling between them and sent it rocketing right into Not-Wally's smug smile.

"Why?" She made a slashing motion and the table disintegrated into ash. "I figure I might as well get used to it!"

"You're not her!"

Vess spoke hate into the world; spitting lip-cracking syllables that rocked Not-Wally back on her feet, stunning her, and in that same moment Vess snapped her fingers and flipped gravity again, and they were both falling. Not-Wally crashed head-first into the stove, crumpling bonelessly for a moment before hitting the kitchen tiles like a sack of wet meat.

It was too much for Vess to concentrate on *and* keep her own feet, though, and she hit the splintered ground hard enough to crack a rib—for whatever that meant in this place. The sympathetic damage this fight was going to inflict was gonna be a real bastard to deal with when she got out.

Out . . . Out to . . . to the *Heights!*

Vess stumbled as memories began flooding back into her mind. Memories of the domain, the specter . . . fifth precinct, and . . . oh gods! Wally! She was still delimited and proxied to Wally!

'Vess! Please! Wake up!'

'I'm here! Wally, I'm so sorry! I'm here!'

Even as terrified as she was, the sound of Wally's—the real Wally's—voice was like water down a parched throat. Vess sobbed as she reach out and grasped the thread of the proxy.

No . . . not the thread.

'Wally?' Not 'thread' singular. There wasn't just one, or even ten. *'Oh gods . . . Wally, what . . . what am I looking at?'*

There were thousands upon thousands of threads. Silver fire burned along every single one of them, and all of them were joined at a single point.

Her.

They were all tied to *her*.

'I'm sorry . . .' Wally sounded drawn so terribly thin. *'I c-couldn't let you go, I h-had to pull you back.'*

Vess licked her lips as she focused her perceptions inward at the impossibility of Wally's astral proxy. Every inch of her was wrapped in burning silver threads. She looked like a marionette wreathed in silver flame. Patches of her astral skin were scorched, and there were deep, dark hollows around her eyes. Her hair hung lank in front of her face, and her whole body hung limp; suspended painfully in the rictus grasp of the proxy that she had refused to allow to fail.

'Don't apologize, Wally.' Tears were tracking down Vess' cheeks. *'Don't you dare apologize . . . not to me.'* She shook her head in disbelief. *'Not for this.'*

'Vess?' Wally's sounded close to tears. *'I wanna go home.'*

Vess nodded shakily. *'Yeah, I'm so sorry Wally, I . . . this should never have happened! I'll be there soon, okay? I'll get out, and we can go home!'*

Extending her arms, Vess breathed out and with that breath bled herself into the matrix of the curse. It was complicated, powerful, and the arcane engineering behind it was particularly devious, but it wasn't perfect.

She would know. She was the one who had written it.

Slowly, the apartment began to unravel. The outermost reaches went first . . . the bedroom, the bathroom, then the living room. It was a slow process. If she collapsed the curse too fast, it could take them with it, leaving the both of them mindless husks. She'd almost done it when Wally screamed a wordless warning just as an ironclad grasp closed around the back of her neck, closed with crushing force, and drove Vess to her knees.

"H-How?!" Vess spat as she stared down at the floor. "That curse should've turned you inside out!"

Not-Wally chuckled, it was a wet, animal rasp coming from a torn throat. "Do the math, Misery, how do *you* think I survived getting an inversion curse spat into my face?"

Vess' mind reeled. She'd inverted the focus of the curse in a local area around Not-Wally. It was a nasty *'taste of your own medicine'* trick to deal with spectrals that liked to curse people by briefly hijacking the miasma that made up their bodies and turning it hostile.

The problem was that the theory behind inversion was childishly simple and any half-decent sorcerer could undo the effect by flushing their lambda system—the magical equivalent of flexing and taking a deep breath. Sure it might burn like a motherfucker for a second, but most would do it by instinct the same way a normal person would try to put out a fire that had spread to their shirt sleeve. It only worked spectrals because they were dead. They didn't *have* a lambda system, meaning . . .

"You're not . . . not real," Vess muttered hollowly as she turned her head slowly to look over her shoulder. "You *can't* be real!"

Not-Wally looked less like Wally than she ever had. The left side of her face was slack and broken, the skin was hanging like a torn and badly fitted mask, while the right was pulled taut, giving her a grotesque, hangdog leer.

Those eyes, though.

It was those eyes that had first captivated her; strange and unique, mismatched and odd. They made their owner stand out even as the 'imperfection' of them had turned her into a pariah. Left eye green, right eye blue. Mismatched, heterochromatic eyes that gave her stare a strange, sick, fae quality. Those same eyes were staring out of the shattered facade of Wally Willowbark, strands of blonde poked through where her scalp had been torn by the combination of spell and impact. The glamour she was wearing was disintegrating around her, leaving behind the thing underneath to glare balefully down at Vess.

"I told you I'd find you!" she rasped, and Vess started to thrash and scream.

There were no rational thoughts left in her mind, just pure animal terror choking her thoughts and filling her nose with the smell of dragonroot as she scratched and clawed at the hand gripping her neck and holding her in place.

"Didn't I tell you?!" She bellowed. "When I gave you that ring?! *DIDN'T I TELL YOU I'D ALWAYS FIND YOU?!*"

For a brief, brief moment, Vess truly thought she'd gone insane. She was sure of it. She was absolutely sure that she had already gone completely mad. Then silver fire exploded around her, and Vess got a brief glimpse of a figure in a scorched tunic and leggings and covered in burning threads hitting the ground before—

"Get away from her!"

A barstool swung over Vess' head and cracked against the thing above her, and Vess hit the ground as the pressure around her neck finally let up.

Shivering, shaking, and curled into a miserable ball on the floor, Vess forced herself to look up.

Wally Willowbark stood protectively over her. Her astral form was scorched black in several places, and the threads tying the two of them together were spinning and twisting gracefully around her like a weavers loom, threading and unthreading, creating warp and weft in a manner that Vess had never envisioned for the proxy.

"Stay down," Wally snarled as she brandished her broken bar stool. "Or I swear I'll kill you!"

CHAPTER 32

Cassidia carried the glaring rage of Ys in her charge as she thundered towards Dolin with Truelight bared and flashing before her.

Tendrils of shadows, claws, and hissing, snapping jaws filled with heterogeneous teeth and fangs crashed around Cassidia as she wove between the deadly attacks. Years of combat experience, trained and live, showed through her footwork and economy of motion as she swept claws from knobbed wrists, twisted heads from oily necks, and severed lashing pseudopods where they neared her. Every advance began that way. Her expertise carried her, step by step, towards the man at the center of the undulating mass of darkness, but each step grew harder, more labored, and covered less ground until finally she was forced to a standstill, and then forced back.

Not this time.

"On your right!"

Polly dove past her, her smaller, more compact frame getting through spaces that Cassidia could never hope to fit. She spun on her axis, rotating like a whirling dervish as her machetes flashed around her, mincing half of the malformed entities that were crawling out of their master's distended shadow.

"Keep up, tin can!" Jemma slipped past her left side spitting noxious syllables that bent the space around her.

For a heretic, her will was truly ironclad. As a paladin, Cassidia could appreciate a brute-force approach to problem-solving better than most. For cult-priests like Jemma who worshipped the Master of Daemons, such approaches were not only appreciated, they were practically doctrine.

Runes flashed into existence in front of Jemma as she advanced, and each one was met by a ritual blow from Jemma's hammer, literally and symbolically beating her power into existence. Each rune was an imprecation to her foes as much as it was a declaration to man, god, and spirit alike that her name was Jemma Corsivo, and she was unashamed. She was like a battering ram; the barricades of her conviction and her will to power moving her forward. Claws and teeth scraped across the sickly violet light that surrounded her, inflicting bruises and abrasions where muscle should have torn and bone ought to have broken.

"Away with you!" Jemma swung her hammer and it struck one of the gibbering masses of teeth.

Where her ritual tool struck, unholy flesh boiled away like water on forge-fresh steel. Unearthly screams filled the air around them as Cassidia moved like the tip of a spear aimed at the heart of the wretched mass before her. The light of Ys filled her and it demanded one thing, and one thing only, of her.

Illuminate all shadows.

"Shit!"

The man they called Dolin was actually backing up. He was cursing and swinging his arms, casting more and more of his noisome spectrals at them.

"Die! Die! *Why won't you just die!*" Dolin spat. "Why won't you just—*Aaaaahhh!*"

His scream was shrill and sharp as Polly made use of her size to squeeze past half a dozen of his gnashing protectors, and with a flicker of her blade, sent his right hand flying away trailing a stream of thick, black, rotten blood.

"Get away!" Dolin shrieked. *"Get away from me!"*

He lashed out with his severed wrist and darkness exploded out of his putrid veins.

"Polly!" Cassidia closed the distance and threw herself over her elder sister, driving Truelight into the ground as a wall of fangs, hooks, and talons fell over them in a fleshy mass.

Light flickered around them, and Cassidia dropped to a knee as she gripped the hilt of Truelight with one hand, and raised the other—fingers splayed—in forbiddance. A golden dome held off the darkness around them, but it wouldn't hold for long.

"Holy shit," Polly muttered. "What . . . What the fuck was that?"

"I don't know," Cassidia replied tightly.

Polly shook her head. "It came from *inside of him!*"

"You think I didn't see that?!" Cassidia snapped a glare at Polly. "You always do this! Diving in with no thought nor discipline! You may be immortal, *sister*, but the rest of us are not! So have a care!"

"I have plenty of care, but unlike you, I actually trust my team to have my back!" Polly retorted.

Before Cassidia could get a word in, the sickly sound of ripping leather and tearing flesh filled the shadowed dome, and suddenly new light flooded in.

"Will you two get out of there before the Master has had his fill?!" Jemma growled.

Her arm was at full extension and painted across her open palm was a wide and intricate sigil—the Maw of Akur. Inside of the maw, however, was not the dark skin that surrounded it, but a deep, hollow, hungry void that pulled at the core of Cassidia's being. She resisted it, but the spectral mass that had been chewing away at her conjured dome of protection was not so fortunate.

Dull, sepulchral screams vibrated around the three of them as Jemma fed the miasma making up Dolin's minions to her hungry master, and Cassidia took the moment to scoop up her sister in an underarm carry, grab her blade, and bolt through the opening that Jemma had given them.

"Finally!" Jemma snapped her hand closed and back-pedaled several steps before falling in at Cassidia's side. "Anyone wanna tell me what the hell kind of spectral does *that?*"

Cassidia shook her head as she dropped Polly, who landed deftly on her feet, shaking off the manner of her extraction with a sideways glare.

"It can't be a spectral," Polly said.

"Polly's right," Cassidia replied, as much the agreement irked her. "A spectral can manifest something like flesh, but not like that. It had a physical presence." She turned and eyed the roiling mass of shadows down the street cautiously.

There was movement within, the figure of a man who was not really a man anymore if Cassidia's instincts were right. What that made him, she wasn't sure. She could name a hundred different classifications of corpse and spectral off the top of her head but this *thing* baffled even her.

"As loathe as I am to rely on . . . cult expertise," Cassidia began slowly before turning to Jemma. "Are there any corpses in the wider reach of your knowledge that could occupy a living body that way?"

Jemma's raised an eyebrow. "You're actually asking? I didn't know your pride existed in swallowable form, paladin," she said.

"Enough of your barbs, heretic! Yes or no!" Cassidia snapped, and Jemma took a step back.

Fear lashed across her face like a whipcrack, and for a moment there was a glassy, childlike terror in her eyes. An instant later Polly was between them, her gore-stained machetes held with casual violence at her sides as she eyed her sister gravely.

"Raise your voice at her like that again," Polly said, "and you're making your next charge into those teeth *alone.*"

"It's fine." Jemma put a hand on Polly's shoulder and pushed her out of the way, took a step forward, squared her shoulders, and met Cassidia's gaze.

She was scared. It took Cassidia longer than she wanted to admit to realize that, but Jemma really was scared of her. She could see it in her eyes; feel it in tension that surrounded her. Cassidia could actually *feel* Jemma's fear.

"No," Jemma said. "I've communed with the blind sages of Akur's Citadel many times for knowledge of the dead, and I've never heard of a corpse doing something like that."

"I see . . ." Cassidia turned to look back at the twisting shadows that were Dolin, then said, "thank you for . . . for answering my question, I apologize for losing my temper."

Apologies had never come easy to her. They came with even less grace after her ascent to the position of Knight Commander.

"So . . ." she looked back over her shoulder at them as she gestured at Dolin with her blade, "shall we try again?"

Jemma and Polly shared a look.

"Wait . . ." Jemma put a hand of Cassidia's arm, "what if those things . . . what if they're not spectrals at all?"

Cassidia frowned, then looked back up at the thrashing mass as it began to slowly congeal back. She could see him underneath it, pale and drawn, glaring back at her with hate in his eyes. His once rakish hair was matted to his scalp and over his eyes, and that black, viscous ichor dripped lazily from the stump of his wrist.

"Explain," Cassidia said as she raised Truelight between Dolin and the others.

"Jem?" Polly eyed her friend carefully. "What are you saying?"

"I'm saying that there isn't a single spectral I know of that's capable of something like that," she pointed down the street. "But . . . but there are a handful of daemons that *are.*"

Cassidia's heart went cold at that word.

"Daemons?" she repeated. "You're sure?"

"Of course I'm not sure," Jemma shot back. "But it's the only thing I can think of! A daemon can possess a mortal by force if they're strong enough, or with almost no effort at all if they're invited in!"

"I know he's not high-grade, but would that even work on a reflector?" Polly asked.

Jemma nodded. "Yeah, reflectors turn back pure magic and curses are just that, but a daemon physically merges with you, so a reflector's talent isn't as effective at hedging them out."

"Okay." Cassidia blew out a breath and gestured towards Dolin. "Let us assume that we're not dealing with spectrals like we thought, but a daemon. Theoretically, how strong would a possessing daemon have to be to do . . . that."

The notion put a knot in Cassidia's stomach. Daemons were rare for a number of good reasons, the largest of which being that they simply couldn't survive in the Real for more than a few moments without a properly desecrated sanctum or, at the very least, a host. Their bodies obeyed no natural law of the world, even simple things like thermodynamics didn't apply to their physiology, so when they entered the real, material world, and were suddenly subjected to those laws, well . . .

The world tended to win that particular metaphysical argument.

"There are a few problems with that question," Jemma said as she moved up next to Cassidia and readied her ritual tools. "The first is that a daemon doesn't necessarily have to be strong to possess someone if they were invited in."

"And the other problems?" Polly asked as she took position on Cassidia's left.

Jemma chewed her lip, then said, "Daemons don't use spectrals like that," she nodded at the roil and torment of shadows that hung around Dolin, "and they also can't just generate new flesh without being on desecrated ground."

"Except it did, so give me a theory to work with, her—" Cassidia bit her tongue, then amended herself to— "Corsivo! Tell me how it *could* happen!"

For a long moment, Jemma was silent. Dolin still wasn't attacking. Either Polly had wounded him more severely than they had thought, or the monster sharing his skin was keeping his leash.

And Cassidia watched the coin drop behind Jemma's eyes.

"The exclusion," Jemma muttered softly. "It's dredging power from the exclusion!" Her voice slowly rose in pitch as she pointed her hammer not at Dolin but at the housing block. "That's why it won't move more than a certain distance from the Heights! It's not a spectral, it's a daemon, and so are those little bastards surrounding it! That's not a shadow around Dolin, that's a gods damned hole in the Wall of Sleep! The planar barrier is actually *torn!* It's summoning its minions which is why it never runs out, but the further it gets from the exclusion, the more solid the Wall becomes and weaker it gets! That's why it stopped you from closing the exclusion! That's why it won't let us near it!"

"Oh." Cassidia turned to stare back at the twisting wound in reality with new eyes as she absorbed what Jemma was saying. It made a certain sense. According to lore, daemons slain in the Real weren't killed, their spirits were just banished back to whatever plane spawned them. So they were faced with what amounted to an endless army pouring through a pinhole.

"And we wounded its host," Jemma continued quietly. "Dolin is probably dying as we speak . . . he's probably *been* dying in slow motion for days, or maybe weeks, but the daemon is keeping him alive."

"Can we save him?" Polly asked.

Jemma shook her head.

"No," she replied grimly, "between the daemon reshaping his body to its needs and forcibly healing him through the process so that he'll survive the transition, his lambda system is probably a rotten, necrotized mess. The moment that daemon is out of him, he'll fall apart . . . maybe literally."

"Damn it, Dol, you fucking moron," Polly muttered.

"It's probably struggling just to keep him upright by this point," Jemma said. "There's no such thing as infinite magic. Constantly summoning that many daemons would kill any diabolist." She gestured to the snapping jaws and claws in the shadows around Dolin. "The thinning of the Wall around the Heights and the sheer power of the daemon inside of him is the only reason he's not just meat on the ground."

"It doesn't matter, we can't afford to try even if he could be saved," Cassidia said flatly. "Colvus can't afford it either."

Polly grimaced. "She has a point," she admitted. "Now that we know what it is, I have an idea as to Mizer's plan . . . which means we need to go hard, ladies, because once Dolin's rider pulls him back from the brink it'll start looking for threats and we need it to see us, not Mizer."

"We established that it likely can't move from that spot," Cassidia countered. "Why not just wait?"

"I didn't say it *can't* move," Jemma replied. "I said it won't . . .

it's perfectly capable of moving, it just gets weaker the further it is from the exclusion, but—"

"—but if it suspects Erik's working will result in its death anyway, then it would make its play all the same," Cassidia finished. "I recognize my error, then."

They would have to push Dolin and his rider hard enough to force its focus solely on them. This was more than just challenging some possessing spectral, now, though. A daemon was in a category all its own. Each one was unique and the codification of daemonic powers was, at best, unreliable.

"Polly, before we . . ." Cassidia looked over to her sister. "Why did you forsake us? Your oath, your duty? Truelight ought to have been yours, so . . . why?"

"A week wouldn't be long enough to explain that shit, Cass," Polly replied. "I'm not even gonna try right now."

"Then after this, you'll have your week, and I'll have my answer," Cassidia said sharply as she brandished Truelight. It was easier to say that to her. Easier to tell it to her that way than to tell Polly to be careful. To not die. There was too much distance between them for that. Sisters or not, there wasn't enough left of their childhood bond for Cassidia to force the words out.

But Polly nodded all the same.

"You good, old man?"

Siobhan stood steady at Mizer's side while he sat crosslegged behind the protective bulk of his employee. Sweat rolled down the corded muscles of his neck and between his furrowed brow as he took slow, steady, metronomic breaths.

"I'm good," Mizer replied after a moment. "How are they doing?"

"They're going in again," she said.

Mizer grunted his assent as every muscle in his body reported agony and strain, and his heart labored under the weight of the spiritual energy he was attuning himself to. As much as he wanted to worry and stress, he didn't have the luxury. Anything that might cause his mind to wander too far from the task at hand could quite literally kill him because that thing out there was stronger than anything he'd ever felt. Stronger even than the daemon of Bressig. The last time he'd felt something that hostile and powerful was two decades ago when he and Polly had been tasked to enter that slice of hell called Geddenheim, and to feel that kind of malignance in the middle of Colvus? He didn't have a choice. This wasn't something he could pull punches on.

"Mizer, you sure about this?" Siobhan asked quietly without looking away from the battle. "You know what that's going to do to you."

It wasn't a question. It was a statement.

"They can't win against that thing, Vonnie. I'm not even sure Vess could win against that thing without delimiting fully."

"That doesn't make it easier to watch you do it." Siobhan's dark, inhuman eyes were sharp with judgment.

"I know," Mizer said. "But you understand, don't you? You understand why I have to. You can feel that thing just like I can. You didn't lose everything when you died."

"Not everything, no," Siobhan rasped. "So yeah, I know what you mean. I can feel it whispering at the edge of my hearing like . . . like freezing needles in my soul. Gods, I'd forgotten what the cold even felt like."

Mizer nodded. That thing they were fighting was more than just a monster. More than a daemon or a spectral. It was a cancerous and profane existence. It was an *abomination*.

"How much longer?" Siobhan asked.

"The waters of this city run deep, ten more minutes, maybe."

Siobhan let out a quiet huff, then said, "they might not have that many."

"They'll find them," Mizer replied as he closed his eyes and reached deep, deep beneath Colvus to begin the final preparations for attunement. "Polly always does."

"What if it gets inside?"

"You know the answer to that question, Vonnie."

Siobhan tightened her ever-present grip on the haft of her axe.

"Yeah," she said after a heartbeat's hesitation. "I know."

• • •

Jemma followed Cassidia like a shadow in the wake of the rising sun, leaving night in its footsteps.

"Your turn to keep up, heretic," Cassidia said as light flooded her limbs and suffused her armor, and suddenly, she seemed to blur.

No. Not blur. Jemma's heart lurched into her throat as Cassidia *moved*. There was a subtle *thump* of displaced air, and her armor wrenched and howled with a scream of metal on metal as Cassidia's body momentarily exceeded the limits of her silver-steel plate, and suddenly she was several meters ahead of Jemma and within the shadowy roil of torn space that surrounded Dolin. Blowing out a breath, the paladin planted her feet in textbook perfect form, and swung Truelight like a stolen sunbeam up and out, splitting through the heart of the shadows with bellowed oath, and a split-second later a pillar of light slammed down from the sky like a bolt of lightning to meet the highest stroke of her sword.

The Divine Smite.

Only a handful of paladins in a generation ever acquired the level of blessing required to execute one due to the steep toll it demanded from the users body and soul. It was, in truth, a form of sacrifice. Divine smite channeled the unmitigated power of a god through the physical body of the warrior invoking it. It was temporary, but a mortal body even being fleetingly touched by the pure spark of the divine was something that was never meant to happen.

The finite was never meant to touch the infinite.

When the light faded, the shadows were left frozen in a peeled explosion like a rotten fruit dropped on the concrete, leaking their noisome fluid across the street.

"YOU BITCH!"

Dolin staggered back, stripped of his dark armor. His shirt was scorched to fragments by the gaze of Ys, and there was a wide, bloodless scar splitting him crosswise, hip to clavicle. It would have been a mortal blow if the miserable rotter was still mortal.

"Polly!" Cassidia barked as Dolin lunged at her, his wrist

stump was briefly bleeding shadow and ichor until suddenly it wasn't, and an inhuman, sickle-edged claw erupted from the gore.

The blade came within a handspan of Cassidia's armored flank before a compact flash of motion crossed between them, and the wickering of blades passing through flesh, muscle, and bone, hissed through the air and sent the unholy limb flying.

His shriek shook the air around him as he staggered back, his elbow hemorrhaging steaming bile while Polly landed in a low, bestial crouch below him, her arms crossed over her chest and her machetes resting against her shoulders. It was a predatory stillness that lasted less than a heartbeat before she moved again, her blades flashing in the sunlight cast from her sister's blade as she barreled into Dolin, cutting deep, killing furrows in his chest, across his legs and arms, and over his face in a sequence of strikes that Jemma's eyes couldn't even follow.

Behind her, Cassidia dropped to a knee. Her sun-kissed skin was pallid and drawn tight. The blowback from channeling that smite left her looking like she hadn't slept in days, and Jemma came to a skidding stop by her side to get an arm under her.

"Don't give out on me now, tin can!" She snarled as she pulled Cassidia away from the twisting coils of darkness. There was no telling when they would come back to life. For now, Polly was keeping Dolin and his rider's focus completely on her, but that would change soon.

"You never understood!" Dolin snarled as he finally found his feet and planted them.

The grievous wounds covering his body snapped shut all at once and began knitting with gut-wrenching undulations that flowing beneath the skin.

"You never understood me!" The bilious corruption falling from his severed right arm suddenly began flowing backward, then hardened into a sharp, wickedly knotted limb. "None of you!"

"Ungrateful brat," Polly spat as he lunged at her before dodging back in a fluid, acrobatic roll onto her back before planting both feet in his diaphragm, beating the wind from his lungs.

Pushing herself up into the air, Polly spun out her momentum, snapping her blades twice each across Dolin's chest, cutting four deep, horizontal lines across Dolin's chest, each barely a knuckles-width apart from one another, before her feet hit the ground. She'd barely touched the asphalt before she was spinning again, her spiral strikes cutting deep, vertical slices across the wounds she'd just laid into him.

Cassidia narrowed her eyes. "Why bother with the pattern? It's a needless waste of energy and showmanship."

"Shows how much you know," Jemma said calmly as Polly landed, and Dolin staggered back, breathing hard as his front was drenched in black gore. Except unlike the other wounds, they weren't healing. The flesh was moving, struggling, and shifting, but the wounds weren't closing.

"It's called crosshatching," Jemma said, pointing at Dolin. "Deep, straight cuts made parallel to each other won't heal right, and that's if they heal at all." She made the same pattern in the air with her finger that Polly had made in Dolin's chest—a five by five grid. "The muscle and tissue pulls at itself during regeneration, reopening one wound as it tries to close another, only to rip open the wound it just healed trying to mend the next one."

"That works on the dead?" Cassidia asked, for once sounding quietly impressed. "And the damned?"

"So long as it has to mimic human biology, yeah," Jemma said. "But not many people can do it, your aim has to be perfect, and you have to be fast enough that the thing you're hitting can't heal up between your hits. It's not something you can magic up, it's pure physical speed and skill." She smiled as Polly flicked ichor from her machetes and smirked at Dolin. "It's Polly's specialty. A regenerator that can turn off her enemy's regeneration."

Dolin scraped his fingers over the wound, trying to hold the flesh shut as he stumbled back another few steps.

"You're . . . You're nothing!" He spat. "Even now! You're nothing! This—" he gestured to the ruin of his chest— "means *nothing!*"

"Give up, Dolin, you've been a loser all your life . . . some two-bit cult magic isn't going to change that," Polly said flatly as she advanced on him. "We tried to make you feel welcome! We tried to give you place of your own, but it was never enough for you!"

"Bullshit!" Dolin screamed. "You were always looking down on me! You," he pointed one his remaining fingers at Polly, "and her!" He spat blood and glared at Jemma who met his look with a glower of her own. "Both of you! Mizer too! And Gibson most of all! That . . ." he grit his teeth as blood and black foam pooled around his lips. He trailed off, looking winded as planted his feet again and stood straight, sucking in a breath that sent another slow torrent of ichor flowing from wounds that refused to heal. "You all looked down on me . . ." He spat a gobbet of black mucus on the ground. "But now . . . now I'm stronger than any of you!" he cast his arms wide, one ruined and ending at his elbow, the other notched and bloodied with flesh wounds. "Now, I'm an avatar of the Sunfall's Ephorate! I carry Dark Star Mizrahi herself in my flesh! You stand no chance against me!"

Jemma heart grew cold at that name. It was a name that no Oreliaun dared speak aloud for fear of drawing the attention of its owner.

Dark Star Mizrahi. Disaster Mizrahi. Queensbride Mizrahi.

The legendary consort of the Sunfall Queen and an elven cursemonger of immeasurable power. Stories of the Dark Star were almost in the realm of myth. It was said she could speak the nightmares from your head and turn them real with a word. That hosts of the dead walked in her shadow, each specter damned into her service with a uniquely tailored curse. The blood of tens of thousands of elves dripped from her fingers, and at her feet lay the ruin of a kingdom.

Normally, Jemma would have scoffed at the idea that a being like that would deign to share a body with a roach like Dolin, but, seeing the power he was outputting . . .

It was possible.

"Gods . . ." Polly whispered, and Dolin sneered.

"Now, you fear me," he laughed. "Now you respect me!" Ichor-blackened spittle flew from his lips. "Only now that you're scared does it occur to you to show me the respect I *deserve!*"

Polly shook her head. "No, Dolin, I'm not . . . I was just thinking, you really are pretty fucking stupid, aren't you?"

"What?" Dolin stared, and even Jemma was wrong-footed.

"That's not Mizrahi inside of you right now, Dol," Polly said quietly. "I promise you that. I promise that, whatever is in there with you, it's not the Dark Star."

He sneered again, but it wasn't quite so confident this time.

"And how would you know?"

"Because," Polly replied, "the Dark Star was a cursemonger, and curses make spectrals and corpses, and those things—" she gestured down to the shadows around his feet and to his arm— "that you're fucking around with? Those aren't the dead, Dol . . ."

Finally, some semblance of rational fear seemed to penetrate his mind.

"What? No . . . y-you're lying," Dolin licked his lips as he looked down at his own bare feet before looking back up at Polly. "No they're just . . . th-they're—*Ah!*" Dolin flinched violently and staggered back, and he coughed up a gobbet of something meaty before dropping to a knee.

"They're daemons, Dolin," Polly said softly. "You're not proxying with an astral, you utter, *fucking* buffoon. You're possessed by a greater daemon . . . and you didn't even notice!"

"Th-That's not true!" He looked almost feral. "Right?! She's l-lying! Right?!" He wasn't talking to Polly anymore, or anyone that Jemma could see. There was only one being he could possibly be conversing with. "She's lying!" Dolin gripped his head as he spasmed violently. "You're her! You're h-her! You're Mizrahi! Right?! RIGHT?! TELL ME WHO YOU ARE, YOU BI—"

Dolin's head snapped to the side with a sickening crunch of bone, and the light went out of his eyes in an instant. The rise and fall of his chest stilled, and, moving like a marionette, he lowered himself to his knees, and slowly bent backward at the knee until he was folded almost double, with his bare chest arched up, and his head hanging boneless and grotesque from its broken neck.

"Damn it, Dolin." Polly shook her head, and turned to

Jemma. "Hey, Jem . . . you're about to be up."

Jemma nodded and moved from Cassidia's side, and the paladin slumped to a knee.

"Wait." A mailed hand caught Jemma's and she looked down to find Cassidia staring up at her with those eyes that were so familiar, and yet not. They were sharp and bright, but Cassidia's had a shadow to them that Polly's didn't.

"What?" Jemma asked, keeping her words clipped.

"Keep my sister alive." Cassidia's tone had a quiet plea to it. Jemma scoffed, but nodded. "As if I need you to even to ask."

"And you, too," Cassidia added, startling Jemma met the paladin's eyes again out of sheer shock. "You're not allowed to die either, heretic . . . and that's an order."

Yanking back her hand, she forced a smirk on her face as she stepped away from Cassidia. "You ass," but she laughed quietly, then said, "yeah, fine, this once . . . maybe."

Putting her back to the Ysari paladin, Jemma walked over to Polly's side while Dolin's brutalized body began to spasm and contort. The grid that Polly had carved into his chest exploded from the inside in an apocalyptic swelter of bone and muscle, and the deafening sound of shattering ribs. There was nothing human left of the flesh that had been Dolin McIntyre, and Jemma had to swallow her gorge at the rancid smell of rotten meat wafting up.

Gods, he'd been dead the whole time. The daemon had just kept all his organs running on manual—squeezing his heart to make it beat, and his lungs to let him breathe, but all the same he'd been rotting and he hadn't even noticed. It hadn't allowed him to notice. Not until Polly finally hit him hard enough to knock some sense into his thick skull, and the moment he'd started to realize what was happening the daemon had killed him.

"Come out!" Jemma shouted. "By the Master of Daemons, I compel you to declare your allegiance!" Jemma raised her hammer and chisel. "From whence amongst the lower hells and the shadowed realms do you hail?!"

No answer still, there was just a bubbling fountain of bile and viscera flowing up from what used to be a corpse.

Grimacing, Jemma brandished her the symbols of her dark faith at the gory mess. "Thrice I demand and be done! Name yourself!"

"Oh, very well . . ." A smooth, rich voice flowered out of the corpse and with it came a body like a sinful nightmare.

Her skin was stained dark from the liquid she came crawling out of, and the thick black braids that trailed from her scalp were matted down against her bare back. Long, delicate fingers ended in almost dainty claws, and when she finally emerged it was to lay seductively across the ruined meat of her host like it was a chaise lounge.

Jemma's stomach rebelled several times before she got it under control. The woman was beautiful, terrible, and hideously powerful, and her eyes were the least mortal thing about her. They were gold coins burnished like they'd been stuck in a forge almost to melting.

"My name," she purred, "is Hadria Mercutia . . . Or rather—" she uncoiled herself from where she lay, and set her clawed feet on the ground, and stood— "shall I introduce myself as 'Legions' Mercutia, fourth of the Ephorate." She swept her arm across herself and bowed mockingly deep, though she kept her head up and her gold-coin eyes on Jemma and Polly. "And it is my very great pleasure to meet you."

CHAPTER 33

WALLY HAD NEVER, AND would never, consider herself to be a brave person. Bravery and courage just weren't things she had in her most days . . . or any day, really. She was a coward and she had made peace with that a long time ago. Some people had that immutable quality that let them stand up to something objectively horrifying and dangerous, and then raise their fists in challenge. Wally was not one of them. Every single hardship and challenge that had ever come her way was one that she had shrunken away from. It had always been easier to just ignore it. It had never been worth it to fight because why try when she was just going to fail anyway?

Why spend the energy when it wouldn't make a difference?

"Stay down," Wally snarled. Her limbs ached, her body was screaming, and every inch of her just wanted to lie down and sleep for a thousand years, but she couldn't. Not yet. This time, Wally wasn't going to just let it happen. "Or I swear I'll kill you!"

This time, she was going to make a difference.

The barstool only had two of its three legs left, the third having come off when she'd clubbed the thing wearing her face away from Vess. The other two legs were only barely attached, and the seat wobbled as she brought it up between them. She didn't have much left in her. How she'd even managed to cross the illimitable darkness that had been driven between herself and Vess by the curse, she had no idea. All she knew was that she'd heard Vess screaming in a way that Wally hadn't imagined the stalwart woman was even capable of, and suddenly she was just . . . there.

Wally had gone from floating in silverfire shadows to standing in the middle of a disintegrating kitchen watching the woman who'd stolen her heart get *manhandled* by a twisted specter wearing her face. Admittedly, hitting it with a barstool hadn't been her smartest move, but at least it had worked.

"W-Wally?"

The voice that came from beneath her was tiny and barely recognizable as belonging to Vess, but Wally looked down to give her the best smile she could. "It's okay," Wally said shakily. "You're gonna be okay."

She said that, but . . .

"Magnificent." The thing wearing her face stood up. Half the flesh of its head hanging like wrapping paper from a flayed skull, and raised its arms up and out towards Wally. "Truly magnificent! Every time I think you can't get more incredible you just tear past my expectations!"

It ran its fingers through its hair, back to front, pulling the torn skin of its scalp taut and revealing patches of bright golden-blonde hair and tan skin beneath.

Wally took a step forward, raising her barstool between them. "I don't know who you are, but if you try to hurt Vess again I'll . . . I'll kill you! If it's the last thing I do!"

And it probably would be, given how much her noodly arms were trembling. Main physical strength had never been Wally's forte and apparently that translated over to whatever—and wherever—this place was.

"Wally, don't!" Vess staggered to her feet, got a hand on Wally's shoulder, and tried to pull her back. "Don't! That's not what you think it is! She's . . ." Vess trailed off as she looked up Wally's doppelganger, then swallowed thickly as she paled further.

The thing wearing her face chuckled and brushed away a lock of ragged hair that fell across her face. "Hurt her?" It echoed.

"I would never hurt her, and her name—" its mismatched eyes fixed on Vess' face— "is Misery."

"Stop calling her that! Can't you see she hates it?!" Wally snapped, advancing a step forward. "I don't know what you are, but if you want her then you're going to have to go through me!"

"Want her? I've had her." The way her own deformed face contorted into a lascivious smirk twisted Wally's gut into knots. "Lots of times." It grinned, cocking its head playfully. "And *vigorously.*"

Blood boiling, Wally lunged forward, swinging the stool at her double's head only for the creature to vanish as if she'd never been.

An arm settled over her shoulder.

"Has she spread her legs for *you* yet?" It hissed against her ear, and Wally spun around, swinging wildly through the air and hitting nothing.

Warm pressure fell against her back, and arms identical to her own slipped around her waist in a mockery of a loving embrace.

"She's like that you know," the voice continued sibilantly. *"Easy."*

"Stop it!" Wally swung about again, and again there was nothing and no one behind her. "Stop talking about her like that!" Wally yelled. "You don't know anything about her!"

"Don't I?"

Wally's guts turned to ice as Vess let out a shattered squeak of terror, and she whirled about to find her double had appeared behind Vess with one hand gripping her chin and the other settled sickeningly on her thigh.

Pressing her lips flush to Vess' ear, she grinned and said: "You know who I am, Misery, but does she? Does she even know who *you* are?"

"Get. Away. From her." Wally advanced with murder in her eyes.

She had never in her life been so righteously angry. As horrible as the words that were coming out of that creature's mouth were, even worse was the look they put on Vess' face. Wally had never imagined that she would see Vess look so broken; so fragile and defeated. It was like every word from that thing chipped away at her, carving a pound of flesh with each whispered sentence.

The Vess that Wally knew stood tall with her shoulders squared and her chin jutting out at the sharp, belligerent angle like she was daring the world to take the first swing so that she could show them precisely where they stood. Not now, though. There was no power in her now. She could cast, Wally knew that much. Vess had the power to fight back, but she wasn't. She couldn't.

Because driving gives me anxiety, okay?!

Vess was scared. So scared that her mind couldn't form the complex arcane calculus needed to summon her magic. Wally could feel the impossible strain of that terror was putting on their connection. If it weren't for her, the proxy would have disintegrated long ago, but she couldn't let that happen. Not here.

She might never get Vess back if she let her go in here.

"She's so charming, isn't she?" It said. "Beautiful and clever and brilliant, but all that charm is just another one of her tricks." It smiled with Wally's lips, and all Wally wanted to do was swing at it, but she couldn't. Not when it was that close to Vess.

"She'll draw you in," it dragged Vess tighter against it, "and then once you're there she'll treat you like garbage. She'll yell at you every time things don't go her way then give you the silent treatment until you've convinced yourself that it's all your fault and you beg for her forgiveness. Then she'll kiss you and be all charming again until the next time she wants something, and the cycle will repeat."

Tears were streaming down Vess' cheeks from wide eyes that were locked on a point somewhere on the horizon. She was shaking like a rabbit caught in a trap as that thing whispered poison in her ear, and not once did she raise a word to her own defense.

"I can see her already working on you, Wally, and it breaks my heart," it continued. "You're so protective of her. I was too. I still am. But unlike you, I've known her long enough to know that she's not the person she acts like." It idly moved its hand up Vess' thigh to settle on her hip. "Little Vess Misery is just a miserable bully, and, like every bully, the moment someone really stands up to her . . . she crumbles."

"You're wrong," Wally spat. "Vess isn't like that."

"Oh?" Its lopsided grin widened as it jerked Vess' head up so she was staring at Wally. "And how would you know? You don't even know her name."

"I . . ." Wally started to argue, but the words stuck fast in her throat.

Did she know Vess' name? She was over a century old, surely her name wasn't actually *Gibson*. Was it? It could be but the odds weren't high.

"I told you," it continued gleefully. "Her name is *Misery.*"

"Please, Wally, just go!" Vess finally broke through her silence. "Just . . . Just leave me here, okay? Just get out! Cut the threads and go!"

"I'm not doing that and you know it," Wally said quietly. "Even if I don't know your name, I don't care!" She moved towards them, holding the barstool high. "If that thing thinks that it can take you away from me, then . . . then I'll show it that I don't care!"

It smiled so wide that the skin around the corners of its mouth split.

"You want to tell her, Misery, or should I?" it cooed, then looked up at Wally. "Come on, say it with me." It moved its mouth around each syllable slowly, like it was teaching a child to speak. "Mis. Er. Ee."

"Shut up!"

"Miz. Er. Ee."

"That's not her—!"

"Miz. Ra. Hi."

Wally froze.

"Kids can be so cruel, but you already know that, don't you, Wally Willowbark?" Her double said calmly. "They'll turn anything into a joke, but especially a name, and especially if it's a name that sounds like something else." Misery. Misery. Mizrahi. "A childhood nickname can stick with us for a lifetime. Miserable Vess Mizrahi. Poor little Vess Misery. Orphaned, alone, and angry, with a chip on her shoulder the size of the Dragonsback mountains."

"You're lying," Wally whispered.

It scoffed as it finally let go of Vess who dropped to the floor in a crumpled heap.

"Why does everyone always say that?" It shook its head and laugh. "I don't lie, Wally. Lies are a waste of my time when the truth hurts so much more."

Wally drew in a shuddering breath, then looked down at Vess who was curled up on the floor in a pathetic little ball. Her auburn hair veiled her face, and what it didn't cover was covered by her hands, and every few seconds tinny little sobs squeaked out of her.

"Vess?" Wally started softly. "Vess? Please . . . she's lying, right? That's . . . That's not your name, is it?"

The silence was deafening.

"Vess—?"

"I told you," Vess hissed pitifully.

"What?"

Wally swallowed hard as she lowered the barstool. The threads around her were pulling to their absolute capacity. Vess was already falling apart, if Wally lost it too, then the connection would die and . . . no, she couldn't let that happen.

"What did you tell me?" Wally begged.

"That I'm a bad star," Vess mumbled.

Wally's heart dropped out of her chest, past her stomach, and settled somewhere between her toes. A bad star? *A bad star?* Vess wasn't *a* bad star. She was *the* bad star. That epithet only came into use in reference to Dark Star Mizrahi. It was like calling someone a walking, talking storm of bad choices and worse luck. Someone who brought . . . who brought misery to everyone who met them.

"You see?" It grinned as it knelt and reached out to pet Vess' hair, and Vess went rigid at the touch. "She's a liar and a scoundrel and a rake . . . they invented whole wartime laws in response to the things she did." Crouching over her, that thing wearing Wally's face pressed her lips to Vess' ear and said, "She's a monster."

Crack

The thing staggered and stumbled backward as Wally split the seat of her barstool across its temple. "Get away from her!" Wally snarled again, and finally her double looked surprised.

"Wally?" Vess looked up in shock.

Crack

Wally dove over and past Vess to shatter the remains of the stool against her double's shoulder, sending her spinning to the ground.

"Maybe she is a monster!" Wally spat as she adjusted her grip on the two broken stool legs she had left, wielding them like clubs. "But even if she is—" **Crack-Crack**— "then she's *my* monster! You hear me?!" She raised both spars of wood over her head and silver fire exploded around her. "SHE'S MINE!"

Her double threw its arms up in a panicked guard between herself and the descending meteor of silver flames that coruscated across Wally's limbs, licking around her shoulders and hair, and clinging to the fragile wooden legs of the barstool as she brought them down in an explosion of palpable fury. A nova of silver broke across the room, searing whole patches of the remaining realm while leaving both Wally and Vess untouched. The legs of her sturdy little barstool were scorched black in her hands as Wally stood up straight. She was shaking, and there was tears on her cheeks and she was fairly certain she was getting a little snotty. She really did hate crying.

Swallowing back her anger, Wally reached behind her with a hand open towards Vess, then looked over her shoulder pleadingly.

"I trust you," Wally said softly. "I . . . I still trust you."

Vess stared at her like she couldn't quite believe what she was seeing, but after a moment, she reached out and took the proffered hand, and instantly the threads reconnected, and time seemed to slow.

'I'm sorry, Wally,' Vess' thoughts slipped across the thread. *'I'm sorry I didn't tell you. I'm sorry you found out like that! I . . . I never meant to be that person, I swear it!'*

'I believe you,' Wally sent back. *'Now how do we get out of here?'*
'We have to break her hold.'
'Didn't I already? I . . .' Wally looked down at the burning corpse beneath her, then looked back at Vess. *'I killed it!'*

Vess shook her head.

'Look closer.'

Wally did, and what she saw turned her stomach. She saw her own face, brittle, scorched, and deflated, in the flames, along with the rest of her body. Her empty, and hollowed-out body. It had sacrificed the glamour like a snakeskin to slip away from Wally's attack.

'Where is it?' Wally looked back at Vess. *'How do we find it?'*
'I don't know . . . she might not even bother to come back out. She might just wait. Now that you're here she has nothing but time, after all.'
'What do you mean?' Wally knelt and took Vess' hands in hers. *'Vess, what do you mean?'*

Vess was quiet for a moment, and the crack and hiss of burning wood filled the silence as she sat up and shivered. Wally reached a hand out to lay it across Vess' cheek, but stopped short. She wasn't sure Vess would want to be touched.

As it happened, she needn't have bothered. Vess leaned forward almost desperately to lay her cheek against Wally's fingers.

'It's me,' Wally sent the calming affirmation to Vess as she stroked her cheek. *'It's not that thing, this time, it's really me.'*

Vess nodded and pulled herself closer, seeking affection in a silent manner that still seemed so alien to the normally proud woman.

'How do we get out?'
'Unless she shows herself, we don't.'

The finality of that statement settled over Wally's shoulders like a granite slab. That wasn't fair! It was just going to hide until she could keep the proxy stable anymore? And then just . . . win by default? That wasn't fair! Wally pulled Vess closer, wrapping her arms around the shaking, emotionally-crippled woman that had captured her heart so neatly, and whose heart that, Wally trusted, she had captured as well. As crazy as it sounded, Wally truly believed everything she had said.

'*You're really her, aren't you?*' Wally sent. '*You're really Dark Star Mizrahi? I thought she was an elf.*'

There was no denial, just a silent, desperate squeeze of her hand. So it was true. Dark Star Mizrahi, second of the Ephorate. The speaker of a thousand curses.

'*Later,*' Wally assured her, and herself. '*We'll talk when we get out.*'

'*I told you, Wally,*' Vess' stress strained the brittle threads connecting them, '*there's no way out . . . I know you want there to be, but trust me, I know her, and this is what she does. If she's shown herself, it's only because the deck is stacked and she knows she's won. Now she's just playing out her hand until we die of exhaustion or the proxy disintegrates on its own.*'

'*Isn't there a spell you can cast to get out?*' Wally pleaded.

'*If there was, I'd have used it, but this seal is airtight.*'

'*Then how did I get in?*'

Vess chuckled weakly and shook her head. '*That was impressive, but you only managed it because this seal is a trap. Traps don't keep people out. They keep their victims in once they've stepped in it, which we've both done.*'

Burying her face against Vess' warm, auburn hair, Wally sighed softly as the apartment smoldered around them. '*Can I ask . . . where are we?*'

Another broken laugh escaped Vess as she leaned against Wally and sighed. '*Just a dream . . . a dream where I was normal, and we were together and happy. It's a clever, horrible curse because the trap is subtle. It keeps you in it but it also convinces you to stay until you wither and die. I've seen people realize they're trapped, then just ignore it. They just live their little dream in willful ignorance while their body fails.*'

'*Your dream was . . . me?*'

Vess nodded and curled a little closer.

That was too cruel. The notion that the place where Vess would have been happiest was in a quiet and unassuming life with her, of all people, only to be trapped in a death-curse wearing its skin, was too cruel.

'*That's why you have to go, Wally,*' Vess sent after a moment of silence. '*Let the proxy go. Cut the thread. I should have died over a century* ago, so this . . . this is just time catching up to me.'

'I can't,' Wally hugged Vess tight and let out a broken sob. 'I can't just walk away and let you die.'

'It's okay, it was always going to happen because people like me don't get happy endings.' Vess laid her hand on Wally's cheek and gave her a tragic little smile. 'But I met you, and I got to kiss you, and . . . and I even got to tell you I love you, and that's not so bad, right?'

'There has to be something!' Wally cried. 'Some spell! A trick! Something! You're so powerful and so . . . so much smarter than me! There has to be something!'

Vess shook her head.

'What if you were fully delimited?' Wally asked.

There was a brief moment of rigid fear that slashed through Vess' posture, then she relaxed, let out a weak laugh, and shook her head. 'Maybe, but I can't lose my last limiter, Wally. That would require me to wear you.'

'And?'

'And wearing requires me to use your physical body, and it isn't here.'

Wally sagged against Vess, her final idea neatly shot down. It didn't escape her notice that Vess had seemed singularly relieved that she'd been able to shoot down the idea, though, which was frustrating, but ultimately trivial. Whether or not Vess was happy about it was irrelevant since they couldn't reach her—

'Vess? I got . . . I got in here because things can get in but not out, right?'

It took a moment for Vess to respond. There was a cold, heavy hesitation behind her words when she finally said, 'Yes . . . that's mostly true . . . why do you ask?'

'So could you summon my body?'

The tension bled out of her, and she shook her head. 'No, Wally, I can't summon your body. We're in a sectioned-off marble of pseudo-reality beyond the Wall of Sleep. I'd need a way to lock on to you, like a physical token.'

'You can't just use me?'

'No, we're proxied, the lock-on equation wouldn't be able to differentiate between you and me.'

'Then what if you did it the other way around?' Wally pressed, the idea scratching more heavily at the back of her mind. 'What if *you locked on to something of yours?'*

'You don't—' The thought-stream cut off sharply as Vess finally latched on to what Wally was saying.

Her coat.

She was still wearing Vess' coat.

'Wally, no!'

'So you can!' Wally pulled back and glared down at Vess. *'Right? You can pull me through and we can drop the limiters!'*

'Wally, it will kill you!'

'You don't know that!'

'It's killed everyone I've ever worn!' Vess seized desperately onto her collar. *'Wally, please, for the love whatever you hold holy, do not ask me to do that! You can't ask me to kill you like that!'*

Wally seized Vess' wrists and practically threw her next thoughts into Vess' mind. *'Then what gives you the right to ask me to kill you?!'*

She flinched back, then licked her lips and slowly let go of Wally's collar. Wally released her wrists gently and leaned in to press her forehead to Vess', and let she let out a quiet, shaky breath.

'You don't get to ask me to watch you die, either, Vess. Tell me, if we do this, and I die, will you get out?'

The answer came hesitantly. *'No, probably not . . .'*

'Do we have any other options?'

Another beat of hesitation opened between them before Vess sighed and said, *'No.'*

'Then at least this way, either we both live, or we both die.'

'Why?' Vess sent in a mental whisper that was heavy with regret and self-reproach.

'Wouldn't you risk your life to save me? To protect me?'

'In an instant.'

Wally put her hand to Vess' cheek and pulled her up just enough for their lips to meet. It was a warm, soft kiss full of longing. Full of fear for a life they might have that may never be. Full of a want for more months and weeks. More days and hours and minutes, and even seconds.

Because no amount of time would ever be enough.

When they parted, Wally just smiled, and said aloud, "Me too."

Taking a deep breath, Vess nodded, and together they stood amidst the burning dream that surrounded them. *'I guess you're really making me do this, huh?'*

'I guess I am.'

'I really am dogshit at saying no to you.'

Wally sobbed and laughed silently, but nodded.

'You really, really are.'

A bark of laughter escaped Vess, and she leaned against Wally as she shook, and pressed her forehead to Wally's as she whispered, "You're a louse, Wally Willowbark."

Smiling, Wally just leaned in, pecked a kiss on her lips, and said, "And how."

Closing her eyes, Vess took Wally's hands in hers and began to whisper.

"Wally Willowbark, do I have your full and knowing consent to lift all restraints and join as one, body and soul, til battle is done and the foe is made silent?"

"You have my consent."

Vess' eyes snapped open, glowing lambent blue in the silver firelight, and her mouth began to move in perfect ritual cadence. "Invert the Ro Invocation, release all processes to begin from zero, the song is unsung, the harmony unmade, releasing limiter restraints two and one in three . . . two . . . one."

With a snap of her finger, Vess called from beyond the Wall of Sleep, and the familiar energy sunk deep into every fiber of her coat answered.

CHAPTER 34

Polly's left arm struck the ground in three distinct pieces before she or Jemma could make a move. One moment, the thing was introducing itself as Legions Mercutia—the storied diabolist of the Sunfall Ephorate—and the next it was between them, and Polly was swearing up a storm as she tucked down and rolled away while Jemma scrambled much less gracefully in the other direction.

It was only a combination of terror-fueled reflex and pure adrenaline that had Jemma swinging her hammer in a wide arc in front of her, carrying a veil of solid violet energy with it as she threw the whole of her convictions into her will to survive. That terror saved her life as a claw the size of Jemma's torso slammed into the veil with crushing force, and sympathetic echoes of pain were beaten into her body. A blood vessel popped in her right eye, washing her vision pink and red even as she doubled over with vertigo. She tasted bile and copper as she rocked back on her feet for a brief moment before forcing herself stable.

Mercutia grinned as she turned her head lazily to look Jemma up and down. "You're strong, child."

Jemma spat blood and shook her head. "My strength is legion . . ." she hissed, *"for legion is the strength of my convictions!"*

"Legion, you say?" Mercutia grinned. "What fortuity."

The moment Mercutia had her head turned, Polly was up and running. Her arm stump flared viridian with biomantic power as the missing limb erupted back into existence, first the bone, then muscle and tendon, then skin, all in a matter of heartbeats.

Without looking, Mercutia gave a distracted wave of her free hand in Polly's direction, and that hand—and the arm with it—exploded into dozens of greedy, grasping claws. Too many fingers bearing shearing claws stretched out towards Polly, who roared as she carved through them, and ichor flew alongside hunks of meat and gristle before the main mass of the mutant arm caught the near-immortal regenerator.

Bone crunched and skin split as Polly thrashed in place, held aloft by evershifting hands and claws. Not even her freakish regeneration could push her through the sheer daemonic muscle that was holding her place.

"That's a good girl," Mercutia cooed. "Now, where were we . . . ?" she turned back to Jemma and favored her with an almost maternal smile. "I must say, I've watched your work from the back of that little weasel's mind—just peeking through some memories and such, you know how it is—and I'm impressed."

Jemma shuddered as she turned her body, autonomous of her arms. They were like separate entities, twisting and writhing in place where they sprouted from her shoulders.

"A disciple of Akur, aren't you?" she prompted.

"Akur takes no disciples, but I walk the crimson road behind him all the same," Jemma said. "If you are the stronger of us—" she raised her chisel and thrust it through her shield, deep into Mercutia claws, sending a jolt of power through her arm— "then come and have me!"

The elven diabolist shuddered in what looked like ecstasy.

"Is that what you want then?" Mercutia husked as she drifted towards Jemma with a venomous smile. "For me to 'have you'? Tell me, Jemma . . ."

Burning trails erupted in Jemma's mind, and suddenly she was sweating. Her heart was pounding a thousand times a second, her mouth was dry and her hands were shaking, and everything felt far too warm.

'I can feel your desire. I can give you everything you want~' Mercutia's voice was digging into the meat of Jemma's brain, filling her soul with rich perfume and toxic promise. *'She will never look at you the way you want her to, but I can make her love you. I can make it real. I can make the impossible, possible. Isn't that what you want? Or are you going to give up? Admit to failure? Will you fight with every ounce of your being, use every weapon at your disposal to make her yours, or—'* The perfume turned to searing gas in Jemma's lungs, driving her to the ground as the ground cracked beneath her. The skies split and the city of Colvus was plunged into an anarchic vision of fiery apocalypse as Mercutia towered over her in fiendish glory *'—will you fail?'*

Jemma screamed as the daemon's voice grated and scraped across her mind and soul.

'Will you fall to your knees again, Jemma Corsivo? Will you beg her for scraps of affection just like you begged for your life from the templar who came for your brethren? Will you be happy to lick her boots while she claims another woman's lips, knowing you could have had her for yourself if you had but the courage to ask?!'

"Begone from me, daemon," Jemma snarled trembling lips. "I . . . I will not treat with you. I deny you for you offer only the erosion of strength!" She snapped her head up to stare into Mercutia's bright, gold-coin irises.

"Strength?" She spoke with her true voice, and it echoed richly as she leaned in—her body still dripping with gore and ichor from her host's grisly death. "You speak of strength but cower in the dirt," she said as she dug her claws deeper into Jemma's shield, cracking her ward like armored glass. "You speak of which you know *nothing*, child. The strong do not speak of strength, for they have it already."

Jemma coughed up blood as Mercutia pressed almost playfully against her shield. The daemon was right. As wrenching and galling as it was to admit . . . that thing was *right*.

If it wanted to, it could shatter her barrier with a single blow. It could break through at any time, but it hadn't. It was playing with her, pushing against the bulwark of her will as if it were little more than sheer silk just to make it buckle more slowly and prolong the sympathetic pain that her spell reflected back into her. Licking her lips, Jemma forced her shaking legs straight as she stood. Every breath in her aching lungs burned, inside and out, and her vision was swimming, but if she was going to die to this thing then by Akur's thundering arse she'd do it on her own two fucking feet.

"Maybe you're right," Jemma rasped through bloody teeth. "But you aren't offering me strength . . . and I'll be damned if I end up like that walking chode—" she jerked her head towards Dolan's corpse— "over there."

The daemon's laughter was a narcotic cascade across Jemma's synapses and muscles. It was like her mirth was spilling over out of her soul and into Jemma's, and before she could stop herself she was laughing too. Cackling, really. It was desperate, breathless, and hysterical, and she just couldn't stop!

This was it.

She was really going to die.

"Oh, *child*," the daemon simpered as it swept its hand dismissively, blowing apart the remains of Jemma's shield and cutting the strength from her legs at the same time.

What exactly, the thing hissed into her mind, *makes you think you have a choice?*

Jemma screamed as the daemon's mutated limb coiled around her. Spines and claws scraped her flesh even as its alien mind peeled her psyche like an orange. Blood leaked from her eyes, mouth, and nostrils, and for a moment the entire span of her sanity was stretched to a single cord of steel pulled taut to the precipice of snapping.

You will deal, Jemma Corsivo. Its words poured over her gored mind like salt and lemon. *Or you will weep and shatter and break . . . and then you will deal.* Jemma's scream became a low, animal moan as the daemon writhed around her. *But you* will *deal, and—*

The weight, agony, and hissing words vanished without warning, replaced by an almost equally painful light, but the difference between the two was practically ecstasy in itself. Jemma collapsed as she was dropped to the ground in a heap while pounds of daemonic flesh and muscle sloughed off of her, rotting away with sickening speed as its grip on reality failed along with its physical connection to Mercutia.

"Get up!"

Jemma startled and stared up at the armored form of Cassidia, standing over her with Truelight bared and held between the daemon and the pair of them.

"Damn you, heretic, *get up!*" Cassidia barked. "I cannot hold it at bay for long!"

Swallowing back her gorge, along with enough blood to make it want to rise again, Jemma forced herself back to her feet.

Cassidia slid a foot forward, claiming another stubborn inch of ground as she forced her blade—the symbol of her faith—forward and Mercutia another inch back as her flesh boiled in the light. Darkness bled from the daemon, gnawing at the edges of Truelight's false dawn. Worse was that, inch by inch, the darkness was winning.

"Thought you . . . were sleeping back there . . . paladin," Jemma panted.

Cassidia spat on the ground and muttered an oath. "I'll sleep when I'm dead, Corsivo, and that will be sooner than later if you don't get your feet under you and *help me!*"

And she needed help. Her face was still pale and drawn from the strain of channeling pure divinity. The fact that she was standing and fighting at all was a testament to the monolithic will and reserves of strength that the woman possessed. Anyone else would have been left bed-ridden for days, but not Cassidia Truelight.

Jemma licked her lips. "Right, then I need you to . . . to buy me time, we need to free Polly."

"Buy you—" Cassidia bit down on her words. "Do I dare to hope that you actually have a plan?"

"Sure, that's a word for it," Jemma replied as she coughed up another mouthful of blood. "How much longer can you hold her?"

"Twenty-four seconds and counting."

"Good."

Reaching into her jacket, Jemma pulled out the steel case containing her special inks. It was dented from the rough treatment but still intact. Popping it open, she didn't bother with the brush, instead, dipping her fingers into the precious and expensive liquids, and scooping them out.

Shucking her jacket off, Jemma smeared a hangdog death's head across her face with her palms and finger, then started hastily scrawling crude gods of aversion across her chest and collar.

"Ten!"

"I get it!" Jemma snarled as she scooped more of the inks and started on her arms.

"Five, four—" The darkness was snapping and biting at the edges of Truelight's aura like a ravenous eclipse— "three!"

She jerked up her muscle shirt and slapped last of the ink across her core, painting her abdomen with a single glaring eye protecting the center of her spiritual focus.

"DROP IT!"

With a bellow of rage, Cassidia poured the last of her strength into Truelight and thrust it forward, pushing the dark back just long enough for her to backstep.

Gripping her hammer tight, Jemma barreled forward and at the same moment reached out with the bruised and bloodied span of her will and found what she was looking for; the chisel she had buried deep in Mercutia's arm.

She'd never performed this spell without her focus, but now she had no choice. It was possible, obviously. A focus was just that; a paradigm. A manifestation of intent that allowed her to cast without as much burden. Every magus, cultist, priest, and practitioner in the world used *some* kind of focus. Most used several. In all her time working magic Jemma had only ever seen one woman cast universally without the use of one and while she would never be the calibre of caster that Vess Gibson was, the demands of Akur were clear. Be stronger than you were a year ago. Be stronger than you were a month ago. A day ago. A moment ago. Be stronger with every single breath and beat of your heart.

Grow. Change. Evolve. Strengthen.

Be. Better.

Jemma screamed her defiance as she swung her hammer,

seeing clearly in her minds-eye the head of her chisel in each ritual point before her. The hammerhead struck the air with a dolorous tone of metal on metal as she beat the first runic syllable of Akur's name into the air at the same moment that Mercutia rallied and surged forward.

She was fast, but not quite fast enough.

The burning rune seared into existence and Jemma's soul erupted from her body like a shooting star. A shadow of her hammer was carried in her right hand and its head was lit with searing corpusant as Jemma aimed herself straight for the cold, familiar metal of her chisel.

'YOU WANT STRENGTH?!' Jemma howled into Mercutia's mind as she wrapped her burning soul around the miasmic mass of the daemon. *'I'LL SHOW YOU STRENGTH!'*

Mercutia let out something between a hissing scream and an ursine roar as Jemma used her chisel as a lever to tear open the gates to the daemon's flesh. The mind of a daemon was a fractious, chaotic thing. They could not be controlled nor possessed—not even the ones that were once mortal. Their flesh, however, was another matter. A daemon was a spirit, not a form. Without a host, their flesh was no more than ephemeral matter made real by their own twisted magic, and that method of existence created a pair of very specific problems.

The first was that such a body would be doomed to disintegrate from the start. It was made of energy and energy decayed. The longer the daemon chose to exist beyond the Wall of Sleep without a host, the more power took for them to remain coherent.

Secondly, that flesh was not their body. It was a construct. Like a vehicle quickly fashioned from spare parts, and vehicles could be hijacked.

'Get out!'

Jemma's body rocked back on its feet as the soul it was tethered to was dealt a ringing blow by the daemonic spirit she was wrestling with. The ink charred and cooked on her skin as it absorbed the brutal impact, and several meters away Mercutia's body writhed and twisted abominably.

There was nothing of beauty left to the facade of Legions Mercutia. Its torso bulged and distended as Jemma stormed beneath her skin, fighting the body's creator with all the rage and mongrel fury she had in her. Flesh warped and tore. Bones snapped, realigned, fused, then snapped again as a battle was fought inside the daemon. The whole time, Jemma kept a hard metaphysical grip on her chisel. It was her anchor. The focus of her strength. Mercutia had been arrogant to let her bury it, although in her defense it was likely that no one but Jemma was insane enough to try to wage a soul war against a greater daemon.

Somewhere in the throes of the battle, Mercutia lost control of the arm that was caging Polly, and with a twisting jerk of motion and will Jemma seized control of it, cocked back the mutant arm, then hurled Polly's mangled body at Cassidia. She was alive. Jemma had felt the woman's biomantic regeneration fighting against the damage that Mercutia had been inflicting. Cassidia dropped Truelight and caught her sister open-armed with a deafening clang, and even in the midst of her fight, Jemma mentally winced; Polly was definitely going to feel that head-first impact with her sister's hauberk in the morning.

'Oh, you wretched little girl!'

'Fuck you, you withered crone!'

Mercutia shrieked as she released the power that was maintaining her body. Her violently twitching form detonated and the explosion tore the chisel from Mercutia's body, taking Jemma with it. Her projected soul crashed back into her body, and she collapsed to the ground, twitching and aching. Her nostrils filled with the stink of cooked ink and burnt skin, but worse was the absolutely leaden sensation of her limbs. Metal-clad fingers closed around her arm as Cassidia dragged Jemma towards her. The paladin dropped to her knees, turned just as a wave of black, miasmic fire rolled over them. It crashed against Cassidia, and she bellowed in agony, but she held.

"You still live, heretic?" Cassidia grunted.

"For certain . . . definitions . . . of the term."

"Can you move?"

Jemma grimaced. "No," she replied after a moment. "I'm

... I think I'm done . . ."

Cassidia sighed as she pulled Jemma upright and cradled her in the crook of her arm. "You did well, Corsivo," she said quietly, and Jemma's eyes widened at the blatant compliment. "Better than I expected of you and that . . ." she pinned her lips shut as she shook her head and held out a hand.

A faint gold light spilled from the paladin's palm and it sank into Jemma's chest, soothing torn muscles and knitting the most grievous of the damage she'd taken. Almost immediately, Jemma felt a weight lift from her lungs and she began breathing easier.

"You could have given in to her," Cassidia said quietly. "Holier women and men than you would have, and have done, but you stood firm in your convictions and courted death before corruption." Cassidia lowered her hand and looked Jemma in the eyes. "I confess that I am . . . humbled."

Jemma opened her mouth in search of something to say, some response in the face of the paladin's unexpected sincerity, but found nothing. In her periphery she watched as the discarded flesh of Mercutia reformed and reshaped as the daemon expended yet more of its power to anchor itself in reality again, and finally she found it in her to huff out a dry laugh that caused her chest to rattle painfully.

"I think you're only saying that because we're about to die," Jemma said, nodding towards Mercutia.

The three of them were utterly spent. Polly was unconscious, Jemma couldn't even move, and Cassidia looked like the weight of her own armor was about to drag her to the ground.

Neither of them had anything left.

"Well! I must say that was more than I expected!" Mercutia said brightly as she reformed with a subtle clap of power.

The daemon stepped out from the disintegrating body it had violently shed to free herself of Jemma's attack, and smiled. Its skin was dark and unblemished, and its long braids were free of ichor and fell in three thick tails down its back. Robes of rich, lustrous purple and black silk edged with gold hung around it like the vestments of royalty and flowed faintly in the chill wind of the early Colvus morning as it fixed its gold-coin eyes on the trio.

"I understand now, why my sister is so enamored of your little motley." Mercutia flicked her fingers down at the ground, and shadows bled out around her, and in moments her aura of gnashing, snapping lesser daemons was around her again.

Gods, how much power did she have? Without a host, she should have been rejected from this reality long ago, but she just kept anchoring herself again and again! Even allowing for drawing supplemental power from the Heights exclusion, it was unheard of.

Mercutia advanced one step, then another, then paused as a curious look passed over its fair, elven features. It wasn't looking at them, though. It was looking past them.

The scent of clean water washed over Jemma, chasing away the stink of blood, gore, and daemonic ichor. Her aching muscles relaxed, and she nearly sobbed with relief as a broad shadow fell over them, and a wide palm settled on top of her head.

"You did good, kiddo, but I'll take it from here," Mizer said calmly.

She stared up at him, and even Cassidia looked stunned at what she was seeing. He was bare-chested, and whorls of azure light flowed beneath his skin the lengths of mighty rivers. That same light suffused the air around him with a calming aura that left behind a soothing chill in her pain-scorched muscles.

"Can you get them out of here, Cass?" Mizer asked as he moved between them and the advancing daemon.

Cassidia looked between Jemma and Polly, then clumsily scooped Polly up and threw her sister over her shoulder before pulled Jemma closer. "Arms over my shoulder, please, or I'll just drop you on your ass, heretic."

"I think I'd prefer that," Jemma grumbled, but she was too tired and burnt out to argue.

"Erik!" Cassidia called out. "Are you sure you can do this?"

He answered by snapping a hand out, and the air was suddenly filled with the roar of water, and Cassidia staggered back. The streets trembled that roaring rose to a deafening pitch, and at that same moment, a deep and terrible premonition sank into

Jemma's chest like a dagger.

"MIZER!" Jemma jerked weakly in Cassidia's iron grasp as she was dragged haltingly towards the hearse. "MIZER DON'T YOU DARE! DON'T YOU DARE!"

Siobhan strode past them, axe settled over her shoulder and her countenance fixed grimly on the storm brewing in front of her. Jemma saw something in the dreadnought's eyes that drove that dagger deeper.

It wasn't fear or worry.

It was grief.

"So." Mizer let his arms fall to his side as he walked forward. "Legions Mercutia, huh? I've heard stories about you."

"Have you now?" It purred.

"They say you know the names of ten thousand individual daemons," Mizer continued. "That you have a grimoire penned with the names of a hundred thousand more."

"Mmm, yes, storytellers do like their big, even numbers, don't they?" Mercutia replied wryly.

"I've heard other things, too, though . . . of the power you hold, and the *Word* that you learned."

Mercutia's eyes narrowed. "Oh? So she told you about that, did she? Color me surprised. Did she tell you about her Word, too?"

"She did," Mizer replied.

The daemon's expression didn't change so much as the air around her did. The atmosphere grew colder and more hostile, and Mizer grit his teeth against the sheer *wrongness* of it all. The elementals of Colvus were in a frenzy. Spectrals and corpses were one thing; the elementals disliked such beings, but they were still born of the world. This creature—Mizer refused to refer to it by any word so mortal as 'woman'—was of a place wholly divorced from the world. She was a sickness eating at the edges of reality and it was more than just her nature as a daemon.

She was steeped a power older than anything that Mizer had ever tasted.

"I know you, as well, Erik, bastard of Iosev." Mercutia's voice was the whisper of steel from an oiled sheath. "You, of the oldest faith. Not the ritualistic hubbub of the temples, but the deep faith that these modern sophists—" it gestured dismissively at the city around her— "call pagan magic. I admit I was surprised to learn the shamanistic ways of the elements still persisted . . . even in my time they were dying."

"I'll give you one chance, Mercutia," Erik said, ignoring its jab at his parentage. "Return to your realm. Go back, and we will have peace."

"Peace?" It echoed with a viperous hiss.

Suddenly she was gone, and a heartbeat later she was in front of Mizer, her arms twisting into curved, scabrous blades of gnarled bone as she spun and struck out like a dervish.

Mizer moved with the flow of the elements suffusing him and in that moment ceased to be Erik Mizer. He was the storm in the air and the snow in the sky. He was the River Colvus flowing deep and cold and strong for generations before and generations to come. He flowed around Mercutia's withering barrage of killing strokes, each one missing him by a hairs-breadth.

The daemon's grace was unearthly. Its body moved and twisted with gut-wrenching bonelessness, as if its joints weren't connected properly, but Mizer was patient; he let the river speak through the motion of his body, until finally he found the moment—the path of least resistance—and he flowed through that narrow space with the exorable pull of a riptide.

Four fingers held sharp in a dagger-thrust punched deep into Mercutia's abdomen, driven by the quiet rage of the waters of Colvus. Black ichor spilled from Mercutia's gullet as showed her first expression of true pain.

"W-What?!" Mercutia gasped.

Her voices sounded almost childlike. She actually sounded *scared*.

"I warned you," Mizer said as he closed his fist around something approximating a spine.

"G-Get away!"

Mercutia raised her arm, only to find the bone blade she'd shaped it into melting into that same black slurry. She struggled, snapped, and snarled, kicked and bit and cursed as Mizer dragged her closer and the sound of surging river rapids grew louder and louder in his ears until it was so deafening that it drowned out even the screams of a daemon.

The air around them whipped into a frenzy, carrying the lashing spite of whitewater and the cloying weight of drowning seas with it. The winds turned into a liquid vortex, spinning faster and faster about them with each passing moment as moisture was dredged from the water-rich atmosphere of the city. Mizer could feel the whole city around him and within him. He felt the canals like arteries and veins, and the streets like capillaries. Energy, life, people; everything flowed. It was all water and air and earth and fire. It was the fundamentals of all things. Everything was flowing, and now, it was all flowing through him and into Mercutia.

The daemon's scream became a keening wail of anguish as the elementals of Colvus raged through the unnatural body of Legions Mercutia, tearing great chunks of power from her too fast for her to be able to keep her body coherent. The comparative trickle of miasmic power she was siphoning from the exclusion was nothing compared to what she was losing.

Or to what she had already lost.

As he grit his teeth against the torrential forces pouring through him, Mizer had a moment of wan appreciation for his team and for Jemma especially. She was young, fiery, and easily lost, but when the chips had been down she'd done exactly what he had trained her to do. She had been exactly has fantastic as he knew she could be. Without her actions, Mercutia might have retained enough power to have an option outside of the one last resort he knew she would take.

"Bastard shaman!" Mercutia shrieked as she shunted the whole of her remaining power into her body, reforming it, solidifying it, then driving her claws deep into the flesh of Mizer's arm. "You think a mere channeler can break me?!" Her body began to melt and distort.

'I am a daemon beyond daemons,' her voice hissed viciously inside of his mind. *'Your soul is wide open and if you think these irate puddles*

have the will to keep me out of you then you're—' Mizer bared his teeth in a tight grin as the last of her flowed into him and spat a word in the tongue of the lords of water '*—WHAT?!*'

The word had many meanings, all deriving from the same source. It meant to Choke, Throttle, Hold, and Bar.

To Dam.

Mercutia scrabbled to eject herself from his body but it was far too late. The elementals raging in the vortex that surrounded the two of them crashed in over Mizer, and the world vanished with a sickening lurch as the elements followed his last command and sealed away every one of his meridians—and his connection to the elements and magic itself—forever.

"Water flows, Mercutia, but it can also sit, still and stagnant, rotting for all time," Mizer said wearily.

THIS IS NOTHING! she shrieked into his mind. *YOU ARE NOTHING! I WILL CLAW MY WAY OUT OF YOUR FLESH INCH BY INCH IF I HAVE TO!*

"I know," Mizer laughed. "You're predictable like that . . . *Siobhan!*"

He stood, turned, and threw his arms wide as the dreadnought came roaring out of the mist and fog of Colvus, and Mizer threw his will wholly against Mercutia's as she raged to take control of his body. He wasn't strong on his own, but he was enough to hold them both in place while the smile of Siobhan's cursed axe came down with a sickening crunch.

CHAPTER 35

Quiet. Everything was so . . . quiet.

She stood in the eye of a storm of silver fire that tore the world apart around her, remaking it with every breath only to tear it apart again, anew. It was the cycle writ small and cast into fast motion. The endless ritual wheel of creation, stagnation, and destruction spun past her eyes a thousand times and thousand times.

Life, death, life, death, life, death . . . It was all so impossibly big and yet so simple. So small and simple. It was all a game. A dream. The Dream Eternal, eternally dreaming of different worlds and different lives. Different existences. It dreamt it was a tree growing high upon the summit of a mountain until it was killed in a stroke of lightning. It dreamt it was a mountain, driven to divine heights by the inexorable crash of tectonic plates only to be ground to gravel by the passage of time. It dreamt it was a dragon swimming deep beneath the blackest stretch of the seas.

It dreamt that it was a girl, hiding beneath a table as monsters warred above it. Those monsters were great and terrible, like storms of power given names and voices.

One was a vortex of madness and hunger, its eyes—familiar and dark—burned hatefully as it opened its titanic maw and drew in the screaming essence of innocent souls. The Dream dreamt that it watched that monster kill an entire town for the sake of power, snuffing out lives like meager candles, all through the eyes of a child.

It dreamt, then, that another monster came.

This monster was crowned with horns of light and righteous curses that billowed in its wake like a cloak. The mist and miasma parted before her like an obedient sea. The world shook and cracked in her presence, and made the first monster seem crude and unfinished. Most strongly of all, the Dream dreamt of eyes that were like meteors. Like supernovas.

No.

They were like stars.

Dark. Stars.

Wally Willowbark opened eyes that were not hers and looked out at the false dining room that she had been sharing with Vess a moment ago. Had it only been a moment ago? She tracked the passage of time in her mind in a way that, a second ago, would have required concentration. Now, though, she simply pulled the information out and decided that, yes, it was just a moment ago. A handful of seconds at most.

For perhaps the very first time in her life, she felt calm. Perfectly calm. It wasn't the calm before the storm, either. That was an anxiety all its own. It was true calm.

It was 'Certainty'.

Her head turned, and she was vaguely aware that she was the one who had commanded it to do so. At the same time, she knew that it hadn't been her. That it was someone, or something, else.

Vess. That's right. Vess was with her now. Or . . . Or she was with Vess. Or she *was* Vess. Or maybe Vess was her? It was hard to tell. Hard to know the difference. Where did Vess Gibson end and Walythea Willowbark begin? Was there a difference anymore? Did it even matter?

Gods. Did it even matter?

"Incredible." The word came out in something very much

like Wally's voice, but layered with a rich contralto. "This is incredible," she repeated as her hand lifted and her head turned to examine it. "Fits like a glove."

Lines of white traced across her dusky skin. Echoes of another body—another form—lay just beneath, shining through now and again. She brought both hands up and wondered at them. Wondered at how easy it was to move. There was no pain. No restriction. No sense of confinement or pressure.

In fact, it felt like for the first time in years, she was able to truly breathe. Able to truly *think*.

All her life, her mind had been a buzzing hive of anxieties and neuroses, fears and doubts. Now, though? Now it was quiet. They were gone. They were all *gone*. The million buzzing blowflies of stress that had always filled her brain every moment of every day were suddenly *gone*.

And she could finally think!

Her hand swept up to brush a few strands of hair from her eyes and her fingers caught on something. Frowning, she flicked her fingers out and tugged a few strands of stray astral matter out of the dimensional matrix around her, tethered them, and commanded them into the shape of a mirror.

In the space of a breath, her mind wheeled through the calculations—energy coefficients, logarithms, and a thousand other tiny equations—without stuttering once, and the mirror shaped itself into a perfect silver oval in front of her.

"Oh!" Her voice again. No, not quite. It was Wally's voice and Vess' voice, together. "Would you look at that?"

She touched her own cheek and smiled. It was Wally's face, but only almost. Burning blue irises peered out from a face that was familiar and not. Lines of brilliant white light traced geometric patterns of symbological power. Monads and Gods' eyes decorated her cheeks while alchymic glyphs glowed along the laugh lines of her mouth and lips.

Most noticeable, though, were the dozen delicate horns forged of blinding white light that rose from beneath her hair like a crown.

"Wally, this is amazing," her own voice said to her. "It's like

... like nothing I've ever felt! Oh, Gods' hooks! Are you okay? Wally?!"

She was fine. She was perfectly okay, and Vess knew it the moment that Wally had the thought.

"Oh thank fuck." She blew out a relieved breath then straightened out and waved her hand again. The mirror expanded, drawing more matter from the space around it with only the smallest modification to the spell matrix. It was elegant, really. Wally finally understood how it was Vess could cast and modify her spells so gracefully.

It was because Vess never actually finished casting anything.

Every single equation was left open-ended, like a looping spiral. Like Pi, it just kept on calculating and calculating out to infinity until Vess needed to modify it, then she would insert the modifications, only to let it continue to spin and spiral. The spell that created the mirror would normally be cast and with set borders and circumference. Instead, it just kept on calculating its own dimensions until Vess wanted it to be a different shape.

It was a self-checking spell.

"So?" she asked. "How do we look?"

Oh, wow. Had she grown? Had she always been that tall? No, it wasn't that she was taller. Not really. She was just standing straight. Her shoulders were set and her posture was high and regal the way that Vess always held herself. Vess' greatcoat, which Wally privately thought looked a little baggy and silly on her smaller frame, actually fell nicely around her shoulders when she stood properly. The collar framed her face in a way that brought out her mother's strong jaw which was really only noticeable now that she was standing like Vess always did; with her head held high and her lips curved into a bellicose smirk.

The lines of her face were highlighted with runes of power and symbols of ancient grace, and the crown of horns on her head shone like a constellation. The light was balanced by the dark as the greatcoat trailed into wisps of darkness around her calves. That couldn't be her, could it? That couldn't be Wally Willowbark. That woman looked calm, confident, and *powerful*; three words that had never applied to Wally in her entire life.

"You doing alright, Wally?" She was, and Vess nodded as the thought formed. "Okay then, you ready to tear this dimension a new asshole?"

She was also ready for that, and Vess smiled at the vindictive shades of her thoughts.

"Alright, this isn't just me on this, Wally, you know that? This is us. Both of us. Right here and right now, this is all just . . . us. If we get out of this—no, when we get out of this, it won't be me saving us. It will be *us.*"

Warmth pooled in her chest and swelled up and out through her limbs. The way she said the word 'us' moved something in Wally that she hadn't even known was there. Something real and very much like hope. It had been so long since she'd really felt it that she almost didn't recognize it.

How long had she been alone? Truly alone?

"Wally, stay with me."

How long had she been completely empty of anything but the animal need to survive? To put one foot in front of the other going nowhere but to her next footstep.

"Okay, we're uh, gonna unpack *that* later, but I really need you to come back to me, Wally, please!" She put the thoughts away. She put the darkness away. Another time. Vess was right. That was for another time. She could . . . *They* would deal with that at another time.

"That's right, Wally," Vess said quietly. "And we will, I promise, but right now that monster is still here with us and she thinks she has us trapped."

But she didn't. Nothing could trap them now.

"Damn right." Vess raised their arms and turned out their palms, and that wonderful, incredibly brilliant mind of hers began to calculate. "And if you keep complimenting my mind like that I'm really going to blush. You really are a charmer in here, you know that?"

Once upon a time, realizing that someone else was sharing every single thought she was having would have mortified her. It didn't scare her anymore. At the very least, it didn't scare her right then. The only one who could see her thoughts was Vess, and that was alright.

"I am gonna kiss you so hard when I have a body again," Vess said, grinning.

Then their hands met in a thunderous clap of power. Brackish energy flared between their fingers as Vess moved Wally's lips around strange and noxious words. They tasted like oil and loam and peat on her tongue as she pulled their palms apart. Her fingers moved with subtle, twitching patterns, catching strands of energy and flicking them out in tiny echoes, instructing the world around them how to breathe and flex and exist, and then changing those instructions in slight but deeply profound ways.

It was incredible. She was fighting for control of an entire marble of reality that was, itself, controlled by a being strong enough to manipulate it like a smaller god. Wally could sense the tension. She could feel the malevolent consciousness behind the walls of the false apartment straining to keep control.

Straining . . . and losing.

Cracks appeared first; small ones so faint that they were almost imperceptible. Vess changed the spell, checking and re-checking and altering the tiniest variables to widen those cracks.

It was, at its core, simple maths.

What Vess did was no more and no less than what any other practicing magus did when they cast their spells. The only difference was proficiency—or rather mastery. What took others hours or days to calculate, Vess managed in seconds. Where others required totems, fetishes, and other foci to serve as crutches for their arcane equations, Vess computed every variable manually.

There was a phrase used to describe the idea of mathematical perfection. It was the high-minded concept that all the worlds and all the stars in all the universe were, if one thought about, just math.

Divine Calculus.

And Vess was just such a divine calculator.

Reality peeled apart, snapping like panes of fractured glass put under pressure. The cracks widened and Vess took hold of the magic, bled power through her fingers, and wrenched the whispering curse of domesticity that had caged her soul as much as her mind apart with a tortured shriek. Time warped and twisted about them as the Wall of Sleep bled from the wound it had been dealt. It would heal, given time, although Wally suspected that, if anyone ever rebuilt the Stymphalian Heights, it would experience a significantly higher-than-average rate of hauntings.

Wounds like that left scars, after all.

Tile and timber flew up to build a path beneath Vess' feet as she stepped forward. Silver fire and cloying darkness raged around them, and their face bent in an annoyed grimace as Vess gave a dismissive wave and banished the storm. Space and time drifted like a silent nebula in the distance. Clouds of memories passed over them while storms of dream and nightmare seethed on the horizon, and Vess scowled as she furrowed her brow and took in a deep breath.

"OPHELIA!" Vess roared. "COME OUT AND FACE US!"

The answer to her challenge came almost peacefully.

One moment, they were standing alone on the precipice of eternity staring out into the space between spaces that lay past the Wall of Sleep, and then . . . *she* was there.

Her appearance was heralded only by the soft taps of her shoes settling on a platform some meters away that hadn't existed a moment ago, and pain shot through Wally as she swore she felt their shared heart skip a beat. On the heels of that, though was grief, pain, and anguish . . . it was betrayal and choking bitterness.

"Hello, Misery." Her voice was strong and rich and had the quality of someone used to speaking loudly and being listened to.

She was on the pale side of bronze-skinned, with the long and gracefully tapering ears and high, sharp cheekbones of a full-blooded Oreliaun elf. Short, dirty blonde hair, styled in an almost punky, swept-back pixie cut crowned her head over a pair of eerie, mismatched eyes. All told, she was startlingly handsome and so androgynous that her elfin features seemed almost fae.

Most startling, though, was her outfit.

Where Vess wore dark colors and wore them well, this woman wore stark white trimmed with gold. Her coat, Wally realized, was almost the twin to Vess', but in opposite colors. Beneath the coat was a suit tunic of creamy silk that only accentuated her androgyny. Everything about her made her seem like a strange mirror to Vess Gibson. Bright, where Vess was dark. Gaudy where Vess was understated.

Frankly, Wally sort of hated it.

"Phee," Vess said quietly. "You should have stayed in hell."

"Oh, you know me," the woman that Vess called Ophelia replied dryly. "Restless legs and all that. I never could sit still for long."

"I'd ask how you got out, but I don't really care," Vess continued. "All that matters is that I put you back in your fucking box."

"Says the girl in the soup can. I love that, by the way. Hilarious. You found a good one."

Wally bristled at that.

"Don't you talk about her!" Vess hissed.

Ophelia shook her head. "I'm serious, you must have noticed by now that that girl is something special."

"She *is* special, but I get the feeling that we're not talking about the same qualities here." Vess bared their teeth and took another step forward, her movements synchronized perfectly with Wally's.

If Ophelia wanted them both mad, then that's what she would get.

"Oh, don't be coy, Misery, you've always been attracted to power and that girl is practically *oozing* with it."

Power? Their face fell in a frown that echoed Wally's confusion as much as Vess'.

"You're blowing hot air, Phee. Your trap failed just like your rebellion." Vess' tone was tight with barely contained anger as she stalked around Ophelia.

"*My* rebellion?" There was laughter hiding under her voice as she pretended to examine her nails. "You say that as if you're not the one who started the whole thing." Her face settled into a self-satisfied smirk. "Remind me again who it was who murdered my father and his pompous court in their sleep? Who spoke her dweomer into the dreams of King Constantius Invictus Oreliaus until his nightmares clawed their way out of his flesh?"

Their stomach flipped, but Wally refused to balk. She knew who Vess was. She knew full well the horrible things that were attributed to Dark Star Mizrahi during the Sunfall Rebellions, but she wasn't going to let the woman that war was *named after* get under her skin. Vess would tell her everything. She'd promised.

"You're right, and I did it for you," Vess said shakily. "I did everything for you because you told me that it was necessary, and I believed you because I was stupid and in love."

Ophelia shook her head and sighed. "It's always someone else, isn't it, Misery? Even after all these years, you haven't changed a bit." She eyed Vess pityingly. "Even after all these years, you're still *using* the people who love you."

Vess bared her teeth, snapped out a hand, and there was a thunderclap of pressure as the space around Ophelia violently compressed. Crushing force wrapped around her, but stopped a handspan from her body as she spread her hands and caught the folds of power. She was still as powerful as Vess remembered, Wally could feel the thrum of memories—memories of the powers that Ophelia once wielded.

"You *never* loved me!" Vess growled as she pushed the bands of force down. "You only ever loved what I could *do!*"

Grunting, Ophelia pressed outward against the immense weight, fighting the spell of compression. She wasn't quite losing. Not yet. The spell was beginning to fracture against the waves of magic and countermagic flowing between the two.

"Keep telling yourself that, Misery, I'm sure it makes your betrayals of personal convenience easier to justify."

'Shut up!'

The air around them rippled and Ophelia staggered as the strain redoubled, and the bands of compression solidified and snapped tighter, nearly closing around her before she caught them again, although it nearly didn't matter because Vess almost lost the spell entirely as her control of the Wearing shuddered. Numbness shot through her limbs like venom only to fade as Wally actually *pushed* beyond Vess' control.

"My my, would you look at that." Ophelia's voice was strained but still strong. "Every gods damned time, you surprise me. I don't know why I keep underestimating you."

"Wally?" Vess whispered. "That's not . . . how are you—? We're melded! How did you do that?!"

She didn't know. One moment they had been synced up, the next Wally had been so angry that she'd just . . . lashed out.

"You still don't understand the extent of her power," Ophelia said with a dry laugh. "She's just a toy to you."

"You don't know anything about her!" Vess roared.

"I know *everything* about her!"

Conjured power slammed into the field of energy surrounding her, spearing through Vess' spell and shattering the bands. Vess staggered with a bark of sympathetic pain as gold light spilled from Ophelia's body like a venomous sunrise.

"You've always been arrogant! But this is beyond the pale even for you!" Ophelia struck out with a bolt that scorched the half-light of the disintegrating dimension around them, leaving a painful after-image burnt into the air.

Vess and Wally moved as one and batted the bolt away with a pulse of brackish light.

"I won't let you manipulate her like you did me!" Vess snarled as she pulled pure power from the crackling air.

"Manipulate her?!" Ophelia roared with laughter as she ascended on ethereal winds. *"I'm the one who created her!"*

The bottom dropped out of Wally's stomach, and Vess staggered as Wally reeled back, then rallied as she clung to Vess like a security blanket.

"Liar," Vess said quietly as she rose up with her coat billowing out around her like great bat-wings.

"I told you, Misery, I never lie. It's pointless when truth always hurts so much more."

The strain of their bond was beginning to pull at the edges of the Wearing, and Vess grimaced. "She's lying, Wally," she whispered. "She's just trying to get under our skin."

"Oh don't give the girl false hope, Misery, that's just cruel," Ophelia jeered.

"Shut up!" Vess snapped. "You have no idea what she's been through!"

"I know exactly what she's been through," Ophelia replied flatly, all humor fading from her fae features. "Walythea Wilhelmina Willowbark, daughter of Anathea Rhumina Willowbark and Gaven Lasthammer." She fixed her eyes on Vess' but it was clear it wasn't Vess that Ophelia was looking at. "Born in the year of the blue serpent two weeks early, diagnosed at age four as a powerful astral potential, entered primary school at age five, and at age nine was caught in the Bressig exclusion event, the largest of its kind in over a century."

With every word, Wally grew colder and more afraid. It was all basic knowledge, but it wasn't something that someone like her could or should have access to! Everything about her childhood had been sealed!

"How could you know any of that?" Vess breathed. "You were still trapped when she was born!"

"Was I? You always did put too much faith in your own magic, Misery." Ophelia smirked as she tugged her lapels straight.

"You couldn't have—"

"—you may have trapped me," Ophelia spoke over her with a deadly edge to her voice, "but you didn't trap *all* of me . . ."

She held up a hand and showed her ring finger, bare of jewelry. There was just a shadow. A tan line where a ring must have been worn for quite a long time. Ice sluiced down Vess' spine, and it must have shown on her face because Ophelia's grin widened.

"Finally put the pieces together, did you?" she lowered her hand and chuckled dryly. "You always did think you were ten steps ahead, but that's your problem, Misery! That's always been your problem! You're sitting there trying to play five-dimensional Shatranj while I'm across the table playing Goblin Three-Card! You know how to plot and scheme, but it all goes out the window when I make a bet that you're not ready for!"

Vess drifted back. Her ears were buzzing and her brain was filling with fog. Wally was thrashing—panicking to the point of madness. Ophelia was getting into her head just like she used to get into Vess'.

"It's okay, Wally, I promise," Vess whispered. "It's okay. Whatever she's saying, it's just to hurt you! To hurt us! To break us apart! We can't let her win!"

Let her win? She knew things she couldn't possibly know! She claimed to have created . . . no. That was insane. She was insane! Right? Except . . . Wally had seen Vess do things that she hadn't even imagined was possible—move magic in ways that should have *been* impossible.

Was it so unlikely?

"Wally, I swear to you," Vess hissed as she reeled back while Ophelia advanced. "I swear that when we get out of this I will dig until I find the truth, but right now? Right now we can't let her win!"

Vess' words echoed through their shared mind, and, in that moment, Wally was more grateful than ever that she wasn't the one in control. Vess could have restrained her mind—Wally knew that instinctively. This wasn't the proxy. That had disintegrated with they had merged. Now, Vess was the one with control but Wally knew just as firmly that she wasn't going to exercise it because Vess would never do anything to hurt her, which meant that if they failed it would only be because Wally had held them back.

If Vess died, it would be *her* fault.

The strain receded and a bone-deep anger that Wally hadn't realized that she possessed boiled up into their veins, and Vess bared her teeth reflexively.

"I'm going to find that ring," Vess whispered. "And I am going to throw it in a fucking smelter! And you're never going to control her or *me* ever again!"

"You can certainly try," Ophelia said calmly. "But you seem to misunderstand why you're here, Misery."

"I'm here because you brought me here!" Vess snapped.

"No," Ophelia replied. "The only reason that you're here is because *you*—" she pointed at Vess— "are glued to *her.*"

She gestured more broadly, and Vess frowned as she looked down at their shared body. Without warning, Wally felt horror seep into her soul from Vess as she looked back up at Ophelia whose smile was widening viciously.

"That's the look," she hissed. "That's what I wanted to see . . . that bovine realization of how badly you've fucked up! Gods, but you always were slow on the uptake!"

"ENOUGH!"

White and silver fire streaked with black exploded out of their body as confusion and horror sublimated into pure fury, sweeping Wally's mind along in a surge tide of righteous wrath. She thought she had known rage before, but no; she had known anger, or something approximating it in the same way that exhaustion felt very much like being drunk if one had never been well and truly plastered. Wally had never been plastered, but she had been *angry*. Anger exhausted her. It drained her. It was an arid heat that sank into the bowels of her soul and dried out everything worthwhile, leaving her empty and spent and ugly.

Rage was no meager heat. It was volcanic, dynamic, and soaring. She was *soaring*. Soaring forward, arms wide and body spinning on gales of spite and killing intent. Vess laughed and Wally laughed with her, their voices twining like the bodies of lovers as lambent stars of harsh blue flickered into life around them by the dozens. In the depths of wrath, Wally heard that wretched woman curse. Ophelia dove away, riding streaks of noxious sunlight that flashed off of her gaudy coat as she tried to evade them.

There was no evading them. Not this time. She had tried to break them. Tried to weasel between them with poison words and needling suggestions.

How dare she.

How dare she.

Those midnight stars orbiting them flashed once, then twice, then exploded into pinpoint supernovas carving slashes through the skin of reality as they sought out Ophelia who spun, darted, and bolted every which way.

"What's wrong?!" Their voices rang out in tune. "Don't you know everything?! *Didn't you prepare for this?!*"

This was funny, wasn't it? Wasn't it just too funny? That Ophelia. That miserable woman. She had been talking and talking and talking. Shatranj and Three-card. Hah! Made a bet they hadn't been prepared for had she? Maybe her hand wasn't as good as she *thought!* They pursued her, laughing, through the disintegrating realm. Reality was falling apart, cracking at the fractures that Vess had left in the walls of Ophelia's domestic little dream-curse. They chased her through drifting shallows of nostalgia that Wally batted away with a flick of their hand, cooking it into so much smoky residue of false recollection.

Laughter spilled from them again, high and ecstatic, and they spun playfully through the air, sending ravening beams of sharp blue light slicing through the air. They were one. They were together. They were as close as two people could possibly be and it was glorious! Finally, she didn't have to think! She didn't have to question and counter-question, and chew on her every decision for hours before and months after the fact! She could just *do*.

Vess could do it, so she could, too. It was so much easier like this.

They rollicked through shoals of sharp introspection, the wicked edges of minds looking inward, reflecting and refracting the worst of oneself. Vess caught them in the tide of her brilliant mind, sharpened them with the ease of a master bladesmith into hundreds of knives of bleeding-edge doubt that were sent wickering towards Ophelia who barked out a command as she spun to face them. Light exploded in flashbangs around her, searing the doubts to nothing with the zealotry of blind arrogance as they reached her.

But the nature of blindness had an edge all its own.

The blades vanished and the light with them, just as Vess and Wally burst through the searing veil that Ophelia had erected around herself. The stink of scorched hair and fabric filled their nose, but the sweet sound of Ophelia's desperate incanting choking off into a pathetic wheeze as their hand closed around her throat made up for it. They tightened their grip as Vess conjured a wall of hard stone out of astral junk behind her, slammed her into it, and chains of cold iron ripped from the stone to lash around her, binding her, and birthed shackles that bit into her wrists.

"You're finished, Phee," they snarled, and a thrill went up Wally's spine as she heard her voice roll perfectly across Vess'. "You're no match for us, not without your dweomer, and you don't have enough power to speak it without a host."

"I . . . d-don't need it," Ophelia spat with a weak laugh. "Y-You really think I'd . . . risk everyth—*urk!*"

They tightened their grip, cutting off her words. Don't listen. Can't listen. She speaks lies. She only ever speaks *lies!*

"I'm done listening to you." Vess' voice rolled up to the fore, rich with pain. "I'm done letting you hurt me, and I will never let you hurt *her!*"

Their lips pulled into a sadistic smile. She deserved to hurt. She deserved everything that happened to her. Here she was real until she either escaped her little marble of reality, or she died and her wretched soul went back to wherever it had come from. For the time being, though, they enjoyed themselves as Ophelia tried to choke out words from her abused throat.

Vess turned their head, leaned forward, put an ear towards Ophelia's lips, and said, "I'm sorry, I couldn't hear that. You'll need to speak up."

They let up some of the pressure, and Ophelia licked her lips, drew in a ragged breath, then gave a bloody smile as she gasped out a single word.

"Harder."

Rage—blinding and choking rage—blitzed their senses and Vess whirled on Ophelia. With a command of will she forced the chains taut, pinned the woman to the wall, and let out an animal roar as she raised their fist and struck Ophelia across the jaw.

Again.

And again.

Ophelia's form flickered, her androgynous beauty shattering with every blow. Jaw. Cheek. Brow. Vess was screaming. Wally was screaming, too. The noise wasn't enough. It didn't drown out the sound of knuckles splitting skin and breaking bone, and memories filtered unbidden into Wally's mind. Memories of a fist crossing *her* face and a voice telling *her* that she was worthless and meaningless. That she was a mistake. The voice was hard and dark and masculine, but here and there her memories bled across into the present.

She heard Vess' voice. Saw Vess' fists.

Hers and his. Vess' and her father's.

Wally saw and heard that same unrighteous rage mirrored in eyes that were drunk on hate and spitting into the faces of everyone around them while the dull crack of knuckle and bone punctuated icepick lances of memory.

'That's right . . . think . . . what are you missing? Think little girl.' Ophelia's mental voice found the incidental crack between them and slammed between her and Vess like a wedge, and Vess froze. *'You remember don't you?'*

She did remember.

The night of the exclusion. The night it all went wrong. Her father had been doing something. Hurting someone. She remembered blood. She remembered seeing her father in the garage, kneeling amidst a gory mess.

She remembered a circle scrawled in red onto the floor.

'A little more.' The wedge drove deeper *'Come on. A little more!'*

She remembered the magic spilling out of it and out of everywhere else, and wrapping around him. Tendrils of dark power bored through his flesh and crawled down his throat. It changed him . . . warped him into a bloated storm of horror and abhorrence. A wraith and a daemon. She remembered how he killed the town in moments, filling it with miasma and excluding it. It happened so fast. So very, very fast.

'You're so close now. So close . . .'

She remembered choking on the darkness and cowering beneath the ruined furniture of their small dining room feeling sicker than she'd ever felt in her life while the world died around her.

'And? What else?'

In that moment, when she was sure that things would never be good again, she remembered something else. A light in the darkness. Something pierced the shadows—a new daemon, but this one forged of something more than just hatred, tearing through the miasma like a titan of myth and crashing against her father's bloated and repulsive wraith, and how she had screamed in terror at their battle. Gods, how had she forgotten? How had she forgotten how the daemon of light had turned its head to look down at her while it grappled with the daemon her father had become. How had Wally forgotten how it had fixed those cursed-star eyes on her, and how that beatific face had softened, and how she had felt the painful tell-tale pinch of connection pierce into her young mind.

How had she forgotten the very first words that Vess Gibson had ever spoken to her? Words that had imprinted into her mind in a repeating, subconscious mnemonic her entire life.

Five simple words.

'I'll protect you, I promise.'

CHAPTER 36

The air of the collapsing dream was cold in Wally's lungs. Cold and sharp and painfully real, and the pain didn't end there. Every inch of her body felt bruised and broken, her eyes burned and her throat felt like she'd just spent the last three hours screaming her lungs out.

All of that registered in only the most distant manner because beneath the threads of agony and cold, sharp air Wally knew that she shouldn't be feeling anything at all. Vess was in control, wasn't she? That was the nature of being Worn. Vess had inhabited her body, yoked control of it to herself, but then shared that yoke with Wally, which begged the question: Where the fuck was Vess?

"Oh, you made it out, good."

Ophelia grinned up at her through split, bloody lips. Bruises were already forming—psychosomatic reflections of the damage inflicted on her by Vess' mad assault. Therein lay the problem with manifesting a full astral form. A body was a body and it was as real as you believed that it was. The more real you made it, the more durable it was and the more punishment and strain it could take. And the more it hurt.

"Thank the gods, I really wasn't sure that gambit would work, Miss Willowbark," she continued, coughing up a gobbet of blood. "But it did, and you know what they say about idiocy and heroism, right? It's only idiotic if it fails."

It took Wally several moments to grapple with her seemingly total shift in personality. The snide, sneering, abusive mannerisms were gone, and in their place was a bruised and beaten young woman wearing a smile of utter relief.

She smirked and then winced as the expression stretched her lips. "Since you've ah, got me as a captive audience," she made a vague shrug, rattling the chains that were still binding her, "I'll take this moment to apologize for some of the egregiously offensive shit I was saying, you'll understand it was just to pry her off you, right? Like a barnacle."

"A barnacle?" Wally whispered. "What . . ." belatedly, she realized she still had her fist raised and poised to continue the ruinous thrashing Vess had been meting out, and her fingers were still around Ophelia's neck, albeit without much strength in them.

"You have no idea how dangerous she is," Ophelia said calmly. "And she had her hooks in you as deep as she possibly could have . . . if you were anyone else, it would have been over."

"Shut up!" Wally snarled as she pushed Ophelia back against the stone wall Vess had conjured. "What did you do to her?!"

Ophelia frowned and confusion painted features that were still handsome even despite the blood and bruising. "I didn't do anything but offer you a hand, Miss Willowbark, you're the one who took it and pulled yourself out," she said.

Wally swallowed thickly and drifted back, letting go of the woman that history called the Sunfall Queen. She was chained and shackled and beaten to within an inch of her life and she was also looking up at Wally with a surprising amount of softness. That relief was still there, and Wally realized it wasn't that she was relieved that the pain had stopped. If anything, she looked relieved that Wally was alright.

"If you had let her, she would have consumed you like she's consumed so many others," Ophelia explained through labored breaths.

"LIAR!"

Wally surged forward and slammed her fists against either side of Ophelia's head. She gasped as the chains constricted, tightening around their captive with a sickening crackle of bone and cartilage. Wally startled back, and almost as if they were following her, the chains relented, and Ophelia gasped.

"What . . . th-that's Vess' spell! How did I—?!" Wally looked up at Ophelia who shook her head.

"Because she's still in there," Ophelia replied as she spat blood. "It's just that you're in control of the Wear right now, Miss Willowbark. Her power is *yours* to command, which means, uh . . . so are these chains."

"How is that possible?"

"Simple," Ophelia replied. "Because the Wear is just an incredibly complicated type of curse, and you're a reflector."

"That's not how reflection works!" Wally snapped.

"And how would you know that?" Ophelia countered.

"Because—!"

Wally's argument died on her tongue, largely because she realized she didn't actually have one. What was she supposed to say? Because she was one? Being a reflector wasn't a skill, it was a talent. It was inherent. She didn't 'reflect' magic anymore than she commanded her heart to beat or her lungs to breathe. Moreover, reflectors were vanishingly rare. Even rarer were reflectors of any great potency. There simply weren't enough samples to compare with to give anyone an objective understanding of what a reflector could do or even how they functioned.

"Reflection is so much more than just turning back ill will," Ophelia said softly. *"You* are so much more than just a vessel for a selfish sorceress! And it breaks my heart that you don't realize that!"

"What are you talking about?" Wally breathed. "Tell me!"

She had never tried anything like what she was about to do before, but she had seen Vess do it from the background more times than she could count anymore. So Wally raised her hand and mentally reached for the thrumming power of the conjured chains, and then closed her grip.

"TELL ME!" Wally snarled.

The chains constricted.

"I'll . . . t-tell you!" Ophelia gasped, and Wally uncurled her fingers, and the chains slackened. "N-No need to get violent, Miss Willowbark, although I'll admit I probably deserved that last bit."

"Why?" Wally asked carefully. "Why would you tell me anything? And why should I trust you?"

Ophelia shook her head. "You don't know me, so you shouldn't, but it's like I said . . . I don't lie because there's no reason to. I'm here for you. To save you from her. And I'll tell you everything you want to know, just uh . . . maybe make it quick?" she nodded up at the fracturing realm around them. "Not a lot of time."

She was right. A marble of this complexity wasn't going to collapse quickly, but Vess had done a number on it. It *would* fall apart, and soon with the amount of magic that they'd been slinging around.

"Tell me how to get Vess back," Wally said. "Now!"

Ophelia sighed.

"She's controlling you, Wally, the same way she controlled everyone!" She pressed her lips to a fine line, then shook her head. "I'm sorry . . . that's the one question I won't answer. I won't let that monster go free again. Call me selfish if you want, but I can't have that on my conscience, even if it means dying here."

"You murdered hundreds!" Wally roared. "The Burroughs! The Heights! And how many others?!"

"You're right, I did," Ophelia agreed, and Wally startled back at the bald-faced admission.

"But you—"

"I traded eight hundred and forty-seven souls in total via a series of objectively horrible rituals, all for the purpose of giving me the strength to get here so I could draw her in and finally make up for my greatest sin by taking her out of this world." Ophelia raised her head and squared her shoulders inasmuch as she could. There was no apology in her eyes, just grim, confident surety.

"You're lying," Wally whispered.

She had to be lying. She simply *had to be*. Wally could see, in her mind's eye, the horrors that had been wrought on the Burroughs. So many dead.

"No," Ophelia said flatly. "You just want me to be lying."

Wally shook her head and repeated herself, enunciating each syllable with as much venom as she could. Trying with her ounce of breath to push those words into reality and *make them real.*

"You're. LYING!"

The chains started to constrict again, but Ophelia didn't flinch. She didn't move a muscle or ask Wally to relent. Not this time. She just met Wally's eyes, set her jaw, and waited for Wally to kill her. Metal ground on metal as the chains rattled in place, twisting about as they responded to Wally's inner turmoil. "Why would you kill that many people?" she asked finally. "What could possibly be worth that?"

Ophelia's sharp, glittering eyes hardened, and she said, "because eight hundred and forty-seven, is better than half a million."

Numbness crept into Wally's fingers.

"Half . . . Half a million?"

"They call it a war now, but it was no war." Tears trickled down Ophelia's cheeks as she bit out the words piece by piece. "My rebellion was supposed to end an age of stagnation, misogyny, and oppression, and usher in a new, modern era! But Misery didn't care about reasons. She only cared about blood . . . about avenging that mountainous chip on her shoulder!"

Liar. Liar. Liar. She was lying! She had to be lying! Vess wasn't like that! She didn't do that! She couldn't have—! But couldn't she have? Wasn't she Dark Star Mizrahi? Wasn't she the most reviled cursemonger in centuries? Her name was spoken in epithets and imprecations from Silverdawn City to the floating academy cities of New Ghereve. Even among the monstrous Ephorate of the Sunfall Queen, Mizrahi had stood out as a singular monster. Her infamy overshadowed even the queen herself.

"I don't even know what she wanted, in the end," Ophelia

said quietly. "First it was to prove herself. To prove that she was better than her parents. Better than a fortuneless orphan. That ambition . . . that 'never say die' attitude along with her brilliant mind is what I fell in love with, and it's who I married." She turned her head away in shame. "But somewhere along the way, she changed. She became hateful, wicked, and angry. She used her powers to carve a gory furrow in my people's history and I let her do it, and I will never forgive myself for that."

"I don't believe you," Wally said quietly.

She couldn't. She had promised Vess she would hear her out. Wally had *promised*.

But what if that was exactly what Vess wanted? Gods, what if? What if, in the end, she was just like her mother. Just another spineless doormat sitting by and happily nodding her head while her partner fed her lies and committed atrocities because she'd convinced herself she was in love.

"I know you don't," Ophelia said quietly. "Because even now, she won't let you . . . she's in your head, Wally, and I don't mean that metaphorically. I mean, all this time, she's been in your head!"

'I'll protect you, I promise.'

"That day in Bressig," Ophelia pressed, "she wormed her way into your mind, and seared a promise to protect you into your mind so you would never doubt her!"

Something tickled at the edge of Wally's mind. Something was wrong. Something about those words she'd just said was very, very wrong. Her mind was spinning. She was exhausted, in pain, and stretched to her limit, but . . .

"She's controlling—!"

"—how did you know that?" Wally spoke over her as she looked up sharply. "What she said to me that day?" Wally continued, her voice growing hard. "How could you know what *specifically* she put into my head and how she did it?"

"I . . . well . . ." Ophelia started, then pinned her lips shut and sighed. "Well, shit, yeah, I probably laid it on a little thick there, huh?"

She moved faster than Wally could have imagined with the

damage that had been dealt to her. Ophelia turned her hands up, snapped her fingers, and the chains exploded off of her, link by link, in a flash of golden light. She made a lazy flick of her fingers and the chain links swarmed Wally's body, spinning around her in a vortex as they clicked back together and snared her like the web-strands of a monstrous spider.

Wally cried out as the chains tightened painfully, twisting and pulling her limbs in different directions as Ophelia drifted contemptuously forward.

All traces of kindness melted away like cheap cosmetics. Her distinctive eyes—which had been soft with understanding and relief a moment ago—were suddenly hard and calculating, and under the bruises that sneer had settled back across her lips.

Gods, it was like watching a shapeshifter, except with emotions. She controlled her expressions so perfectly and so minutely that they looked completely genuine. If Wally hadn't watched her face change in real time, she might not have believed it. Worse was that it clearly wasn't magic. It was just . . . practice.

"You know, I'll admit it, I overplayed my hand," Ophelia said casually. "But it was honestly for your own good because this whole thing—" she gestured between them— "is going to happen whether or not you agree to it, it would just be a lot easier on us both if it was voluntary."

Wally struggled against the chains, trying to will the power she'd commanded a moment ago into them.

SLAP

"Stop that."

Wally blinked as a new pain bloomed across her cheek and jaw. Ophelia hand still hovered threateningly, poised to cross her other cheek at a moment's notice.

Sighing, Ophelia shook her head. "You may have Misery's power, but you don't have her skill, *Walythea,* and you never will. My Misery is a singular woman, and you might be powerful, but you're not what I'd call a precision instrument."

A burning ache settled across her face as Wally turned to look up at Ophelia whose gaze practically dripped with disdain.

"Where is she?" Wally whispered.

Ophelia rolled her eyes. "You really are a dense one, aren't you? I told you, she's right—" she jabbed a finger painfully into the middle of Wally's forehead— "there. Not that it matters, since you've handily put her to sleep. Thanks for that, by the way."

Cold fingers gripped her jaw and wrenched her face back up, and Wally started to shake. She couldn't do this! Not without Vess! Vess was the only reason she had any courage at all! All her life she'd been a useless coward and then Vess had come along and seared all that away by being magnificent and brazen and perfect, and now . . . now Wally had ruined it, just like she ruined everything else!

"Look, Wally?" Ophelia began. "We both know you're a failure at basically everything you do. I could give you all the power in the world and you'd only blow your own kneecaps off with it, so let's make this easy."

Both of her hands, cold and hard and utterly ruthless, settled on Wally's cheeks.

"Just give up," she said. "You've already done it once, just do it again." She had given up, hadn't she? That moment was etched into her skin forever, now. "No one would blame you either . . . no one would ever know."

Wally clenched her eyes shut. It would be easier if Ophelia's words were as honeyed as they had been moments ago. They weren't. There was no cajoling or enticing softness, just hard, pragmatic truth. Hadn't she said it so many times already? She didn't lie. Why lie when the truth was so much more painful, after all? And the truth was that Wally was weak.

She had always been weak.

"You can't win, Walythea, but you can lose as gently as possible. It doesn't have to hurt. Just close your eyes and let it go black, and nothing that comes after will be your fault. Nothing will be your fault ever again."

"No . . . I w-won't just l-let you win," Wally said through gritted teeth.

"Let me?" Ophelia narrowed her eyes and scoffed. "I'm offering this out of courtesy, not necessity."

She dragged Wally up towards her, and the chains bit into her skin. Wally gasped as her joints strained and her muscles screamed, and she swore she heard something pop around her shoulders.

"Don't mistake me, Walythea Wilhelmina *Willowbark*," Ophelia said with arid contempt. "You are not an obstacle, you're barely a snag, so I'll forgive you for misunderstanding your place in all of this. Let me explain by just—"

'Do you see?' Ophelia's voice was thunder in the meat of her brain as Wally's skull was suddenly splitting. It was like the vague pinch of mindspeak connection but turned up by a thousand times. Her jaw wrenched open as she labored to scream, but couldn't even get enough air into her abused lungs to manage that much. Blood leaked from her eyes, ears, and nose, and filled her mouth as the overwhelming presence of *gold* blinded every other sense she possessed. *'You're already hollowed out for me. Misery did her job well, and, as usual, she didn't even know she was doing it. Thanks to her, your body will survive my presence, but your sanity? Well, that's more . . . hit or miss.'*

She laughed aloud as she withdrew, and Wally sagged against the chains that were now the only thing left supporting her. The absence of pain after that all-consuming agony was almost euphoric, and it left Wally sobbing with relief.

"I will admit," Ophelia began after a moment of silence, "that this is not my spell, it's Misery's, and without her dweomer I'll never be able to use it right, but—" she grabbed Wally by the chin again and jerked her back up— "I can sure as hell use it *wrong*."

"It w-won't work!" Wally gasped out.

"Sure it will, think of it like this." Ophelia made a vague gesture and conjured a scalpel. "Misery is like a trained surgeon, right? She makes a painless incision and goes in, while I," she banished the scalpel and conjured a rusty hacksaw, "am more of back-alley sawbones . . . I'll get the job done, but it's not gonna be pretty."

Sharp, cruel eyes met Wally's and she knew without a shadow of a doubt that Ophelia wasn't lying. Of course she wasn't lying. Ophelia didn't lie. Why would she?

"I'm trying to be kind here and you're being very unappreciative," Ophelia said. "I could saw my way into that pretty head of yours right now, and while I can't say how much of your psyche would be left intact by the time I'm done, I can at least guarantee you it will enough that you'll be aware."

She let go of Wally's chin and Wally fell slack again and this time Ophelia lowered herself into a crouch to look up into Wally's exhausted, aching eyes. Even without Ophelia trying to burrow into her skull with a metaphorical hacksaw, she was just so tired. So tired and so finished. What could she possibly do? Resist her? For what? All of a minute or two? Then she would fold and crumple and wouldn't even die. She would suffer endless torment on what? Principle?

"Look, I'm just saying, if it's all the same to you, I'd *really* rather not spend the time and energy it takes to lock up the screaming vestige of your amputated consciousness into the rear quarters of what will soon be my mind, alright?" She reached up and pinched Wally's cheek fondly. "Besides, you owe me your life anyway, so just think of it as paying a debt!"

"W-What?" Wally mumbled. "You . . . I what?"

"When your organs shut down from necrotic shock after Bressig, whose magic, do you think, brought you back?" Ophelia let go and then slapped her across the cheek just hard enough to hurt. "Who do you think stationed the disciple that called the priests on your suicidal ass—" she slapped Wally again, this time with a backhand— "when you tried to off yourself ahead of schedule, hm? Whose cult do you think made sure that job ad ended up in *your* mail?"

With every word, Wally's world was fractured and broken. All her life she had been watched. All her life she had been moved towards this moment. Had anything she'd done mattered?

"Let's be hypothetical for a moment here, Willowbark," she sneered, "and assume I give up all of my plans and designs and ambitions and let you go . . . right?"

She grabbed Wally by the forearm, wrenched it up, and pulled back her sleeve to expose the ugly scar, and Wally tried to close her eyes, but she couldn't. Too many of those words were worming into her brain. It was too much!

"You'd give up inside ten years, and that's being generous," Ophelia said as she dropped Wally's arm. "So just cut out the middleman and give up *now*. This is your last chance."

Give up? It would be that easy, wouldn't it? Just give up and no one would ever know and she would never have to deal with anything ever again. The world could just fade and so could she.

"Going once!"

Wally ignored the finger that that Ophelia held up between her eyes. Gods, it would be easy. Just to give up. Even Vess had warned her against that feeling deep in her heart. So why shouldn't she?

"Going twice!"

Ophelia was right. After all, she'd almost given up to Vess in the practice room on *reflex*.

"GOING THRICE!"

Given up . . . to Vess. What had she said about beats and intervals?

"Well?" Ophelia hissed.

That's right. She'd called it *torpor*.

So Wally gave up.

Cursed blue stars ignited in the core of Wally's soft brown eyes as Vess' slumbering consciousness came roaring back to life. Wally was plummeting into the abyss of her own subconscious, drowning in herself as Vess Gibson seized hold of her body and slammed herself back into place; a syncopation within the beat of Wally's yielding lifeforce.

"Shit!"

Ophelia rocketed back as the chains Vess had conjured and which had turned against her when she'd fallen into her own dark torpor detonated, flying apart in all directions. Shrapnel lit with brackish fire peppered and slashed across Ophelia's body as Vess exploded back to life. The phantasmal patterns of light that had decorated her face effervesced, channeling and controlling her unbridled power.

"I'll kill you!" Vess bellowed.

"Wuh-oh."

Spinning away, Ophelia took off like a golden comet and Vess lit off in pursuit. Shadows and cold, blue fire trailed from her as blue veins crawled up her face and down her hands. Power bled from her hands as she cut through the disintegrating dream of domestic bliss, an echo or a shadow of something she might once have had. Animal screams of inchoate rage spilled from Vess as her passage ruptured the air around her while pitch streaked across her cheeks as she spat words of power and twitched her fingers through runic shapes.

"GET BACK HERE!"

Spiraling hard, Vess snapped her arms out and finished the spell, conjuring chains of a wholly different source. Each link was scribed with a name, and each name bore a grudge—a curse.

Legends told that Dark Star Mizrahi knew a thousand curses, but oh, she had so many more than a thousand. Every death. Every sin. Every life she had taken was imprinted into the soiled patina that coated her pitch-black soul. She was Vess Mizrahi, and she was drowning in the blood of a kingdom.

Ophelia screamed as one of the many chains finally hit its mark. The dark metal spike on the end punched through the meat of her arm and out the other side, only to split into quarters and anchor itself in her, and she jerked to a halt. It was one of many. The second took her in the thigh, the third, fourth, fifth, and sixth went through her abdomen. Each one anchored its barbed links cruelly into her, and Vess spat another command as she jerked her arm back.

Tainted blood gushed from Ophelia's astral body as its systems began to fail, and Vess hauled her back like a rag doll, spinning her body around herself like a lasso with her right hand, and with her left she flicked her fingers through another conjuring. Fragments of the dissolving apartment congealed back together into hodgepodge walls of concrete, cheap tile, and light fixtures, all arranged in a row.

"I'm not letting you go that easily!" Vess roared.

Swinging her arm down and around, Vess sent Ophelia

arching into the walls with a wet, meaty crack that warped into the sickening sound of splintering stone, wood, and plastic. Each wall exploded in turn as Ophelia was swung through them until she struck the final one where Vess had left all the sharpest leftover crap she could find, including the two objects she'd been most interested in pulling into place. Blood rolled down Ophelia's lips as she stared at the two fractured barstool legs that Wally had been bludgeoning her with not too long ago, and which were at that moment sticking out of her chest, puncturing through some relatively important organs.

"This is over," Vess hissed as she rose to float before Ophelia.

"Is it?" Ophelia rasped. "You know you haven't gotten me . . . not really."

Vess seized her by the temples, thrust her thumbs into Ophelia's eyes, and screamed. Ophelia screamed with her as clawed nails dug in until there was nothing but a ruin left of the sockets.

Ophelia sagged, breathing in wet, labored heaves as Vess let go.

"I don't care how long it takes, I don't care how many years I have to spend, but I will find every last scrap of you!" She grabbed Ophelia by the chin and jerked her head up.

The once-Sunfall Queen stared up at her with gored and empty eyes. Vess remembered the day she'd looked into those mismatched eyes past a silk veil. She remembered the falling flowers, thousands upon thousands of petals harvested and thrown in celebration for the new queen and her bride. She remembered how hard her heart had been beating and how wide she'd been smiling. Most of all, she remembered how Ophelia had lifted that veil and promised her the world and everything in it.

Every sin. Every atrocity. Every bloody corpse.

It was all hers.

"And when I do," Vess whispered as she blinked away bilious tears, "you'll finally, *finally* be gone."

Ophelia smiled weakly and coughed, and blood spattered across her pale lips as she leaned just so. Just enough to brush her cheek fondle against Vess' thumb that was gripping her chin.

"Gone? No." She raised one hand weakly to brush her fingers over Vess' face, tracing lines in the black tears on her cheeks. "The people who love you are never really gone."

She tightened her fingers around Vess' and smiled, and Vess began to shake. Even now, with the monster from her nightmares dying right in front of her, it was like nothing had changed.

"No matter what, I will *always* be with you, Misery," she said quietly.

And Vess screamed.

She screamed and roared and poured every ounce of her rage, her pain, and all of her heartache into a hurricane of pale fire. The curse-born storm scorched skin, muscle, and bone into ashed, shredding it to nothing along with everything else, but it wasn't enough. The world had to burn. This false dream of what might have been; it all had to burn! The Wall of Sleep groaned as the wound that the excluded domain had inflicted on it began to close, the infection cauterized by Vess' hatred, and blackness slowly closed in around her.

Vess sobbed brokenly as she curled up in the grim nothingness of nowhere while reality reasserted itself, and when it did, and when Vess opened her eyes again, it was in what once might have been a normal living room. The furniture was burning silently with that same pale fire she had used to burn away Ophelia. The floor was on the edge of collapse, and so was the rest of the building for that matter. The domain was gone, and with it went the unnatural physics that had been keeping that part of the heights upright, and in the very middle of it all—right where Ophelia had been moments ago—was the remains of a young woman's spirit.

Her spectral form, barely coherent, was threaded with rotten veins from a curse that had maintained her through Ophelia's hijacking, and she was cradling a beautifully-crafted bass guitar with one scorched arm, the other had rotted off and was lying beside her. There was little left. Maybe not even enough to rejoin the cycle of life and death, but despite that, Vess did what Wally would have done. She went to the woman's side and knelt.

"Are you her?" The woman's voice was so faint that it was

barely there. "Are you the Dark Star?"

Vess pressed her lips to a thin line. On the one hand, this was the person responsible for everything that had happened in this place. She and her ilk had been the ones who had given Ophelia a strong enough foothold in the world to come back, even briefly. On the other hand . . . she was so young; Wally's age, or a little older, and from the look of her ruined home she had little to hold on to. Her life must have been miserable.

"Yes," Vess said softly. "That's me."

"M-My name is M-Myriam," she whispered. "Myriam Wates."

"Hello, Myriam, my name is Vess."

"Vess . . ." she smiled faintly. "I . . . I'm going, aren't I?"

"You are."

"Can I ask you something?"

"Shoot."

Myriam swallowed, although her spectral body no longer needed such things, then asked, "W-Who does Misery love?"

Vess' eyes widened at the question. She almost lashed out.

"Why would you ask that?" she asked.

The woman was fading, but she tightened her grip on her instrument, and slowly she began to cohere. Just a little. Just enough.

"I always t-told myself," she said, "that . . . even if n-no one else did, at least . . . at least Misery loved me."

Vess sat down beside her and reached out to card her fingers through the woman's lank, greasy hair. "Oh, well . . . if it's any consolation, you and I have that in common."

"Yeah? Jazzy . . ." Myriam smiled. "That's . . . that's j-ja—"

The arm that had been cradling her bass; a rare Ulverike 1092 Special, fell limp, and the instrument clattered to the ground as she faded to dust with a quiet sigh.

Who does Misery love? Vess hung her head as the walls and floors and ceiling cracked and started to crumble around her. Who indeed.

And who, in their right mind, could ever love Misery?

CHAPTER 37

Dawn crept inexorably across the districts of Colvus, illuminating a street that looked more like an urban battlefield than a part of a peaceful city. The asphalt and concrete surrounding the Stymphalian Heights was cracked and torn by the forces that had been summoned there; forces that hadn't been seen since the pinnacle of the Sunfall Rebellion. Vess could smell the blood and miasmal stink of diabolic conjuring as she stepped out of the crumbling building wearing the flesh of Wally Willowbark. The taste was a familiar one. Only one person conjured with that particular flavor of dark magic. Her one-time sister-in-arms, one of four, and a woman she had once counted amongst her finest and most steadfast friends.

Adjusting the strap of the bass guitar she had slung over her shoulder, Vess scanned the street with Wally's eyes, and her heart leapt into her throat. In the middle of the road was a sight that cored her.

"No." The word left her lips and, without thinking, she slipped through the space between spaces and appeared just behind the dejected dispersers of sixth precinct. Jemma was sitting crosslegged on the ground with Siobhan across from her. Between them was Polly resting on her knees, and the three of them were surrounding the man that each of them, even Vess, had viewed as something between a father and an older brother.

Erik Mizer's head was resting in Polly's lap, his eyes closed, and every vein in his body scorched black by miasma. Buried in his chest was the heavy, cursed head of Siobhan's axe. It had been broken off where metal met wood, and Siobhan gripped the rest of the weapon in her right hand, right where it always was.

"Wally?" Jemma looked up at her, then snapped her head back to the hearse, then back up at Wally. "How did you—"

"That's not Wally," Polly said, without looking up. "Is it?"

Vess pressed her lips to a thin line. What could she say? She had failed. By every meaningful metric, she had failed. Ophelia was free—somehow—and even if she hadn't gotten what she'd wanted, Vess had managed to neither capture nor destroy her. Sure, the domain had been safely collapsed . . . but at what cost?

"No, it's not," Vess said, her voice layering hauntingly over Wally's.

Polly looked up at her with red-rimmed eyes. "Is she still in there? Tell me she's still in there, Gibs, or I swear to all the Gods—"

"She is," Vess said softly.

Impossibly, the faint thrum of Wally's lifeforce was still there, buried beneath choking miasma and hundreds of thousands of curses. Her silversheen soul was still protecting her, despite everything. Ophelia had been right about one thing; Vess had had no idea how powerful Wally really was. She still didn't.

Swallowing thickly, Polly nodded and turned back to Mizer.

"Good," she muttered, "that's good."

"Vess?" Jemma stood, her eyes wide with wonder.

"It's a long story, Jem, and this isn't the time."

She hadn't been fast enough. Once again, she'd been slow on the uptake and better people than her had died. Erik Mizer was a better person than most, and he had paid the price for her sloppy technique. Turning back to Polly, Vess knelt and put a hand on her shoulder. "Talk to me, Pols."

"The daemon is contained," Polly said woodenly. "Mizer used the Colver river Elementals to seal her inside of himself, and Siobhan . . . Siobhan did what was necessary."

What was necessary?

Vess grit her teeth as she stared down at where the smile of Siobhan's cursed axe was buried. The weapon of a dreadnought was more than capable of cleaving flesh and spirit alike. It was a clever, if crude, tactic. Mizer was no fool. He must have known what was going to happen. She laid a hand on his arm and let out a shuddering sob. He was so cold. Not just physically, but spiritually. He sealed his own magic, sacrificed everything, all to create a prison for a daemon with Siobhan's cursed axe as the lock.

Not even the magic of Hadria Mercutia could heal that wound.

"Who are you?"

The voice behind the question was strident and hard, and Vess stood and turned to face it.

Cassidia Truelight, sister to Polly Truelight and High Paladin of Ys, stood before her. Her once resplendent hauberk of silver-steel was scored, charred, and badly notched, and her golden hair was stained with ichor and blood, but those eyes of hers were still sharp, even despite the bags beneath them.

"Beg your pardon?" Vess asked.

"You are not the young woman I met in the lobby of the sixth precinct, are you?" Cassidia's voice lowered to a deadly edge. "You are not the flesh you wear, so name yourself."

"Cass, don't, she's a friend," Polly said.

"She's a monster!" Cassidia barked as she snapped Truelight free of its scabbard.

The dawn carried in the blessed blade bloomed across the streets again, casting Wally Willowbark's features in stark light as Cassidia brandished it.

Vess eyed the blade with a raised eyebrow, then looked back up at Cassidia.

"I'm not in the mood, paladin," she said quietly. "I know it goes against the grain, but maybe think this through."

Cassidia squared her shoulders and adjusted her grip.

"I assure you, I have."

"I assure you," Vess echoed. "You *haven't*."

"Whatever you are, I will burn you out of that girl's body like a cancer," Cassidia growled.

Like a cancer? Yes, maybe that was a good word for her. The funny thing was that Cassidia wasn't wrong. She was a monster. She *was* a cancer. She was a blight on the world and she knew it.

But Ophelia was worse, and monsters ought to kill monsters.

"Oh you will, will you?" Vess smiled, and in that moment she saw some of the zeal in Cassidia's eye fade into realization. Maybe some fragment of her gods-blessed powers was informing her of precisely how different the scale of their powers were. Even if Cassidia had been at her peak, she wouldn't have been a threat. Not when Vess had access to the breadth of her magic.

"I—" Cassidia began.

Then the lights went out.

There was no word of power or detonation of dark magic, just the snap of a finger and a sudden, sharp clatter of chains, and Truelight's light was snuffed. Black chains spilled subtly from the shadows around Vess, the runes of their grudge-forged links burning angry red as they coiled around Truelight's blade. The sound of sizzling metal and the stink of cooking iron rose from the weapon, but only for a moment, and eventually, even that fell silent.

"You were saying, paladin?" Vess asked softly.

A hand settled on her arm, and Vess looked down to find Jemma staring up at her with pleading eyes that were bloodshot from tears. It caught her so off-guard she almost dropped the seal from around Truelight.

"Vess, please," Jemma whispered. "Not right now . . . please, Cass is . . . she's just doing her job."

A cold weight sunk into Vess' chest as she looked back at Cassidia whose eyes were wide with horror. She wasn't staring at Vess, though. She was staring at her weapon. At the blessed blade that she and her family had staked their very name on.

The one whose light Vess had snuffed out like it was a toy.

What was she doing? Picking a fight in front of Polly and Jemma after Mizer—Gods, what had she been thinking? Shame welled up inside of her as she turned back to Jemma and nodded.

"Right, sorry . . ." Vess waved a hand, releasing the sealing chains, then looked to Cassidia. "Peace, paladin, I'm not your enemy and I never will be. If I was a threat to this city then Colvus would have been a graveyard over a decade ago. Let me do my job, and I'll let you do yours."

The light of her blade was faded when it returned. Instead of an all-encompassing light, it was wan and yellow, and it illuminated the expression on Cassidia's face far too well for Vess' liking. More than horror, more than hate. Something had broken, just a little, in Cassidia's eyes.

Shit. Vess Misery had done it again.

"Can you . . . ?" Vess looked down at Jemma and nodded towards the paladin.

"Yeah." Jemma nodded back and went to Cassidia's side, while Vess trudged back to Polly and sat down.

Polly Truelight was running her hands through Mizer's dark hair, and her eyes never left his face. Her soft cheeks were streaked with tears, and every so often her chest and shoulders shuddered as she brushed fingers across his still features again.

"I loved him so much," Polly whispered.

"I know."

"It's not fair, Gibs," she continued quietly. "It's just not fair."

"It never is."

"We could have been happy, had a family . . . lived a quiet life somewhere doing something silly and stupid, and entirely meaningless, but . . ." Polly lowered her head as hot, angry tears began to spill, spattering across Mizer's cold brow.

"He loved you, too," Vess said quietly. "More than anything and anyone. And you *were* happy, weren't you? You did have a family . . . you still do." She took Polly's hand and gripped it tight. "You have us. For whatever it's worth, you still have this messed up motley family that you and Mizer made together."

"I don't know how to do this without him," Polly sobbed.

"The same way he would have if he had lost you," Vess said. "One day at a time, and with as much love and help as we can give you."

"But I'm gonna lose them all, Gibs!" Polly cried. "One day I'm gonna lose them all! And I'll keep losing them! Over and over and over!"

Vess pressed her lips to a thin line, then said. "Not all of them." she gripped Polly's hand all the tighter. "You'll always have me, old mum. I'm stuck in that soup can, remember? Death won't come for me either."

Finally, Polly squeezed back, and something inside of her finally snapped as she bent double over the man she had loved with all her heart, and screamed out every hollow edge of her grief born of decades of watching the world pass her by, and in the grim anticipation of centuries of the same to come.

A soft rumble was what eventually woke Wally from the dark places her mind had wandered to. It was a familiar feeling, and one that she struggled to place for a moment.

Opening her eyes was a laborious process, but she finally did it, and when she did she found herself staring up at the ceiling of her room in the sixth precinct. It was dark, the lights were out, and settled on top of her chest, doing her absolute best to help while also making it a little hard to breathe, was Wally's little rumble factory.

"Tipsy?" Wally mumbled through chapped lips.

"You're awake!"

For a moment, Wally was actually groggy enough that she thought Tipsy had replied, but her brain connected the voice to its owner a second later, and she turned her head.

"Jemma?" Wally squinted into the dark and picked out her co-worker as she stood from an easy chair that had, at some point, been dragged into her room, and moved to Wally's bedside.

She tutted over Wally for a few moments, giving her a once over with a critical eye. Part of that was looking over an IV that had been affixed to her arm. That should have horrified her since it certainly meant that Jemma had seen her scars but, for some reason, she couldn't even work up the energy to feel that much.

"Hold still," Jemma ordered as she put a hand to Wally's forehead. "No fever . . . good, look me in the eye and keep'em open, okay?"

Wally obeyed despite her eyelids being as leaden as the rest of her limbs.

"No cataract clouding, no darkness in the sclera, shit, you're a real piece of work, you know that, Willowbark?" Jemma leaned back with a relieved smile then began detaching the IV with practiced fingers. "Still gotta do some bloodwork on you, but I get the feeling that's going to turn up fine, too."

"What do you mean?"

"Possession, Wally, you let Vess fucking ride you! Do you have any idea how reckless that was?!" It was a testament to her grogginess that the first thing the notion of Vess 'riding' her did was put a blush on her cheeks, and it didn't go unnoticed.

"Get your mind out of the gutter, please." Jemma massaged the bridge of her nose and shook her head. "Look just . . . Vess explained everything, and I get that you had no choice, but—" to Wally's surprise, Jemma got down on a knee and took Wally's hand— "please, be careful, okay? I . . . I don't want to lose anyone else. Not even you."

"Anyone . . . else?" Wally echoed dully.

Jemma's eyes widened faintly, then she lowered her head and swore softly.

"Jemma?" Wally said quietly. "What do you mean 'anyone else'?"

She lowered her head and touched her forehead to Wally's knuckles, holding on tight for a long moment. Every passing breath got harder for Wally until finally, Jemma answered her.

"There was someone else. Some*thing* else. It was a daemon, but not like anything I've ever seen . . . she claimed to be Legions Mercutia and I think—" she cut herself off, biting her lip as she rose, then turned to sit down on the mattress beside Wally. "I think she was telling the truth . . . we did everything we could and she just toyed with us, until Mizer . . ."

"No."

"He did what he had to do, Wally, he—"

"NO!" Wally grabbed at Jemma's arm. "You're—! That's not—! Stop saying that!" Despite her weakness she forced herself up, displacing Tipsy, and grabbed Jemma by the collar.

When she faced Wally, it was with eyes that had done a lot of crying in the past however long she'd been asleep.

"I'm sorry, Wally," Jemma said quietly. "I wasn't strong enough. I couldn't even scratch her . . . not really." she bowed her head and started to shake. "I just wasn't strong enough."

Mizer.

Mister Erik Mizer. No, not Mister. He hated being called Mister. He was Mizer. Just Mizer. A good man who had given her a home and friends and a job and . . . and a purpose. He had given her a chance to find meaning in her perpetually empty life that, if that monster in the Heights was to be believed, wasn't even really hers, and now, what? He was gone? Just like that?

"But . . ." Wally licked her lips as her chest felt like it was hollowing out. "But I didn't get to say goodbye." What shallow strength she had mustered to sit up bled out of her as she collapsed against Jemma and started to cry. It was a weak thing, pitiful really, but Jemma wrapped strong arms around her and held onto her all the same. "I d-didn't get to tell him 'thank you'!" Wally sobbed. "I didn't get to tell him what it all meant to me!"

Jemma pulled her closer. "He knew, I'm sure of it."

He was gone. He was gone and she had missed it and here she was being comforted by someone who had loved Mizer like a father. Someone who had known him longer and had memories with him that Wally couldn't imagine. She had known him for a couple of months, and Jemma was comforting *her*.

Selfish.

So *fucking* selfish.

Pulling back, Wally swallowed thickly, and said, "C-Can I have some time? Alone, I mean? Sorry, I just . . ."

"Are you sure?"

Was she sure? To think that Wally had had the audacity to dislike Jemma at one point. Someone she loved just died horribly and she was asking Wally if she was sure she wanted to be alone. "I'm sure." Wally offered Jemma a wan but placating smile. "And I still have Tipsy."

She clicked her tongue and Tipsy popped right back up onto

the bed before worming her way into Wally's lap. Almost immediately, she began purring again and Jemma finally looked assuaged as she stood, and Wally forced herself to smile through the guilt that was gnawing at her throat like a rabid wolf.

Jemma stood and wiped at her eyes, then reached out took Wally's hand to give it a brief squeeze. "You're one of us, you know," she said quietly. "Even if I can be kind of a bitch about it, you're still one of us."

"Thank you." The words almost didn't make it past Wally's lips before her throat closed up. Fortunately, Jemma didn't seem to notice and left the room in silence and darkness.

At least, it ought to have been silent.

Tipsy's purring was almost deafening to Wally, and for once it wasn't as comforting as it ought to have been. Now that she was alone that feeling of sinking into the darkness of torpor—of just giving up and yielding everything including her will to live—came back in force. She told herself that it had been necessary; that if she sank into that place that Vess had warned her to stay out of, it wouldn't matter, and that even if she sank so deep that she didn't wake up, that everything would be okay.

Wally laid her hand on Tipsy's back and stroked her gently.

Tipsy would have been fine. She would have been absolutely safe, Wally knew that for a fact. If nothing else, Jemma absolutely adored her. She would be fed and loved and taken care of. And Vess would have been fine, too. She was Vess, after all. She was always fine.

Everything and everyone would have been fine.

That was what she had told herself.

And suddenly she was choking. The walls were closing in around her, and even Tipsy's presence wasn't enough. She needed to move! She needed to go! She needed . . . needed *air! SHE NEEDED*—

—daylight filled Wally's vision as she stared out over the skyline of Colvus. The city was bright and expansive, and it stretched across the broad, agrarian plains of the Union with all the life and tumult and chaos that any city brings with it as it grows.

And she felt lighter too.

Lighter, and heavier, in a way.

No, not heavier. She felt . . . inconstant. Temporary. In truth, she had always felt that way. Like the world was moving past her and she was watching from some subtle place just outside of everyone else's line of sight. All it would take would be the slightest breeze and she would just fade, and no one would be the wiser, and everything would be fine.

It wasn't fair. None of it was fair. Mizer shouldn't be gone. Neither should Bressig for that matter. Ophelia had blatantly admitted that she had engineered it to produce a new generation of reflectors. Tens of thousands dead, all for the sole purpose of finding one strong enough to survive her taking them over meaning that, for once in her life, Wally was the best at something, for once she was made aware that she was indelibly important, and it was for something like this.

When she'd been younger, Wally had imagined that the gods of fate had some kind of grudge against her, but as she got older she realized how arrogant that was. The gods of fate certainly had better things to do than to poke fun at someone whose lifespan wouldn't measure the length of a cosmic heartbeat.

She wasn't so sanguine of that as she had been before the Heights.

"Wally?" A warm, familiar contralto pulled Wally from her thoughts, and she turned to find Vess hovering just out of reach. Her body was opaque, and the lack of dark veins and ruddy skin meant she must have had a purification bath recently.

Wait. Hovering? Wally looked down, and surprise shot through the caked-on numbness. Vess wasn't the only one who was opaque and hovering.

"You're projecting," Vess said quietly. "I didn't . . . that's quite a feat for a reflector."

Turning back to the city skyline, Wally wrapped her arms around herself and shrugged. "All reflectors are former Astral talents, remember? That's the only real requirement to . . . to make one," she replied. "So, it's not that strange."

Vess drifted up next to her and shook her head. "Of course

you would say that," she said a touch bitterly.

"I didn't choose to be like this," Wally said with more vitriol than she could remember ever speaking with.

To her credit, Vess didn't flinch. She just nodded and remained silent as they watched the light of the early evening filter through the city. It seemed so peaceful now.

"How . . . How long was I asleep?" Wally asked.

"Four days," Vess said. "Polly channeled some of her gift into you to stave off muscular atrophy, but we all knew you'd recover."

"Then Mizer . . . the funeral?"

"No funeral," Vess said, and her voice hardened as Wally turned to stare at her in disbelief. "His body is a cage for Legions Mercutia . . . you can't just burn or bury something like that. The temple of Ys took it to be entombed in the undercroft of the Solar Temple."

A shudder ran through her and Wally grit her teeth as she settled down to the ground. An echo of pressure from touching the ceiling spread through the soles of her feet, and it was faint enough that she could have slipped through it if she wanted to.

"That's too cruel," Wally whispered.

"Cruelty was always her specialty," Vess agreed as she kept pace with Wally, drifting down to stand beside her. "Now, here . . ." she put a hands on Wally's shoulder and turned her until they facing one another. "It's not safe for you to project without training, you could draw all kinds of astral predators."

"I don't want to go back to my room, Vess," Wally said through clenched teeth.

"No worries." She put her fingers to the soft spot just beneath above Wally's navel then twitched her fingers and curled them sharply inward.

The strangest sensation that Wally had ever experienced rippled through her. It was like vertigo. It was a combination of vertical freefall while rapidly rising up from the depths of the ocean. It lasted all of an instant before a sense of crushing physicality slammed Wally to her knees, and she dragged in breath after breath of cold air.

"You okay?" Vess knelt and got an arm under Wally.

Wally shrugged it off. She didn't need to look up to see the hurt on Vess' face. She could practically feel it. But she couldn't. Not right now. Not yet. Maybe not . . .

"I'm fine," Wally said shakily. "W-What did you do? I was projected and now I'm here. Did you teleport my body?"

"No, not exactly," Vess said quietly as she took a step back, and Wally didn't want to admit how much she appreciated the space. "Every astral form has a kind of ripcord, it's how you get back. Give it a tug and you're yanked back to your body, but it uhm . . . it works both ways. If you're strong enough, you can yank your physical body through the astral spaces to you."

"That sounds insanely dangerous," Wally said as she stood on rubbery legs. Biomantic infusions or not, she'd still been flat on her back for four days, and she was stiff as all hells.

"It's not, really," Vess said. "It's just draining, so don't do it over any kind of distance. Moving physical matter takes exponentially more power."

Wally nodded, then finally looked up at Vess. "I know I've said this before but we *really* need to talk about you asking permission before doing that stuff, okay? You always just . . . do it."

"I . . ." Vess started, then lowered her head as she solidified, completing her bilocation spell fully. "I know," she said finally. "You're right, I'm sorry."

"Don't be sorry, just don't do it!" Wally said.

"Is it weird to say that I don't really how to stop?" Vess asked as she looked down. "Solving problems with a spell . . . it's like a reflex for me."

"Was it a reflex when you messed my head when I was a kid?" Wally asked, and Vess blanched.

Turning away from her, Wally walked to the edge of the roof and looked down. It wasn't such a far drop but it was far enough. Sitting down, she dangled her legs over the lip and took another long, deep breath. The cold air was bracing, and it chased away the claustrophobic grip that kept settling around her throat.

"That wasn't rhetorical, Vess," Wally said after a moment of silence.

"Sorry," Vess whispered.

She moved up beside Wally shed her long, black coat, and sat down next to her. The wind moved through the fiery auburn strands of her hair, making them flow around her face like waves of slow fire. It wasn't fair that she got to be so beautiful. It made it hard to be mad at her, but then again, Wally wasn't mad. That's what bothered her, among so many other things. She wasn't mad at Vess, and she knew she should be. She wasn't scared of her either, and she knew she should be that, too.

She should have been feeling so many things, but she wasn't and that, more than anything scared the sprinkles out of her.

"Why did you do it?" Wally asked.

"Because it *was* reflex," Vess replied. "When I was fighting that wraith—your father, I guess?" she asked, and Wally nodded. "Right, well, I was fighting it, and then I looked down and . . . and there's this little girl, hiding under a table," she shakes her head and laughs wanly. "And I knew that the moment she moved she'd draw the attention of the wraith, and then she'd die so fast that she wouldn't even know what had happened."

That much, at least, Wally could understand. After the nightmare of the Heights she could remember enough of that night to put the pieces together with what Vess was telling her.

"So I . . . I reached into her mind and told her I would protect her," Vess continued.

"You imprinted it," Wally said. "Like a . . . a repeating mnemonic in my mind to keep me calm."

"So you wouldn't move, yeah." Vess nodded as she took deep breath and tipped her head up to stare into the darkening sky. "It wasn't supposed to last. I was going to remove it once I saved you, but . . . but then everyone told me you died."

"Because I did," Wally said, and Vess looked sharply over at her.

"What?"

"Necrotic shock into massive organ failure," Wally said. "The temple told me I was dead for a full day, and then, miraculously, I just . . . woke up."

Because of Ophelia. Because somehow, she had gotten some of her magic into Wally, and brought her back. Part of Wally wished she had questioned Ophelia further when she'd had the chance. How had she done it? How had she brought her back from death a day after the fact? Resurrection was amongst the rarest and most powerful of divine miracles, and it was the remit of only the highest-ranking priests of the gods of light and healing.

Wally had the distinct impression that whatever Ophelia had done to bring *her* back hadn't had half so wholesome a source.

"Everyone's records are private and sealed, so I don't know this for sure but . . . I suspect I wasn't the only one to come back," Wally said after a moment.

What was it that Vess had said about Ophelia? That she stacked the deck? Wally suspected that every astral talent possible made it out of Bressig alive—for certain definitions of 'alive'—all so Ophelia had the greatest odds of procuring one that could survive her.

"All my life, I've had this feeling like I was missing someone or something," Wally said. "Like someone was supposed to be there, and wasn't."

"Wally, I—"

"Take it out, Vess," Wally sobbed as she looked back at Vess. "I . . . I need you to take it out."

It wasn't often that Wally saw her hesitate. Vess was normally so certain of herself. So absolutely confident. Now, though, she not only looked torn, she looked scared.

"B-But, Wally it's been in there so long," Vess said.

"I don't care!" Wally snapped.

"What if . . . ?"

"What if what?" Wally said through gritted teeth. "Go ahead! Finish the sentence! What if *'what?'.*"

It would be so much easier if Vess hadn't made her bilocated body so real. If it were more of a facsimile, then she wouldn't be able to cry.

"What if you don't . . ." She choked on her words. Wally could hear the anxiety close up her throat. She knew exactly how Vess was feeling. "What if you don't love me anymore?"

"Is that the kind of love you'd want?" Wally asked. "Because you know who that sounds like, don't you?"

It would probably have hurt Vess less if she'd just gored her with one of Polly's machetes. Some of the light went out of Vess' eyes as she lowered her head, and the tears finally stopped, but only because Wally had the feeling that the pain, at this point, was too big even for them.

"Okay," Vess said quietly.

"One more thing." Wally took Vess' hand and held on tight, and Vess looked up with a sliver of hope. "I believe in my heart that I'll still feel the way I feel, but I need you to take the mnemonic out because, right now, I'm not afraid of you, and right now, I trust you."

"And?" Vess asked.

"And I know that I probably shouldn't."

In a sick and twisted way, Wally took comfort from the agony on Vess' face. If nothing else, that kind of feeling was hard to fake. Seeing her wearing her pain so nakedly was a horrible sort of balm against the barbed words Ophelia had spat into her brain about Vess controlling her.

"And I need you to make me one more promise."

"Anything," Vess whispered.

"That once you take it out, you won't leave this roof until I say you can, or until I ask you to go."

"Done."

"No, not like that," Wally said. "I want you to *swear it.*"

Vess goggled for a moment, dumbstruck, then licked her lips, took in a shaky breath, and said, "You want me to . . . to compel myself? To curse myself?"

"I trust you because you made me trust you," Wally said with a voice full of unspent tears. "And once that's gone I don't think I will . . . so please."

Squeezing Wally's hand hard, Vess nodded.

"Yeah," she muttered. "Okay, I owe you a lot more than that, anyway."

Stepping back, Vess laced her fingers, cracked her knuckles, then began to cast. Like always, it was a wonder to watch, even from the outside. Her long, dextrous fingers passed through intricate runes, and her husky voice echoed faintly with words of power.

On the final syllable, she snapped out her right hand and twisting traceries of brackish violet light bloomed into existence around her wrist and arm.

"Wally Willowbark, I swear I will not leave this roof until you grant me permission . . . or order me to do so." With each word, a rune appeared amidst the streams of conjured light, and when she finished there was a sound like a rope snapping taut

The spell-light snarled around her arm like a serpent, and she winced as it burrowed beneath her skin, searing itself in place, and Wally hated herself all the more for asking. They needed this though. Not just Wally, but Vess, too. They needed to confront this if anything about 'them' was going to survive, and Wally couldn't risk Vess bolting.

Not this time.

"Do it," Wally said.

"The mnemonic is old," Vess warned. "It's seated deep in your psyche. I'll have to go all the way in, and it . . . it *will* hurt."

"I know."

Vess didn't say anything more. There was no use delaying. Cracking her knuckles again—more out of habit, Wally thought, than need—Vess laid the tips of each of her fingers on Wally's head, pressing her thumbpads to Wally's temples.

"Deep breath, Wally, in and out," Vess said, and Wally obeyed.

In and out.

As the air came out, Vess drew her fingers back, and sparks of light flew from them. Light, too, spilled from beneath Wally's hair, which was lank and greasy from lack of showers.

Green light laced with streaks of violet and shadow exploded into life around her and with it came a building pressure on her temples, like Vess' thumbs were digging into her scalp.

"Deep breaths, Wally, deep breaths," Vess repeated.

Wally braced herself as both the pressure and the complexity of the lights dancing around her increased. Synapses. She was looking at her own synaptic activity. Her oldest and darkest memories were laid bare in arcs of bioelectrical light, captured by Vess' spell, and her skull felt like it was in a vice that was closing with agonizing slowness. Every moment it grew tighter, and she cried out as the pain become the next best thing to unbearable.

"I know, Wally, I know," Vess murmured tightly. "But we're almost there, okay? Deep breaths, we're almost there!"

Wally nodded frantically as she struggled not to fall to her knees and scream. The visions around her grew more and more complex and Vess delved deeper and deeper until finally—

"There you are!"

A sharp stab of ice-cold pain shot through Wally's mind as Vess snapped a hand out a grabbed onto something just behind her right ear.

"Wally?" Vess said in a tone so much softer than anything she'd ever heard. "I need to breathe deep and close your eyes, okay?"

"Why?"

"Because this next part is *really* going to hurt."

That much at least, Wally trusted, regardless of the subtle compulsions of the mnemonic. So she closed her eyes and filled her lungs.

"I'm sorry," Vess whispered.

And she tore it out.

Wally didn't even have a chance to scream. The agony was so intense that it instantly transmuted into a sensory whiteout. Her eyes flew open, her jaw dropped, and every sense was replaced by a static feedback buzz for a brief moment before her eyes rolled back into her skull and she blacked out.

CHAPTER 38

Vess held on to Wally for hours, cradling her on the rooftop as the sun dipped slowly towards the horizon. There was nothing more she *could* do. Thanks to the geas, she couldn't leave, not even for Wally's sake.

Fortunately, Wally was fine. Vess had checked her over a dozen times, and her mind was recovering quickly. The mnemonic hadn't been a particularly complex one, and it had never been intended to last. The only reason its removal had hurt so much was because it had been in there for so long, buried under a decade and a half of complexes, neuroses, and memories.

She watched the progress of the sun for wont of anything else to do, and to distract herself from the pain she knew would come when Wally finally opened her eyes. There was no preparing herself for it. So she indulged in the selfish impulse to hold Wally as close as possible for as long as she could.

Gods knew she probably wouldn't get to again.

Of the million and one things she wanted to say to Wally, none of them seemed important enough to give voice to in that moment. Why bother when she wouldn't hear them? Not that she would listen to them once she woke up. Hell, she'd be lucky if Wally even stayed with the precinct. It would hurt in more ways than one if she *did* leave. Losing someone else after losing

Mizer like that was the last thing this place needed. If she wanted to leave, though, then she would leave. Polly would understand, and no one—not even Jemma—would hold it against her.

Not after the things Vess had done.

When Wally finally began to stir and those beautiful brown eyes were glassy and distant when they opened. She stared for a moment, unseeing, up at Vess, and hope flared briefly only to die a breath later as recognition settled in. Wally's pulse started to race, her eyes widened and her features went pale, and there was no warning and no sound as Wally was in her arms one moment and the next she was gone.

Vess jerked and tumbled back as something kicked off against her. Wally's weight vanished from her grip and Vess stood in a panic. She scanned the rooftop as terror gripped her.

Where was she! *Where had she gone?!*

Frantically, she started to flick through different states of vision. Thermal, soul-sight, anything and everything she could think of, but there was nothing!

"Wally!" Vess cried. "Wally, please! I . . . I'm sorry! Please, don't leave! Please!" Wrapping her arms around herself, Vess slowly sank to her knees and started to shake. "Please, don't leave me!"

Until that moment, the notion of Wally actually leaving her behind and never looking back, hadn't sunk it. It hadn't struck her just how desperately she wanted to prevent that until the moment it was upon her, and now? Now, panic boiled in her veins, shattering her concentration. She needed to find Wally! She needed—

"AH!" Vess doubled over and curled around her arm.

Pain seared through her. She'd almost lost hold of her bilocation and begun snapping back to her body when geas had stabbed her in the back of the mind with the force of a red-hot poker. It didn't stop the panic, though. Didn't stop the fear.

"FUCK!"

Vess rolled over onto her back and began scraping at her arm despite knowing it would do no good. It felt like hundreds of needles were burrowing under her flesh, shredding her skin and muscle to mulch. She was actually half tempted to shear her own arm off, but that wouldn't do any good either. The geas wasn't actually attached to her arm, it was part of her until Wally released her from it by permitting her to fulfill its condition.

Another spasm wracked her and this time she had no words to give voice to it, just an inchoate bark of pain as she thrashed on the rooftop of the sixth precinct. It's what she deserved. If Wally left her there for the rest of her gods-forsaken life it would still be what she deserved. Another loss of control, another jab of the poker, and soon Vess didn't have any strength left even to thrash. She just laid on the roof, twitching as her mind desperately tried to claw her back to her body while the geas endlessly dragged her back over a bed of nails with no grasp of time, as she reached out for a hand that she feared might never close around hers again.

The monochrome starkness of the world was a silent storm that gripped Wally Willowbark by the throat. Terror as real and choking as her father's sweaty, stinking fist was throttling the air from her lungs as she stared out over the span of the city and rocked back and forth on her heels.

Back—she was vaguely aware of Vess moving in silent agony behind her—and forth—her vision tipped forward for a brief, vertiginous moment she was staring down at the sharp drop to the hard concrete ground.

In the back of her mind she calculated it; the precinct was two stories, with the upper level given over largely to storage. The garage meant the first floor was slightly taller than a standard sized home. All-in-all, Wally understood, in a distant, clinical way, that she was just a bit over four meters above the ground. A four meter drop would do it. If she hit her head, it would certainly do it.

Back—in her periphery she saw Vess reaching, her hand outstretched towards the last place she'd seen Wally—and forth—the yawning gulf opened up again.

The drop didn't scare her. Nothing about that scared her. Everything else scared her. *Everything* scared her. Her heart felt like it was trying to thunder out of her chest and at the same time her head felt as though it were full of cottonballs made of barbed wire. She wanted to run. She wanted to jump. She wanted to throw up.

Most all, she just wanted it all to stop.

All the pain, all the fear, all the unfair *shit* that kept happening over and over and over. Even her life wasn't her own. Ophelia had said it, hadn't she? She had been kept alive for a purpose. A single, grand, terrible purpose. Wouldn't denying that purpose be better? Wouldn't it be so much better, and so much easier?

It would be.

It would even be noble, in a way. Wally let that notion trickle through her mind. The 'noble' sacrifice. Wouldn't that be better? Wouldn't it be *easier*? Why force Vess to track down and face Ophelia again when it clearly caused her so much pain when there was another, simpler option? If Ophelia needed her alive to be reborn into the world, then it would be smarter and simpler and *better* to just deny that at the root.

One step forward and . . . and it would be done.

Vess wouldn't have to worry about Ophelia coming back, and neither would anyone else, and without Mizer what good was she anyway? What purpose did she serve? None. That was the simple and truthful answer. She served no purpose anymore, except to the enemy, so really, the answer to it all was obvious.

Obvious, and easy, and . . .

'Wally . . .'

It would be easy. The fighting would stop. The hurting would stop. The *fear* would stop.

'Wally, I'm sorry . . . please—'

—all she had to do was—

'—don't leave me . . . please don't leave me.'

Do it. Back and forth and back and forth and back and forth. It's fine! It's better! It's obvious, you stupid, stupid girl! It's obvious and easy and smart and simple and—

'—Wally, please—'

—wrong.

She turned and looked over her shoulder at Vess who was twitching and spasming on the rooftop. Even in her agony, Vess was still reaching out, flailing and searching with her mind to try and find her. She was begging for Wally to come back—pleading—and it all seemed so stupid, suddenly; that rickety belief she'd clung to that she was 'better' or that she had 'changed'. Nothing had changed because she had never *tried* to change it. She had cracked and snapped and broken, then a bunch of doctors had glued all the little pieces back together into the shape of a girl and declared her healed, and she had chosen to believe them because it was easy, obvious, simple, and wrong.

In that moment, all Wally wanted was for the noise and the pain to stop, but she couldn't look away from Vess. She couldn't look away from the woman who, even trapped in her fondest dream—a dream that involved Wally of all people—she had never given up. Not really. She had come back, she had woken up, and she'd done it because Wally had begged her to.

Wally stepped back off the ledge.

She wasn't different. Not yet. Maybe she wouldn't ever be different. Maybe Ophelia had been right about her all along; that she would, generously speaking, be dead inside a decade, but right then, in that moment, Vess was begging her to come back and to Wake Up. Just like she had woken up for Wally.

"One day," Wally whispered into the soundless, monochrome world around her. "Just one more day, and then . . . then maybe I can do it again for one more day." She could try.

For Vess, she could try.

Vess had no grasp of how long she lay there, only that by the end she was mindlessly sobbing Wally's name as she was caught in an endless tug-of-war between pain and terror.

The end, when it did come, was with a soft touch.

"I . . . I'm here."

It was faint enough that Vess thought she might have been imagining it, but when she looked up from where she was sprawled out in a pathetic pile, she found herself staring into a hazy mass of half-seen images; a reflection. It was a reflection of everything around them. Wally wasn't gone, she was invisible. She was reflecting everything; even the spectrum of light. Even magic.

"W-Wally?" Vess mumbled.

"Mhm." It was a noise more than a word, and there was a shake to it that Vess didn't like. It was real, genuine, and utterly normal fear. "I'm here."

"Thank the gods," Vess curled up as the pain began to subside with panic. "I'm sorry . . . I'm so sorry . . ."

"Me too," she said quietly. "I just . . . I was so scared, I—I couldn't think straight. I didn't know what to do or . . . I'm so sorry."

Vess sighed as she felt Wally's hand brush her cheek. "S-So long as you're okay, everything is okay."

"It's not okay, though!" Wally cried. "I'm so scared, even now! I can't shut it off! The reflection! I can't shut it off!"

"But you're still here." That, more than anything, soothed Vess' soul. The fact that Wally was still there, that she stayed and wasn't leaving her behind. At least not yet. Maybe there was still time to fix things.

"Yeah," Wally said, her voice steadying. "I am."

Vess curled up into a ball as her burning nerves finally began to drift back into a semblance of normalcy, and let out a shaky breath before reaching out a hand to Wally. She didn't touch her. They weren't there yet. Not anymore. But she waited and she hoped.

Oh gods, how she hoped.

And for once, it seemed the right sorts of gods were listening, because Wally tentatively laid her hand in Vess'. "I know that . . . that everything is bad right now," Vess started as she closed her fingers around Wally's smaller, more delicate hand. "It's all shit, and it's all my fault, but for whatever it's worth, nothing about my heart has changed, okay?" She lifted her head weakly to look up at Wally properly. "I still love you."

"I know," Wally said quietly. "And I . . . I think I still love you, too."

Vess let out a sound that was halfway between a sigh of relief and a happy sob as Wally knelt and got an arm underneath her, and dragged her gracelessly over to the wall that the roof access door was set into.

Once she was propped up against it, Wally dropped into place beside her with a dull thump. It was still hard to see her. It was like looking at her through a grimy, oil-smeared window, but she was slowly becoming more coherent. Vess was satisfied with that much. The fact that Wally was there at all was a miracle she didn't deserve. That there was a chance to salvage something of 'them' was even moreso.

Turning over the hand that was between them so her palm was up, Vess waited, and, after a moment of hesitation, Wally took it and their fingers entwined. It wasn't as easy or as familiar as before, but it was still there.

"Does this mean I get a second chance?" Vess asked.

"Yeah," Wally said quietly. "Yeah, it does."

"Okay . . . I'll uhm, do my best not to fuck that up."

For the first time since Wally had woken up, Vess heard that charming little snort of a laugh. "Forgive me if I don't hold my breath," she replied.

Vess chuckled weakly and nodded. Perennial fuck-up that she was, that was probably fair, but at the very least that laugh suggested that Wally wasn't going to hold it against her even when she did, inevitably, prove true to her nature.

"I still love you like crazy, Wally Willowbark," Vess said.

"I know."

"Thank you." The words came out in a sudden sob as Vess lowered her head. "F-For the chance . . . thank you."

Vess couldn't see her clearly, but she thought that Wally was crying too. Maybe they both had a few more tears to shed over the matter. At least they hadn't lost everything.

"I guess, we're starting over, huh?" Wally asked.

"I guess so." A fresh start was more than Vess could have hoped for, to be honest. "How uh . . . how should we do this?"

"Maybe learning a little about each other the right way?" Wally ventured, and Vess turned to smile at her and was relieved to see she'd almost fully resolved back into clear existence.

Nodding, Vess licked her lips and said, "Y-Yeah, that sounds okay . . . you wanna go first?"

Wally nodded and turned to look back at the skyline of Colvus. It was almost fully night, and the final sliver of the sun was just barely peeking over the horizon.

"Can I ask something really personal?"

"Shoot."

Vess smiled as Wally squeezed her hand, and she could practically hear the gears turning in Wally's head as she formulated her words.

"When . . . back at the Heights, when I learned your name was Mizrahi," Wally began, "I had a thought, and I wasn't sure, but now I think I am . . . your first name isn't Vezha, is it?"

"No, it's not," Vess replied.

"So what *is* your name?"

Vess sighed. She should have known this would come up but she hadn't had time to think about it. She'd been too worried about a thousand other things in-between sharing bouts of grief with Polly

"That's gonna require some context," Vess said after a moment.

"I'm listening."

Blowing out a long breath, Vess leaned her head back and thumped it against the stone wall. "Far to the east, beyond the coast, there's a chain of sixteen islands. They're uninhabited now, but they're dotted with ruins. The cursed kind. Those ruins belonged to a kingdom that reduced itself to ashes some . . . oh, seven hundred-ish years ago."

"Okay . . . ?" Wally said, clearly following, but uncertain where she was following Vess to.

"The language is dead now, but, in the trade tongue, it was called the Dawning Kingdom, although it was established by a line of Sorcerer Kings and Queens, which actually made it more of a Magocracy in terms of governance."

Wally chuckled, and Vess smiled at the sound before continuing.

"When the kingdom fell, it was because of the usual things. Corruption. Weakness of rule. Civil unrest. When the royal line was expelled, they were driven almost to extinction . . . almost, but not quite." She turned to find Wally staring at her with slowly widening eyes. "My family was that line . . . my mother was the last of the main house while my father was from some distant branch family, I think."

"You're a princess?" Wally said in rank disbelief.

"Yup." Vess popped her lips on the last letter. "Princess of rags and tatters . . . princess of nothing. Except, by sheer happenstance, I turned out to be a genetic throwback. After my mother and father died, I was taken in by the state and evaluated, and they found that my lambda system was freakishly strong. Turned out to be a rare genetic mutation that only a few of my foremothers and -fathers ever had, the first in recorded history being the first of my house, the Dawning Lord himself."

"That's why you can cast so endlessly," Vess said quietly. "Why you never run out of power."

"Yeah, I'm like someone whose muscles never tire out," Vess said. "So there I was, the last of the line of the Dawning Lord, and my mother, who believed that I would amount to no more than a final guttering ember of a great dynasty, thought it would be funny to name me Vesper."

"Vesper?" Wally echoed. "Vesper, as in . . ."

"As in the ancient word describing the evening star . . . or the final light of day." Vess smiled humorlessly. "My mother named me after the death of our house."

"Wow."

"Yup."

"Your mom was a bitch."

Vess snorted and suddenly every ounce of tension snapped free and she couldn't stop herself. She was laughing—not just laughing but cackling! It was the kind of laugh that had tears spilling down her cheeks as she pounded the ground and desperately clawed for air, and, blessedly, after a moment of it, Wally started laughing, too. There was a tinny edge to her laughter. It was a little high, a little thready, and it wasn't nearly as comfortable as Vess was used to, but it was real. A real laugh. One that wasn't tainted by the shadows of her magic.

When the wash of laughter finally subsided, and the two of

them caught their breath, Vess was pleased to find that Wally had collapsed against her. She was less pleased when Wally realized it and jerked reflexively away, but it hurt less than she'd expected.

"Sorry."

"Don't be," Vess said, waving it off. "We're starting over, remember?"

"Right." Wally rubbed awkwardly at her arm where she'd been leaning on Vess. "I still . . . I'm still okay around you, alright? I'm just . . . it's like a raw wound. Like my brain is trying to make up for all the lost time it could have spent panicking about you."

"You don't have to explain," Vess said, holding out a hand for her, which Wally took with more ease than before. "We have time."

"Yeah, we do," Wally said softly. "So uhm, what happens to me now?"

"What do you mean?"

Wally frowned. "I mean . . . without Mizer . . . without the proxy, how do I help you? What can I even do anymore? I don't think I can . . . no, I don't want to be worn again, Vess. Gods' hooks. Please, I . . . I'm sorry, but I don't think I can."

That, at least, Vess had been fully expecting. A safe wearing required a level of trust and intimacy that they simply didn't have anymore. They might never have it again with the damage the mnemonic did.

"You're a talented disperser, Wally," Vess replied after a moment. "Polly isn't going to chuck you out on your ass."

"But they need you!" Wally insisted.

"And without Mizer, we can't proxy anyway, so it doesn't matter." Vess carded her fingers through her hair and shrugged. "I can still consult."

Wally looked gutted, and, frankly, the idea of being reduced to little more than a glorified fact-checker didn't sit well with Vess either.

"There's nothing for it," Vess said. "Without Mizer interceding with the elements, the proxy won't work, and without the proxy, there was no way I can cast without killing myself."

"But you made the proxy, right? Can't you change it?" Wally asked.

"Change it to what?" Vess shook her head. "It's designed to be a maximum safeguard, but I can't use divine powers because they're anathema to me." She turned her hand up and conjured a ball of miasmic power into her palm. "I'd burn through holy wards in a second. Shamanism is neutral, though, which is why it works, but there are no other shamans I know of in Mizer's league, and I wouldn't trust them anyhow."

Wally deflated at that, and Vess understood. It was a tough pill to swallow. Vess had never imagined the sixth precinct without Mizer, and hadn't ever come up with contingencies for that; a weakness that was biting them all in the ass now.

"Wait . . ." Wally looked up over at Vess curiously. "What . . . What if you didn't maximize the safeguards?"

"What?!" Vess held up a hand. "No, that's insane, without those bulwarks my power would overwhelm damn near anyone I touched."

"Anyone but me."

"Right, but you're—"

Vess stalled out as she finally grasped the end of the rope that Wally was throwing at her.

"Wally that's brilliant," Vess breathed, and Wally flushed. "When I designed the proxy it was meant to be generic! To work for anyone! But . . . But if I designed it around you—" she pointed at Wally as a broad smile grew across her face— "then . . . yeah! Your reflector grade is off the charts! You don't need generic protections!"

"So it could work?" Wally asked hopefully.

"Yeah," Vess was nodding as a flare of hope bloomed in her chest, "it won't be the same, but . . . but yeah, Wally, it could work!"

Wally sagged in relief, and Vess had to fight the urge to wrap in the biggest hug imaginable. They weren't there yet either. She was lucky that Wally could still hold her hand without panicking, and Vess didn't want to push her luck.

This was enough. So long as it was Wally, it was enough.

"C'mon," Vess said, tugging Wally's hand, "can we go tell Polly? She could probably use a little bit of good news."

"Mhm."

Wally stood, and Vess stood with her, but as she went to the door, Vess stopped cold.

"Vess?" Wally turned around, to find Vess smiling wanly before nodding down to her right arm. "Oh! Right! I uhm . . . it's okay, you can go downstairs."

Vess let out a sigh of relief as the insistent clench of the geas on the back of her mind finally let up, and then smiled at Wally.

"Will you come with me?"

Dark, slender fingers tightened around her hand, and Wally nodded. Her smile was fragile but real, and Vess swore, in that moment, that she would protect it. Whatever the cost and however many nightmares and challenges, it would be worth it.

"Yeah," Wally said. "I will."

For whatever dreams may come.

CPSIA information can be obtained
at www.ICGtesting.com
Printed in the USA
BVHW050102250622
640661BV00003B/41